W9-AZS-578

Before ever after

Before

A NOVEL

SAMANTHA SOTTO

ever after

CROWN PUBLISHERS NEW YORK

This is a work of fiction. Names, characters, places, and incidents either are the product of the author's imagination or are used fictitiously. Any resemblance to actual persons, living or dead, events, or locales is entirely coincidental.

Copyright © 2011 by Samantha Sotto-Yambao

All rights reserved.

Published in the United States by Crown Publishers,
an imprint of the Crown Publishing Group,
a division of Random House, Inc., New York.
www.crownpublishing.com

Crown and the Crown colophon are registered trademarks of Random House, Inc.

Library of Congress Cataloging-in-Publication Data
Sotto, Samantha.
Before ever after: a novel / Samantha Sotto.—1st ed.
p. cm.
1. Marriage—Fiction. 2. Family secrets—Fiction. I. Title.
PS3619.O87B44 2011
813'.6—dc22
2011003327

ISBN 978-0-307-71987-4
eISBN 978-0-307-71989-8

Printed in the United States of America

Book design by Lynne Amft
Jacket design by Jennifer O'Connor
Jacket photographs: (*book with flower*) Cavan Images/Getty Images;
(*painted wood*) Shutterstock

10 9 8 7 6 5 4 3 2 1

First Edition

For Nico and Cai

While you may see only one name on the cover of this book, this is a gift from Mom and Dad to both of you—so that you will always believe that you can hold your dreams in your hands.

Prologue

Three Years Ago

*J*asmine.

It was not Max Gallus's top choice for his last thought, but it would have to do. He wondered if there was time to say it out loud.

He had difficulty telling which came first: his phone shattering against his cheek, his skin tearing from his ribs, or the flames taking dibs on what was left. He was certain though that the Silence came last. It always did.

Chapter One

Eggs and endings

A RENTED APARTMENT

MADRID, SPAIN

Earlier

Eggs and engagements. Though slightly odd, they were a harmless pairing on most days, even with a greasy pile of bacon on the side. But today was not like most days, because in less than an hour, they would make Shelley Gallus a twenty-six-year-old widow.

Shelley did not know this yet, so for now she was happy to listen to Brad's eighth retelling of how Simon had proposed to him. This was, after all, why she and Max had driven down from London for a holiday with their friends. The last time all four of them had been together was two years earlier, when they had met on a budget European tour. Toasting the engagement was a good excuse for a reunion and excessive amounts of Rioja.

The trip was also Max's chance to continue his long-time pursuit of the perfect Spanish omelet. His passion for eggs almost rivaled his devotion to chickens, though generally he preferred the latter off a plate than on it. Max staunchly believed you could get through anything if you had a chicken, and the clucking kind, in his expert opinion, had far more uses than the ones nesting on warm mashed potatoes and gravy.

Shelley never fully understood her husband's ethos on poultry and chalked it up as just another item on his long list of quirks. His rabid love of the Bee Gees topped that list, while his two-year reign as strip Scrabble champion fell somewhere in the middle. (Shelley was, by default, first runner-up, being the only other contestant in their Saturday-night tournaments.) Still, she loved all of Max's quirks equally, and the sum of them even more.

Accompanying Max on his omelet excursion was to have been the first thing on Shelley's morning agenda, but a rogue prawn from the previous night's paella had other plans. Shelley insisted that Max go on his egg hunt without her, and Simon decided to tag along. She didn't have a hard time guessing why Brad had opted to stay behind and play nurse to his captive, albeit slightly green, audience.

Shelley flushed the toilet and drowned out the last lines of Brad's latest blow-by-blow account from the other side of the bathroom door. She squirted bright pink soap onto her palm during the interlude of her gastric flamenco. The scent of strawberries, or rather what strawberries might smell like if they were made from melted plastic and disinfectant, filled the white-tiled room. She turned off the tap and stepped into the bedroom. "Simon certainly outdid himself. I will never look at cheesecake in the same way again."

"You didn't think that he could hold out for long, did you?" Brad brushed his sandy blond hair from his brow and held up the large Nikon dangling from his neck. His permanent dimpled smirk peeked out beneath the camera. He focused its lens and chased the laughter sprinting across her face.

Shelley's laugh followed its familiar trail up to her aquamarine eyes, flitted through her dark lashes, and settled where the almond slant of her eyelids met the faint crinkles above her golden cheeks. This was the point where most people caught their breath and wondered from which continent she could have been so magnificently misplaced. Shelley was oblivious to the serendipity of her curious beauty and a lifetime on the receiving end of this involuntary half-gasp had left her convinced that everyone she knew was asthmatic.

Shelley's gut twisted. Intermission was over.

"You really should take something for that, you know," Brad said. "I'm sure Simon has some Tums tucked away somewhere."

"I'll try my luck with some tea first. Chewing cherry-flavored chalk can be Plan B."

"Sure thing. One cup coming up."

"Thanks, but I think I'll survive a trip to the kitchen. I'm tired of staring at the ceiling." Shelley made her way to the sunflower-yellow kitchenette. The clicking of Brad's camera trailed her, chronicling the swish of her wavy dark ponytail against her nape.

She stood on tiptoe to reach inside the cupboard, then pulled out a tea-stained cup and set it on the counter. She scoured the pantry for a tea bag.

Brad snapped a portrait of Shelley's sole find, capturing the flutter of a cobweb on the ancient jar of coffee creamer sitting on the shelf.

Shelley sighed, picked up her phone, and pressed the speed dial.

Black coffee with a hint of gravel answered. "Miss me already, luv?"

Despite the din of the Madrid rush hour in the background, Shelley could tell from her husband's voice that he was grinning. After two years of marriage, she still got butterflies when that flash of mischief crossed Max's dark and scruffily handsome features. Unfortunately for Shelley, butterflies and toxic crustaceans, as a rule, do not get along. She stifled a groan and grasped the counter. Her fingertips nudged the teacup closer to the edge.

"Are you all right, Shell? You sound worse."

"I'm fine."

Max eyed the train door. The last of the passengers were filing in. He pushed through the crowd. "Are you sure?"

"Yes. I just called to ask if you could get some tea on your way back."

"Simon and I can head back now," Max suggested as he trampled on more toes.

"No, don't. It can wait."

Brad found his next subject. Two clicks immortalized his now empty pack of peppermint gum that Simon had, as usual, promptly polished off.

"All right." Max stopped squeezing between shoulders. The door began to slide shut just as he reached it. "I'll be back soon."

"Oh, and Max, please make sure you get . . ."

"Jasmine," Max was about to guess correctly. Something grazed his foot as he stepped back from the door. It was a blue backpack. Or was it purple? Colors tended to look the same when they exploded.

Shelley's hand slipped from the counter.

The teacup shattered on the floor.

Click.

Chapter Two

Sundays and surprises

LONDON

&⁊❦ *Three Years Later*

Breathing is not an optional activity—but Shelley found the opposite to be true. To live without Max, she had to stop.

Her final breath had been the gasp she had taken when the bomb shredded Max to pieces. It was the last lungful of air she would take as Max's wife and in it was all she had left of him. If she exhaled, he would be gone. And so she didn't.

Shelley held her breath and mimicked the motions of life with a white-hot pain in her chest. Walking and reading the paper were activities that were easy to fake, carrying on a conversation, not as much. Eventually she learned that most people were satisfied if she logged in the appropriate number of nods as they spoke. With some practice, she became proficient enough to keep even her nosiest neighbor, Mrs. Pond, happy.

Shelley's ability to go through the motions wasn't surprising considering that she had been schooled by the best. Her mom had never quite gotten over the death of her own husband, and Shelley grew up watching her paint on the brightest smile with a berry shade of Revlon lipstick. There had been days when her happiness had seemed so real, so genuine, that Shelley had almost believed it. In the months and years since Max's death, Shelley's mime repertoire had grown to rival her mother's, expanding to include what in the beginning was too excruciating to even consider.

Online Scrabble was far tamer than the strip version she and Max used to play, but a milestone nonetheless. Shelley had whipped off countless bras to reward her husband's triple word scores and ruined several tiny metal clasps in the process. Surrendering her underwear had always been easier than challenging Max's more obscure words and enduring his discourses on their definition, etymology, and Latin conjugations. She later discovered the wonders of Velcro. Regardless of who won, tumbling naked on a letter-littered floor was how their games always ended anyway, along with the loss of yet another vowel. *E*'s, in particular, were in dangerously low supply.

Chicken and eggs were Shelley's next hurdles to a semblance of normalcy. In her case, it was the egg that came first. She had banished eggs from her kitchen when Max was killed. It was how she had managed to survive Sundays without him.

Sunday mornings had once been her favorite time of the week. It was only then that not waking up in Max's arms made her smile. The sight of his empty pillow meant one glorious thing: Paris was bubbling in the oven.

Shelley had fallen in love with Max's baked eggs and cheese almost as soon as she had fallen in love with Max himself. They were in Paris when he first made the dish for her and the tour group she had hastily joined. Since then each forkful tasted like that morning—warm, buttery, and bursting with full-fat promise. But Max was gone, and now Sundays coated her mouth with ash and gritty bits of grief.

She both dreaded and longed for the hour when sleep thinned enough to peer through. She would smile at Max's empty pillow, believing its false hope with every half-asleep fiber of her body. The waking dream was less than brief, but it lasted long enough for the smell of sharp cheese melting into a layer of eggs and cream to crush her when it drifted away.

She learned to cope by bypassing most of Sunday with the help of marathon nights of online Scrabble. But after countless days of rising at noon, she finally found the strength to wake up to the emptiness inside her. She found it, of all places, inside a box couriered to her home one Saturday afternoon. It was from Brad.

Brad had told her that he would be sending a draft of his new project. Photography had always been a hobby of his, but he had only ever shown his work to Simon. After Simon was killed, Brad had wedged his camera between himself and a world that did not have his fiancé in it.

Shelley realized that it was now a year since Brad had closed their wedding-planning business to see if his art could feed him (and still satisfy his occasional Prada cravings). She had helped convince him that he could always scrape by as a paparazzo if money ever got tight. Luckily for the celebrities of New York, Brad's new career was keeping him well fed and fashionable.

She tore the box open. Inside were pieces of a teacup scattered over a kitchen floor. The title of Brad's new book was printed on the black-and-white photograph.

MARCH 2010 MADRID

One day before. One year after.
A STORY TOLD IN PHOTOGRAPHS
BY BRADFORD JENSEN

The shards of porcelain cut into her hands, slicing open old wounds. Shelley dropped the book on the hourglass mosaic inlaid on her foyer floor. She slumped down beside it.

Simon beamed up at her from the open book, his black mod glasses, as always, slightly askew. Shelley stopped herself from nudging them back into place. There was nothing she could do. Simon was dead and his glasses would remain sitting crookedly on his nose.

Tears rolled down the page. She tugged at the edge of her sleeve and dabbed Simon's face before drying her own. She stroked his damp cheek, lifted the corner of the wet page, and turned back time.

Shelley was in Madrid the day before the world had changed. Her fingers trembled. She gripped the book tight as Brad's printed words led her through frozen seconds of ignorant bliss.

Max and Shelley's battle-scarred luggage
on the sofa bed
Simon cleaning his glasses
Shelley handing Max the dental floss
Simon finishing the last of my mint gum

Shelley lingered over the tiny nothings, worrying that the slightest breeze might blow them away. These were the mundane specks that leave yawning gaps in shattered lives; no matter how well you think you've put all the pieces back together.

She turned the page to the last photo in the series. Her heart broke all over again.

She and Max were asleep in each other's arms on the sofa bed. The pale light streaming from the window told her that the moment was stolen at dawn, a few hours after they had collapsed in bed after a night of spicy tapas and one too many bottles of wine. They were lying on their sides with Max's lean muscled form fused into the curve of her back. He was in his jeans, naked from the waist up save for a thin silver chain around his neck. A blank Scrabble tile hung from it and rested beneath his collarbone. She had given the necklace to Max on their first anniversary to celebrate all the vowels they had lost so far.

Shelley slammed the book shut and lay back on the floor, staring at a ceiling that was falling upward and away. Liquid darkness closed around her as she sank into a well of salty tears. The stale breath she had lived on bubbled from her lips. She curled into a ball, closed her eyes, and waited for the death of her body or her soul, wondering which would save her first.

Max's breath tickled the back of her neck. He pulled her closer to his chest. His skin was warm against her back, melting her into him like butter. He wove his fingers through hers and placed her hands over her heart. It stirred under her palms. Shelley felt it beat again.

Max kissed the secret spot behind her ear. "Good night, luv."

Shelley closed her eyes and began to drift into sleep. "Good . . . bye, Max."

Wisps of sunshine swirled above her. Shelley burst through the surface of her dream and drew in three years' worth of air.

It was Sunday morning, her first real Sunday since Max had died. Brad's book was in her arms, creased from a night in her embrace. She smoothed out its pages and carried it to the kitchen, driven by a long-lost though still familiar feeling: peace and a desperate craving for baked eggs.

Without a sliver of an eggshell in her kitchen, Shelley made do with a breakfast of burned toast slathered with trans-fat-free disappointment. She went through the rest of Brad's book with oxygen in her lungs and a chipped floral cup of jasmine tea nursed in her hands. The second half of the book was called "One Year After." It was a diary of the healing hum-drum Brad had fashioned from the old and the new.

A full pack of mint gum
Notes from last week's support group meeting
Simon's framed photo by the bed
An email from Shelley
Broadway tickets for two

Shelley closed the book. It didn't end with "happily ever after." And now, after three years of crying herself to sleep and one night curled on her foyer floor, she knew why: The story went on.

She took a deep breath. It was time to try to write the rest of it. She had said good-bye to Max the night before, but as she closed her eyes and felt his kiss on her neck, something told her that he wasn't far away. He was there, holding her hand, steadying her fingers as she turned the pages. She would start small, she decided. A paragraph—she bit her lip—or perhaps something smaller. Shorter. A list. She rummaged through a drawer for a pen. She pressed its tip to paper. *Milk. Bread.* The pen shook. She gripped it tighter. *Eggs.*

LONDON

🌿 *Now*

The rubbery yellow mess in front of her would have made a less determined person give up on the idea of re-creating Max's Sunday breakfast staple, but Shelley was made of sterner stuff. She pinched her nose and shoveled in a mouthful of what used to be eggs. Waste not, want not.

Strictly speaking, she would have to waste an inconceivable amount of eggs before she would ever want for anything again, at least moneywise. Max had seen to that. Shelley had gotten the second biggest surprise of her life when she found out how much Max had left her in his will. The biggest surprise was going to come three years later—today, in fact, in exactly three minutes and thirty-two seconds.

00:03:30

Max had willed to Shelley an obscene amount of money and a diverse investment portfolio ranging from office blocks in Stockholm to a private island in the Venetian lagoon. The only explanation Shelley had ever gotten from the solicitor was that Max had inherited his estate years before and that she was one of the two beneficiaries stated in his will. The other was an orphanage in Cambodia.

00:02:15

Shelley struggled to understand why Max would keep such a secret—not that there was anything to complain about in the life they had shared. He had operated a small tour company and spent his weekends at his small free-range chicken farm. When she wasn't in their 1970s Volkswagen van traveling around Europe with Max or helping him run after chickens, Shelley worked on her mosaic commissions. It was an art Max had introduced her to on their first trip together, and it had instantly become a passion. Working with the chaos of pebbles and broken tile reminded her that almost everything made sense after one took a few steps back.

00:01:24

In spite of her new status as one of the wealthiest women in the U.K., Shelley didn't scoop up the nearest castle on the market. Nor did it even cross her mind to move back to the States. With Max gone, she wanted to keep everything else in her life as unchanged as possible. She did, however, sell the chicken farm. Chicken chasing just wasn't the same without Max.

00:00:58

Shelley also continued to make mosaics. Her career as an artist had given her the fulfillment she had craved since she had first channeled Bridget Jones, quit her advertising job, and signed up for Max's tour five years ago.

00:00:45

She considered what had gone wrong with this batch. Definitely more edible than last week's, but perhaps it could have done with a bit less cream and a little more tarragon—or perhaps a dash of cayenne?

00:00:37

The doorbell rang.

She swallowed the mouthful she was chewing, belted Max's plaid blue bathrobe around her, and padded to the foyer in her furry purple slippers.

00:00:24

If Shelley had known what would be standing on her doorstep that Sunday morning, she might not have laughed off Brad's constant prodding to hire a butler. He had never given up trying to persuade her to live the whole lady-of-the-manor lifestyle he had dreamed up for her. She ignored him, but she promised to rent the same Scottish castle Madonna had used for her last wedding reception when he kissed the right frog someday. Brad had found a couple of promising ones hanging around his watering holes lately.

00:00:05

Shelley was still preoccupied with planning next week's baked eggs and cheese attempt when she opened the door.

There, waiting patiently behind it, was the surprise—or rather the shock—that would change all that she knew.

00:00:00

Max.

Shelley blinked.

And blinked again. She tried to speak, but the stars swirling around her whisked her away.

"Mrs. Gallus?"

The voice called to Shelley from somewhere far away. She could not place its accent, though she was almost certain that it sounded like hot chocolate, the dense and dark kind you slurped rather than sipped.

"Mrs. Gallus? Are you all right?"

Shelley nodded through the haze in her head. She kept her eyes closed to keep the constellation at bay. She felt the cushions against her back and wondered where she was. She vaguely recalled that she had recently been lying down on something much harder.

"You had me worried there," the voice said. "I'm really sorry to drop in on you like this."

Shelley's thoughts began to take form. Eggs. The doorbell. The door. Max.

She sat up. Her living room spun around her. Her stomach lurched. She squeezed her eyes shut until the sofa came to a halt. She peeked through her lashes. Max's warm amber eyes gazed back at her. She covered her mouth to stifle a scream. It didn't work.

The ghost stumbled back from Shelley's high-pitched shriek and fell on the mosaic on the floor.

Shelley peered over the edge of her couch. She gasped when she realized her mistake. The very much alive man on her floor wasn't her dead husband after all.

The man was in his early thirties, the same age Max had been when he died three years previously. His face was almost identical to Max's—Shelley swallowed—but now she could see the subtle differences between them. The stranger's brown hair was a shade lighter than Max's. The bow of his lips curved more deeply. His chin bore the hint of a cleft. Still, the man looked similar enough to Max for her to be almost certain that they shared more than a few strands of DNA.

The stranger picked himself up and took a step toward her.

Shelley scrambled to the far end of the couch. She wasn't a huge fan of strangers showing up at her home not carrying a box of pizza and change. "Who are you?"

"Who am I? Yes, right. Good question." The man moved closer. "I'm not really sure how to answer it though."

"*Try.*"

The man dug into his pocket.

Shelley's chest tightened. She inched her hand toward the jar on the table beside her, ready to defend herself with her Mexican pottery.

The man pulled out his wallet and took out a photograph. He held it out to her.

Shelley kept her fingers wrapped around the clay jar. "What's this?"

"Your answer."

Shelley glanced at the picture. It was yellowed and worn around the edges, but she could see the two figures in it clearly: A grinning man with sideburns and bell-bottom jeans was holding a ruddy-faced toddler in his arms. They were standing in front of St. Peter's Basilica. Shelley flipped the photo over. A date, written in an all-too-familiar hand, was fading in the bottom left-hand corner. *Aprile 1978.* She gasped. "What sort of sick joke is this?"

"So you recognize him?"

"Yes. I . . . mean, no. No, I don't."

"Are you sure about that?"

Shelley felt the stranger's eyes bore into her. "Who are you? Why are you here?"

The man took a deep breath. "I'm Paolo Rossi. I'm the boy in the picture. And I'm here because the man carrying me is my grandfather and . . ."

Shelley loosened her grip on the jar. *His grandfather—of course.* She felt foolish for even thinking for a moment that the grinning man in the old photograph was—

"Max," Paolo said, "your husband."

Hearing her thoughts spoken out loud made them sound a thousand times more absurd. It gave Shelley the strength to deny them.

"Mr. Rossi, my husband died three years ago, and he wasn't much older than you. I think you should go now or I will have to call the police." She reached for the phone.

"Wait. You don't understand." Paolo fumbled with the zipper of his leather messenger bag. He pulled out a manila envelope. "There's something else you need to see."

Shelley arched a brow.

"Open it," he said. "Please."

Curiosity won over caution as it often did with Shelley. She kicked herself for what she was about to do. She took the envelope from Paolo and opened it. "More photographs? What is all this?"

"Proof."

Shelley flipped through the stack of photos. She darted looks at Paolo to make sure he stayed glued to her couch. The photos were of her husband's doppelgänger and the same boy taken on various occasions—birthday parties, Christmases, vacations. The boy grew taller and older with each picture, evidence that the pictures were taken over a period of several years. The man beside him aged as well. His hair turned grayer and at some point he started wearing glasses. By the time the boy was in his teens, the man's hair had gone completely white and he sported an equally white full beard.

Shelley set the last picture down and exhaled. If the photos had proven anything, she decided, it was that Paolo was a very disturbed young man. "Mr. Rossi, thank you for sharing your lovely childhood memories with me, but I'm afraid that I'm going to have to ask you to leave. Now."

"But the pictures . . . Didn't you see . . ."

"I saw that your grandfather was an old man whom, I will admit, looked very much like my husband when he was *younger*. But I assure you that unless my husband discovered some damned good face cream and magical Viagra, they were not the same person."

"No. Look at them again. Look closely at my grandfather's face."

"Please go." Shelley handed the pictures back to Paolo and stood up. "The police will not ask you as kindly, so I suggest you hurry."

"No. Wait. I'll go, I promise. Just look at them one more time. Please."

Shelley rubbed the crease that was digging deeper into her forehead. She now believed that the stranger in her living room was more annoying than dangerous. She snatched the pictures back.

"It might help if you laid them out next to one another," Paolo said.

Shelley glared at him but then decided that the fastest way to get the stranger out of her house was to play along. She spread the photos on the coffee table, not expecting to see anything different. Looking past the graying hair, the beard, and her own perceptions of how the world worked, she now saw that unlike the boy in the picture, whose face subtly aged over time, the face of the man did not.

A thousand questions careened into one another on their way to Shelley's lips. She did not know which stunned her more—the fact that this man was frozen in time or that, defying all logic, he was indeed Max.

Paolo reached for one of the photographs. "This was taken ten years ago when I was attending university in the States. My grandfather flew in from Italy for my graduation. He died a week later."

Shelley glanced at the top of Paolo's head. She thought that it was funny that she had just now noticed that his hair was twinkling.

Shelley woke up with the pain of the morning's events lodged behind her tonsils. She coughed and swore to have her blood sugar checked. She did not like fainting.

"Would you like me to get you some water?" Paolo asked.

She nodded. The pain in her throat prevented her from doing anything else—like continue screaming.

"I'll be right back."

Shelley watched Paolo as he walked toward the kitchen. His stride was identical to Max's. He was a fraction shorter than Max's six-foot-three frame, but he had the same lean build. Max was this man's dead grandfather, she thought.

Paolo returned with a glass of water. She gulped it down, wishing that it were a much stronger drink.

"Feeling better?"

Shelley stared at him blankly. In the time it had taken her to empty her glass, she had decided that she had gone mad and that Paolo and the morning's events were part of some delusional episode. It was all those eggs that did it, she thought. "Salmonella."

"I'm sorry, did you say something?" Paolo asked.

She couldn't help but smile. So this is what it felt like to fall off your rocker. Not too bad, really. She could have done much worse, hallucinating a circus of pink elephants and creepy clowns. Paolo at least looked like Max. She was now in fact quite proud that her subconscious had whipped up such an entertaining storyline. It would make a good plot for a book she could write someday. This was assuming, of course, that this was only a temporary bout of insanity. If the madness was more permanent in nature, well, Shelley didn't want to think about that right now. She distracted herself by studying the imaginary fellow in her living room. Nice smile and a good behind. He was Max's grandson, though. Slightly perverted, but three years of celibacy could do that to you.

"All of this must be quite disturbing," Paolo said. "Believe me, I know. But I'm afraid there's more. Do you have a computer I could borrow?"

"A computer? Certainly. Follow me." Shelley let her hallucination run its course, not really knowing what else she could do. She led Paolo upstairs to Max's old office.

Paolo walked over to the laptop. "May I?"

Shelley grinned.

Paolo sat down at the antique mahogany desk and tapped away on the keyboard: T-h-e-B-a-c-k-p-a-c-k-i-n-g-G-o-u-r-m-e-t. Reggae music played as the website loaded.

"Mrs. Gallus . . ."

Shelley put her hand on Paolo's shoulder and smiled. "Please, call me Shelley."

"Uh, okay. Shelley. I have to warn you that what I'm about to show you will be a . . . well, a bit of a shock."

She doubted him. Sanity was overrated. Going mad was surprisingly refreshing. In fact, she should have done this earlier.

Paolo clicked on an archived entry. "I also have to tell you now that I can give you no explanation for what you are about to see."

Shelley liked what she had seen so far and grinned even wider. She wandered through the familiar sun-kissed landscape of Paolo's face, pausing to admire the flawed perfection of his slightly hooked nose. She sighed, wondering why she couldn't be hallucinating about her husband and not just his facsimile.

"Shelley? Did you hear what I said?"

"What? A shock? Oh, yes." She turned to the computer screen. A picture of baked eggs and cheese appeared in front of her. There was a caption beneath the familiar dish:

"Sundays with Shell," an unforgettable masterpiece I found on my recent trip to Boracay Island.

Shelley frowned, trying to comprehend what she was seeing.

"Go on. Read the rest of it." Paolo let Shelley take the seat in front of the desk. She was going to need it soon enough.

She skimmed over the article that praised the dish as the surprising find on the anonymous blogger's backpacking trip to Boracay, a resort island in the Philippines. The dish was served at The Shell, a rustic café perched on a limestone cove overlooking the sea.

```
I was lucky enough to find an old friend in Boracay,
which brought back all of the memories of my very first
backpacking adventure. And then there were the eggs. Be
warned: The Shell is only open on Sunday mornings and
only serves eggs, so don't make the mistake of dropping
in at any other time, because my friend has made it
```

clear that he will not throw the rope ladder down even
if you are drowning or being feasted on by sharks. Check
out the gallery to see the pictures from my trip.

"I don't understand. Why did you show me this?" Shelley asked. True, the baked eggs looked uncannily similar to what Max used to make. True, it was an odd coincidence that the dish shared her name— then again, shells weren't exactly unheard-of on tropical beaches. But what did a café halfway around the world have to do with Paolo's preposterous claims about Max? It began to dawn on her that perhaps she was not experiencing a mad delusion after all, and that she had just let a very strange man into her home.

"Go to the gallery and take a look at photo number three," Paolo said.

"All right. But after that you'll have to go. I mean it."

Shelley clicked on the gallery button. A dozen thumbnail pictures appeared on the page. She double-clicked on the third picture in the series.

An uncropped photo of the baked eggs and cheese dish filled the screen. In the background was a shirtless man sipping a mug of coffee. His face was turned sideways to the camera, the profile of his slightly hooked nose distinct against the sunlight. Catching the sun on his tan chest was the chain and Scrabble pendant she had given Max. The date printed at the bottom of the picture showed that it had been taken less than two months ago.

It was an hour before Shelley spoke again. There was a bitterness in her voice that hadn't been there before. "How is this possible? Max is dead. He's been dead for three years."

"That's why I came looking for you, Shelley," Paolo said. "To find answers."

"Answers? You came to me for answers? Jesus, I don't even know what damned questions to ask. How? What? Why?"

"Actually, 'who' might be a good place to start."

Shelley looked out the window. The row of brick town houses across the street looked exactly as it always did. And so did the parked cars and the people walking past them. This was odd, she thought, considering how her world had just turned upside down. She had half expected to see at least one goldfish fly by.

"You do know that this is mad, right?" Shelley said. "I can't believe we're even letting ourselves think for one second that what you're suggesting could be true. There must be some logical explanation. A relative, perhaps? A look-alike? A . . . er . . . clone?"

"A clone? This isn't science fiction, Shelley."

"Oh, and your theory that I was married to a remarkably resilient and well-preserved old man is more plausible?"

Paolo walked over to her and held her by the shoulders. "Shelley, when you saw that photograph on the computer, you knew in the same way I did that that was the person we loved and lost. I know it's him. And so do you."

Paolo was right. If there had been any doubt in Shelley's mind of the identity of the man on her computer screen, the pendant around his neck had torn it into a million pieces.

But knowledge and acceptance are two very different things. Shelley rejected the truth not because it challenged reason but because admitting that Max was alive was more painful than believing he was dead. That he was alive only meant one thing—that he had *chosen* to leave her—and that she could never accept. She buried her face in Paolo's chest and wept.

Shelley shoved the remnants of her breakfast down the drain. She had half a mind to jump in after them. She couldn't be shredded more than she already was. "Tell me everything," she said, "from the very beginning."

Paolo stared at her from the kitchen island. "Are you sure?"

"Yes."

"Very well." He inhaled deeply. "The short version begins with the eggs and cheese your garbage disposal is grinding away. The long version begins with a car crash along a blind curve in Naples. Which one would you like to hear?"

Shelley looked at the mush disappearing in her sink. "Car crash."

"Car crash it is," Paolo said. "My parents were in a car accident when my mother was pregnant with me. My father died instantly while my mother survived long enough to deliver me through an emergency C-section."

"Oh, I'm sorry. Um, maybe we should have started with the eggs instead."

"It's okay. Chickens saved the day."

"Pardon me?"

"French chicks, to be exact," Paolo said. "Luckily for tiny premature me, as my grandfather often liked to remind me, the French chicks and their ingenious incubators at the Paris zoo inspired a doctor in the late 1800s to develop a similar incubating apparatus for humans. And so here I am today, fully indoctrinated with my nonno's fervent belief that you can get through life's tightest jams if you are fortunate enough to have a chicken on hand."

Shelley smiled despite herself, remembering the way Max had doted on his hens. "Well, Max did love his chickens."

"And eggs." Paolo grinned. "Nonno made absolutely the best baked eggs and cheese. It was sort of a tradition with us. The last time he made the dish for me was when he attended my college graduation," he said. "A week after he returned to Italy, his fishing boat was found capsized on the lake. They never found his body."

Shelley thought about the empty casket she had buried at Max's funeral.

"Soon after that, I learned about the will Nonno had left and its conditions," Paolo said. "'A trade,' as he liked to call it. Next to his philosophy on chickens, you see, the importance of learning that nothing came without a price was something that Nonno took pains to teach me since I was a toddler crying for juice. Before I learned how to speak, I mastered how to hoard stuffed toys to exchange for the things I wanted."

"I assume his will did not require you to produce a teddy bear," Shelley said.

"No, but Nonno did ask for two things. The first condition was that I hold down a stable job for at least three years. The second was that I care for Alessandra in the lifestyle she had grown accustomed to."

"Alessandra?"

"His pet chicken."

"Of course."

"Nonno's conditions weren't surprising. What really shocked me was my inheritance. I couldn't—and still can't—grasp the amount of money he left me. I remember thinking then that he had apparently known a whole lot more about trading than just dabbling in the stuffed-toy market."

Shelley nodded. She did not feel like volunteering information about her own inheritance or about her life with Max. She did not trust herself to stay as calm as Paolo if she did.

"I tried to comply with his wishes as best I could," Paolo said, "not because I wanted the money, but because I wanted to make him proud. After graduating, I decided to remain in the States. I found a job at a publishing company in New York and read Alessandra a story every night. She and I lived happily enough together, and I put her eggs to use in my attempts at re-creating Nonno's baked eggs and cheese.

"I didn't have much luck in my cooking though," he continued. "It became an obsessive hobby of mine to hunt down the perfect baked eggs and cheese recipe. That's how I discovered the Backpacking Gourmet. I literally fell off my chair when I saw the picture of Nonno posted on the website. Since I knew that my last name was definitely not 'Christ,' I convinced myself that it was insane to think that my grandfather had somehow been resurrected from the dead. I did my best to just push the whole thing out of my head."

"Let me guess," Shelley said. "It pushed back."

"Hard. I kept seeing that man's face as if it were scorched into my eyes. I went through a thousand rational explanations for what I saw but wound up rejecting every single one of them. I finally decided to prove to myself how silly I was being. I looked through our old photo albums, hoping to get a good laugh at my own expense. But as I scrutinized each picture, seeing the same, unchanging face, I realized that it was far from funny."

Shelley looked at him with a question she was not sure she should ask.

"Why didn't I see it before, right?" Paolo said. "How could I grow up with a man and not notice that he wasn't getting any older? I asked myself the same thing. But I suppose if you see someone every day, you don't really notice him getting older or, in this case, staying the same."

She was surprised that Paolo could read her so well. His similarity to her husband did not end with his looks.

"Nonno was always just Nonno. He was certainly fit for his age, but I didn't really think much of it," he said. "The disproportionate number of female customers in his secondhand bookstore didn't seem to mind, either. They were always quite pleased to learn that he was a widower."

Shelley's face fell. She had been so caught up in the morning's whirlwind that she had not even given a thought to what should have been very obvious from the beginning: Grandmothers were a prerequisite for grandsons. Max had been married to someone other than herself. Her stomach churned.

"My grandmother died long before I was born," Paolo said. "Nonno didn't talk about her much."

Shelley rushed to the sink to throw up.

"Uh . . . are you okay?" Paolo asked.

Shelley watched the water wash away her last meal as Max's widow. *Max's widow.* It sounded like a bad joke. She wondered now if she had ever even truly been his wife. She cupped her hands under the tap and filled them with as much clarity as they would hold. She dove in.

When she emerged, she knew what she had to do. She opened the drawer next to her and groped through it. Inside was the only option she had left. Her fingers found what she was searching for. Her fist tightened around its familiar shape. She drew out her last recourse: her emergency stash of obscenely expensive organic tea. After Madrid, she had made a point of always having a tin of loose jasmine leaves close by. She put the kettle on.

Shelley poured out two cups of steeped calm and offered one to Paolo. Then she took a long sip and braced herself for the rest of his story. "Please continue."

Paolo stared into his tea. "Seeing the truth was like losing Nonno all over again, but I still couldn't accept what was now in front of me. That is, until Bradford Jensen's book found its way to the publishing company I work for. The concept of his book seemed promising. I looked through the photographs and was instantly drawn into his story." He glanced up at her. "And then I saw you . . ."

"And Max." Shelley clutched her chipped floral teacup.

"There was no denying what I saw this time," Paolo said. "I called your friend and asked him about the pictures."

"You decided to find me . . ."

"Yes."

Shelley drained her tea. She began to accept what she needed to do, defying the million reasons why she shouldn't. She and Paolo needed answers and they were not going to find them in her kitchen.

A FLIGHT TO THE PHILIPPINES
❧ *Now*

F ish!"

Shelley and Paolo's chorus jostled the flight attendant's practiced smile. It wobbled momentarily, teetering between annoyance and disdain. Then the woman blinked and plastered it back. She handed them their choice of steamed sea bass fillet, leaving the offensive roasted chicken breast and potatoes on her dinner cart.

Shelley inhaled the entire contents of her tray. The last of the adrenaline that had fueled her had been spent in the sprint to the airport. It was only now, as she was licking the remnants of tapioca pudding from her spoon, that she was beginning to comprehend how she had come to be strapped into a coach seat on a flight to the other side of the world.

She had made the decision to fly to Boracay that evening with the same blind haste she had on her first and last attempt at a do-it-yourself Brazilian bikini wax. If there was anything the home kit had taught her, it was that there were certain things in life that did not allow for even a half-breath's hesitation. But unlike her inadvertent foray into masochism, no amount of anti-inflammatory cream could take away the realization stinging her now.

Frantic scenes of herself mindlessly packing, jumping into twice-worn jeans, and stumbling out the door with Paolo replayed in Shelley's head. It dawned on her that she was on the most important journey of her life with a backpack containing only her passport, Max's plaid bathrobe, a pair of gym socks, and a container of dental floss. The last item was arguably packed more out of habit than haste, the legacy of her reminding Max to floss every single night for two years. She chewed on her plastic spoon. This was the last time, she swore, that she would pack without a list.

"This is going to be a long flight," Paolo said. "It's a good thing that we have a lot to do to pass the time."

Shelley set the mangled utensil down and scanned through the in-flight movie selection. She had already seen most of the films. "Cards?"

"That's not what I meant. I've told you my story," he said, "now it's your turn."

"Well, you've pretty much got the gist of it already, right?" Shelley said. "Girl meets boy. Girl marries boy. Boy dies, but not really. Boy opens café on a tropical island. Girl searches for boy with boy's grandson. Your standard love story, I would think."

"I'm serious, Shelley," Paolo said. "We might be able to find some clues to this mystery if you could fill me in on a few more details of what you knew about Nonno."

The flight attendant drifted by with pots of coffee and tea. Shelley leaped at her chance for a reprieve. "Tea, please."

She stirred a packet of sugar into the steaming amber liquid. She took a sip and burned her tongue. Paolo was right. Finding Max without preparing herself would be scalding and beyond horrific. On the other hand, she had once read that you could boil a frog alive without any struggle if you raised the temperature in slight increments. Boil now or burn later.

"It all started five years ago with a bar of soap." Shelley heard the fire crackle under her seat. "I had moved to London from the States and was working as a copywriter. My team was on our eighth revision for a new soy-milk soap ad campaign. Our lovely client, you see, had the notion that their sales were somehow directly proportionate to the number of times their brand name was mentioned in the copy. This left me with two choices. The first was to write a commercial that began with 'new' and fill up the rest of the thirty seconds with 'Smilky.' The second, and my personal preference, was to tell Mr. Appleby exactly where he could shove his moisturizing bar. Fortunately, Sister Margaret talked me out of it."

"Sister Margaret?" Paolo asked.

"My old Catholic-school teacher. The real Sister Margaret is in retirement in a nuns' community in Florida, but for better or worse, hers is still the voice of my inconvenient conscience."

"I take it that the two of you don't get along?"

"Let's just say we've learned how to compromise. That's how I wound up churning out the requisite number of Smilkys—twenty-four to be exact—and stapling it to a resignation letter that was, to be honest, tons more creatively fulfilling. I left my masterpiece on my boss's desk, grabbed the plastic potted plant from mine, and hurried to catch my train before the euphoric cloud of freedom I was floating on could drop my unemployed butt on the pavement. I needed my hoard of dark chocolate to cushion the fall."

Chapter Three

Campers and caveats

LONDON

❧ *Five Years Ago*

Shelley hugged her fake fern. It offered as much sympathy as plastic leaves could—support that did not include making the escalator's descent into the tube station less excruciating. A bicycle with two flat tires could have made a faster getaway.

The first drop of regret had hit her as soon as she stepped out of her office building. It snaked down her back. As she sprinted to the tube, the trickle of afterthought burst into a downpour. She hated being drenched with hindsight. It seeped through her skin and settled into her marrow, making her joints ache with cold. It was the very reason she made lists.

Some people carried hand wipes for emergencies. Shelley made lists. Since she was without a clear long-term plan, they were her best, though not necessarily successful, attempts to navigate life. Things to do. Things not to do. What to do if she did. The latter was particularly important, as she often found herself with a shopping cart full of chips and chocolates despite her best efforts to make a beeline for the yogurt aisle. Still, she tried.

Whole wheat bread. Jasmine tea. Ignore half-off frozen waffles. Check.
Phone Mom. Chatter brightly. Fake yawn. Check.
Flee Ohio. Move to London. Get a job. Check.

Unfortunately, Shelley's last list didn't have an exit plan. She considered the upside of returning to the States and moving back in with her mother. Pressed clothing was always nice. No longer having to subsist on instant ramen was even better. The nostalgia over her mom's grilled lamb chops, however, fell a dollop of mint jelly short of convincing her that heading home was for the best. She conjured a memory of rosemary baked potatoes. They smelled good, but not good enough. As much as her mother's dinners were lovingly made, Shelley was all too aware that they came with strings of the thick apron variety. London was as far as she could run to avoid being ensnared in them while still being able to order takeout without needing a dictionary.

Shelley sighed. She knew she couldn't blame her mother for her vise-like grip. It was her father's fault. He was the one who had died. She had been ten when cancer ate him away and her mother had started embracing her tighter. Shelley had learned two things growing up pressed flat against her mother's grief: how to hold her breath and how to squirm away as soon as she had the chance. It wasn't that she didn't love her mother— she just couldn't bear to listen to the echo inside her chest. Nothing was lonelier than the limping beat of half a heart.

A blast of Italian expletives knocked Shelley to the present. A young couple was manhandling a map of the London Underground a few steps below her on the escalator. She considered helping them but changed her mind. *Gelato al cioccolato* was the full extent of her Italian vocabulary and would not be of much use in getting them to their destination unless they wanted ice cream. The woman grunted, snatched the map, and threw it in the air. It flapped against Shelley's face. The man hollered an apology Shelley's way and chased after his companion.

Shelley pulled off the map, relieved to be irritated at someone other than herself. She scanned the map of multicolored lines, envying the order of preordained stops. She wished that making her way through life was as simple as tracing a thick blue line from Piccadilly station to a reasonable mortgage, a car, and a medium-size non-shedding dog and/or cat. Sensible. Straightforward. Allergen-free. The route itself wasn't complicated, she admitted, except for her habit of jumping off trains. She cradled her fern and remembered why it was in her arms. She had leaped off another one. She had not followed her list. Again.

Sit. Grin. Bear it. Damn.

Advertising had been slightly tolerable while it lasted. And so was her fleeting stint at a golfing magazine before it. At the very least, these jobs had paid the bills. Shelley groaned into her plant. If only eating dark chocolate and running away were financially viable life skills.

She had become quite adept at the art of escape, and not just from jobs that required her to write about soy milk or golf balls. Since moving to London a year earlier, she had developed a talent for making a clean getaway from men who got too close. The last one was named Roger. Shelley had promised herself that she would never end up like her mom, and dumping men just before things became too serious seemed like a reasonable strategy. It followed the same principle as pushing away a dessert after a few bites. Guys like Roger were fun rides that were easy to hop off of miles before she was in any danger of having her heart split in two.

Meet. Date. Run. Check. Check. Check.

(Shelley kept copies of this particular list in her pocket. She had always found accents particularly sexy, and in London there were many opportunities to get distracted.)

Shelley reached the bottom of the escalator. The Italian couple was kissing by a vending machine. She rolled her eyes and made her way to the edge of the platform. Paper rustled against her foot.

A yellow leaflet clung to her heel. Shelley tried to pry it free, stretching the pink tentacles that glued it to her shoe. The top half of the paper tore off. She teetered near the platform gap, hopping on one foot and trying to regain her balance without dropping her plant.

FANCY GETTING LOST? The words leaped from the tattered page in Shelley's hand.

The wind whipped in the tunnel. Her train was approaching. She pulled off the rest of the leaflet just as the train came to a stop. She stuffed it into her handbag and read it on her way home.

THE SLIGHT DETOUR

Veer away from the expected and lose yourself in the
back roads of history on a road trip across Europe. Not
for the prissy or the daft. Nutters most welcome. Good
fun and excellent egg breakfasts included.

It was exactly what she needed—the chance to postpone reality. The fact that the tour was leaving the very next morning was even better. She needed to get out of London as fast as humanly possible. She dialed the number listed on the yellow paper. The phone rang six times.

"Hello! The Slight Detour Company." The man at the end of the line caught his breath. "Max Gallus here. Sorry to keep you waiting. Was chasing after some chickens. How may I help you?"

"Er, hi. This is Shelley Sullivan. I know this is rather last minute, but I was wondering if I could still join the tour tomorrow?"

"You're in luck, luv. It will be tight, but I think we can squeeze you in the boot. Log on to our website for details. You can pay by credit card."

Pack bags. Lock up flat. Escape. Check.

Shelley craned her neck to catch sight of the tour bus. Her hope that it would ever show up flickered along with the streetlamp she was standing next to. The website had said that the pickup time was 1:30 A.M. That was twenty minutes ago. She shivered in her light coat. A vintage electric-blue Volkswagen van sputtered around the corner and put the brakes on her dismay. It stopped at the curb. Its driver stuck his head out of the window.

"Ms. Sullivan?"

Smiling at her was the scruffier, though no less charming, version of the fairy tale she had dreamed up when she still believed in happy endings and had married a hundred times over in her wedding finery of crocheted doilies and her mother's high heels. Her heart, without any consultation with Sister Margaret, leaped. Shelley chewed her lip. This was dangerous. She stuck her hand in her pocket and fumbled for her list. *Meet. Date.* She couldn't remember what came next. She vaguely remembered it sounded like "fun."

"Er, are you Ms. Shelley Sullivan?"

"I do. I mean, yes, I am. I am." Shelley hoped her collar was pulled up high enough to hide the blush creeping up her neck.

"I do apologize for being late. The old girl was feeling her age this morning." The driver patted the side of the Volkswagen. "But she's raring to cross the continent now." He stepped out of the vehicle. He towered over Shelley's five-foot-four frame. "I'm Max, your humble servant for the rest of the tour. We spoke on the phone."

Shelley shook Max's hand as firmly as she could, battling the visceral human impulse to stick her tongue down his throat and have his children. "It's, um, lovely to meet you, Max."

"Likewise." Max took her luggage and headed to the back of the van.

She followed him, admiring the ease with which he carried her suitcase.

He loaded her bag and took a step back. "Watch your step, luv."

"Huh?"

"It took a bit of clever space management, but I managed to find a place for you next to the toolbox."

Shelley willed her mouth to close. It would not.

"Joshing, luv." Max chuckled, putting his arm around her shoulders and giving her a quick squeeze. "I apologize. I couldn't resist."

"Is this a preview of the rest of the tour?"

"Absolutely."

Good. Shelley smiled to herself and hopped aboard the van.

The inside of the van was roomier than Shelley had expected, though she still had to duck to avoid the disco ball hanging from the ceiling.

"Good morning" came a chorus from the back.

She twisted around. An elderly couple waved at her from the backseat. A gangly red-haired man was squeezed in next to them, his long legs tucked at an angle that made her heart go out to his knees.

"Oh, hi. Good morning," Shelley said. "Didn't see you there."

"We're the Templetons. I'm Jonathan and this is my wife, Rose," said the bear-size man. His thick white mustache and beard gave Shelley the distinct impression that he was of the polar persuasion. The way he circled his lips around vowels, however, placed his roots south of the Arctic Circle. Cardiff, perhaps.

"We're on our honeymoon." Rose twittered like the canary Shelley's grandmother used to own, and was only marginally larger.

The young man seated next to Rose tipped his Red Sox baseball cap at Shelley and flashed a toothy grin. His smile was wide and came easily enough, but there was something about the way it was cast across his freckled face that made her wonder if it was boyishly lopsided or . . . broken. "I'm Dex," he said with an accent to match his cap, "and not on my honeymoon."

Shelley nodded back, undecided about Dex's grin despite the lilting humor in his voice. "Hi, I'm Shelley. Recently unemployed and avoiding reality."

"That's lovely, dear," Rose said. "We all need to take a proper break once in a while. Life's too short." She smiled and grew ten inches taller in Shelley's eyes.

Max strapped himself into the driver's seat. "Shelley, did you happen to see two other Americans around? They're supposed to be meeting us here."

"No, I'm afraid not."

"It will just be us five happy campers then." Max turned the key in the ignition.

A tall figure appeared in the dark street. His sandy blond hair flopped over his forehead as he sprinted toward the van. A chestnut-haired man ran alongside him, his glasses jostling on his nose. Prada suitcases rattled behind them.

"Max, wait!" Jonathan said.

Max looked in the rearview mirror and grinned. He put the Volkswagen in reverse and met the two men halfway. He hopped out of the van and slid the dented passenger door open.

"Thank God!" The blond man slipped in next to Shelley. A Nikon camera swung from a black strap around his neck.

His companion took the seat beside him and closed the door. He panted as he nudged his glasses higher on his crooked nose. "Thanks for waiting."

A wisp of peppermint drifted Shelley's way.

"Wouldn't dream of leaving without you," Max said. "Didn't think you'd fancy the swim across the Channel. The water can be rather nippy at this time of day."

"I'm Brad and this is Simon," said the man with the camera.

The group traded handshakes and hellos.

"Campers, may I have your attention, please," Max said. "There's a standard little speech I need to make before we get to the point of no return." He pulled a folded piece of paper from the pocket of his khaki shirt. It was his little yellow leaflet. He flipped it around and cleared his throat. " 'Greetings, campers,' " he read out loud. " 'I do hope you read my little leaflet before you signed up for this trip; otherwise you might be in for a very, and I mean very, long trip. But just in case you did manage to do the unfathomably stupid feat of blindly signing up, allow me to give you one last chance to salvage your holiday. We don't give refunds, but if you decide to drop out at this point, I want to leave you with the warm and fuzzy feeling that you will be making a young Cambodian orphan very happy with the generous donation that I will be making of your payment. For anyone who thinks they are climbing the Eiffel Tower, cruising down the Danube, or climbing the Spanish Steps, little Seng Kong Kea would like to say *"Awkun ch'ran"* from the bottom of his heart and hopes you can visit him on your next holiday.'

"As clearly stated in my leaflet, we will not make any stops of popular historical significance. For that, you can dust off your old history books or watch those highly informative BBC documentaries. Or, better yet, you can make a mad dash for the Go Europe! coach parked across the street." Max looked around at the group. "So, does anyone have that cold knot of panic in their stomach yet? Ah, good. Looks like increasing the font size to fourteen paid off this year. I formally welcome everyone then to Whips, Welts, and Wenches, the U.K.'s premier sex tour. You can call me Master Max."

Rose squeaked. She clutched her little peacock-blue handbag to her chest. Jonathan bundled her close.

Max grinned. "Anyway, for those of you who really didn't read the leaflet and are now trying their very best to put on a brave front and make a go of this trip, I'm proud of you. I'm counting to ten before I turn the key and we reach the point where you're stuck with me."

The group stole glances at one another as Max counted out loud.

"Eight, nine, ten. We're off!" Max restarted the van. "Oh, and don't worry, I'll still be making a donation to the Cambodian orphanage on your behalf even if you are joining the tour."

Brad leaned toward Shelley's ear. "I wouldn't trade the Eiffel Tower for this guy's buns, would you?"

Shelley giggled, agreeing fully.

Max tilted the rearview mirror to look at her. "What's so funny, luv?"

"Oh, er, nothing," Shelley said. The edges of her mouth were still twitching.

"Already we have secrets between us. Well, let's see what other secrets await us on this trip, eh, campers?" Max turned a knob on the stereo and filled the Volkswagen with the falsetto of the brothers Gibb. "First stop, Paris."

The mirrored ball showered flecks of sunlight across her eyelids. Shelley stirred from a dream about French carbohydrates. The warm buttery scent grew stronger, teasing her awake. She rubbed the sleep from her eyes and leaned out of the van's window. The wind tousled her hair and carried with it a sonorous pleasure: the ensemble of croissants calling her name.

"Bonjour, campers!" Max said. "We are now in gay Paree. We'll be making a stop at our accommodations so we can have some breakfast before we begin our little adventure."

An assortment of yawns, grunts, and crackles of joints answered him. Dex sounded particularly creaky.

Shelley caught Max's eye in the mirror and smiled. He gave her a wink.

Max drove the van through the Right Bank and down a cobbled street lined with grandes dames decked in their finest wrought-iron lace. He parked in front of one of the regal buildings. He stepped out of the van and rang the doorbell. A round old lady answered the door and bounded onto the sidewalk.

"Maximilian!" The woman kissed both of Max's cheeks.

"Marianne, *comment ça va?*"

"*Ça va très bien, merci!*" Marianne's ample chest heaved with delight.

"*Et les poulets?*" Max asked.

And the chickens? Or at least that's what Shelley thought he asked. Her French wasn't as good as she had thought.

"*Très bien! Et toi,* Maximilian?" Marianne's eyes darted over Max's face. "You look the same as always," she continued in French.

Max smiled. "There are seven of us who will be bothering you this time," he said, reverting to English. He signaled the group to join him.

"You no zat eet ees nevah a bozzer, Maximilian." Marianne's accent coated each syllable of her English like a layer of marzipan. "Welcom, evree-won. I am Marianne, zee caretakah ov zeez hom. Please com eenside."

Unless the local YMCA had done some major renovations, Shelley thought, this was not the budget hostel she had expected to be staying in for the price she'd paid for Max's tour. The building she walked into had fallen out of step with time, preserving an elegance more likely to be seen cordoned behind the Louvre's velvet ropes. She couldn't help feeling that her jeans and red Chuck Taylors were an affront to the parlor's gilded ceiling, silk-covered walls, and crystal fixtures. "Are we washing dishes to pay for this?" she asked Max.

"Yes, but you'll need to wear your French maid's uniform first," he said. "Marianne will show you where you can change."

Marianne giggled and took Shelley's arm. "Come. I weel show you to your rums." Her cheeks puffed as she led the group up a carved staircase.

To her credit, Shelley managed to behave like an adult long enough for Marianne to close the door of her room behind her. She shed all such pretense when she heard it click shut. The room was a jewel box. She guessed it had once belonged to the dark-haired girl whose faded portrait hung on one of its walls. The quiet smile in the girl's amber eyes made Shelley feel welcome. She launched herself onto the canopied bed and sank into a sea of pillows and silk. Highly inappropriate thoughts of a certain tour guide stirred inside her. She fiddled with the button on her jeans and considered locking the door. She closed her eyes.

"Amore," Max whispered in her ear.

Shelley bolted upright, then heaved a sigh of relief. Max was not there. His voice had drifted in from the small garden below her window. She peeked out.

Max was singing—opera—impressively. Shelley watched him sing as he collected brown eggs from a small henhouse tucked in the corner of the garden. Two clucking feather balls darted around him like puppies. Smug satisfaction curled in the corners of her mouth. She had not forgotten her French after all.

A whiff of strong coffee lured the group from their rooms, but it was the warm, savory scent that made them scamper down the staircase. They bounded into the kitchen.

"Feeding time at the zoo." Max pulled the oven door open and flooded the white brick kitchen with promise. "Rooms all right, campers?"

"Boudoirs, Max, boudoirs," Brad said. "Between your donations to orphanages and setting us up in this palace, I can't figure out how you're making any money on this tour—not that I'm complaining. I love being on the receiving end of charity."

"The owners of this home are friends of mine, mate. They like that I drop in and keep an eye on the place for them once in a while." Max drew a large earthenware dish from the oven.

The group followed Max and their noses to a rustic wooden table. It groaned under the weight of freshly baked bread, croissants, jams, coffee, and fruit. Max set the dish at the center of the table, revealing a golden crust of cheese topped with a sprinkling of fresh herbs. It bubbled an invitation.

"I only had time to whip up some baked eggs and cheese this morning, but it should be enough to sustain you through our adventures today," Max said. "I was worried that I might find you chewing one another's appendages off if I attempted anything more elaborate. To be honest, it was a bit of a mess to clean up the last time that happened."

"If your cooking is as lovely as it smells, I don't think you'll have to worry about any of us snacking on body parts today." Shelley was lying, of course, since nibbling on Max seemed like a perfectly good alternative to breakfast—at least that's how she felt before her first forkful of his baked eggs.

She sank her teeth into melted cheese and summer, unleashing a silk stream of eggs and cream in her mouth. A buttery earthiness lingered on her tongue. She gulped orange juice to keep from moaning from the world's first egg orgasm.

Rose gave Shelley a knowing look. "I came as well, dear. Twice."

Jonathan sputtered, turning a shade brighter than the raspberry preserves on his baguette. "Ah . . . um . . . yes, yes, wonderful eggs, Max. *Très magnifique.*"

Shelley did not recover quite as elegantly, and was still choking on the juice that had spurted out of her nose and onto Max's shirt. Max came to her rescue with a couple of solid pats to her back, a napkin, and a grin.

Shelley watched Jonathan mop up the last of his eggs. She sipped her coffee and made a mental list of what she knew about her traveling companions so far:

Dex was a freelance writer, chewed slowly, and had a wheat allergy.

Jonathan was more than happy to save Dex from his croissants.

Rose was not, and religiously reminded her husband to take his anticholesterol pills.

The honeymooners argued about Jonathan's diet but agreed on the care of hydrangeas—so much so that they got married at the flower club where they met.

Brad and Simon did not belong to a garden club, were not allergic to wheat, and did not have high cholesterol, but were thrilled about their new wedding-planning business.

That about covered it except for Max.

Shelley set her cup on the table. It was the second she had drained while waiting for her guide to volunteer information about himself. She decided to take matters into her own hands. "And how about you, Max? Is this what you do full time? I recall that you were chasing after some chickens when we spoke over the phone. Married? Um, happily?"

Max smiled. "Maximilian B. Gallus. Tour operator by profession, chicken farmer by passion, and single on account of the vow of celibacy required by the Poultry Club of Great Britain. It is a curious fact that jealous chickens do not lay as many eggs as their emotionally secure counterparts, you see." He turned to the group. "And now, campers, if you're done with breakfast, it's time we made our way to the first of our two destinations in Paris. Let's meet in the parlor in ten minutes, shall we?"

The group gathered beneath the ornate Metro sign at the top of the steps leading to the subway.

Dex eyed the sign and pulled a small Lumix camera from his backpack. He adjusted his baseball cap and took a deep breath. "Um, can I take your picture, Shelley?"

Shelley obliged by default, too lost in her own thoughts to manage anything more than a blank stare. She was busy relishing the breakfast that had settled lazily in her stomach and the fact that, celibate or not, Max was single. She smiled to herself.

Dex angled his camera and framed Shelley below the subway sign's green art nouveau arch.

"Now listen, campers," Max said. "Take note of this place in case you get lost during our field trip and need to find your way back home. If you don't think you can remember where we started from, you can purchase a baguette and leave a trail of bread crumbs. Oh, and before we head off, there are three things you must remember. First, don't talk to strangers.

Second, you need to be aware that your travel insurance does not cover acts of stupidity or alien abduction. Please do your best to avoid them. And third, hold on to your mates."

The couples in the group took Max's instructions to heart and proceeded hand in hand down the stairs of the station.

Dex glanced at Shelley, his cheeks as red as his hair. He held out his arm to her. "Um . . . I suppose he means us."

"No, I don't, actually." Max grinned at Dex.

"Oh, uh, well . . ." Dex's arm snapped back into place.

Max turned to Shelley. "You're in luck, luv. Not only am I skilled at rescuing damsels from drowning in orange juice, but you'll find that I'm also rather adept at mating."

Shelley raised a brow. "Mating?"

"Mating," Max said, "from the word *mate,* a word derived from the Old Dutch word *maet* or *companion,* which shares the same root as *mete,* which means 'to measure.'"

"I see," Shelley said. "So what you are in fact offering me is a measure of companionship, correct?"

"Indeed." Max stuck out the crook of his arm. "The length of my arm to be exact. All in accordance with the guidelines of the Poultry Club, I assure you. You won't get lost, I have a place to rest my arm, and the chickens are secure in my fidelity." He shrugged at Dex. "I'd offer you my other arm . . ."

"Er, that's okay." Dex stuck his hands in his pockets and marched down the steps. "I'll take my chance with the bread crumbs."

Simon looked up at the name of the station from which they had emerged. "Père Lachaise. That's the cemetery where Jim Morrison is buried, right?"

"That's correct," Max said. "The Cimetière du Père-Lachaise was the site of a Jesuit residence and was converted into a cemetery in 1804. Apart from Mr. Morrison, it is home to other famous residents such as Héloise and Abélard, Oscar Wilde, Maria Callas, and Frédéric Chopin, to name a few."

"And who among that distinguished set shall we be paying a visit to today, Max?" Jonathan asked.

"You'll meet her soon enough."

Père Lachaise was a village, Shelley thought, minus the village. There were no charming country houses along the tree-shaded streets, only crumbling mausoleums, each more sadly beautiful than the next. Brad snapped away with his camera, capturing the eternal mourning of the stone angels that stood watch over them. Occasionally, he trained his Nikon at an aging rocker that strode past them, focusing on a thinning gray ponytail or a tear in his jeans. She guessed that these leather-cuffed devotees were not searching for Oscar Wilde.

As much as she liked the Doors, however, she could not fathom why anyone would come to Père Lachaise of his or her own accord. She loathed cemeteries. They broke her heart like posters for missing dogs and ice-cream cones dropped by little kids. But it wasn't the yellow Labrador puppies, vanilla melting on the pavement, or the dead beneath the grave-stones that made her sad. What tore her up was the thought of the people who lost them. That, and soggy grass—the kind your heels sank into after an hour of steady rain.

Shelley could still feel the way the grass had squished under her feet that gray morning she stood at her mother's side watching raindrops splatter over her dad's coffin. She did not know at the time that she was attending three funerals: one for her dad, the second for her ruined ballet flats, and the third for the twinkle in her mom's eye when her dad walked through the door.

Shelley blinked back tears. She looked around, searching for dry and solid ground. Apart from the clicking of Brad's camera, her little group walked in silence, their feet shuffling along the same path, their thoughts wandering on more distant roads. Dex seemed to have drifted the far-thest away. He glanced toward her and caught her looking at him. He flashed her the same fractured smile he had when they had met in the van. It was bright, but it still made Shelley wonder if something less sunny was hidden beneath.

"This way," Max said as he grabbed Shelley's arm. Leaves rustled above the thin dirt path, leading toward a stone wall. Shelley didn't notice them. She was busy trying not to trip over their fluttering shadows. Walking arm in arm with Max had the unfortunate effect of making her knees wobble.

"Has anyone here heard of the Bloody Week?" Max asked. "And just to be clear, I am not referring to that nasty union strike at the tube last month."

"If memory serves me right, I believe that was the week when the French government reclaimed Paris from the Communards who had taken over the city in the late 1800s," Jonathan said.

"Well done, Jonathan," Max said. "That would be a somewhat sanitized definition, but, yes, technically correct. Although the twenty thousand men, women, and children who were brutally murdered that week might think that 'mass indiscriminate slaughter' was a more apt description. Semantics." He shrugged. "Ah, there it is." He pointed to the perimeter wall of the cemetery and doubled his pace, dragging Shelley along with him.

A large cement plaque was affixed to the wall. It was engraved with the words AUX MORTS DE LA COMMUNE 21–28 MAI 1871.

"The Wall of the Communards, the final resting place of the doomed Bohemian dream that was, for two months in 1871, the Paris Commune," Max said. "It is also the approximate site of the execution and mass grave of one hundred forty-seven souls who were rounded up and shot against this wall. They were the lucky ones."

"The lucky ones?" Dex asked.

"Living among the dead and scavenging for food like wild animals could not have been a pleasant experience for the survivors who were forced into hiding here after the slaughter," Max said. "But I am getting ahead of myself. I could begin our story on the day an overindulged thirteen-year-old named Isabelle debated with her father, Julien, on the merits of having a cat, but I'm afraid I might lose you somewhere in the midst of their frequent puberty-fueled quarrels. I have therefore decided to begin our tale with the far less complicated subject of the Franco-Prussian War. Any objections?"

"Gee. Sounds like fun." Brad groaned.

"Hardly," Max said. "War never is—especially when you are on the losing end—which is exactly where the French dangled precariously from, on January 28, 1871. They had lost their long war with Prussia over the Spanish throne. Starving Parisians surrendered after months of being under siege and blockaded within their city's walls. Among the terms of armistice was a ceremonial entry by the Prussian army into Paris."

"I bet that the French weren't too thrilled by that," Simon said.

Max nodded. "The city's working class was particularly upset. The war had brought countless deprivations and sacrifices—hunger, poverty, death—and now, adding the humiliation of defeat to the hardships they had already endured stirred up the proverbial hornet's nest. But they were too busy hiding the cannons that they had used to defend the city from the Prussians to mope.

"Prussian troops paraded through the city. They were later withdrawn when France agreed to pay five billion gold francs in war indemnity. Following the Prussian withdrawal, the French government decided to relocate to the landscaped gardens of Versailles, believing that the farther away it was from the grumbling Parisians who had to shoulder the bulk of the reparation payments, the better," Max said. "The government, however, had one of those did-I-leave-the-iron-on? moments when it occurred to them that four hundred cannons were probably not such a good thing to leave at the disposal of an angry mob. It decided to seize them. It was not one of its best ideas."

"Why not?" Simon asked.

"Well, getting Paris back and winning over its residents wasn't a simple matter of saying please," Max said. "The soldiers from Versailles found themselves face-to-face with the citizens' militia—the National Guard—as well as throngs of Parisians who were, quite understandably, not eager to part with their only real means of defense. When ordered to shoot at the crowd, the demoralized soldiers turned around, shot their commander, and joined the rebellion. The remaining loyal troops scampered out of Paris, leaving a city of two million people without a government.

"When the smoke cleared, a town council, or 'Commune,' was formed by the citizens themselves. The Commune was comprised of ninety or so people, almost half of whom had barely gotten over their teen acne. Among them were clerks, journalists, teachers, and of particular significance to our story, one veterinarian."

Max said this last word with such distaste that it reminded Shelley of the time she made the mistake of asking her grandmother for a sip of the cod liver oil she took every morning. Moments like those scarred you for life.

Max sighed. "This is the part where I always regret not talking about Isabelle's cat earlier. We will now have to leave the birth of the Paris Commune for a moment to discuss the matter of a girl and her sickly cat. Isabelle had eventually won the debate with her father about getting a pet cat. She had unleashed the weapon against which all hapless fathers have no defense."

"Let me guess," Shelley said. "A hug, a kiss on the cheek, and a sugary 'Please, Daddy, please?'"

Max smiled. "How did you know?"

"It's listed on page ten of 'A Daughter's Guide to Manipulating Her Father.' We're issued that manual at birth," Shelley said.

Brad smirked. "No wonder I'm still waiting for the pink pony I asked for for Christmas."

"As it turned out, Isabelle had more luck than you, Brad. Or perhaps, I should say, less. She got her cat," Max said, "and in the process met the veterinarian she would elope with four years later."

"That doesn't sound too bad," Simon said. "Unless, of course, her husband turned out to be a total jerk."

"He was worse," Max said. "He was an idealist. In any other place and time that would have been forgivable, but not in Paris in 1871. Teen-age infatuation and daring idealism were a volatile combination then. It was not a good time for a young girl to go behind her father's back to elope with her cat's veterinarian, Stephane, a man who would later be an elected member of the hastily formed Paris Commune. And so, as Isabelle's wealthy friends and neighbors fled the city once armistice had been reached with Prussia, Isabelle faithfully made her bed with her new husband and his reformist beliefs. Julien had no choice but to stay in the city and watch over his daughter as best he could while waiting for the end he knew was coming. The Versailles government would retake the city—at whatever cost. It was just a matter of time."

Max led the group through one of the smaller lanes in the cemetery and stopped in front of a white marble building. The small mausoleum was noticeably well preserved compared to some of its disintegrating neighbors.

"Here we are. I hope you aren't too disappointed that we aren't visiting dear old Jim." Max fished a key from his pocket and unlocked the mausoleum's iron gates. They were well oiled and hardly made a sound when he pulled them open.

The group followed him inside.

Marble columns stood in each corner of the ivory room, effortlessly holding up the weight of the world. A woman with a child's face slept in the center of the mausoleum. The marble folds of her dress flowed over her stone bed. Across her chest, her carved hands clasped a freshly cut bouquet of small purple flowers.

"French-Roman hyacinths," Jonathan said. "An interesting choice."

"Yes, very sad, indeed," Rose said.

"Sad?" Shelley asked. "How so?"

"Every flower has a specific meaning, dear," Rose explained. "Red roses say 'I love you.' Pink carnations say 'I'll never forget you.' And purple hyacinths, well, they say 'please forgive me.'"

"Oh." Shelley wanted to ask Max who the dead girl was, but he was no longer by her side.

He stood in front of the wall on the far side of the mausoleum. The entire wall was covered with an intricate mosaic of an olive tree. He gazed up at its canopy as though studying each of its leaves.

The tour group shifted on their feet. Jonathan's bunions began to throb. He cleared his throat. "So, Max, who exactly are we paying our respects to here?"

Max turned from the mosaic and walked over to the marble woman. "Well, campers, if you haven't guessed by now, this is Isabelle's tomb or, to be more precise, this is where her memory has been laid to rest. Her body lies at the foot of the Wall of the Communards, the place where she was executed more than a century ago."

"Executed?" Shelley gasped, glancing at Isabelle's childlike face. "But she was only a girl . . ."

"She was seventeen," Max said softly.

"What happened to her family?" Shelley asked. Isabelle, she thought, looked terribly alone in her marble tomb.

Max gestured to the mosaic. He stepped aside and let the group approach the wall.

Names, painted on glass tiles, sprouted from the olive tree's limbs. *Adrien. Pavel. Ionus.* Shelley squinted at the topmost tier. The two names, from which the family branched, had faded beyond recognition. Her eyes drifted to a pale yellow flower forever falling to the ground. The name it bore was barely a whisper over the glass petal. *Isabelle.* Shelley reached out to touch it. Fingers closed tightly around her wrist and pulled her arm back from the wall. She looked up. Max was glaring at her.

"The mosaic is very fragile," he said.

"I'm . . . I'm sorry." Shelley could feel her face burning with embarrassment. Her throat tightened. She wondered if it was possible for shame to cause anaphylactic shock.

"You didn't know, dear." Rose patted Shelley's arm. "Isn't that right, Max?" A grandmotherly reprimand was hidden in her soft voice.

Max drew a deep breath. "Yes, yes, of course. No harm done."

Shelley looked away, undecided if she would ever speak to him again.

Dex caught Shelley's eye and winked. He tapped Max on the shoulder. "Um, excuse me, Max. At the risk of sounding like the ignorant ugly American, I have to ask: Who is this Isabelle, anyway? I mean, are we supposed to know her? Is she famous or something?"

Max flashed a grin. "I'm appalled. Don't they teach you anything in America? Well, not to worry. You didn't miss class when Isabelle's story was taken up. As I mentioned back in London, this tour will not take you down the well-trodden-tourist-trap path. Our characters do not make any cameo appearances in history books, so don't even bother looking them up later," he said. "All right, Shelley?"

The sound of her name startled her. It sounded different. No one had ever said it so gently. She looked up at Max. His amber eyes smiled at her. Her injured pride wrestled with the sides of her mouth to keep them from smiling back. He hadn't even said he was sorry, and she would not give in so easily. Max, she decided, was like a golden full-fat mozzarella stick fried in butter. Irresistible, unapologetic, and off-limits.

Shelley felt Max slip his hand over hers. He gave it a quick squeeze then let it go. Something soft and paper-thin was now in her palm. She drew her fingers open and saw the crumpled petals of Max's purple apology. She tucked them in the pocket of her jeans and smiled. "All right, Max."

Max smiled back. "Now where was I? Ah, yes, the characters in our story. You will find that they are no different from you except for the fact that they lived their lives before the invention of frappuccinos and when many more things were punishable by a horrible death. But, unlike the lot of you, who I'm certain still get a decent number of greetings on your birthday, our characters are now forgotten. This of course is not to say that, in due time, you will not be forgotten as well—because you will— unless of course you somehow earn a footnote in history by inventing something as brilliant as, shall we say, an egg incubator or as unspeakably evil as Facebook."

Shelley smirked. "I won a gift voucher for suggesting we ban plastic swizzle sticks in the office. Does that count?"

"I am sure the planet will be eternally grateful to you, but I doubt that your valuable contribution will be immortalized anytime soon. But don't fret. I, for one, do not think that makes you an inconsequential blip in time."

"I'm glad you think so," Shelley said. "I would hate to be forgotten so easily."

"I didn't say you wouldn't be forgotten, luv."

"Ouch."

"I said you weren't inconsequential. No one is. We change at least one person's life just by being born. If you don't believe me, go ask your mother. The fellows who write history books may not think that's so special. I happen to disagree. Isabelle and her family may be long gone, but because they lived, regardless of how small their lives may have been, I believe they are worth remembering, even if only by strangers."

"I can only hope that someone returns the favor when my time to be forgotten comes," Jonathan said wistfully.

Rose leaned into her husband's chest. "I don't think that's something you should be worrying yourself about, dear."

"I agree. Fretting over how life ends, or anything else for that matter, is a complete waste of time," Max said. "I don't know about you, but when I got my hands on those Harry Potter books, I simply had to sneak a peek at their last pages."

"Er, Harry Potter?" Jonathan arched a thick silver brow.

Max nodded. "I, for one, believe that in order to really enjoy any story, you need to get the ending out of the way as soon as possible—which is why I've brought all of you here. You are here to learn the conclusion of one family's story so that you may better appreciate how it began and the cast of characters you will meet along our way." Max gently stroked a lock of Isabelle's marble hair. "You have just met the last descendant of this family."

Shelley shivered, uncertain if it was Max's tone or the air in the tomb that had turned icy.

"Isabelle is how our story ends."

Chapter Four

Daughters and dragons

PARIS

ᚕᚖ *May 21, 1871*

Isabelle slipped from Julien's arms. She was falling, but not as fast as one might expect a small girl to fall to the ground. But she was not four anymore. She was six, or perhaps seven. No, not seven. She was older now. Nine. Twelve. Seventeen. She fell, beyond his grasp, beyond saving, shattering his heart into pieces. A fragment flew up and slashed his face, waking him from his nightmare.

Julien touched his cheek. It was wet. Sticky. His fingertips found a glass shard. He pried it from the paste of sweat and blood on his skin. He wiped his hand on the bedclothes and rose. Heat sliced through the ball of his foot. Blood trickled from his sole, hiding the sliver embedded in it. He squinted through the weak light. The floor glittered with the jagged pieces of a broken dawn. Screams poured through the shattered windows. He stepped around the maze of glass and peered outside. The Versailles army was swarming through the streets. Julien whispered her name: *Isabelle.*

This was the first time since he had stolen her from her father that he regretted his decision. That night, seventeen years ago, had been rancid with her mother's misery. It had soured the air with a stench worse than milk left in the sun. It was on her breath, on her skin, and in the tears she spilled over her newborn's cheeks when she abandoned her at the door of a once grand home. Julien could not blame her. The house belonged to her daughter's father and its wet stone steps were still better than the lice-infested bed her baby was born in. Leaving her child in the rain was a mercy. She could never offer her daughter more than that.

But Julien knew that Isabelle's father would give her even less. He had made choices that made Julien forget that he had once been bound to him, however distantly, by blood. The man was a gifted drunkard, but a far worse gambler—an unfortunate assemblage of talents that Julien correctly predicted would, sooner rather than later, send him to the bottom of the Thames with a rusty knife twisted in his back.

She had been so small, Julien remembered. He thought he would break her, as he ran from her father's house, through the cold night rain, to the ship waiting for them at the dock. Once they were safely onboard, sailing toward Paris, Julien looked into Isabelle's bright brown eyes. She was all that he had left and that was more than enough.

He grasped for the chain he wore around his neck and slipped it off. A crude locket made of two small half-shells of beaten gold dangled from it. It had been another child's once, a token of protection. Julien could no longer recall when he last believed in any shape of superstition, but in his daughter's eyes he found a new reason to have faith. He tucked the locket inside her coarse blanket. Tiny pink fingers reached out and grazed the tip of his slightly hooked nose. He breathed her in. Spring and promise. Untainted. He nuzzled her cheek, hoping to remember the smell of her skin forever.

Tonight, however, as the streets of Paris ran with blood, a part of Julien wished that he had never intervened. If he hadn't saved her that night, she would now be hungry and hard—a whore like her mother. He could live with that kind of guilt. At least in London his precious girl would be somewhere else, anywhere else, but here.

Julien dressed, clothing himself in the thin hope that the army had not yet reached Isabelle's home. He tucked two pistols into his coat and a dagger into his waistband. He raced downstairs. The courtyard was still dark. He called for Alessandra. She emerged, happy to see him. Julien gathered her in his arms. His fingertips found a passing calm in the softness of her feathers. Her eggs had been better currency than gold during the war when Paris was living off rats and moldy bread. He squeezed his eyes shut, tightened his fist around her small neck, and snapped it. He took his dagger and slit her throat. Blood gushed out. Julien stained his white shirt crimson and plunged into the chaos outside.

The sun erased the shadowed corners that had sheltered Julien. It left him with only one place to hide: in plain sight. The Versailles soldiers had little interest in bloodied corpses slumped against walls, and Alessandra's blood made it easy to pretend to be one of them.

Julien watched the army sweep through the makeshift barricades with brutal efficiency. They tore through walls of houses, outflanking the barricades and killing all defenders and whoever else had the misfortune of standing nearby. By midday, all of the roads to Isabelle's home were blocked by the carnage. He could do no more than to stand shoulder to shoulder with the city's defenders and keep his daughter safe for as long as he could. Shots flew over the barricade. Julien's shirt turned a brighter shade of red.

ACROSS THE CITY

Isabelle! Get up!" Stephane knelt beside the bed and shook his wife awake.

"What is it? What's wrong?" Isabelle was unsure if she was still asleep. Dawn had barely crept into their small bedroom. Stephane's hand trembled against her skin, but the dark kept her from seeing the terror in his blue-gray eyes.

"We have been betrayed." Stephane choked on his anger. It hardened the angles of his plain face, erasing the gentleness that Isabelle had fallen in love with. "The army breached the walls last night. Soldiers are pouring into the city."

Isabelle closed her eyes. This was the nightmare her father had warned her about, the one from which the morning could offer no escape. She shut her eyes and hoped that when she opened them again, she would be curled in Stephane's arms.

"The council is assembling at the Hôtel de Ville." Stephane stood up and grabbed his coat.

Tears seeped under Isabelle's eyelids, forcing them open. She rose from the bed. "I'll get dressed."

Stephane shook his head and held her firmly by the shoulders. "Stay here. Keep the windows shut and lock the door." He turned to leave.

Isabelle grabbed her husband's arm. "Please let me come with you, I beg you. Do not leave me alone!" Her nails dug into Stephane's arm while the rest of her froze with panic.

"Your father will be here soon. He will keep you safe," Stephane lied. He did not know where Isabelle's father was or if he was even still alive. What he did know was that Isabelle was safer in their home than in the chaos outside. Once the Versailles soldiers were pushed back, he would come back for her. He had to. He kissed the small swell of her growing belly and ran out of the room before his tears could wash away his resolve.

Isabelle curled into the shape her husband had left on the sheets of their bed. It was still warm from the night he had spent lying on his side, stroking her belly until she fell asleep. She ran her fingers over her stomach. She would not follow Stephane to take up arms with his comrades, but she would do whatever it took to protect their child. Parents were supposed to keep their children safe. Her father had taught her that.

She reached for the gold locket beneath her nightclothes. It was far less elegant than any of the other jewelry her father had given her, but there was nothing she treasured more. The charms inside it tinkled softly when she walked, whispering that they were always close by, keeping her from harm. Perhaps today, Isabelle thought, she would find out if they truly worked. Her father had never given them the chance to protect her. That was his job. He had always hovered close enough to scoop her up before she scraped her knees and rescue her from towers guarded by fire-breathing footstools during her childhood games. But her father was not with her now, and all she had to protect her was the faith he had clasped around her neck.

Stone and wood clattered beneath her window. Isabelle cracked the shutters open and peered outside. Tables and chairs were being dragged across the street. Her neighbors were building a barricade. She clutched her belly. The barricade would keep them safe until Stephane returned home and her father joined them. She rushed outside to help.

The faces of the people around Isabelle could not have been grimmer. They spoke little as they erected a wall out of whatever they could pry off the ground. The bed she and Stephane had made love in the night before was wedged between what used to be their kitchen table and a neighbor's stool. They were unrecognizable now, stained with sweat and dread.

Children, no higher than her waist, tiptoed to pile paving stones. The younger ones believed it was a game, laughing as they raced to gather rocks. Isabelle ruffled their hair and cheered them on. It helped her pretend that the tangle of pillows, cobblestones, and prayers would keep the bayonets from ripping through their skin. Fingers tapped her arm.

Isabelle lived in that second of buoyancy and belief. In that moment, anything was possible. Stephane had returned. Her father had found her. Either—no, both—were a breath away from where she stood. She was saved. She turned around, ready to throw her arms around them and never let go.

A thin hand held out a brick to her. A shy smile peeked over it. The boy—no more than eight—pressed the brick into Isabelle's hands, grazing her skin with his. His fingers were as rough as the stone he offered. She fought back tears. Rescue had not come. She pushed the brick back into the boy's palm and closed his fingers around it. "Keep it. Hold it tight. When the soldiers come, it may serve you better than this wall."

The barricade could go no higher. Courage had run out soon after the stones did. The rain began to pour down on them, washing away what little hope Isabelle had left. She did not seek shelter. Rain, unlike the silence that filled her home, was an old friend. Each drop was like a tiny mirror, reflecting how she felt inside. When she was little, she had looked forward to the rain. It had made her bed feel warmer as she listened to the lullaby tapping on the roof. Her father had always hovered closer when it rained. He would come in right after a flash of lightning, just before the thunder cracked, to make sure that she was not afraid. She never was.

Until now.

Today the skies cried with her. Isabelle touched her cheek and wondered where her tears ended and the raindrops began. A blade of pain, hot and sharp, twisted in her belly. She bit down on her lip and clutched her stomach. She breathed slowly, waiting for the rain and hurt to stop.

Had it been hours or days since Stephane had left? The rain swept away the barrier between days. Only the sound of fighting gave Isabelle any sense of time. It grew louder with every breath. She longed for her enemy's gunfire to put an end to her misery. Her clothes had already been stained dark gray with dirt and sweat, an appropriate color for her own funeral.

The National Guard huddled behind the barricade. A number of them had fallen back and brought news and instructions. Isabelle strained to hear their whispers. A last stand would be made at Père Lachaise. The group drew lots on who would stay and who would defend the walled cemetery. She scoffed at their efforts. Did it really matter where they fell? They were already dead. Including her. She wrapped her arms around her stomach. Her hands froze over the swell. Her baby. She had forgotten the reason she needed to stay alive.

Hope stirred in her womb. She saw the faces of Stephane and her father among the graveyard's defenders as clearly as though they were standing next to her. She pushed her way to one of the National Guard bound for the cemetery. "Please, sir, could you take me with you? My family could be there."

Another man's blood had crusted in the lines on the officer's face. He opened his mouth to say no. Death would be swifter at the barricade, he thought, kinder. His friend's blood trickled into his eye and he rubbed it clear. Then he saw her. Standing in front of him, beneath the layer of grime and desperation, was his dead comrade's wife. He nodded, unable to tell her she would not find Stephane.

The rain was falling harder now. Isabelle searched the drenched faces of the two hundred Communards gathered at the cemetery. Filth and fear made them all look the same and yet glimpses of a familiar eye, ear, or tip of a nose made her throw herself into the arms of a startled stranger. A blast tore her from her quest.

The Versailles army ripped through the gates and opened fire. The cemetery's defenders fell into the mud. Bayonets sliced through their clothes and found their flesh.

Isabelle ran, slipping in the sludge of soil and blood. She tripped over a broken headstone, tumbling against the foot of a carved angel. She glanced up. Its gray face was a blur through the rain in her eyes. It held out its hand. She grasped her answered prayer. It was rougher than she thought marble would be. And warmer. She remembered where she had first felt its touch.

"Hurry." The thin boy from the barricade pulled Isabelle to her feet. "This way."

They ran hand in hand toward a small mausoleum. Its iron gate hung from its hinges. They crept inside and pulled the gate closed. They huddled behind it, unable to breathe.

The sound of gunfire swelled. Isabelle held the boy tight, waiting for it to fall on them.

And then it ebbed.

Isabelle shuddered in the lull. It was then that she could hear what was really happening outside. Shouts. Scampering. Surrender. And then more shots—deliberate and cold. But even that faded with the rain. The cemetery grew quiet.

Footsteps nearby broke the silence in the crypt.

Isabelle and the boy clung to each other, trembling as one.

"We are safe here." She pulled the boy closer, pressing him against the child growing inside her. She did not like lying to either of them.

Wet grass and mud sloshed under the heels of heavy boots.

Isabelle felt a wet heat flow through her dress, soaking her skin. The boy looked down in embarrassment at the urine on his trousers.

"It will be all right." Isabelle reached for his hand. His fingers were clenched around the brick from the barricade. It cut into his palms. She wondered if he had ever let it go. His will to live was stronger than hers. It was her turn to feel ashamed. Tears welled in her eyes and rolled down her face.

The boy wiped her cheek and looked into her eyes. His smile was back, less shy and more determined. It quivered with the last of his courage. "Do not cry," he said softly. He gripped the brick tighter. "I . . . will protect you."

Isabelle saw the boy speaking, but it was her father's voice that she heard coming out of his mouth. She still believed her papa's words: parents were supposed to keep their children safe. But she was not a child anymore. The boy huddled next to her, however, was. She took her locket and slipped it over his head. Its charms clinked softly, the sound of her faith in the man who had never let her down. "My father gave this to me," she whispered. "It will keep you safe. I promise. Papa will come. He will save us. You'll see."

The boy clutched the locket and looked up at her. Isabelle had never seen eyes filled with so much trust. She reached out to stroke his cheek. A sharp pain stabbed her womb. She gripped her stomach and screamed. The terror of hearing her voice echo in the mausoleum was almost worse than feeling her thighs grow sticky. Boots trampled nearer, summoned by her cry. She looked down at her skirt and watched it turn crimson. It was a comrade's blood, she told herself. It had to be. But as it pooled thick and hot beneath her on the floor, she could no longer pretend. Her child, the one she hoped would have Stephane's smile and her eyes, was gone.

Isabelle could hear the soldiers searching the crypts nearby; it was only a matter of time before they were discovered. In her heart, she had known from the moment he said good-bye that Stephane would never be coming back. There was no time to mourn or feel pain. She cupped the boy's face in her hands. "Whatever you see, whatever you hear, do not move. Do not make a sound. You will grow up. You will grow old. And when you do . . ." She kissed her locket and tucked it beneath the boy's clothes. "Remember me."

Isabelle gathered what little strength she had and dashed out of the tomb. If she could not protect her own child, she would save someone else's. "I surrender!"

The soldiers grabbed her by the arms and led her away from where her gray angel was hiding. She was no longer scared. She was now drifting away from the stench of gunpowder and blood, away from the choices that had led her to this lonely end. But perhaps she would not be alone anymore, she thought. She remembered how Stephane had kissed her good-bye days before. She would see him soon, with their child. And Papa—she smiled—he would be waiting for her, too.

She did not look back. She kept her eyes focused ahead of her, beyond the rows of graves and trees, at a wall at the end of the path.

PARIS

🖋 *May 28, 1871*

THE PART OF THE STORY MAX DID NOT TELL SHELLEY

It was Sunday. One last barricade remained on the Rue de Belleville. It was held by a single man for a quarter of an hour before he fired his last shot and walked away.

Julien met a young soldier weeping on the street as though it was his side that had lost. The soldier saw his face and fell back at the sight of his amber eyes—the eyes of the dead girl that had taken his soul with her to her grave. Duty was not supposed to feel this way. The soldier told the man where he had left his daughter. It was only because the man was too numb from grief that he did not kill the soldier where he stood.

That evening, when the rains had driven everyone else away, the man stood over an acrid lime-filled grave in the northern corner of Père Lachaise. He clawed at the mud until his fingers were raw. He dug deeper, in a blind, frantic search for something he was desperate not to find. And then he saw her. Lying in the rain as she once had on stone steps a lifetime ago. But he could not save her this night. He wiped away the wet dirt from her face.

"She said you would come," a small voice said from behind him.

The man stumbled back and drew his pistol. A boy stood over him in the rain. The child reached for a chain around his neck and drew out a locket of beaten gold. He slipped it off and pressed it into the man's hands. "She was right. It kept me safe."

The boy had scampered back into the shadows of the graves when the man found the strength to move. Tears streamed down his face and onto his daughter's. "Forgive me," he said, though he did not feel worthy of forgiveness.

But it did not matter. There was no one left to absolve him. He had failed to keep his family safe. Once again, he was utterly alone.

Chapter Five

Girlfriends and guinness

A FLIGHT TO THE PHILIPPINES

🌿 *Now*

And that was it," Shelley told Paolo. "That's all Max told us about Isabelle."

"And Julien?" he asked softly.

She frowned. "What about him?"

Paolo reached under his collar and hooked his fingers around a gold chain.

Shelley thought she heard a wind chime. A tiny one.

Paolo drew the chain from his neck. A weathered locket dangled from it. Charms clinked against the round gold shell.

She swallowed hard. "Where . . . where did you get that?"

"It was a gift . . . from Nonno." He clutched the locket, his fingers trembling around it. The charms rattled louder.

Shelley steadied his hand with hers. The locket grew quiet. Paolo did not. Shelley heard him drag every breath into his lungs, each one heavier and more ragged than the one before it. Her own breath caught in her throat, and she realized she was breathing just as hard.

"I cannot remember a day when this was not around my neck. Nonno told me that it was my father's." Paolo's voice shook. "But now . . . I believe it might have been someone else's." He bowed his head and closed his eyes.

His neck, Shelley thought, seemed to be straining under a much heavier weight than the thin chain that hung from it.

"Shelley, I think Julien was . . ."

Shelley willed Paolo to stop speaking. There were certain things that were never meant to be put into words: your age after you turned twenty-five, your weight after the holidays, and how the man you married could possibly be more than two centuries old. She jumped out of her seat and ran to the lavatory, hoping to outrun what Paolo was going to say next.

Absurdity and possibility collided against each other and bounced off the walls of the airplane's lavatory. Shelley ducked and hit her head on the stainless-steel sink.

Paolo knocked on the door. "Shelley? Is everything okay?" Concern replaced the trembling in his voice.

She found his question highly amusing. Max was Julien and she was anything but okay.

"Shelley?"

"I haven't flushed myself off the plane, if that's what you're worried about." She had in fact tried to but had only squeezed half a foot into the bowl when Paolo's theory about Julien and Max had ricocheted over her head like shrapnel. Shelley unlocked the door. Paolo stood outside, the locket tucked beneath his shirt.

"You better not. You can't bail out on me now." Paolo eyed the reddish bruise forming on Shelley's forehead. "Do you, uh, need some ice for that?"

"No." She brushed past him and marched to her seat. She pulled out the in-flight magazine and flipped blindly through its pages. Max's voice and his stories rang in her head. She was certain that they had grown loud enough for the other passengers to hear. She forced herself to look at the magazine. Sand. White, like baby powder. And palm trees. Boracay. She slammed the magazine shut and took a deep breath. "If Max was Julien, and I'm not saying that he was, why would he tell complete strangers about his story? Why would he risk letting his secret out?"

"It wouldn't have been much of a risk, would it?" Paolo said. "I mean, you and I can now see the similarities between Julien and Max—his sense of family, his protectiveness . . ." He paused, tracing the shape of the locket beneath his shirt with his thumb. "But I don't think any tourist would believe that their tour guide was actually sharing with them an autobiographical account of events that happened more than a century ago, right? To them, what he shared was just a story."

Shelley's chest tightened. Max had left her with more than just one story—each gilded with razor-sharp details waiting to carve out more of the husband she remembered. "Paolo, Julien was just one of many men and some of them weren't like Max at all."

PARIS

Five Years Ago

The tour group trailed Max out of the cemetery like a procession of mourners leaving a funeral.

"Why so glum, campers?" he asked. "I told you we needed to get the end of our story out of the way. Now that that's done, it's all tales of randy sex and comedy from this point on. Well, at least most of it is."

"Max, what planet are you from?" Brad said. "I mean, really, how many happy pills did you pop this morning?"

"Yeah," Dex said. "And where can I get some?"

"Turn left down that street and look for a man in dark glasses," Max said. "Tell him I sent you. He'll give you a good price. As for the rest of you, we're off to our next stop." He offered Shelley his arm.

She clung to it, eager to leave the cemetery and its ghosts behind. "Where are we going next, Max?"

Max stopped. He opened his backpack and took out a small leather drawstring pouch, then handed it to Shelley.

"What's this?" She felt the weight of the bag in her hands.

"Go on, luv. Open it."

Shelley dug into the pouch. Her fingers brushed against something cold. She pulled it out. Louis XVI turned his gold double chin up at her. She poured more of the gold coins into her palm. "Are these real, Max?"

"Of course, luv. You can pass it around so the others can have a closer look," he said.

"This is no small change, Max," Simon said. "Why on earth are you carrying this around with you?"

Max shrugged. "Pocket money."

"Seriously, Max," Jonathan said, "whatever is all this gold for?"

"A bribe, or at least it was intended to be one."

"Okay, I'll bite," Dex said. "And what exactly was this bribe for?"

"Patience, mate, patience. You Americans are always in a rush."

"I'm guessing you'll keep us in suspense until we get to our next mystery stop, then?" Shelley asked.

"Does my lady protest?" Max touched her chin lightly with his fingers, grazing her lower lip with his thumb.

A current ran from Shelley's lip to her crotch. "Not . . . not at all. By all means, lead the way, good sir."

"But first a slight detour," Max said. "Our morning's adventure has made me rather thirsty."

The group stood on the stone bank of the Seine. Shelley watched the wide brown river ripple in the wake of a bateau-mouche. Tourists waved at her from the boat's glass-covered deck.

"So, who else is up for a drink?" Max asked.

"Max, you disappoint me," Shelley said. "Are you telling us we'll be joining one of those river cruises that come with free lunches? That hardly qualifies as off-the-beaten-path in my book."

"I agree, but this might." Max shielded his eyes from the glare of the sun bouncing off the river. "Here's our ride."

The name *Isabelle* was painted on the side of the red barge. Shelley wondered if it was a coincidence.

"Quick!" Dex grabbed her by the shoulders and angled her in front of the approaching barge. He raised his camera. "Say 'cheese.'"

"Er, cheese." Shelley knitted her brow. "Dex, don't you want to be in the picture? I can take your photo if you'd . . ." Bright green billowed at the corner of Shelley's eye. She turned in its direction.

The emerald sundress blew in the wind, clinging to the tall fiery-haired woman who emerged on the barge's deck.

"Miren!" Max waved at her.

Miren waved back as the barge came to a stop beside the embankment. Max led the group aboard. He gathered Miren in a tight embrace and lifted her in the air. Miren laughed and ran her fingers over Max's smile. Her years creased at the sides of her green eyes but did not diminish her beauty.

Shelley bit her lip and considered reporting a certain wayward member to the Poultry Club of Great Britain.

Max set Miren back on her feet. "Everyone, I'd like you to meet the owner of this fine boat, Ms. Miren O'Loughlin, the finest Irish lass on French waters." He held Miren's hand as he walked over to the group.

"Welcome aboard the *Isabelle,* floating pub by night and my humble abode by day," Miren said.

The group introduced themselves and Max guided Miren's hand to shake everyone else's. Shelley realized that Miren was blind.

Miren ushered the group to a hatch leading belowdecks. A bulky, stern-looking man nodded hello from the helm then quickly turned his attention back to steering the barge.

"That's Paul-Henri, the *Isabelle*'s captain," Miren said. "He's fairly new here and still painfully shy, I'm afraid."

Shelley followed Miren down the steps and through a narrow corridor. Miren opened a red door. If not for the portholes that ran along the length of its dark oak walls, Shelley could have sworn that she had strolled into her neighborhood pub. All that was missing was Charlie, her favorite bartender. She could have used a pint's worth of his time to rant about the stunning copper-haired woman whose arm was still linked with Max's.

The group gathered around the bar. Shelley hopped on a stool. She looked hopefully at the stool next to hers. She clenched her teeth when Max followed Miren behind the counter. Dex took the empty seat.

"So, what can I get everyone?" Miren handed out bowls of peanuts. "Guinness all around?"

"Thank you, but I think it's too early in the day for me to be drinking," Jonathan said. A peanut disappeared behind his white beard.

"I'll have a pint, dear," Rose chirped.

Jonathan choked on a half-chewed nut. "Oh, all right. I'll have one, too."

"That's the spirit." Brad grinned.

"How about you, luv?" Max asked Shelley.

"Well, you know what they say—when in Paris do as the Irish do," Shelley said. "I'd hate to be the only one not sick all over your van tomorrow." She knew, however, that she would not feel the slightest bit guilty if she contributed her share of bile onto the Volkswagen's green shag carpet. Seeing Max standing next to Miren did not bring out her considerate side.

Miren smiled and began pouring beer into mugs.

"Ah, yes, the dreaded hangover," Max said. "Did you know that in Myanmar the phrase for hangover means 'clapper of the temple bell'?"

"On second thought, I'll have a Coke," Shelley said. Jealousy was not worth a pounding migraine.

"Trust me," Max said, "no one has to worry about hangovers or clanging bells with Miren around. In fact, that's why we're here. There's a little potion she makes that I'd like all of you to try."

"It's what this old tub is famous for," Miren said, beaming, "that and our perfectly poured Guinness and potato pancakes. This is the only place the blokes can drink themselves under the table and not worry about their heads exploding in the morning—thanks to Max and his secret recipe."

"Well, it's not my recipe, really," Max said. "It was Adrien's."

The name was familiar, Shelley thought. Where had she heard it before? Then she remembered that she had not. She had seen it. The memory crept back to an elegant cursive, painting gold letters on an olive leaf. It was one of the names on the mosaic in Isabelle's tomb.

"Who's Adrien?" Simon asked.

"Isabelle's great-grandfather. It is his story we shall entertain ourselves with next," Max said. "But first we drink."

Shelley watched Max help Miren prepare their drinks with choreographed ease. She wondered how many times they had done this before. She felt a pain in her throat thinking of what else Max had done—and might still be doing with this woman.

"How about a toast?" Brad asked Miren.

Miren raised her mug and smiled broadly. "To your wives and girl-friends," she said, "may they never meet."

The group laughed. Shelley did not.

Miren drained her mug in one swig and licked the froth off her upper lip. "Excuse me for a moment while I whip up Adrien's little potion." She left the bar through a door in the back of the room.

Max leaned his elbows on the counter in front of Shelley. "Miren's an old friend."

"Of course." Shelley immediately regretted her clipped tone. "I mean, yes, that's lovely. Old friends are lovely. I have a lot of old flames, er, friends, myself."

Brad nudged Simon's knee under the counter. "Why don't we finish our drinks outside? I'd like to take some pictures from the deck."

"Uh, okay." Simon shrugged and got to his feet.

"Splendid idea," Jonathan said. "I think we'll join you."

"Max, would you be a dear and call us back in when Miren returns?" Rose asked.

Dex sipped his beer.

Rose tapped his shoulder and smiled. "Coming, Dex?"

"Oh. Um, sure." He stood up. "Shelley?"

Shelley shook her head and dove into her beer. The rest of the group filed out of the room.

"Darts?" Max asked Shelley.

"Sure." Picturing Miren's face on the dartboard, she thought, could be mildly satisfying. She walked over to the corner of the bar where the dartboard was set up. She picked up a dart, got a feel for its weight, and threw it directly at Miren's nose.

"I used to live on this barge," Max said.

Shelley flinched. She could have sworn her dart was headed straight for the bull's-eye, but somehow it had made a U-turn and pierced her chest. Or at least it felt that way. "So . . . you and Miren used to live together. I suppose this was before you took your vow of celibacy?"

"Lived together? No, no, luv. I didn't even know her back then," Max said. He threw a dart. It landed next to Shelley's. "I sold the barge to Miren and her husband, Rhys, when I got tired of bobbing along canals."

"Miren's married?" Shelley tried not to look too happy.

"Was," Max said. "Rhys died a year ago."

"Oh." She took another sip of her beer and winced. Guilt left a fishy aftertaste.

Max pulled their darts off the board. "He had been sick for a while," he said. "That's why he and Miren bought this barge from me. They wanted to squeeze in one last adventure doing the most absurd thing they could think of. A floating Irish pub in the heart of the wine-drinking capital of the world fit the bill. I gave them the hangover recipe because I thought they would need it after their business sank to the bottom of the Seine. As you can see, they proved me wrong. Rhys lived long enough to show his doctors that a dream and a pint a day can sometimes be better than what they used to shove up his veins."

"It must be difficult for Miren, though, with Rhys gone." She threw another dart. It landed on the wall. Aiming was harder without a compelling target. Her chest felt heavier as she thought about Miren sailing alone down the Seine.

"The pub keeps her busy. She once told me that the love Rhys gave her was enough to last her several lifetimes." Max threw a dart. He hit the bull's-eye. "Do you believe that's possible, luv?"

Shelley was about to disagree when Miren walked into the room. In her experience, love, or what passed for it, was like a good beer buzz. Fizzy and fleeting.

Miren balanced a tray of shot glasses half filled with a dark green liquid. "Have your friends abandoned ship, Max?"

"They're on the deck," Max said. "I'll call them back in."

Shelley stowed the darts away. "Can I help you with that, Miren?"

Miren smiled. "That's all right. Just grab a glass for yourself."

Shelley took a glass from the tray. She gave it a sniff and gagged. The smell, she was certain, would have made vomit vomit.

"Horrid, isn't it?" Miren said. "Don't worry, it tastes even worse. But the way my regulars drink it, you'd think it was nectar from the gods." She set the glasses down on the counter.

"In front of each of you is the beginning of our next tale," Max said when the group had taken their seats at the bar. "But there is something we need to do first."

Miren reached under the counter and pulled out a basket of eggs. "Crack an egg into your glass right before you drink it." She broke an egg on the rim of Dex's glass and poured the egg in. "Like so."

"Um . . . thanks, I think." Dex took his glass from Miren. He arched a brow at Max. "Does our travel insurance cover voluntary poisoning?"

"I'm afraid not," Max said.

Dex took a deep breath. "Oh, well. Bottom's up."

The group gulped down their shots. Coughs and colorful swearing (mostly by Rose) racked the bar.

Shelley could still feel the liquid making its languorous course down her throat like an oyster clinging to life. "Now I know what all your gold coins are for, Max—lawsuit settlements," she choked. "You can start with mine."

Max grinned. "I truly apologize, luv, but I just wanted everyone to get their money's worth and have the most authentic experience possible."

"Yes, well done, Max. Very authentic. Do let me know if this story of yours involves guillotines, okay? I'm rather fond of my head," Brad said.

"I'll do my best to remember that." Max turned to face the group. "I'm sure you'd like to know what you have just bravely imbibed. As I mentioned earlier, the credit for this wonderful elixir goes to Adrien. He and his business partner, Antoine, were wealthy wine merchants in the 1700s who discovered that plying both poison and cure made for a very profitable enterprise."

"I can believe that," Simon said. "That's how Bill Gates did it."

"Touché," Max said. "It was also because of this creation and their generously discounted wine that they managed to become fixtures at the French court despite their lack of royal pedigree. They became particular favorites of a cake-loving queen who often requested the pleasure of their company at her frequent gambling and drinking parties. The queen's impending misfortune, however, proved to be somewhat contagious."

"Why?" Dex asked. "What happened to them?"

"Well," Max said, "it was ultimately because of these parties, or rather what happened after them, that the luck of our protagonists was altered considerably."

Chapter Six

Birthdays and bribes

VERSAILLES, FRANCE

April 1778

The bed's canopy kept out the pale morning rising in the garden. Antoine slid away from an embrace and shivered. The blankets called him back. He pushed the thought of warmth aside and set himself to the task of finding his clothes.

He groped around the parquet floor and knocked over an empty wine bottle. It crunched over broken eggshells as it rolled under the bed. He followed its trail. The bottle came to a halt next to his rumpled breeches and a wig of white-blond hair. The wig's ornamental birds nested in the crotch of his pants. He shook the uninvited feathered guests off and stood up. His ruffled shirt was hanging from one of the bedposts. He pulled on his clothes and slipped out of the queen's bedroom.

Antoine strode into the bedchamber of the queen's favorite lady-in-waiting and marched up to her bed. He grabbed a foot sticking out from under the silk sheets. "Rise and shine, Adrien."

"Go away." The young man's voice was muffled by the large breasts piled over his face.

"We need to go," Antoine said sternly.

Adrien disentangled himself from a pair of fleshy legs. He yawned and rolled out from under the covers. "Oh, look." He glanced at his morning erection. "Shame to waste it. Won't be a minute."

Antoine dragged Adrien off the snoring woman. "When will you grow up?"

"You first. It is your birthday, after all."

"My birthday? Clearly, you're still drunk. As I recall, it was your birthday we toasted last night."

"Well, I thought that since you don't like celebrating your own birthday, I'd share mine with you. Consider it a present."

The woman mumbled in her sleep.

"How kind." Antoine threw Adrien's shirt at him. "But can we continue this conversation when you're wearing a little bit more than just an idiotic grin?"

The grass was still wet with dew when they emerged from the Petit Trianon. Dawn was Antoine's favorite time of day, and the sprawling grounds of Versailles did it justice. The dim light veiled the garden's colors, but Antoine could already smell the flowers, their scents flitting in the air along with the gurgle of distant fountains. Yellow. Pink. Peach. Everything was still so new, he thought. It was easier to be happy.

"So how do you think we should celebrate your birthday?" Adrien plucked a rose from a bush and pressed it to his nose.

"I told you, I don't like celebrating my birthday."

"I've never understood that." Adrien threw the rose away. "Birthdays are fun. Don't tell me you didn't have a good time last night."

"Birthdays are better when they're someone else's," Antoine said. "When you get to be my age . . ."

"Your age? You're hardly over thirty, my friend, though sometimes I feel that you carry the burden of a much older man. You don't always have to be so serious."

"Believe me, I'm trying."

"Good. It's settled then."

"What's settled?"

"Today is your birthday, and tonight we drink."

The wine swam in Antoine's head. He fluffed up the pillows behind his neck, regretting that he had let Adrien have his way. It was pointless arguing with Adrien on matters involving wine and women. It wasn't a question of winning the debate—it was a matter of not wanting to. Losing had its own rewards, however brief. And now it had passed. Antoine pushed himself off the bed and threw up in the bucket beside it.

He wiped his mouth with a wet cloth. He knew he was not setting the best example for Adrien, but youth was for making such mistakes. With any luck, Adrien might even learn from them. Who was he to stand in the way of Adrien's education? He was not in a position to preach. In many ways, he saw himself in Adrien. He found Adrien's lust for life—or anything in a corset, really—infectious. It helped him remember a time when he had felt the same way. Well, almost. The memory was always beyond his grasp, slipping away right before he could smile at his past willfulness. He contented himself with viewing the world through Adrien's eyes. They were young and had yet to be jaded. He, in turn, provided Adrien with the occasional, though necessary, whack on the head. It was a good partnership.

Antoine had grown to know Adrien well in the course of their working together. But they were more than just business associates. They were friends. When Adrien's parents had passed away, Antoine asked him to join him in his trading company. Adrien had jumped at the opportunity. Running his family's apothecary was not something Adrien had particularly enjoyed. He liked to pound his pestle in the midst of fancier surroundings, preferably one with a canopy above it and silk sheets beneath. He was, in fact, off doing just that. Antoine had declined to accompany him. The thrill of Versailles' bedrooms was not what it used to be.

Adrien's elixir was another thing Antoine had passed on that evening. For once he wanted to wake up the next day and feel something. A pounding headache was better than nothing at all. He was tired of feeling numb, of pretending that having a woman in his bed made him feel less cold inside. Whether he woke up in a royal bedchamber or in his own room, the day ahead was always the same. He was a day older and more alone. He closed his eyes and sighed. "Happy birthday."

"Out with it." Antoine leaned back in his chair and put his feet up on the carved writing desk. He was still nursing his hangover. "What did you do this time?"

Adrien looked at him across the desk. "I don't have the slightest idea what you are talking about." He turned his attention back to his account books.

"I know you, and I have the misfortune of being well acquainted with that look."

"What look?" Adrien widened his amber eyes.

"That look," Antoine said. "The look of someone who has just stolen the crown jewels and stuffed them up his ass."

"Nonsense." Adrien returned to his work.

"Very well, if you say so. Just don't expect me to come running with a spade to dig you out from the latest pile of excrement you've managed to bury yourself under."

"Oh, come now. I thought you enjoyed our little adventures."

Antoine rolled his eyes. "It's late. I'm going home. Lock up the office when you're done, will you?"

"It's nothing, really," Adrien said.

"It always is." Antoine sat down.

"She was sleeping when I left."

"Who was sleeping?"

"The duchess. She was sleeping when I left her side." Adrien shifted in his seat.

"So? You always leave while she's snoring away."

"Exactly! She's always been a heavy sleeper, right?"

"Adrien, please, feel free to get to your point anytime in this century."

"The point is . . . well, she woke up."

Antoine drummed his fingers on the desk. "I'm waiting."

"And saw me getting out of bed."

"Still waiting." Antoine folded his arms over his chest.

"I was getting out of her cousin's bed."

"Ah, I see."

"I told you it was nothing," Adrien said. "Although the duchess did appear to be the tiniest bit cross with me. But then again, I could be mistaken."

"Mistaken? How so?"

"Well, I was rather busy dodging the various heavy brass objects she was throwing my way to really pay attention to what she was saying."

"Of course."

"Do you suppose we're still on for cards with the queen tonight?"

Antoine leaned back in his chair and rubbed his chin. "Adrien, my friend, I think it would be safe to assume that you can make other plans for the evening."

"Oh."

"And if I might make a tiny suggestion as to the nature of these plans . . ."

"Yes, please."

"They should involve a rather urgent business trip and a very fast horse. I will come by your house at half past the hour."

Antoine knew what it was like to flee, to shed a life as though it were a cloak. He had learned to pack light. The less he had, the less he had to leave behind. It was a lesson Adrien would have to learn. Quickly. Antoine did not look forward to teaching him. There was only one thing he liked less than running away: getting caught.

He knocked on Adrien's door. It was ajar. He held his breath and swung it open. A servant was cowering in a corner of the room. She did not have to speak for Antoine to realize what had happened. He was too late. The king's soldiers, on the strength of a *lettre de cachet,* had already taken his friend. Antoine was not surprised. The royal warrant had stolen others away for lesser crimes. He swore under his breath and swung back on his horse. He chased after the arresting party, hoping he was wrong about where they were heading.

MIREN'S BARGE

THE SEINE, PARIS

Five Years Ago

Max glanced out of a porthole. "We should be moving out to the deck now."

"Wait," Shelley said. "You can't stop now."

"I would never leave you unsatisfied, luv," Max said. "I just thought we could continue outside. There's something thrilling about doing it outdoors, wouldn't you agree?"

Shelley felt her ears glow hot as Max's grin grew wider. In a minute she could throw steaks on them and get a nice char.

"Absolutely, dear," Rose said. "Remember that time in Tahiti, Jonathan?"

"Er, ah, yes." Jonathan blushed. "Of course, dear."

The barge drifted beneath one of the old stone bridges crossing the Seine. The bridge stood firmly anchored in time, oblivious to the water and years flowing beneath it. The air was cooler under the shadow of its unchanging arch.

"This is the Pont de la Concorde," Max said. "The parapets of this bridge are built from stones salvaged from what became Adrien's home for the next eleven years of his life."

"Adrien's home?" Dex asked.

"Yes," Max said. "The Bastille."

PARIS

✴✷ *April 1789*

Adrien had hoped that Louis XVI, or rather his milled likeness, might do a better job than Antoine at pleading his case to the Bastille's warden. Unfortunately, it turned out that the gold sovereign was as adept at buying his freedom as the real king was in ruling France.

He stared at the ceiling. In the eleven years that he had lain under it, he had come to memorize every whorl and crack across its beams. It had not changed much over the years except, it seemed, for its height. When he was first imprisoned, it had pressed down on him until he couldn't breathe. Today it was less asphyxiating. The ceiling must have gotten higher, Adrien thought, or perhaps he had learned to do with less air.

He had, in fact, gotten quite used to his accommodations. Sleeping in his own bed, being surrounded by his own furniture, and having his needs tended to by his manservant made it easy to imagine he was in a well-appointed apartment—that just happened to be locked from the outside. Adrien was happy to learn that, far from its dreaded reputation as a house of horrors, the Bastille was the rather luxurious confinement for the country's wayward elite. While it was a lesson he would rather have not learned firsthand, he was relieved nonetheless.

A knock on the door interrupted his reverie. His manservant showed Antoine in and took his coat.

"Happy birthday," Antoine said. "How was the party?"

Adrien shrugged. "The wine was good, the women not as much, though they did seem to get better the more I drank."

Antoine took a seat on the couch. "I see that the years of incarceration haven't changed you much."

"Just keeping the sword sharp, my friend." Adrien waved his servant away. "Rusty blades have a tendency to fall off, you know."

"And sharp ones thrust in the wrong places tend to be locked up."

"*Touché.* My beloved duchess does know how to hold a grudge, doesn't she?"

"And so do the people of France, it seems," Antoine said. "Their grumblings grow louder outside these walls. There are whispers of revolution."

"I've heard the warden speak of such things, too," Adrien said. "With my luck, the masses will rise up and forget that I'm locked in here."

"Perhaps," Antoine said. "But I will not. I will never forget you. You have my word."

Adrien embraced Antoine. He thought it was ironic how their years apart had brought them closer. He had grown to appreciate his friend's company more now that they were not busy emptying their wineglasses or unlacing corsets. He had more time to listen to Antoine's stories. His tales of basilisks, ancient monasteries, and war were the highlights of Adrien's week. He liked the stories with chickens the best. Earlier, he had worried that Antoine would run out of stories to tell, but he never did. Adrien had learned that his friend had a vast and wild imagination, but real or not, Antoine's tales made him laugh and, sometimes, even cry.

"We are family." Antoine drew away and ruffled Adrien's hair. He handed him a satchel. "Here. I brought you more books in case you find some time between your card games and dinner parties."

"Thank you. I enjoyed last week's selections immensely. The three Bibles you sent were difficult to put down."

Antoine grinned. "I thought they might comfort you in these trying times. But I think you'll find the history books I have for you this week more to your liking. They are absolutely hilarious."

"Antoine, I do believe that you are the only one I know who finds history books comical," Adrien said. "So will you be staying for dinner? The new chef makes an excellent roast, and I think we shall be having some fruit tarts for dessert. They are always quite delectable."

July 14, 1789

Adrien rapped his knuckles against the inside of his door. "Hello? Is anyone out there?"

One of the Swiss mercenaries contracted to guard the prison answered from the hallway. "What do you want?"

"I do believe it's time for my walk," Adrien said.

"Prisoners are not allowed out of their cells today."

Adrien heard the guard walking away. "Wait. Why?"

"It is for your protection."

"From what? Tripping on a rock in the courtyard? Come now. Let me out."

"I can't."

"Then tell me what's going on out there."

The guard took a deep breath. He walked back to Adrien's cell and whispered through the door, "A mob—a large one—is gathering outside."

The shouts of the crowd grew loud enough to be heard in Adrien's cell. They demanded that the fortress surrender and give up its cache of gunpowder and arms. Adrien wondered if that was all they wanted. Their voices were ragged. Hungry. Perhaps for justice, or for something more. Would the people see him as a prisoner or as a man of privilege, a symbol of all they despised? Or did it even matter as long as they could find limbs to grab onto and rip apart? Blood, like wine, was intoxicating.

He worried about Antoine. If there was a swarm at the gates of the Bastille, the rest of the city might not be faring any better. He wished he had read at least one of Antoine's Bibles. Maybe he would know how to pray for his friend's safety and his own. He knelt. Outside, wood thundered against the ground, ripping him from his attempted plea.

The drawbridge to the inner courtyard had been cut. Adrien heard the crowd storming over it. He shielded his ears from the gunfire and screams, but it was no use. They crept up his spine.

Then it went quiet, but it was not the kind of silence that lulled you to sleep. It was restless and sharp. It twisted inside him. He could feel the mob's hate seeping through his door. If the silence meant a ceasefire, it was not going to last long.

The stairway to the north tower roared with the angry swarm. A fleeing guard told Adrien that the Bastille's governor had surrendered the prison and opened the gates. Adrien held his breath. His door shook on its hinges as the mob rammed against it. It cracked but did not fall. They tried again. He shrank behind his bed. The door crashed down. The crowd swept into the room. Adrien squeezed his eyes shut, arms wrapped around his legs, ready to be torn apart. Then he was hoisted up, hovering above the crowd. He opened his eyes. The ceiling loomed closer. He frowned. He was either dead and had not quite made it up to heaven or he was sitting on someone's shoulders. He glanced down. Antoine grinned at him from the cheering crowd.

Adrien stared at him openmouthed. "What . . ."

"I apologize for the delay. Some enterprising fellow stole the keys to your cell as a souvenir. I believe he also carted the governor away. I had to get some help." Antoine smiled. "Now, dear friend, be a good symbol of the people and wave. Repeat after me. *Vive la révolution!*"

Chapter Seven

Pierre and pachyderms

PARIS

Five Years Ago

The stones of the Bastille grew smaller as the barge made its way down the Seine.

"Records show that the storming of the Bastille yielded a grand total of seven prisoners: two lunatics, four forgers, and one Irish nobleman imprisoned for debt," Max said. "Adrien and Antoine had left Paris before history could jot their names down for posterity. This suited the two just fine since it was this very anonymity that enabled their safe passage to Scotland. Antoine left Adrien in the care of friends in the French Huguenot community there. Adrien, who had considerably mellowed with age, found country life rather agreeable. He married the daughter of a respected poultry farmer and settled into a long and rich life filled with chickens and children."

The group applauded. The barge slowed and veered toward a quay.

"That was a lovely story, dear." Rose patted Max's arm.

"Yes, great story, Max," Dex said, "but how do you know all this stuff?"

Max shrugged. "Trade secret—or then again, it could just be a load of rubbish."

"What happened to Antoine?" Shelley asked.

"Antoine? I . . . well . . . I believe he continued to travel around

Europe." Max turned to the group. "Campers, this is as far as the story of Isabelle's family goes on this leg of the trip. You can spend the rest of the afternoon doing whatever touristy thing you fancy. Oh, and if you happen to come by an Eiffel Tower snow globe, I'd greatly appreciate it if you could pick one up for me. I'll see everyone back at the house for an early dinner."

A FLIGHT TO THE PHILIPPINES

Now

Paolo took a deep breath. "So Antoine was Max."

Shelley nodded. She felt numb.

"That makes Nonno about two hundred years old and counting," Paolo said. "It gives a whole new meaning to the expression 'midlife crisis,' don't you think? I can totally understand why he would have wanted to hang out with Adrien." He looked pleased with his analysis.

Shelley was not. She looked away. Paris had, like a flower, been safely pressed between the pages of her memory. Now it was drying out and crumbling under Paolo's scrutiny. This was excruciating, but necessary, she thought. As was keeping a single petal of the past to herself. She held it close to her chest.

PARIS

Five Years Ago

WHAT SHELLEY DID NOT TELL PAOLO

Shelley watched the barge pull away from the embankment. She overheard Max giving the Templetons advice on the best place to have lunch near the Louvre.

"Hey, I'm having lunch with Brad and Simon. Would you, um, like to join us?" Dex asked.

Shelley sighed. It was better than eating alone. "I . . ."

"Do you have plans for the afternoon, luv?" Max asked.

Shelley spun around. Max was standing behind her. "Well, uh . . . no." She bit her lip and looked back at Dex.

Dex gave her a small smile. "I'll see you later. Enjoy your lunch."

"Brilliant," Max said. "I'm seeing an old friend and I'd love for the two of you to meet."

"An old friend?" The image of another gorgeous redhead popped into Shelley's head. She winced. "Sure. Sounds like fun."

"He lives up in Montmartre. Let's take the metro. You'll need to save your energy for the race."

"Hang on." Shelley cocked a brow. "What race?"

"Trust me. It will be fun."

"I win." Shelley gripped her burning sides. The race, as it turned out, was a sprint up the two hundred and thirty-five steps to the Sacré Coeur Basilica. The sprawling view of Paris's radiating boulevards and monuments from the city's highest point would have been breathtaking if she had had any breath left to lose.

"Congratulations, luv," Max said, "but I think clinging onto my back for the last fifteen steps may be grounds for disqualification."

Shelley tried not to look too sheepish. This wouldn't have been the first time she had broken the rules this morning, she thought. She was certain that having this much fun talking about everything and laughing at nothing with a man she barely knew was illegal in some parts of the world. But she told herself that Max was just another train she could hop off of anytime she wanted to. Just not right at this very minute. She could do it tonight. Or tomorrow. There was plenty of time. Really. "Fine. A tie, then."

"A tie it is. What's my prize?"

"I think the fact that I let you drag me all the way up here to meet your friend should be reward enough," she said. "We could have taken the funicular, you know."

"But then I wouldn't have had the chance to know how Adam felt, would I?" Max said. "I can now in all honesty say that I don't blame him at all."

"Adam who? And what aren't you blaming him for?" Shelley's face was flushed deeply from the sprint up.

"Eve's better half, of course. I now know why he couldn't help taking a big juicy bite out of that wickedly red apple." Max stroked the side of Shelley's glowing cheek.

"Is that so? Well, sir, I suggest you keep your teeth off my cheeks and your snake in your fig leaf. That's a house of God we're standing in front of, you know."

"I'll try my best." He took her hand and cut a path through the sea of tourists surrounding Sacré Coeur. "Come on, let's go inside. Pierre's waiting."

Shelley found sanctuary inside the basilica's hall. The cacophony in the street faded as she breathed in the fragrance of incense and candle smoke. Her heartbeat slowed for the first time since she had met Max—only to start racing again when he rushed her toward the stairwell of one of the church's towers. She winced as she stared up at the winding stairs. More freaking steps. This was an odd place to meet Max's friend, she thought, unless that friend turned out to be one of the pigeons perched on the tower's ledge. From what she was quickly learning about Max, this was not exactly far-fetched. She was panting when they reached the top.

"Ah, here he is," Max said. "Shelley, I'd like you to meet my dear old friend, Pierre."

Shelley glanced around the empty tower. The loss of oxygen from all their climbing, she decided, must have either made her blind or Max delusional.

"Saint-Pierre, that is." He pointed through the dome's window at a small church standing on the slope beside Sacré Coeur.

"I see . . ." Shelley stuck her head out the window. "It's a pleasure to meet you, Mr. Saint-Pierre. Max has told me so much about you. Though

I have to say that he did give me the impression that you were, well, much more *alive*. But no matter, some of my best friends are town houses. I even have a charming old rail station for an aunt on my mother's side."

Max laughed. "Let's head over there, shall we?"

"Head over there? Are you telling me that we climbed all this way just so that you could point to where we were actually going?" Shelley's cheeks were still blazing.

"Of course not. We climbed all this way so that I could see if you could get even more rosy and delicious."

The street in front of Saint-Pierre was deserted except for the three tourists who had just left the small church.

"What's so special about this place, Max?" Shelley asked. Whatever it was, it seemed to be a well-kept secret.

"It's pretty hard to compete for attention when you're literally standing in the shadow of such a flashy neighbor," Max said. "Still, I thought that Paris's oldest church was worth a visit."

Shelley stared at the eighteenth-century stone edifice and wondered if he was mistaken. Surely there were churches in the city that were older than this one.

Or not.

Her doubts were erased the second she set foot inside the stark medieval hall. She could hear its age.

Shelley had first come to the conclusion that age was a sound when she went hunting for a place after she first moved to London. Most of the places she had seen were white shoe boxes that reeked of fresh paint and lemon air freshener. This was, after all, the easiest way to make a place feel shiny and new. But all the Lysol in the world could never change how a home sounded.

New places snapped, crackled, and popped. The flick of a light switch was crisper, the toilet flushed with a fury, and the drawers slid open with the whoosh of an Olympic bobsledding team. New apartments were like yapping puppies in a pet store, jumping over one another to be picked.

Older places were more restrained. Each sound they made was

thoughtful and deliberate: the slow, echoing plops of a leaky faucet, the falsetto creak of a floor plank, the soft sigh of a breeze through a jammed window. She had chosen the oldest apartment she could find. It was quiet, but not nearly as silent as Saint-Pierre.

Max took a seat in the back of the empty church. "As you can see, Saint-Pierre is much older than its facade lets on. It has been ruined, rebuilt, and repurposed more times than your grandmother's couch."

"How old *is* this place, Max?"

"It was originally built in the twelfth century as part of a Benedictine abbey," he said. "But the site's history goes back farther. The abbey was constructed over an earlier Merovingian chapel that was in turn built on the site of a Roman temple of Mars." He pointed to the choir bay. "Those two granite columns are from that first temple."

"It's beautiful," Shelley said.

Max nodded. "Yes."

"In a sad kind of way."

"Sad? Why?"

"All this history, all the things this church might have seen," she said. "It's a shame that it's been overlooked."

"I wouldn't feel too bad for old Pierre, luv."

"Why not?"

"Well, let me put it this way. It has served as a chapel for a burnt-down abbey, a tomb for a desecrated royal corpse, a telegraph tower for the revolutionaries, a dusty wheat warehouse for the Russians, and even a munitions depot for the Paris Commune. I think it's about time it's overlooked, don't you think?" Max said. "It's earned its anonymity."

Shelley found herself agreeing with him. It was, perhaps, no different from curling under the covers after a long and hard day. "But still," she said, "I'm sure it must get lonely."

He reached for her hand and covered it with his. "I suppose it does."

It was both hidden and highlighted by the sunlight filtering through the trees along the road. Flitting shadows stirred its landscape constantly.

Shelley found it difficult to get her bearings. An eyelid. A chin. A cheek. They changed with every step, with every shift of the breeze. Max's sun-dappled face was the perfect place to get utterly lost, she thought, and so was the maze of Montmartre's crooked little streets. She hoped for such a misfortune as they made their way down the hill.

Shelley could not understand the effect Max had on her. She was turning into a version of herself that she had not been introduced to, and she wasn't sure if she was pleased to make her own acquaintance. A brush of his arm stripped her down to synapses and nerves. Shelley: Acoustic and Live in Paris.

They approached a wall of rough-hewn stone. A sundial was carved into it and a painted blue rooster crowed in elegant script: *Quand tu son-neras, je chanteray.*

"When you ring, I will sing," Shelley said. The inscription was hardly profound, but it made her smile. It gave her something else to think about besides how Max bit his lower lip when he paused to think.

"Ah, you speak French. And here I was thinking I could make you believe that it said something convenient like 'Seize the day' or 'Kiss the man named Max.'"

Shelley cursed Sister Margaret's French lessons. Her knees wobbled, so she leaned on the wall for support. "Ha ha." She willed herself not to melt. There wasn't anything funny about the situation. It was delicious. And terrifying. She pretended to check her watch. The numbers blurred. Everything was moving too fast. She searched frantically for the train door and got ready to jump. "I . . . uh . . . think it's time we head back."

"It is?" Max glanced at the sundial. "The gnomon never lies." He gestured to the iron bar casting a shadow on the dial. "I believe the Greeks were spot on when they gave it that name. It means 'one who knows' or 'that which reveals.'"

"And what exactly does it reveal, Max? Other than the fact that the sun is shining, that is."

"The truth, luv." Max shrugged. "Unlike that wristwatch of yours."

"Hey, don't dis the Timex. It hasn't fallen apart on me yet—even after falling into the tub. Twice."

"I'm happy for both of you. The fact remains though that it is little less than an illusion."

"An illusion?"

"Yes. It helps us pretend that we can put time on a strap and wrap it around our wrist; that we can cut it into bite-size pieces and save some of it if we get up exactly at half-past seven, have breakfast on the train at eight, and are in the office before the large hand strikes nine."

"Well, Max, I could be wrong, but the last time I checked, that's what watches were supposed to do."

"Sadly, yes," he said. "Which is why I appreciate sundials. They aren't nearly as pretentious."

Shelley sighed. "Okay. I am officially lost."

"Look at it, luv. It is the closest we can come to grasping what time really means. It moves on whether you wind it or not. It doesn't have a snooze button you can hit to bargain for an extra five minutes. The earth turns, the sun rises and sets, and there is absolutely nothing you or I can do about it."

"That has got to be the most depressing thing I have ever heard."

"Depressing? I find it very helpful."

Shelley's eyebrow shot up. She wasn't sure if Max was making fun of her. "Really."

"Absolutely. If we accept time for what it is, how it flows and how we flow with it, I doubt very much that we would continue wasting loads of it by constantly checking our watches. The gnomon's shadow falls where it falls—and so do we. Where we are now is where a lifetime's worth of steps have taken us. Are we early for this moment? Are we late? Should we hurry back to the town house because your watch says so or should we linger as long as we can in the second where we stand?"

Shelley was taken aback by the way Max looked at her. His eyes seemed to plead with her to understand. And when she studied the sundial, she did. It did not have hands to tell her if she and Max were half-past acquaintance or a quarter before prudent. It simply cast a shadow that mirrored where hers fell. Both pointed to Max. This was where she was and no other place or time mattered more.

She liked to believe that what happened next was due to Adrien's special brew sloshing about inside her. Before Sister Margaret could object, she clasped Max's face and claimed the only truth she cared to know— his taste in her mouth.

Berries. No. Red summer fruits. And oak. With a hint of vanilla highlighting a surprising freshness before an intense long finish. (Shelley had read something like that once on a label of a Cabernet Sauvignon she decided she could not afford. She had taken home the red sweet stuff that came in a box instead. But kissing Max made it impossible for her to ever pick up another carton again, even at half-price.)

She pulled away to grasp for the safe and familiar, but not before her life had split in two: the wait before Max's lips and the raw yearning that came after it.

A FLIGHT TO THE PHILIPPINES

❧ *Now*

E arth to Shelley. Come in, Shelley." Paolo nudged his seatmate.

"Hmm? Oh, yes, right. Sorry," she said. The sundial she had been standing next to had disappeared, but the taste of Max the first time she had kissed him was still in her mouth.

"So where did you go?" Paolo asked.

"No . . . nowhere. I'm just a little tired, that's all," Shelley said.

"Maybe you should try to get some sleep. It's been a long day."

"I'm fine, really. I don't want to sleep. I can't," she said. "The sooner we're done with this, the sooner I can get rid of all his . . . lies."

Instant coffee, followed closely by fat-free mayo, was the biggest lie ever told to humankind, Shelley had thought. Her life with Max had just leapfrogged over it. All three looked exactly like what they were pretending to be on the outside, but the truth inside was a different matter. She could not digest any of them.

"I understand." Paolo reached over and gently squeezed her hand. "But I think you might be wrong about that."

Shelley pulled her hand back. "Wrong? About what?"

"You don't have to dismiss your past as a lie because of what we are finding out now," he said.

It was like watching a Chinese action movie dubbed in Russian, Shelley thought. She saw Paolo's lips moving, but she couldn't understand the words coming out of his mouth. She didn't like Paolo's kung fu.

"Paolo, I don't even know Max's real name. He is a man who has faked his own death—at least twice that we know of—has abandoned his wife and his grandson, and oh, let's not forget, is hundreds of years old. Please feel free to jump in anytime and tell me which part of my husband was not a lie."

"His love."

"What did you say?"

"His love."

"That's what I thought you said. I thought perhaps that you had lost your mind. Apparently you have."

"Shelley . . ." Paolo fixed his eyes on his lap. "Do you know what it's like to grow up without parents?"

She pressed her lips together. She thought about her dad and the huge box of birthday cards he had written for her before he died. Every year, he still wished her another year of joy and adventure. She could still hear his baritone in his thick handwriting.

Happy Birthday, Seashell. Always, Daddy.

"No, I don't," she said truthfully.

Paolo looked at her and smiled. "Neither do I. I was tucked into bed and kissed good night. I was scolded if I didn't clean up the mess in my room. I was hugged if I fell off my bike and scraped my knee. My parents died, but I was never an orphan. Nonno was my family. He raised me as his son and there was not a single day that I doubted that. Even now. You can make a child believe a lot of things. Santa Claus, the Tooth Fairy, the Easter Bunny . . . just about anything really, except love. You cannot make a child believe you love him if you don't. My grandfather loved me, Shelley. I know that. Whoever else he was or turns out to be, he was and always will be Nonno to me. My childhood was not a lie. And I don't think your life with Max was, either."

Tears burned behind Shelley's eyelids. "You're right, Paolo," she said. "Children know when they're loved. It's when you grow up that you're more easily fooled."

EMMENTAL VALLEY, SWITZERLAND

Five Years Ago

It had become clear to Shelley after the group had climbed the first hill why Max had left the van at the train station. The grassy trail was not suited for anything but mountain bikes, cows, or in the tour group's case, several pairs of blistered feet.

Brad struggled to drag his rolling carry-on up another slope. "Where on earth are we going, Max? I might have missed it, but I don't recall seeing 'trekking to China' in your brochure."

"What I do recall," Max said, "is that I explicitly told you to bring only what you'll need for an overnight stay."

"Don't mind him, Max," Simon said. "He's just beginning to realize that 'travel essentials' do not mean his heavy-duty blow-dryer, ten-step skin-product regimen, waxing paraphernalia, and thirty pounds of clothing."

Brad rolled his eyes. "I'm sorry, but you just can't fit fabulous into a backpack."

"You'll be out of your misery soon," Max said. "We're almost there."

Shelley puffed under the weight of her own overstuffed backpack but was too busy trudging through a forest of thoughts to complain. Max, she decided, was turning out to be more of a mystery than their next destination. She remembered how they had kissed in front of the sundial. The time since then was another matter. Max had all but ignored her, and she was beginning to wonder if she had just imagined everything that had happened between them. She shoved her hands into her pockets. Paper tickled her fingertips. She pulled it out. It was her list.

Meet. Date. Run.

It didn't seem so funny now. Technically, the list hadn't failed her. The principle was still sound. Max had just run faster.

Rose walked next to Shelley. "He fancies you, you know."

"Excuse me?"

"I said Max fancies you."

"Oh . . . well . . . uh . . . I wouldn't be too sure about that."

"Don't be silly, dear. He's just waiting."

"Waiting? For what?"

"For a little nudge from you, of course. Men always need that little bit of encouragement."

Shelley remembered the welcome party thrown by her tongue and tonsils for Max and cringed. It had nudged Max, all right—in the opposite direction.

"Especially if you've kissed," Rose said.

"How did you . . . I mean, why would that be, uh, theoretically speaking, that is?"

Rose smiled. "Raisins, of course."

"Raisins?"

"A kiss can be dreadfully terrifying for the males of our species, I'm afraid," Rose said knowingly. "Sex is easy. All they really need is a few good thrusts. But when they kiss, they open themselves up and let you in. And that, my dear, makes some men's balls shrink to the size of raisins."

Shelley snorted with laughter.

Dex strode up to her. "Did someone say raisins? I'm starving."

"You might try asking Max for some," Shelley said. "I'm sure he has at least two."

Shelley quickened her pace, trying to outrun her thoughts. She found herself beside Max as they made their way up another hill. The tour group trailed behind them. She waited for him to say something. Anything. Hum. Or even whistle. But he remained quiet, glancing at her only to smile as they walked. They hiked in silence until they reached a wildflower bush at the corner of awkward and excruciating. That's when she heard it. Soft padding steps. Shelley turned to see who was following them.

The large gray beast waved his trunk hello. Shelley groaned. This is what the kiss she had given him had become—a lumbering pachyderm, trying its darnedest to be inconspicuous. "Oh, get lost," she mumbled.

"Did you say something?" Max asked.

Shelley was acutely aware that this was the first time he had spoken to her since Paris. "Um . . . I said 'are we lost?'"

"You tell me."

The elephant swished its tail innocently.

"But I thought you were leading the way," Shelley said.

"I am? I had the distinct impression you were the one taking the lead when we were in Montmartre."

The elephant charged. Shelley tripped over a rock as she tried to get out of its way.

Max pulled her up from the grass. "You were the one who kissed me, remember?"

The elephant spun around. It charged again.

Shelley's eyes darted around her, searching for a way to escape. She found one. She had reached the top of the hill. She could not have dreamed up the emerald scene sprawled below her even if she tried. She followed the shadows of clouds as they glided over the valley, tracing a path across patches of wildflowers and fruit trees before floating over the ivory crowns of the Bernese Alps. Only the weathered farmhouses dotting the grasslands hinted of men.

"Wow." Dex walked up behind her and pulled out his camera. He framed her in a shot. "Say cheese."

Shelley forced a smile. She was growing tired of posing for Dex's pictures, but she owed him this much for rescuing her from a raging elephant. "Cheese."

Brad looked over the hill's edge and took a deep breath. "Is this what I think it is?"

Simon nodded. "Yes, Brad, it is."

Brad sighed. "Fresh air! And so much of it."

Max joined the group. "It makes you wonder, doesn't it?"

"About what?" Dex asked.

"How people can even think of giving those horrid canned air fresheners names like Alpine Breeze. There should be a law against that sort of thing."

"Oh, absolutely," Shelley said. Max's words played in her head. *You were the one who kissed me, remember?* She battled the urge to strangle him. "I'd certainly hate to be *misled* like that."

"I don't think anyone could fool you, luv," Max said, "or would even dare to try."

"Especially if that person knew I wouldn't hesitate to push him off—oh, let's say a hill—if he did." She shoved at his chest.

Grass, sky, and more grass. And Max. Or at least parts of him. That was all Shelley saw as she and Max tumbled down the slope. Her push turned out to be less playful than she had intended. She had tried to grab his sleeve when he lost his footing and had gotten caught in a tangle of limbs and backpack straps.

They ran out of hill.

Shelley landed on her back. Max fell on top of her. He didn't move.

"Shelley!" Dex ran toward them. "Are you guys okay?"

Shelley spat out grass. "I'm fine," she sputtered. "Max? Are you all right? Max?"

The rest of the group gathered around them.

"Get help!" Shelley yelled. Max stirred on top of her. She held her breath. "Max?"

Max trembled. Then shook. Panic rose in Shelley's throat. She blinked back tears. A familiar sound rumbled over her heartbeat. She pushed Max off and rolled over in time to see him shaking with laughter.

"You jerk!" Shelley said. "You scared me to death!"

Max continued to laugh. "And you almost killed me, so I guess that makes us even." He stood up and offered her his hand.

Shelley ignored it. She scrambled to her feet and marched away.

Max caught her by the arm. "Wait."

"Why?" She glared at him.

He leaned closer. "You haven't answered my question."

She frowned at him. "What question?"

"I asked you *if* you remembered that you kissed me."

Shelley swallowed. The elephant was back. It peeked over Max's shoulder and narrowed its eyes at her. She looked away. "I . . . uh . . ."

Max pulled a weed from her hair. His fingers brushed the side of her cheek. "Because I do."

Shelley held her breath. She squeezed the crumpled slip of paper in her pocket. *Run. Run!* She couldn't. Her insides were tumbling down the hill again.

Max grinned. "And wouldn't you agree it's about time we lose that bloody elephant that's been trailing us since Paris, luv?"

They walked across the valley. Shelley looked back. No pachyderm in sight. Rose was right, she thought. All Max had needed was a push. He had not left her side since they had tumbled down the hill.

"Ah, here we are." Max smiled and pointed to a farmhouse that was just coming into view.

"Max!" A blond man waved at him from behind the farm's wooden gate.

The man reminded Shelley of the towering pine trees they had passed on the trail.

"Josef!" Max wrestled him in a bear hug.

Shelley was lost in their exchange of rapid German.

"Well, Josef, here are your new recruits," Max said. "Campers, meet Josef, medieval history professor turned gentleman farmer. He will show you to your cows and you can get started."

"I hope they're sturdier than the ones you brought me last time, eh?" Josef said. "That group curdled the milk before they were able to fill their buckets."

"Oh, absolutely." Max put his arm around Shelley. "This one's small, but don't let her size fool you. There's power in those tiny arms. Believe me, I know. Right, luv?"

"Er . . . ah, yes, I suppose so." Squeezing Swiss udders was not exactly something Shelley could bring herself to be excited about.

"Well, glad to hear that, then. Let's get to work, shall we?" Josef rolled up his sleeves and led the group toward the barn.

Brad was as green as the grass under his feet when they reached the barn. Simon offered him some mint gum from a pack that had briefly been his when he bought it yesterday.

Josef swung the barn door open.

"Moooooooo!" Josef's five small children tumbled over one another as they raced to Max. They tackled him to the ground. "Uncle Max! Did you bring presents?"

"Of course!" Max laughed. He struggled to extricate himself from the giggling avalanche. "They're in here." He dug into his pockets.

The children hopped off him and waited on the tips of their toes.

"Aha! Found it!" Max said.

The children surged forward. He scooped up the littlest blue-eyed girl and tickled her tummy. She squealed with laughter. "Who's next?"

The children scattered. Max chased after them.

Josef laughed.

"So no cows?" Brad asked, the color returning slightly to his face.

"No cows." Josef smiled. "Sorry about that. It's a traditional Swiss welcome."

"We seem to be getting a lot of surprises on this trip," Dex said.

Shelley smiled. "But this has been the most adorable so far."

"I'll take cute kids over cows any day," Brad said. "I like my milk to come out of cartons, thank you very much."

The tour group settled into the dining room of the farmhouse. It was early evening, but the sun was still streaming in through the windows, pouring over the folk art paintings that adorned the room's rustic furniture.

"These are absolutely charming," Shelley said.

"They're called *Bauernmalerei*," Josef said. "Or 'farmer painting' as you would say in English. It's a painting style Swiss peasants developed in the Middle Ages to celebrate and record the milestones in their lives. These pieces date back to the sixteenth century. They were made by the man who built this farm. Back then, you see, peasants couldn't afford expensive—"

"Josef, I'm sure our guests must be starving," Ingrid said. Josef's wife was tall and blond like her husband with blue eyes that smiled as brightly as his. "Your history lesson can wait until after dinner."

The hot soup, the roasted veal with potatoes, and the chatter of the Von Allmen children was the balm the group needed to soothe the aches and pains they had accumulated on the hike. Ingrid brought out a platter of freshly baked butter cookies for dessert. Shelley indulged in two more of the warm treats than her jeans would allow. She undid a button and had another.

An inky night had fallen over the valley when the group gathered in the living room after dinner. Josef started a fire. Shelley sank onto a couch and breathed the crisp scent of burning pine. Max sat next to her.

Ingrid set a tray of coffee on the table.

"Dinner was wonderful, Ingrid," Rose chirped.

"Thank you. We do enjoy having company around. Our neighbors are lovely, but they're always in a hurry to leave before dark."

"I'm quite certain that's not on account of your cooking." Jonathan patted his stomach.

Ingrid smiled and excused herself to check on the children upstairs. Without the children's warm laughter, Shelley noticed just how chilly and quiet the farmhouse actually was. The silence magnified the crackle of the fire and the mournful wail the wind made as it wove through the eaves. She shivered.

"Well, actually, you might be right, Jonathan," Josef said. "Our lack of dinner guests may very well be due to the fact that our farm is haunted."

A breeze, touched with the scent of rain, snaked through the window. It swirled over the fire, making it flicker.

"Haunted?" Brad asked.

"I'm afraid so," Josef said. "There's a legend about this place that dates back to the Middle Ages. Would you like to hear it?"

"Well, I'm not so sure . . ." Brad inched closer to Simon.

"I love a good ghost story," Dex said.

Shelley nodded. "Come on, Brad. It can't be any more terrifying than squeezing a cow's jiggly bits, right?"

"I agree." Max placed his arm over her shoulders.

Shelley stiffened. She caught the tour group stealing glances at them while trying to hide their smiles. Even in the dimly lit room, they failed miserably.

Max edged closer to her. He rubbed her shoulder with his thumb. She suppressed the urge to purr.

"Let's begin our haunted tale then."

Shelley noticed the change in the tone of Josef's voice. He was a professor again and all that was missing was the blackboard. She found herself straightening in her seat.

"But first," Josef said, "you need to learn a little bit more about Switzerland's export industry. Would anyone care to guess what our chief export was in the Middle Ages? Shelley?"

"Er . . . I'm guessing that it wasn't cheese or expensive watches," she said.

Josef nodded. "We exported people—mercenaries, to be exact. Switzerland in those days was a very different place from what you see now. It was an overpopulated and poor country. Meanwhile, its richer neighbors, like France, needed soldiers to fight their wars, and Switzerland found itself with an abundance of young men more than willing to do the job. Soldiering became a sort of summer job for farmers who needed a means to tide them over during the winter months.

"Our mercenaries became must-haves in battles, and employers paid a premium to have them fight on their side. There was even a saying back in the day that went 'No money, no Swiss.' But the Swiss mercenary was worth it," Josef continued. "Necessity, you see, had forced the Swiss to be inventive in their military tactics. Without any horses or artillery at their

disposal, they armed themselves instead with long pikes. They reintro-
duced the ancient Greek phalanx and formed deadly sharp and almost
impenetrable porcupinelike columns that charged into the medieval battlefield.

"As there was no shortage of wars at that time, the mercenary trade
grew and became more organized. A prospective employer simply had to
contract trained units of mercenaries through the local Swiss canton
governments. More than two million Swiss men fought abroad during a
span of four hundred and fifty years until the late 1800s. This farm was
built by one of those men. His name was Uri."

"Who, you might be interested to know, happens to be Isabelle's
cousin," Max said, "several generations removed."

Large raindrops began to spatter on the farmhouse's rooftop as Ingrid rejoined the group. "Uri's wife, Esther, was my ancestor," she said as
she shut a rattling window. "This farm has been in my family since Uri
and Esther lived in it in the 1500s, but Josef and I almost sold it a few years
ago when my grandparents left it to me."

"That would have been a shame. It's such a lovely place. Why did
you want to sell it?" Rose asked.

"Josef and I were busy with our academic careers in Zurich. We put
the farm on the market almost as soon as I inherited it. We quickly found
a buyer," Ingrid said. "The week before the buyer was to take over, we
decided to spend one last weekend on the farm. We were surprised by how
much we enjoyed ourselves, and as you can see, several children later, we
are still here."

"Your buyer must not have been too pleased about that," Dex said.

"I wasn't," Max said.

"What?" Shelley's jaw dropped slightly. "You were the buyer?"

"Luckily for us, Max allowed us to buy the farm back from him on
the condition that we keep the barn unaltered and allow him to visit as
often as he liked," Ingrid said.

"I completely understand why you would want to visit this charming
place," Jonathan said, "but why would you make such a condition about
the barn, Max?"

"Because that's where the basilisk tortured Uri into madness," Josef said.

"A basilisk?" Dex asked. "That's one of those mythical snake monsters, right?"

"Not exactly," Max said. "A basilisk is more like a cross between a dragon and a rooster. It stands three feet high with the beak of an eagle, the head of a rooster, the wings of a dragon, and the tail of a lizard. It's hatched from the yolkless egg of a seven-year-old rooster brooded by a toad on a warm pile of dung."

"Sounds charming," Simon said.

"It might just be me, but somehow a three-foot-tall Franken-chicken doesn't strike me as that terrifying." Brad smirked.

"You might live longer if it did." Shadows from the fire danced over Ingrid's face. "A basilisk can kill you with a mere glance and is so venomous that everything in its wake withers into a barren desert. You do not want to cross paths with such a creature."

"Now, well, that ups the fear factor." Brad hooked his arm around Simon's.

"People were so afraid of basilisks that a rooster in Basel, Switzerland, was tried and burned alive for supposedly laying a basilisk egg in 1474," Josef said.

"And thus the rotisserie chicken was born," Brad said. The group chuckled. A loud pop from a smoldering log in the fire shook them back to quiet attention.

"So is that how you kill a basilisk?" Dex asked. "By fire?"

Max shook his head. "The only thing that can kill a basilisk is its own reflection or the crowing of a rooster. Travelers in the Middle Ages brought caged roosters along with them in case of a basilisk attack."

"Something Uri might have done well to carry on his way back home from his last campaign," Josef said. "The story goes that Uri was able to make a good living over the years that he had hired himself out as a mercenary. In between mercenary stints, he was able to build this farm, marry, and have children. By the early sixteenth century, however, the Swiss reign in the battlefield was drawing to a close. For all their bravery and ferocity, the Swiss and their pikes were no match for the new scourge of the battlefield."

"Which army was that?" Simon asked.

"Not an army," Josef said. "Guns. The end of Swiss infantry dominance came at the Battle of Bicocca, where they were fighting for the French against the Spanish and papal forces. The Swiss were slaughtered by artillery fire and those who survived marched home, unwilling to fight any further. Uri was among them. But he did not return alone."

The rain was pouring in earnest now. "What do you mean?" Shelley raised her voice over the howling wind.

"A basilisk had followed him back," Josef said grimly.

"A basilisk?" Brad gave a sharp gasp. "You're kidding, right?"

"I'm afraid not. But the basilisk did not kill Uri. That is, not immediately," Ingrid said. "At first, no one knew about the basilisk. His family just noticed that Uri appeared distant and spent a lot of time by himself in the barn. Except for the cows, he allowed no one else inside it. He spent long evenings in the barn, and the more time he spent there, the more worried his family became. Uri started speaking of being visited by a basilisk and how this basilisk would tell him the strangest tales. His wife was sure that he had gone mad but refused to let anyone else know about it for fear of what they might do to her husband. The Middle Ages, as you know, was not exactly known for its enlightened views in the field of psychiatric treatment.

"When his two children fell ill and died, Uri withdrew from the outside world entirely. His wife begged him to come out, but Uri refused to leave the barn. One night she went to the barn to try to find out what was happening to her husband. What she heard made her run away in terror. It was the basilisk," Ingrid said. "The next day Uri's wife went back to the barn and found Uri lying dead inside. He was clutching a basilisk's tail feather in his hands. But that was not the strangest thing his wife would see that morning."

"Why? What else did she see?" Rose sat on the edge of her seat, her small fingers digging into Jonathan's arm.

"It's late, campers, and we have an early day tomorrow," Max said. "I'm sure Josef and Ingrid are tired."

Rose nodded. "Oh, yes, of course."

"You might want to freshen up first before bed," Ingrid said. "There's a bathroom you can use just down the hall and another one upstairs."

Shelley waited with Max in the living room for her turn to use the bathroom. "Basilisks are tragic creatures, don't you think?"

Max looked surprised. "What makes you say that?"

"Well, they didn't ask to be born that way. They're simply an odd result of an even odder chain of events. They're doomed to be alone. It makes you wonder how much of the villain they really are."

Max stared into the fire. The flames flickered in the amber of his eyes.

"Well?" she asked.

"Well, what?"

"What do you think? Do you think basilisks are evil?"

"It's just a myth, luv."

"I know that," Shelley said. "I'm just speaking in hypothetical terms."

Max sighed. "All right, hypothetically then. Is a basilisk evil? Well, according to the stories, it certainly did bad things—inadvertently or not. Does that make it a monster? To those it killed, I'm sure it does."

She shook her head. "A basilisk didn't ask to be that way. It didn't have a choice."

"Shelley . . ." Max pressed his lips together. "There's always a choice."

"Everyone ready for bed?" Josef carried an armful of blankets into the living room.

"All set for dreamland. Are we sleeping in here?" Brad eyed the spot nearest the fireplace.

Josef looked at Max. "You didn't tell them?"

"It must have slipped my mind." Max grinned and picked up a blanket. "Campers, grab one for yourselves. We're rolling in the hay tonight."

. . .

The group huddled together under large umbrellas outside the barn. Shelley stared up at the tall barn doors, trying to remember their color. Rain washed over them, blending them into the gray of the evening. A basilisk, she thought, would certainly have felt right at home in the wet darkness.

"Very funny, Max. Ha ha." Brad hugged his blanket. "Hey, cute kids, you can come out now."

"Sorry, Brad," Max said. "We really are sleeping in the barn tonight."

"We're sleeping in this barn—this haunted barn—this barn where Uri was killed by a basilisk?" Brad's eyes widened with disbelief. "You can't be serious."

"I'm always serious." Max opened the doors, stepped inside, and disappeared into the barn.

Shelley heard the click of a switch. A faint orange light glowed from inside the building.

"Make yourself at home, campers," Max said.

"No cows?" Brad's face lit up when he saw that the barn was empty.

"The cows are brought up to the mountains this time of year to graze," Max said. "I hope you aren't too disappointed."

"I'll try to get over it," Brad said.

"Choose a spot in any of the stalls, campers. There won't be any . . . er . . . traces of their former occupants," Max said. "Or you can stay in the hayloft if you wish."

The group inspected the stalls. The hay was clean and warm.

Max led Shelley to the wooden ladder to the hayloft. "Watch your step, luv."

Shelley's heart pounded harder with every rung she climbed. Her ears buzzed with a mix of anxiety and anticipation at the prospect of spending the night in close quarters to Max. She realized just how close when she reached the top of the hayloft. There was only room enough for three people—if the third person happened to be half her size and was willing to sleep standing up on one leg. She walked to the edge of the loft and watched the group settle into their respective stalls. "Um, guys, there's . . . uh . . . room for one more up here."

"Sure, sweetie," Brad called back. "We'll be right up." He pulled his blanket over his head and snuggled next to Simon.

"Would you rather sleep downstairs?" Max asked Shelley.

She peered down. The only empty stall was next to Dex's. She plopped her blanket next to Max's before she could change her mind. "No."

"Pleasant dreams, everyone." Rose snuggled close to her husband and disappeared in his huge arms.

"Nodding off already?" Max asked. "I thought you'd all perhaps like to hear a bedtime story first."

Shelley rolled over. "What story did you have in mind?"

"I figured that after the little story that Josef and Ingrid told you, you might want to know what really happened to Uri. But if you're all too sleepy to hear about it now, we can do it some other time. It is rather late." Max yawned.

"You love torturing us, don't you?" Brad said. "If you so much as blink before telling us that story, I will be snoring in between you and Shelley faster than you can say 'slumber party.'"

"Yes, Max." Jonathan sat up. "We'd love to hear it."

"You twisted my arm." Max rummaged through his backpack. He pulled out a flashlight and switched it on. He pointed its beam toward the center of the barn's ceiling just as thunder clapped close by. "Look up."

Brad shrieked. A basilisk stared down at him.

Or rather a disturbingly lifelike painting of one.

"Meet Uri's basilisk," Max said, "the very sight that greeted Uri's wife when she found Uri dead in this barn."

Shelley studied the creature's painted features. It was just as Max had described. It had the head of a rooster, the outstretched wings of a dragon, and the long scaly tail of a lizard. But there was something else—something familiar about it. She stared into its amber eyes. There was a melancholy there that she could have sworn she had seen before.

"Not exactly the last thing you'd like to see before falling asleep," Dex said.

Max switched off the flashlight and crawled toward the edge of the hayloft. He looked down at the group. "Uri was a mercenary. That much is true. As a young man, Uri saw the mercenary life as a means to an end. He was driven by the single, simple dream of returning home with enough money in his pockets to build a better life for his family. No one told Uri, however, that dreams and war cannot coexist.

"On his first campaign, Uri had the luck of finding himself under the command of a captain widely known among the ranks as the Basilisk," Max continued. "No one knew how the captain had earned such a terrifying name and no one, including Uri, had the courage to ask. The captain, you see, was not exactly the most sociable fellow around. He was a tight-lipped, battle-hardened man with the reputation for being equally as merciless to his enemies as to his men. He did not tolerate cowardice and did not hesitate to execute any of his men who showed signs of weakness."

"How terrible," said Rose, snuggling closer to her husband.

"I believe that in medieval times that practice was quite common," Jonathan said. "The Swiss pike formation could only be as strong as their weakest man. I can imagine that if any one of them bolted in battle, the spiked columns would be left with a rather unfortunate gaping hole."

"Bonus points for Jonathan," Max said. "The practice of executing cowards and deserters was part of the Swiss mercenary code and thus an unlikely reason for the Basilisk's name or reputation. In that respect, he was no different from the other mercenary captains. He may have differed, however, in his penchant for staring into the eyes of the unfortunate soul at the end of his pike. You might say this basilisk's glare could quite literally kill you."

"Now there's a guy who wasn't hugged much as a child," said Brad. "I had a boss like that once. No wonder Uri went nuts."

"On the contrary," Max said, "the captain saved Uri's life on the battlefield on more than one occasion. In the end, however, there was one thing the captain could not save Uri from—himself."

Max ushered Shelley down from the hayloft. He asked the group to join them in a circle in the center of the barn. He switched on his flashlight again and swept its bright beam across the ceiling.

Shelley gasped. "What is all this?"

Another world hung over her. Faces. Trees. Life. The mural was painted in the same style as the art that adorned the furniture in the main house.

"This is what really killed Uri," Max said. The beam of his flashlight settled on a scene in the corner of the ceiling. A blond woman was carrying a small, dimpled child in one arm. She stood in front of a barn that was identical to the one the group was in. The woman was looking directly ahead of her, welcoming a visitor beyond the borders of her painted world. Peeking from behind the woman's skirt was another smiling yellow-haired child.

Shelley frowned. "I don't understand . . ."

"Uri was sick, luv." Max illuminated the ceiling with a wave of his flashlight. "And this was his disease."

"Disease?" Dex asked.

"Yes. A terminal case of nostalgia," Max said.

"Nostalgia hardly qualifies as a killer disease, Max," Brad said. "Unless, that is, one waxed nostalgic about the eighties and died from the combined weight of big hair and shoulder pads."

"Nostalgia," Max said, "from the two Greek words *nostos,* which means to 'return home,' and *algia,* which means 'pain.' Before the Swiss doctor Johannes Hofer coined the term in 1688, the oftentimes fatal sickness was simply known as the 'Swiss disease.' It referred to the extreme homesickness that afflicted Swiss soldiers in the sixteenth century that made them anorexic, depressed, and even suicidal. The condition was thought to be triggered by certain mountain folk songs and traditional Swiss soups."

"So Uri was killed by soup. That makes perfect sense. Are you sure this is really hay we're sitting on or should I bring out some rolling paper?" Brad asked.

"Max, please forgive my friend over here for his constant interruptions," Simon said. "I'm afraid he's still in shock from all the clean air flooding his system."

"Don't worry. I've seen this before. RSD—Rapid Smog Detox. I'm sure Josef will let us burn some logs if you really need to take the edge off,"

Max joked. "Unfortunately for Uri, nostalgia wasn't as easy to cure. The
disease was a matter of grave concern for Swiss mercenary employers.
What employer in his right mind would want an army of weepy soldiers?
The French even forbade the Swiss to sing those notorious folk songs at
their garrisons to prevent outbreaks of the disease. Some Swiss doctors,
hoping to dispel beliefs that this condition was a cowardly trait exclusive
to the Swiss, blamed the disease on the difference in air pressure between
the Alps and the lowlands that supposedly compressed the blood and
made the Swiss soldiers more susceptible to this desperate yearning. Blood-
letting thus became a common practice to cure this affliction.

"It took some time before the good doctors finally discovered the elusive cure for the deadly disease," Max said. "After all, who would have even
suspected that the most effective remedy for homesickness was to send the
patient home? Genius. Draining off his blood until his lips turned deathly
white made much more sense. Unfortunately for Uri, he was born before
the disease was even diagnosed, and in his case, not even returning home
could cure his affliction. In fact, it made things more difficult."

Shelley looked up at the scene of the young family welcoming their
father home. "But how could coming home make things worse?"

"You can't return to a place that no longer exists, luv."

Chapter Eight

Barns and basilisks

BICOCCA, ITALY

April 1522

The battle was over, at least for Uri. He limped along with a dusty column of broken men. He had been gone for many months, but now, together with the remnants of the Swiss mercenary army, he was heading home. He wiped the sweat from his brow. A cloud drifted overhead. The air cooled enough for a breath of hope. He had left as a husband and a father, but on each return he felt more and more like a stranger. Maybe this reunion with his family would be different. The sun broke through. Salt dripped into his eyes. More welled in them.

His sons did not know him. His wife, though she lay next to him in bed, felt more distant than when he was lying alone in camp, yearning for her body. He ached for his family every second that he was away, but now, as he grew closer to his farm and his fears, he wanted to run away. A white-hot pain shot through his leg, reminding him why he could not. He could barely walk, much less run.

Uri's leg had been hurt when his captain fell on him during their assault of the Spanish imperial lines. It was the only reason he was alive.

He had been in the thick of one of the two massive Swiss pike columns that had led the charge against the advice of their French employers.

Their unit had not yet been paid for their previous services and had threatened to leave if the battle was not swiftly concluded. They ignored the
scouts' warnings that Bicocca's ditch-riddled terrain would not favor their
infantry tactics.

More than eight thousand Swiss soldiers rushed into battle. A downpour of artillery slashed their ranks in half, turning the battlefield into a
swamp of the dead and dying. The Basilisk lay among his men in the red
mud.

Uri remembered the captain he had served under since his first campaign. He had never grown to like the grim man whose only joy seemed
to be skewering his enemies, but respect came more easily. The Basilisk
would stare death in the face and defy it time and time again, giving his
men the courage to do the same.

But not this time. Uri could still feel the weight of his captain's body.
It had fallen against him, shoving him into an irrigation ditch. He heard
his ankle bone crack before feeling the pain of it breaking. He tried to
push the Basilisk off him, but the captain's body wedged him to the
ground. It shielded him from the hail of artillery. Another body fell over
his leg. He screamed. It grew dark.

His dreams were darker. He was naked. Hands grabbed at him. They
dressed him in his uniform of patchwork silk, cut from the spoils of war.
They raised a needle and sewed the cloth into his flesh. Crimson thread
ran under his skin. He clawed at it. The pain forced his eyes open. He
woke inside another dream. He was being carried away from battle. He
looked up. The Basilisk's amber eyes stared into his. Uri held his breath.
He did not turn to stone.

The morning found him at camp, his leg set in a cast of wheat-paste-
and-egg-white plaster. He hobbled on it now, each step heavier than the
next.

EMMENTAL VALLEY, SWITZERLAND

May 1522

U ri lay on the grass, his face contorted by grief. The children had not run to welcome him. They were not waiting at the farm's gates nor did they peek shyly at him from behind their mother's skirts. They were here. Underneath the grass. He was now forever a stranger to them, unable to make up for lost time.

"How did this happen?" Uri's tears watered their graves.

"It was a fever . . . a few weeks after you left. It took other children as well." Esther wept and embraced her husband.

Uri froze. He could not bear the feel of her skin. She was cold, as if only sorrow ran through her veins. He shrank from her.

Esther held him tighter.

He pushed her away. He was an open wound, flayed raw by the grass that covered his boys. "Woman, leave me alone."

At first, his wife begged him for words. Failing that, she pleaded for his touch. As the days passed, she simply implored him to look at her. But Uri could not. He was blind to everything but his own pain. He regretted not dying in Bicocca. Whoever had saved him had not done him any favor. He had lived only to lose something worse than his own life: his past and his future.

There was not an inch of his house in which he did not feel the absence of his sons. An empty chair. A quiet room. A cold bed. There was no yesterday he could wade through that did not drown him in tears. To remember how his boys laughed when he carried them on his shoulders only made their silence echo louder. But turning his thoughts to tomorrow was even crueler. The years ahead held only promises he could no longer keep, memories that would never be made, and dreams that had turned into dust.

He looked across the table at where his eldest used to sit and ask for more watered-down stew. His heart had broken a thousand times when he had to tell him the pot was empty. He had hired himself out to fight other people's wars so that he would not have to see his children go hungry. Now, because he had not been at their sides when they needed him the most, he would never see them at all. But maybe what he could not do for them in life, he could do for them in death. Porridge for Hans. Fruit for Peter. And bread. Stew. Meat. Milk. Their table would never be bare again. He picked up his paintbrush. Pie.

The light from his oil lamp flickered on the planks of the barn's ceiling. Uri moved closer to the scaffolding's edge. He dipped his brush into one of his pots and painted over the yellow glow.

"Good evening, Uri."

Uri bolted upright, hitting his head on a beam. Wet paint streaked his matted hair. "Who . . . who's there?"

"I see that you've been busy."

"Show yourself!" Uri reached for his lamp. His hand trembled. A pot fell to the floor. Red splattered over dirty hay.

"I didn't know you were this . . . talented."

Uri scrambled down the scaffolding.

A dark figure emerged from an empty stall. The halo of Uri's lamp lit the amber in his eyes.

"Captain!" Uri stumbled backward. "I . . . I thought you were dead!"

"Consider me a ghost then, or a basilisk, if you like. That's what you and the men used to call me, if I remember correctly." The Basilisk stepped out of the shadows.

Uri screamed and fled the barn.

Uri stumbled on the grass at the edge of the light seeping from the barn. What was he doing? Esther . . . his boys . . . they were still in the barn— with the monster that had taken a dead captain's shape. He shouldn't have left them behind. He had to go back. His heart pounded against his ribs as it had done so many times before a battle. He pulled himself to his feet and tightened his grip on his courage. War's drumbeat thundered in his ears, urging him to advance. He flung the barn doors open.

The Basilisk was waiting for him. "I'm glad you came back."

Uri froze. He did not have his pike.

"Come inside, Uri," the Basilisk said.

Uri took a step closer, his empty fists trembling at his sides. His eyes darted over the Basilisk, searching for the best place to strike.

The Basilisk held up Uri's lamp to his face. Uri held his stare, stunned—and relieved—that he did not turn to stone. The light illumined his captain's eyes. They looked weary. Alive. "Captain, is that really you?"

"Yes," the Basilisk said softly.

"But I saw you fall."

"You fell, too, and yet here we both stand. Wounds heal, Uri. At least, most do." The Basilisk glanced over at Uri's leg. "Your leg seems to have set well."

Uri nodded, unable to take his eyes off the man he had given up for dead. "It only hurts when it gets cold."

"Consider yourself fortunate, then. Some pain never leaves, regardless of the weather." The Basilisk stepped toward Uri. "I heard of your loss. I came to offer my condolences."

"Condolences?" Uri asked, looking puzzled. "There has been no death here." A smile warmed his face as he gazed up at the ceiling. "Forgive me. I have forgotten my manners. Captain, I'd like you to meet my wife, Esther. And these are my children, Peter and Hans." Uri waved to the painted children. "Go on, boys, don't be shy. Say hello to the captain."

The Basilisk felt the ceiling close in on top of him. He was too late. Madness was a ditch he could not carry Uri out of. He wasn't sure that he wasn't mired in it himself. In war, they had little in common. Uri had fought to live. He had battled to die. But now they stood on the same ground. Both of them were trying to find their way home.

"Won't you stay with us, Captain? Esther will be thrilled to have a visitor. We have a spare room." Uri pointed to an empty barn stall.

The Basilisk looked up. Uri's family smiled at him. He envied Uri's painted world. It was more real than any peace he hoped to find. "Yes . . . thank you. I think I will."

Uri set up the scaffolding. The captain had been staying with him for a few weeks now. Or had it been months? He wasn't very concerned with the passing of the hours. Time didn't matter much when you were happy to be in the second where you were. He hummed a folk song. He was working on a scene on the left side of the ceiling. Hans and Peter were carrying a large basket. A half-painted Esther waited by the barn. "It looks like a good harvest this year," Uri said.

"Yes, it does," the Basilisk said.

"The boys are really a big help. They are growing taller every day." Uri climbed up on the scaffolding and waved to his sons.

"I can see that."

"So what story shall we have today?" Uri set up his paints.

"What sort would you like to hear?" The Basilisk leaned against a stall.

"All your stories these past weeks have been very entertaining. Not that I believe any of them, though." Uri laughed. He had never imagined that he would one day be at ease in his captain's company or that they would trade stories late into the night. But neither had he dared to hope for such happiness in his family's arms, and yet every day with them felt like a dream. Only better.

The Basilisk smiled. He was equally content. He could not remember speaking so openly with anyone. Uri's loosening grip on reality was a place where his secrets could run free. "To believe my stories would be madness."

"I told Esther about the time you spent in a monastery." He stroked his wife's cheek. Her blush came off on his finger. He touched up the smudge with his brush. "She enjoys your stories as much as I do."

"Does she?" The Basilisk tried to push the image of the real Esther away. He caught glimpses of her from the barn. She never left her house anymore and only came to the window to stare into the meadow where her children lay. He watched her cry.

"Yes, very much," Uri said. "After hearing all your stories, it's actually difficult to believe you are the same man the men called the Basilisk."

"I can understand that."

Uri finished his wife's smile. He glanced down at the Basilisk. "But why did they name you the Basilisk, Captain?"

"They didn't." The Basilisk played with a blade of hay. "I gave myself that name."

"Really? Why? I'm sure the boys would like to hear that story."

"Because that's what I am."

"But you are not a monster. The children love having you around." Uri turned to his eldest son. "Right, Hans?"

"Perhaps. But I have stared at death as many times as any basilisk."

"Boys, go and play in the meadow while the captain and I talk." Uri watched his sons run past the barn.

"Death consumes everything I care about, Uri," the Basilisk said, "and all I can do is stand by and watch its slow feast."

"What are you talking about, Captain?"

"My family. I am here while everyone I have loved is gone. All these years I have wanted nothing more than to join them. But . . ."

"But what?"

"I grew tired of waiting."

"For what, Captain?"

"Death," the Basilisk said. "So I decided to seek it out." He let out a heavy sigh. "I have led more men to battle—to their deaths—than I can even remember. But war was comforting, at least for a while. Feeling my pike tear through my enemy's flesh and hearing it scrape against their bones made me feel . . . *alive*."

Uri nodded. He remembered how he had never wanted to live more than when he stood in front of an enemy's pike. "I understand."

"But the desire to live would always pass," the Basilisk said. "Each time I won the right to live, I stared with envy into the eyes of the man I had killed and wished . . ."

"That it was you who was going home instead."

"Yes."

Home. Uri closed his eyes. The word fell like a pebble into a well. It plunged through the stillness in his mind. Splash. His thoughts stirred, catching reflections of a reality he had chosen to forget. They grew stronger, swelling into a clarity that lapped at the edges of his painted peace. Paint dripped on his cheek. "My boys . . . they didn't welcome me when I came home . . ."

The Basilisk took a deep breath. "No, they didn't."

"Why, Captain?" Tears streamed down his cheeks, washing away his world. "Why were they taken from me? After all the sacrifices, all the blood I spilled for them . . . my sweet boys . . ."

The Basilisk nodded.

"And Esther . . ."

"Is alive," the Basilisk said. "She has been waiting for you to come home to her. Go home while you still can, Uri."

"Home. Yes, you are right, Captain. I must hurry home." Uri looked at the painted picture of his farmhouse. Madness and reality lapped over it, swirling into visions of muddy graves, empty supper bowls, and blood. He tried to open the door in the haze. It would not move. He needed to break it down. His children were calling for him from beyond his painted world. He needed his pike. Where was it? He looked at his wooden brush. He pressed the sharpened edge to his chest and called to his boys, "Wait for me! Papa's coming home!" He pushed himself off the scaffolding and fell on the brush's point. The hay turned red beneath him.

"Uri!" The Basilisk rushed to his side, but once again he was too late. Uri had left him.

The Basilisk cradled Uri in his arms and wept as Uri had for his sons. He stared up at the painted ceiling and through his salty grief he saw the barn for what it really was. It was a tomb long before Uri had died in it. He looked into Uri's glassy eyes and saw his own amber eyes staring back at him. He watched his tears fall for the things long gone, a home as empty and imagined as Uri's painted world. The Basilisk died at the sight of its reflection.

At dawn, a rooster crowed and the captain walked out of the barn. But before he left, he took the bloodied brush from Uri's hands. What he could not give Uri in life, he would give him in death. He climbed up on the scaffolding and painted a myth over Uri's madness. When he was done, he wrapped Uri's fingers around a black rooster's feather, leaving him the only dignity he could.

EMMENTAL VALLEY, SWITZERLAND

Five Years Ago

Dex's snoring punctured the quiet in the barn, but that was not what kept Shelley awake. The Basilisk did. She could not stop thinking about him. Uri had found peace. She wondered if his captain had ever found the same. She hoped so. She searched the ceiling for him. She made out the outline of wings in the darkness. She could not see his eyes, but she felt their loneliness. She rolled to her side. Another set of amber eyes met hers.

"Jesus, Max. I thought you were sleeping. How long have you been awake?"

"A while."

"I can't sleep, either. I have a hard time falling asleep when I'm away from home."

"Me, too."

"But you're a tour guide! How do you ever get enough sleep, then?"

"I don't. It's better that way."

"Why?"

"I don't like dreaming."

"Nightmares?"

"No. I . . . dream about home."

"That doesn't sound too bad."

"It's not," Max said. "It just makes it difficult to . . . wake up."

"Oh, well, um, go easy on the Swiss soup before bedtime, then. I heard that it can give you a bad case of homesickness."

Max chuckled. "I'm glad you're awake, luv. It's nice to hear another voice in the dark. Especially a voice that makes me laugh. I don't think I've ever even smiled inside this barn until tonight." He leaned closer and tucked a lock of Shelley's hair behind her ear.

Shelley inhaled sharply and caught the scent of a rare evening, the kind of warm night when the most important thing you had to do was lie on freshly cut grass and count stars. And maybe eat jellybeans. She closed her eyes and filled her lungs with the scent of Max. She sighed, reluctant to release him.

"May I ask you something, luv?"

"Sure. Anything."

"Do you regret the kiss?"

"Why? Do you?" Shelley held her breath.

"Yes."

She was grateful for the darkness. It hid the pain burning in her eyes.

"I . . . I regret that I didn't kiss you back."

Her heart stopped. "You know, Max, it's not good to have regrets."

"I agree."

Shelley closed her eyes and brought her lips closer to his.

"I can't." Max pulled away. "Not here. Not in this . . . place."

She turned from him, embarrassed by her eagerness.

He sat up and ran his hand over her leg.

Shelley felt the sparks through her pajamas.

He whispered in her ear, "But there is something else I'd like to do . . ."

She told herself to breathe. The technique looked easy enough in her cousin's Lamaze video. *Hee hee hoooooo.*

Max's fingers glided down her thigh. His palm was warm around her naked ankle.

Hee hee hooooo. Shelley grabbed the blanket to stifle her imminent moans. "What . . . what would you like to do, Max?"

"Well, if you aren't ticklish . . ." He grinned. "I'd be happy to give you a foot rub." He kissed her big toe and pressed his thumbs into her sole.

A FLIGHT TO THE PHILIPPINES

Now

Paolo remained silent, and Shelley had a feeling that it wasn't because he had a hard time picturing his nonno massaging her toes. She wasn't in the mood to talk, either. Thinking of her husband as the bloodthirsty basilisk made her stomach turn. She was sure that if she opened her mouth, she was going to throw up. She heard Paolo taking a deep breath.

"Shelley, this will sound strange, but of all the things I've discovered about Nonno so far, accepting him as the Basilisk has been the most difficult . . . and the easiest," Paolo said.

"What?" She choked. "You're kidding, right? Unless he chased you around with a pike when you were a kid, I cannot, for the life of me, understand why you would feel that way."

"No, I didn't spend my childhood running away from pikes." He almost smiled. Instead, his lips quivered, and he seemed to have difficulty regaining control of them. "But I did have other adventures. A boy can go many places and see many things sitting on his grandfather's lap. Nonno told me stories, Shelley. Many, many stories."

"Your point?" she said.

"He told me they were fairy tales, fables. But even as a boy I sensed there was something different in Nonno's stories from the ones I read in books. Now I realize what it was."

Shelley watched Paolo wrestle with the muscles in his face. They twitched beneath his skin as he struggled to keep them set in the calm and smooth lines she had grown used to.

"They were real, Shelley. Nonno yearned for those places and the people in them. I could hear his longing in every word." Tears crept into his voice. "He missed them, the way I missed him when he died."

She sat helplessly as Paolo let his tears fall.

"That's why I didn't go back to Italy after Nonno died," he said. "I couldn't. Like him, like the Basilisk, I had nothing to go home to."

Shelley watched him sob, unsure whether to hold him or run away. Since she met Paolo, she had fought hard to ignore how much he reminded her of Max. His eyes. His laugh. Even the way he smelled. But now that battle was lost. In this moment of vulnerability, he and Max could not have been more alike. She looked at Paolo through her own tears. His face blurred, swirling and changing into different men who shared the same pain. The Basilisk. The captain. Nonno. Max. She reached for Paolo's hands. They were warm, just as Max's had been. She held them tight, no longer able to deny that the hands that had once wielded a pike were the same hands that had kneaded the balls of her feet into oblivion every night.

Chapter Nine

Sand and shopping

"You certainly work magic with eggs, Max." Jonathan helped himself to the remnants of scrambled eggs.

Shelley was disappointed that Jonathan had beaten her to the morsels. They were almost as fluffy as the cloud she floated on when she woke up in Max's arms. She consoled herself with another slice of *zopf*. She slathered the golden plaited bread with butter and marmalade.

"That's the real reason why we look forward to his visits," Josef said.

"And I thought it was my charming personality that kept me welcome all these years," Max said.

"So where are we headed to next, Max?" Dex asked.

"I trust that you are all familiar with the Fountain of Youth?" Max asked.

"The one Ponce de León was searching for in Florida?" Simon asked.

"I'm no whiz in geography, but I think Florida would be quite a detour for a European road trip," Brad said.

"Indeed." Max grinned. "But while Ponce de León went looking for the secret of eternal youth, we are going in search of the opposite. And for that, campers, we shall have to make our way to Austria."

VIENNA, AUSTRIA

꧁ *Five Years Ago*

The group arrived in Vienna just as the cafés were filling up with the afternoon crowds. According to Max, there was only one criterion for choosing a café in Vienna—the ruder the staff, the better the coffee. But with most of the cafés already overflowing, he had to relax his standards. He led the group to the back of a 1950s-style café that had enough empty seats.

Shelley waded through the hum of conversation and the clinking of coffee cups. She settled into a dark bentwood chair. The troposphere of cigarette smoke coiled over her head. She tugged at her ponytail and sniffed; she was going to have to shampoo twice that evening.

The waiter smiled and politely offered her a menu. She resigned herself to a cup of freshly brewed mud.

Max ordered a round of mélanges.

"So where is this mysterious Fountain of Old Age, Max?" Jonathan arranged his heft on a chair made for someone half his size. "I, for one, would like to keep a fair distance from it."

"Oh, come now, Jonathan, I'm sure a splash or two won't hurt. What are a few good years in exchange for a little adventure, eh?" Max said.

"That, my young friend, would determine how many years I can still spend out of adult diapers," Jonathan said. "But why go all the way to Austria to learn how to grow old when you have two fine elderly specimens right here?"

Rose turned up her chin. "Speak for yourself, dear."

The waiter returned and gingerly set their cups on the table.

Shelley braced for sludge and took a sip. The brew of steamed milk and strong coffee had not been diluted by the waiter's charm. She licked the froth off her upper lip.

"If you don't mind my asking, Jonathan," Simon said, "I was wondering if you feel any different now than when you were younger?"

"That's an interesting question." Jonathan took a sip of his coffee.

"I've certainly never been happier than I am now, though I think that has more to do with finding my Rose than with my age." He gave his wife a squeeze. "She keeps me young."

"Spinach blended with wheatgrass and carrots helps, too." Rose winked. "And sex—at least thrice a day. Or four when there's nothing good on the telly."

Dex snorted coffee onto his lap.

The group's laughter stirred the cloud of smoke hovering over their table.

"To reruns." Brad raised his cup.

Max tipped his cup to Shelley and grinned. "I'll drink to that."

The evening's church bells pealed through the cobbled Austrian streets. It echoed, Shelley thought, from a time and place far more distant than the monastery Max parked in front of.

Dex whipped out his camera, then positioned Shelley in front of the compound's yellow and cream facade. She tried not to look too irritated as he snapped away. His little crush on her was starting to get annoying.

"Campers, welcome to the *Benediktinerabtei unserer Lieben Frau zu den Schotten*," Max said.

"Um, Max, you lost me at Beneweinerschnitzel." Dex set his camera down.

Shelley escaped to Max's side.

"The Benedictine Abbey of Our Dear Lady to the Scots, also known as the Schottenstift or the Scottish Monastery," Max said, "which is rather curious considering that it has never had a single Scottish monk in it."

"Why the name, then?" Simon asked.

"The monastery was founded in 1155 by Duke Heinrich II and was run by Irish monks who came from a monastery in Regensburg, Germany. At that time Ireland was known in Latin as 'Scotia Major,' or 'new Scotland,' and so the Germans called the Irish 'Schotten' or 'Iroschotten.' During a period of reform in the 1400s, the Irish monks were replaced by Benedictine monks from Austria," Max said. "Thus we have standing before us an eight-hundred-and-fifty-year-old misnomer: a Scottish monastery without any Scots, founded by German-Irish monks given the boot by the Austrians who presently occupy it.

"As this is a working monastery, campers, I have to inform you that their accommodation guidelines are, shall we say, conservative," he continued. "Only married guests are allowed to share rooms."

Simon smirked. "Don't worry about it, Max. I'll be happy to fall asleep to the clanging of bells instead of Brad's snoring for once."

"And I for one am positively ecstatic at the thought of not waking up in a puddle of Simon's drool," Brad said. "Plus, any place without hay is a welcome upgrade from sleeping in a cow stall."

Shelley bit down her disappointment. "You certainly have a penchant for choosing the most unusual places for us to stay in."

"Isabelle's ancestors were a diverse lot, as you probably know by now," Max said. "And at one point in this monastery's colorful history, one of them happened to be its abbot."

Shelley studied the ceiling. It was white, like all of the walls in the spartan quarters of the Benediktushaus, the monastery's guest facility. Her room was bare except for the hard bed she was lying on, a pale wooden desk, a nightstand, a crucifix, and the quiet that filled every inch of the small space. The silence soaked through her faded college sweatshirt, under her teddy bear pajamas, and deep into her skin. It drew her into herself and into a place of pause—which might have been a good thing, Shelley sighed, if only she could reflect on something other than Max's long fingers. Foot rubs would never be the same again.

Mustard-slathered bratwurst. The thought popped into her head randomly and Shelley grabbed on to it like a lifeline. She forced herself to ponder how she might actually resemble the sausage if she walked over to the room's only window in her red sweatshirt and wrapped herself in the yellow drapes. It was either that or succumb to less pious fantasies involving the same window, Max, and her—without the sweatshirt or anything else. She grabbed a Bible and attempted to lose herself in the book of

Genesis. The fact that she did not understand a word of German made it more challenging. A loud knock startled her from chapter 2, verse 18. She fell off the bed.

"I think I may have heard the distinct sound of a bottom getting bruised," Max said when Shelley opened the door.

"I, uh . . . dropped the Bible." Shelley ignored her throbbing tailbone. "You're not supposed to be here, you know."

"Glad to see you, too." He ran his fingers through her hair. His fingertips grazed her nape. They lingered there.

All thoughts of bratwurst vanished along with Shelley's ability to string words into a sentence. "Did . . . you . . . um, anything . . . want?"

"Yes." Max shut the door.

A FLIGHT TO THE PHILIPPINES

Now

"Oh . . . I see," Paolo said, "so that's when you and he . . . uh . . ."

"Talked," Shelley said, "until morning."

"Of course." He grinned. All traces of his earlier strife were gone. He seemed as relieved as she was to move farther away from the Basilisk.

VIENNA, AUSTRIA

Five Years Ago

Shelley had steeled herself for a confession about three wives, a mistress, and ten illegitimate children when Max had said that there was something he needed to tell her. He, unfortunately, was not in any rush to put her out of her misery. Her insides twisted as they sat wordlessly on her narrow bed in the only way two grown adults could fit—with Max leaning against the headboard and her back wedged tightly against his groin.

The beginnings of a cramp twitched in her thigh. She shifted to her side and let her face rest on Max's chest. His heart echoed in her ear. Its

rhythm soothed her, lulling her to the edge of sleep. Talking didn't seem
so important now.

"Egg timers," he said.

"Hmm?"

"Egg timers. They're absolutely brilliant, don't you think?"

"Um, I guess so." Shelley yawned. The miniature hourglass had not
helped her cooking much, but it was quite handy when she played Boggle.

"It reminds you of what's really important."

"It does?" she asked. Max's revelation was turning out to be less than
anticlimactic, but she would take his musings on egg timers over confes-
sions of a sordid past any day.

"Absolutely, luv." He fished a tiny hourglass from his shirt pocket.

"Uh . . . you carry an egg timer with you?"

"Doesn't everyone?" Max turned the timer on its head. The white dust
began to spill through the glass funnel, and he held it in front of her.
"What do you see?"

"Sand."

"Yes," Max said. "And?"

"More sand?"

"And the past," he said.

Shelley furrowed her brow at the timer.

"Tiny grains of choice bumping into one another, flowing into what
happens next." Max set the timer on the nightstand. "It's fascinating to
watch."

"And all this time I was just waiting for eggs to boil." She watched
the sand free-fall and realized that there was a strange truth in what Max
had just said. The smallest of the decisions she had made in the last few
days had helped to funnel her to this place—to this bed—grains away
from whatever was going to come next.

Max leaned forward. Shelley felt his breath on the side of her neck. The
tip of his nose traced the curve of her shoulder to the soft spot behind her
ear. Her pulse throbbed in her throat.

He tilted her face to his.

Shelley closed her eyes and wondered if a monastery was a more suitable place to kiss than a hayloft. She bit her lip to stop it from quivering. Max kissed it free and explored its edges. She ached for more. If he kissed her any more slowly, she was going to burst from need.

Max saved her. He teased her mouth open and drank her in—deeply and urgently—with a thirst Shelley thought she would never fill. She pulled away, panting. She glanced at the egg timer. The sand had settled at the bottom of the glass. "What happens . . . next, Max?"

He whispered into her hair, "It starts again." He flipped the egg timer over.

She closed her eyes, then took an extra deep breath for good measure and waited to be drained a second time.

Sand continued to pour.

She peeked through an eyelid.

Max reached for the egg timer and set it in her hand. He leaned back against the headboard. "Yesterday flows into tomorrow, tomorrow tips over to yesterday."

Tomorrow? Yesterday? She exhaled. Perhaps he really had come to talk. Perhaps they were not yet as far from the barn and the Basilisk as he would have liked. Would they ever be? She rolled the glass between her fingertips, finding its narrowest point. "And how about today, Max? Where is 'now' in your egg timer?"

He smiled and wrapped his arms around her waist. "You're holding it, luv."

Shelley felt the thin, delicate nature of the glass tube. She felt the sand rushing past the tips of her fingers. Three minutes had always been an eternity while waiting for breakfast to cook, but as she lay in Max's arms, she saw how brief the seconds actually were. This was how fleeting the years with her father must have felt for her mother, she thought. Her fingers trembled. The hourglass slipped from her grasp, scattering sand all over the floor.

A FLIGHT TO THE PHILIPPINES

Now

"Have you ever been in love, Paolo?" Shelley twisted the gold wedding band on her finger.

"I've had a few girlfriends. Why?"

"Did you ever imagine spending your life with any of them?"

He shifted in his seat. "Um, to be honest, I'm not sure if I'm built for that kind of commitment."

"That's another thing you have in common with Max, then."

Paolo frowned. "Huh? What do you mean? Max married you . . ."

Shelley pulled off her wedding ring, revealing the pale band of skin where the ring had embraced her every second of the last five years. She handed it to Paolo. "Look at the inscription."

" 'Now,' " Paolo read out loud.

"Most people promise each other forever when they get married. Max and I promised each other 'Now.' "

"Why?"

"Because it's breakable," she said, "and the only thing you can really hold in your hands. It's where the gnomon's shadow falls on the sundial. Back then, I thought that it was romantic."

"And now?"

"Now I realize that it was the only promise Max could make."

VIENNA, AUSTRIA

Five Years Ago

The group convened early the next morning outside the monastery's library. Shelley rubbed her eyes. She had found it difficult to sleep after Max had left her room, and when she did, she dreamed of sand slipping through her fingers. Breakfast had been a supreme struggle to keep from taking a nosedive into her muesli. A black-cloaked monk unlocked the library's door.

Ginger steeped with cloves. She caught its scent in the spiciness of the weathered leather-bound pages that surrounded her. The smell reminded her of her father's evening ritual up until the time he needed to use a feeding tube. Her mother continued to brew it for him just the same. And when he had gone, she still set a cup on his bedside table. Shelley remembered watching and breathing in the fragrant and frail wisps of steam rising from it. That was the only time she allowed herself to miss her dad. Her mother mourned him enough for the two of them. She didn't think their house could hold any more grief. She was glad to get away. She scanned the library, desperate to remind herself of how far she was from home.

Shelley tilted her head upward to take in the bookshelves that reached as high as the rows of white columns along the library's two-story-high marble hall.

"This, campers," Max said, "is where we will find the elusive secret of growing old."

"Not as elusive as I would like," Jonathan said. "It seems to have found me quite easily."

Max smiled. "I stand corrected. You are quite right, Jonathan. Growing old is arguably neither a secret nor elusive. What we are here to discover is not the secret for aging but for escaping youth."

"I'm not sure that's something I want to find," Dex said.

He smiled, but the stiffness in his tone told Shelley that he was genuinely less than thrilled about Max's next story. She could understand why. She wasn't a big fan of aging herself.

Since she'd left Ohio, she felt she had been playing catch-up with life. She thought that life in London would be different from the one she had left. She would be different. Living with her mom had been like living in a vacuum-sealed time capsule. Every cup, saucer, and vase had stayed in the exact same place ever since her father died. In London, Shelley was determined to do the opposite—to move, to breathe, to rearrange furniture. Living in a shoe box that only contained a futon, a microwave, and an old couch she had found in the street proved to be somewhat of a design challenge. She made do by moving around cushions and plastic plants—anything to make her believe that she wasn't stuck. She was done with a life that alternated between the pause and rewind buttons.

Max pulled out one of the books from the shelf. He handed it to Jonathan. "This is only a reproduction, of course. The original is kept in the archive because it's now too fragile to handle."

Jonathan opened the book, revealing its illuminated pages. "It looks like a prayer book."

"It is. It's a book of hours. It contains the monk's daily prayers," Max said. "Please turn to the last page."

"It's in Latin," Jonathan said. "Is this another prayer?"

"It's an exact copy of the original's explicit, a personal message a scribe would write after he had completed a book," Max said.

"Was this written by Isabelle's ancestor?" Dex asked. "What does it say?"

"It was written by one of the novices under him. It is the secret we have come to discover," Max said.

"Well, come on," Shelley demanded, her voice tense. "Tell us what it says."

"What's the rush?" Max took the book back from Jonathan and stuffed it into his backpack. "It's such a lovely day I thought we might do a little shopping first."

"I don't think the monks will be too thrilled with that." Simon eyed the book peeping out of the flap of Max's bag.

"Shopping?" Max asked. "Why would they object to that?"

"I was referring to the book you are about to steal," Simon said.

"Don't be silly, I'm just borrowing it for the day," Max said. "I just haven't told the monks yet."

"But . . ." Simon said.

"Oh, will you relax, Simon? I'm sure Max will return it when we're done," Brad snapped. He turned to Max with a conspiratorial grin. "Now, Max, what were you saying about shopping?"

•　•　•

The air buzzed with sounds and smells spilling over from the striped canopies of the Naschmarkt, Vienna's oldest and largest outdoor market. The fresh scent of organic produce was as crisp as the thrill of finding a good deal. Shelley breathed in the bustle.

"Let's meet back here in half an hour, campers. Here are your lists and shopping money." Max handed out little sheets of paper and euros. "Rose, you and Jonathan are in charge of the vegetables, herbs, and spices. Simon, you and Brad will get the figs and grilled octopus. Dex, your assignment is the cheese and wine. And, Shelley," he said, "you're getting some old cock."

"But I thought Jonathan was coming with me?" Rose winked.

"I do hope you are referring to another Austrian misnomer, Max," Shelley said.

"I suppose you'll just have to wait and see."

The heady scent of Eastern delicacies mingled with the warm aroma of freshly baked artisan bread. Shelley walked through the market's endless lanes, finding it impossible to decide which stall carried the freshest, ripest of, well, anything, really.

Max took a strawberry from a vendor whose cheeks were as plump and red as the fruit she sold. He offered Shelley a bite.

The sweet pulp gushed in her mouth. "Hphmhfly."

"I didn't quite catch that, luv."

She swallowed. "Heavenly."

"We'll take one basket," Max said to the vendor.

Shelley took another bite.

"Er, make that two," Max said.

Shelley held on to Max as they wove through the crowds. She was certain they had nibbled through at least a half pound of free cheese, olives, and sausage samples before Max found the stall he was looking for.

"Here we are," he said.

Shelley read the sign on the small store's orange canopy. "Zum Gock-elhahn."

"They have the best poultry this side of the Rhine." Max walked over to the refrigerated glass cabinet at the front of the store.

Three ostrich eggs dwarfed the spotted quail eggs on the cabinet's top shelf. The second shelf held a spread of packaged whole turkeys and goose pâté. Shelley wondered what he was planning to purchase. There was no cock, old or otherwise, in sight.

Max spoke in German to the barrel-chested man behind the counter. The large man disappeared into the back of the store and then reappeared with a football-size package wrapped in brown paper. Max weighed the package in his hand, smiled, and paid the man.

"So is this the mysterious 'old cock'?" she asked.

"Hardly anything mysterious about an unwanted rooster past his prime, luv."

Shelley grimaced. "Sounds delicious."

"I find that in certain instances, older is better," Max said. "And so did Isabelle's distant uncle, Abbot Thomas."

The group unwrapped their treasures on the counter of the monastery's kitchen. Max laid the book he had taken from the library next to them, then opened it to the page containing the explicit.

"I'm feeling slightly sick imagining a dish that would call for a geri-atric rooster, dried figs, and a grilled octopus," Brad said.

"Me, too," Max said. "It's a good thing the octopus and the figs will be long gone before the rooster's done." He put the figs into a bowl and passed it around. "Here. Something to munch on while we cook." He slid the octopus onto the platter. "And this is for lunch later."

"And the rooster?" Rose picked a fig from the bowl.

Max placed the rooster on the chopping block. He raised the butch-er's knife over it. "It's getting ready for a hot bath."

Chapter Ten

Secrets and soup

SCHOTTENSTIFT MONASTERY
AUSTRIA
1210

The hen's head fell into the basket on top of a growing pile of the day's discards. The wet smell rising from the refuse wrestled with the stench of burned chicken feathers. Brother Aidan picked up the hen's limp body from the bloodied chopping block and dropped it into his cast-iron pot. "Make soup, he says."

Abbot Thomas's instructions had left the younger monk feeling more than slightly frustrated. He had gone to the abbot with a serious question, and all that he had received from his superior were two words. *Make soup.* Technically, the old abbot had used four words, the younger monk conceded. *Make soup. Use chicken.*

But the request for chicken soup was not what irked him. He had learned well enough to follow orders in his two years at the monastery. What irritated him was the fact that he had already cooked the broth four times this week, and each time it had been met with the same response. He could already picture what would happen next when he brought Abbot Thomas his dinner in the infirmary.

First he would help the elderly abbot sit up in his straw-filled bed. Once he was comfortably upright, the abbot would smile and ask him if he still wanted to know the answer to his question. "Yes, Abbot," he would reply, though less eagerly than the first time he had asked it. "I would like to know what it feels like to grow old."

"Did you make the soup?" the abbot would say. "Yes," he would respond, "with chicken." He would then give the abbot a spoonful of the hot broth. Abbot Thomas would close his eyes and sip the soup slowly. When his spoon was empty, the abbot would lean back on his bed. A gentle curve would form on his thin lips, communicating his disappointment in the kindest, and most excruciating, way possible. Brother Aidan had grown to dread that smile. The abbot would finish the rest of the soup and thank him. "And the answer to my question, Abbot Thomas?" he would ask, still daring to hope that the old man might finally give him a proper response. "Make soup. Use chicken," the abbot would say and then bid him good night.

Brother Aidan could not understand what was wrong with his soup. He had been, up till then, fairly confident in his culinary skills. None of the other monks, pilgrims, or passing crusaders had ever complained about his cooking. He had tried another variation of vegetables and herbs for this latest attempt, but he knew that he would soon run out of ideas on how to prepare the soup to the abbot's liking.

Brother Aidan found this barter of soup for knowledge quite odd but was still convinced that the abbot's answer to his question would be worth it—even if it meant emptying out the monastery's henhouse. To reach the abbot's advanced age these days was a rarity that fascinated him. Abbot Thomas was the oldest man he had ever met. The younger monk wanted—needed—to know what it was like to be on the abbot's winter journey . . . before it ended.

"Good evening, Brother," Abbot Thomas said when Brother Aidan entered the infirmary. He was propped up in a chair next to the window.

"Good evening, Abbot." Brother Aidan noticed the faraway look on the old man's wrinkled face. "Is everything all right?"

"Yes. I was just remembering what the courtyard looked like."

"Remembering?"

"I lost my sight completely today, Brother."

Brother Aidan could not detect any bitterness in the abbot's voice. He set the soup bowl on the table and knelt by the blind man's side. He looked into the gray veil that shadowed his eyes. He remembered that they had once been the same bright shade of amber as his own. He held the old man's gnarled hands. "I'm sorry."

"There's nothing to be sorry about, Brother." Abbot Thomas patted Brother Aidan's hands. "Everything I should see, I have seen. God has darkened the world outside so that I could see better by the lamp of my memory. Now is the time for me to reflect on the sights God has chosen for me to remember."

The younger monk felt ashamed that it was he who was in need of consoling. "So you are . . . at peace?"

"Perfectly content, Brother. In fact, I am already finding that every sound, texture, and scent unleashes a stream of recollection. Why, even your voice . . ." The abbot's brow creased.

"What is it, Abbot? What's the matter?"

"You . . . your . . . It's nothing." The abbot dismissed his thoughts with a flick of his wrist. "I smell soup."

"Would you like to have your dinner now?"

"Yes, please."

Brother Adrian fed the abbot a spoonful of the broth. He held his breath. The abbot did not close his eyes. There was no longer a need to. But as the sides of the old man's lips began its familiar trail upward, Brother Aidan realized that despite the abbot's new condition, the rest of their soup-tasting routine would remain exactly the same. The abbot was still not satisfied with what he had made. His chest sank.

"Do you still need an answer to your question, Brother?"

Brother Aidan nodded, then remembered that the abbot could no longer see. "Yes, I do."

"Then . . ."

"I know, I know. Make soup. Use chicken."

. . .

"No, I'm sorry, Brother. I cannot give you any more hens this week," Brother Placidus said. The thickset man stood between Brother Aidan and the monastery's henhouse.

"Just one more, Brother. Please," Brother Aidan said.

"I cannot help you," Brother Placidus said. "Only the Lord can make the chicks grow any faster. We need to keep the remaining hens for their eggs."

"You don't understand . . ."

"Besides, Brother," Brother Placidus said, "and please take this suggestion in the kindest way possible, we all love your chicken soup, but having it every day can get a little . . . weary. Why not try cooking something else today? Lentil or barley stew, perhaps?"

Brother Aidan sighed and walked away as a half dozen plump hens rejoiced happily in the yard.

Abbot Thomas took a whiff of his dinner. "Ah, you've made something different today, Brother Aidan."

"Yes, Abbot. Barley stew."

"Does this mean that you have grown tired of asking your question?"

"No, Abbot. It is Brother Placidus who has grown tired of me raiding his henhouse."

"Perhaps the Lord wishes that we set aside your question for a moment so that we may talk about other things?"

Brother Aidan thought about the possibilities of this rare invitation. The Benedictines did not take a vow of silence, but social conversation was decidedly limited. Approaching the abbot with his previous question had already been an unprecedented act of boldness, if not presumptuousness, on his part. Now that he had a chance to speak freely with the abbot, he was strangely at a loss for anything to say.

"I have lived a long life," the abbot said.

Brother Aidan was thankful that the abbot had taken the reins of their conversation. "You have been blessed."

"Are the extension of life's years truly a gift?" Abbot Thomas asked.

"Is that not your belief?"

"What I believe, Brother, is that it was I who was asking you the question. I am still waiting for your answer."

"Oh . . . uh . . . well," Brother Aidan said, "a long life . . . can be a gift . . . if steered by purpose."

"And what purpose steers your life, Brother?"

Brother Aidan missed the empty niceties between himself and the abbot. He realized that he did not enjoy answering questions as much as he liked asking them. He recalled his three vows: obedience, chastity, poverty. He had always been glad that honesty had never been a promise he had to make. And yet he did not wish to lie to the old man sitting in front of him. "God's work," he said. The scope of such work, he decided, was sufficiently encompassing to qualify as a truthful answer.

The abbot smiled. "Indeed."

"Your stew is getting cold."

Abbot Thomas sipped his stew. "This is delicious."

"Thank you." Brother Aidan was genuinely happy at the compliment and for the diversion dinner provided.

"But I am not hungry," the abbot said. "I would much rather continue our conversation, wouldn't you?"

Brother Aidan was glad the abbot could not see the pained look on his face. "As you wish."

"Thank you for indulging an old man's need for some company."

Brother Aidan braced himself for another round of questions.

"What do you think about immortality, Brother?" the abbot asked.

"Everlasting life is the Lord's promise for all mankind." Brother Aidan felt confident mouthing the prescribed pious response. Standard questions like this were easy.

"But what if eternal life did not have to come at the price of death?"

"I do not grasp your meaning, Abbot." Brother Aidan avoided the abbot's blind eyes.

"Would you like to live forever, Brother Aidan?"

Obedience. Chastity. Poverty. Brother Aidan repeated his monastic obligations. Did he owe the abbot anything more than that? "No," he said.

"Neither would I, Brother," Abbot Thomas said. "Neither would I."

Brother Aidan peeked under the pot's lid to check on his lentils. Brother Placidus had yet to lift the moratorium on culling hens. Brother Aidan considered asking someone else to deliver the abbot's dinner that evening. He was in no mood to answer any more of the abbot's questions.

"Do I smell lentils?" Abbot Thomas asked.

Brother Aidan wondered how soon it would be before he regretted his decision to serve the abbot his dinner. "I remain under strict orders to keep at least ten paces away from Brother Placidus's chickens, Abbot."

"Then it seems that God wills us to have more time to discuss other matters, Brother."

Brother Aidan rolled his eyes. "Wouldn't you like to have your soup first?"

"Dinner can wait. I, on the other hand, cannot. Waiting is a luxury for the young, wouldn't you agree, Brother?"

"Yes, Abbot."

"But something tells me that you are a very patient man." The abbot looked directly at Brother Aidan with his blind eyes.

Brother Aidan fidgeted in his seat. "It is . . . a virtue worth striving for."

"And one of the hardest to gain," the abbot said. "The years that forge it also melt it away."

"Do you consider yourself a patient man, Abbot?"

"By the mercy of God, I try not to be."

"Why?"

"When you are this close to the end, Brother, patience can be a slow poison."

"What do you mean?"

"It can lull you into waiting for the end to come, living out your last days as if you were already dead," the abbot said. "This is not how I wish to die. I would like to row myself to shore, pulling my own oars with urgency until the very end of my journey."

Urgency. The end. Brother Aidan struggled with their meaning. They were as real to him as the distant lands he had read of in books, as wistful and imagined as Heaven.

"The lentil soup last night was excellent, Brother," Brother Placidus said.

"Thank you," Brother Aidan said. He eyed the plump chickens clucking in the henhouse. "But I need chickens."

The poultry keeper frowned and planted himself firmly between the other monk and the chickens. "The chicks have barely sprouted two more feathers since you last asked me for another hen."

"I don't mean to pester you like this, but it's not my fault, Brother. It's the abbot. He won't answer my question unless I make him chicken soup."

"And what question might that be?" Brother Placidus asked. "I might be able to help you without killing any more hens."

"I don't mean to be disrespectful, Brother, but I don't think you can." Brother Aidan knew he was not endearing himself to the man at whose mercy lay his quest.

"Then I suggest you return to your kitchen and leave me and my chickens in peace, Brother." Brother Placidus turned on his heel.

"No, wait," Brother Aidan said. "I'll tell you the question."

"I'm listening."

"How does it feel to grow old?"

"What kind of a question is that?" Brother Placidus threw up his hands and marched back to the henhouse.

Brother Aidan sighed and picked up his sack of lentils from the ground. He made his way to the kitchen.

"Brother!" Brother Placidus called from the henhouse. He had a black feathery bundle tucked in his arm. "Here, take this old rooster. It's as useless as your question." He shoved the bird into Brother Aidan's hands. "I pray that it will help you find your answer so that you can stop bothering me."

Brother Aidan stared at the elderly rooster. He resigned himself to another pot of disappointment.

Brother Aidan started cooking dinner early. He wanted to have enough time to prepare an alternative in case the rooster proved to be less than edible. He had been simmering the bird longer than usual, hoping to soften the aged meat. He skimmed the scummy film that rose to the top of the broth as he waited. The broth was getting clearer and more intense in flavor. The young hens he had cooked would have turned to mush long before they infused the soup with such richness, that is, if they even had this quality of flavor to yield. He replaced the lid on the pot. He guessed that it would be a few minutes before the rooster's meat was tender enough to be pulled off the bone.

Abbot Thomas was coughing violently when Brother Aidan entered his room. The abbot's dinner sloshed in its bowl as he hurried to the abbot's side. He rubbed the old man's back. He almost recoiled when he felt Abbot Thomas's bones protruding through his woolen clothes. He had not realized how frail the abbot had become. He held him until his grating cough stopped.

The abbot wheezed. "I see that you have your answer."

Brother Aidan frowned. "What do you mean, Abbot?"

"The answer to your question." Abbot Thomas smiled. "You've brought it with you."

"You mean the soup?" Brother Aidan felt guilty about using an old rooster for the broth.

"Yes. Let's have a taste of it, shall we, and find out for sure."

The ritual began again. The abbot let the soup sit in his mouth. He swallowed it with great deliberation. Brother Aidan's chest began to sink as the sides of the abbot's lips began their familiar curl upward. But then the lips took a sudden detour, stretching toward the sides of his face, lighting it up with a wide grin.

"What did you use to make the soup?" the abbot asked.

"Oh, um, chicken."

"Yes, but what kind of chicken?"

A perfectly plump hen in the pink of health, Abbot. Brother Aidan could not summon the lie. He sighed. "An old rooster, Abbot."

"Very good, Brother," the abbot said. "So, are you pleased with your answer?"

Brother Aidan wondered if the abbot had finally become senile. "Are we still talking about the same question, Abbot?"

"Was there any other question, Brother?" the abbot asked. "A different question might require you to make another soup entirely."

"I think you should rest now, Abbot." Brother Aidan set the bowl down.

"Growing old is to be set free, Brother," the abbot said. "It is a slow and long-simmering process that extracts from you what you are really made of. But it requires acceptance. You cannot put a flailing chicken in a boiling pot. You must accept the heat and the pain with serenity so that the full flavors of your life may be released."

The abbot started coughing.

Brother Aidan reached out to stroke his back.

The old man waved him away. "I'm all right, Brother. You may see this as decay, and it is. But it is also much more than that. As the body rots, so does the cage that traps us in our worldly concerns. When my legs became too weak to carry my body, I stopped pacing with worry. When my fingers became twisted, I stopped pointing blame. When I lost my sight, I stopped seeing illusions. It may be dark in the pot that I am simmering in, but I can see more clearly than I have ever seen in my life. I can see you, Brother," the abbot said, "and I know who you are."

It was Brother Aidan's turn to feel weak. "Excuse me, Abbot. I need to take my leave. The other monks are waiting for their supper."

The shore was in sight. Abbot Thomas rowed closer to it every day. It had been two weeks since Brother Aidan had left his side. But he did not fret. Being blind made it easier to wait. There was no sun or shadow to hurry him either way. He was content in the certainty that Brother Aidan would return before the end came.

Days passed like dreams. It required effort to tell the difference between wakefulness and sleep, so he did not bother to try. He welcomed both sides of the hour. Memories churned rapidly, distilling truth. He waited to share it.

Knuckles rapped against wood. Abbot Thomas turned to the door. He smelled soup. "You've returned, Brother."

Brother Aidan set the soup aside and took a seat beside the abbot's bed. "How are you?"

"Very well. Dying suits me." The abbot smiled weakly. "I'm glad you've returned to finish our conversation. You left so suddenly the last time you were here."

"I apologize."

The abbot put his gnarled fingers on Brother Aidan's hand. "It's all right. I understand. As I told you before, I know who you are, Brother."

Brother Aidan took a deep breath. "I don't know what you—"

"I have almost no memory of my life before entering the old monastery back in Ireland," Abbot Thomas said. "I was very young when I was donated, just as a number of our brothers are. But, unlike them, it was not my parents who gave me to the monastery. I was told later that I was left in the monastery's care by a relative who took pity on me when he found me orphaned by disease. He did not leave his name. I have always regretted that I have been unable to put a face or a name to the man to whom I owe my life. But I no longer have such regret."

"It is good to let go of regret," Brother Aidan said.

"But I did not let it go, Brother. I told you the day I lost my sight that the darkness allowed my body to remember things that my mind had forgotten. I heard a voice that day I went blind, a voice that made me see something that my eyes could not. I heard your voice . . . and I remembered."

Brother Aidan's breathing was almost as labored as the abbot's. "What did you remember?"

"I remembered a quiet good-bye at the gates of a monastery, the voice of the man who saved me. It was deep and gentle, but not without grit, very much like *yours*."

Brother Aidan stiffened in his seat. The abbot tightened his grasp on his hand.

"Is that not true, Brother Aidan?" the old man asked. "Was it not your voice that bid me farewell? You are my stranger—the immortal angel God sent to watch over me. You were the one who guided me into this life, and you are now my last companion as I leave it. Speak now and tell me if that is not the truth. Speak before I reach the shore."

Brother Aidan took the abbot's hand and kissed it good-bye. "Think of me when you get there."

The abbot smiled·and closed his eyes. "Where will you be? Will you not follow?"

"I will be here," Brother Aidan said. "As always."

Chapter Eleven

Lists and longevity

🍃 *Five Years Ago*

Abbot Thomas succumbed to senility or was, at the very least, delusional in his last days," Max said, "and Aidan did not have the heart to kill a dying man's faith."

"But why was Aidan acting so evasively? What was he hiding from the abbot?" Shelley asked.

"Let's just say that he had entered the monastery for less than pious reasons. He did not come to follow the Cross but to chase his own curiosity. He did not want the abbot to find out that his becoming a monk was an academic exercise and not the religious experience he pretended it to be. Aidan had questions, and he thought that the monastery could provide him with answers. And this is the answer he found, the same secret that we have pursued." Max tapped his finger on the explicit.

Shelley squinted at the book. The ancient language lay dead on the page. And then she saw it—a format—so teasingly familiar it danced on the tip of her tongue. Numerals. Steps. Measurements. She laughed. "Max, this is Aidan's rooster soup recipe, isn't it?"

Max grinned. "Well done, luv. You have in your hands the elusive secret for escaping youth."

"I'm not convinced." Dex folded his arms in front of him.

"It is a recipe, and quite a good one, I assure you." Max checked on his cooking pot.

Dex sat up straighter. "I'm sure it is, but what I don't buy is the merit of rotting into a husk. With all due respect to the older members of our group, if I had a choice, I would rather stay young. I don't want my mind to slip away. I don't want my memories of the life I've shared with the woman—with the *people* I love—to be ripped from me. If there really was such a thing as a fountain of youth, believe me, I'd be the first in line with a bucket."

"Not if I beat you to it," Brad said. "Dying sucks. I'd love to live forever."

"Forever, Brad?" Shelley said. "Don't get me wrong. I don't enjoy getting wrinkles, but I imagine that living forever would be like being the last person at a party—and then watching the room fill up again with people you don't know, playing music you can't stand. You wouldn't even have anyone left to remember the good old days with. Think about it, Brad. Could you imagine eternity without Simon?"

Brad pressed his lips together.

"Shelley has a point." Jonathan squeezed his wife's hand.

"How about you, Max?" Simon asked. "Is immortality your cup of tea?"

Max looked at Shelley. "Perhaps with a bit of honey."

"Come on, Max," Shelley said. "Be serious."

"I am," Max said. "In my humble opinion, forever is a bitter brew. In many ways, I envy and admire Abbot Thomas. He accepted death for what it is."

"Which is?" Simon asked.

"Rest," Max said.

"I suppose death must seem that way when you've lived that long," Shelley said. "Life, I imagine, looks very different when you're standing at the very edge of it. I wouldn't know how I'd feel or what I'd do if I suddenly found out that I was dying."

"But you are, luv," Max said. "It's a path you've been on since the day you were born. I'd say you're almost a third of the way through."

"Once again, thank you for such a pleasant thought." Shelley slumped back in her seat.

"That may be true, Max," Simon said, "but I think Shelley was talking about a more imminent end. What if you found out you only had a few months to live? Or even weeks? Do you whip out your list of 'things you need to do before you die' and race to check things off? Or do you lock your loved ones in a cottage somewhere and hug them until they can't breathe?"

"I like the hugging part." Max slipped his arm around Shelley's waist. "But I can think of more interesting things to do in a secluded cottage."

"You're impossible." Shelley slapped Max's bottom.

"Like that, for example," Max said.

"We are in a house of prayer, in case the two of you have forgotten." Brad closed his eyes and clasped his hands together piously. "Brother Bradford. It has a nice ring to it, don't you think?"

"You'd be excommunicated faster than you could spell the word," Simon said. "But while we're on the subject of impending demise and bucket lists, I have a question for the group. What would be at the top of your list?"

"Well, I suppose I would like to see the world and have a trunk full of photographs to show for it. Retiring on a tropical island would be good, too." Dex looked at Simon. "How about you?"

"Well, if I had to prioritize," Simon said, "I suppose it would be to settle down and have a family."

"Oh . . . uh," Brad stammered, "me, too. Right after I went naked skydiving over the Grand Canyon."

Simon rolled his eyes. "How about you, Rose? What would you like to do first?"

"Well, I've already skydived without my knickers, but I suppose it would be more fun if Jonathan joined me the next time around."

"I've jumped out of an airplane behind enemy lines for my country, Rose," Jonathan said. "That was enough for one lifetime, I believe."

"So if donning a parachute and not much else isn't your thing, what else remains on your to-do list, Jonathan?" Dex asked.

"When you get to be my age, you would hope that there wouldn't be much left to cross off. And that's exactly how it was before I met Rose, to be honest. I was nearly done with my short but respectable list. But now," Jonathan said, "my list has grown quite long. Afternoon tea, quiet walks, rainy mornings—nothing I haven't done before, but everything I need to do now with my Rose as many times as I can, while I can."

"Jonathan . . ." Rose embraced her husband, her tiny arms barely reaching around his chest.

Dex hurried to dab at the corner of his eye. "I can't think of a better list than that, Jonathan. That certainly beats hurling yourself from an airplane any day."

Brad elbowed Shelley. "Your turn."

"Oh, come on." Shelley threw up her hands. "You can't expect me to give my answer after that, do you?"

"Go on, dear," Rose said. "We'd love to hear it."

"Well, um, okay." Shelley chewed her lip. "The funny thing is, I actually do have a list. Several, in fact. But there's a couple that I always carry with me." She pulled out a leather-covered notebook from her bag. A faded pink paper was tucked in its sleeve. "This is the first one I ever made. I was a kid. It's silly, really."

"That's too cute!" Brad said. "Let's have a look."

Shelley unfolded the list. "When I wrote this one afternoon in our kitchen, I obviously wasn't thinking about dying. What I was thinking about was my mom and her scrapbooks. After my dad died, my mom's favorite way to pass the time was to wedge me by her side and go through all her mementos of their life together. Love letters. Flowers. Concert tickets. Everything. She never tired of telling me how she met my dad and how they fell in love waiting in the rain for their bus. It sounded like a fairy tale, a story of how a prince met and married his princess, but then . . ." She glanced at Max. He smiled at her, but all she could see was an hourglass shattering on the floor.

"But then what?" Dex asked.

Shelley took a deep breath. "I realized just how sad the story actually was. It was the story of a princess left to live alone on the blank pages of an unfinished book," she said. "That's why I wrote this. It's a magical spell my younger self made to make sure that what happened to my mom would never happen to me. I didn't want the 'ever' that came after happily. I didn't . . . don't want to be the one left behind." She read from the pink page.

1. Find a frog. (No warts, please.)

2. Kiss the frog. (Eeew.)

3. If he turns into a prince, keep him.

4. Make him promise not to catch a cold or die. Or eat flies.

Shelley busied herself refolding the list and tucking it back into her notebook. A grocery list slipped out and fell to the floor. She took her time picking it up. She wasn't in a hurry to see the group's reaction to her list. Especially Max's.

Brad grinned. "So have you kissed any good frogs lately?"

Shelley turned to Dex. "Um, could you please pass the figs?"

Dex pushed the bowl toward her with a sympathetic smile. Shelley stuffed two figs into her mouth.

"I hate to be the one to break this to you, but I think you might have some difficulty finding a prince to sign that kind of a prenup, Shelley," Simon said. "Except maybe for the part about eating flies."

Rose clasped Shelley's hand and gave it a squeeze. Shelley was taken aback by how frail the older woman's hand felt, only slightly more substantial than cobwebs or a passing thought.

"My dear," Rose said, "you might be surprised at how much happiness you can find in the pages of the shortest of love stories. Unlike penises, their length truly does not count."

Now

Scribbling a soup recipe at the back of a prayer book sounds like something Nonno would do, all right," Paolo said. "He always did have an odd sense of humor."

"I guess you'd have to be if you were immortal."

There, she'd said it. Fast, flippantly, and coated in a gel capsule of glib. It was the only way she could swallow the truth without choking. Max was immortal, and she was an immortal's widow. It was a paradox too cruel to understand.

"So do you really think that's what he is?" Paolo asked.

"Julien, Antoine, the Basilisk, and Brother Aidan, Abbot Thomas's guardian. All of them . . . they were all just one man," she said. "What else could Max be?"

"I don't see any bite marks on your neck, so I guess that rules out the other possibility."

"Very funny. You're just like him, you know," Shelley said. "He never took things seriously—not even his own death, it would seem."

"I'm sorry, but I have to find some humor in this whole experience. The more I learn about who Nonno was, the more I find myself wondering about who I am. You married an immortal, but I am his grandson. What does that make me, Shelley?"

She could hear the strain in Paolo's voice. Guilt dropped in her gut like a heavy pasta dinner. "I . . . I'm sorry. I've been so focused on myself, I haven't stopped to think how you must be feeling. I promise that I'm not as idiotic in real life."

The tension in Paolo's brow smoothed over. A hint of the smirk hovered at one corner of his mouth.

Shelley inhaled sharply. She had caught another glimpse of Max in the dimple that deepened in Paolo's olive cheek.

"Real life," Paolo said. "That sounds kind of funny now, don't you think? As bizarre as things are, do you realize that this moment is actually the closest either of us has actually come to the truth? Life has never been more real, Shelley, and as profoundly unnerving as it is, I'm actually . . . glad."

She rolled her eyes and turned toward the seat in front of her. What kind of person could be pleased in a moment like this? And what kind of person would choose to upholster a plane in scratchy, unattractive plaid?

"After thirty-two years," Paolo continued, "I'll be able to look into the mirror and truly know who it is I'm looking at. The pieces of Nonno's puzzle are mine, too. All of his lives . . . all the people in them are part of whoever—or whatever—I turn out to be."

The air roared out of the cabin. Shelley gasped and grabbed for an oxygen mask. She clutched at the empty space above her head. She wondered why no one else was panicking. She drew her arm back from the ceiling and slid down in her seat. It dawned on her that she had been the only one who had gotten the wind knocked out of her lungs.

Paolo had spelled out the terrible and enviable difference between them. They were on the same plane, seated inches from each other, but they had never been on the same journey. By discovering who Max was, Paolo was coming into his inheritance—his own identity. She, on the other hand, was drifting farther away from the life she thought she had, and there was no way to turn back.

Paolo took her hand. "Is everything all right?"

It was so easy to imagine Max's fingers closed around her hand, Shelley thought, to curl up into a time when that was all she needed to feel safe. All she had to do was close her eyes. She fought hard not to blink. She needed to face the truth, that as warm as Paolo's hand felt, she was alone on a one-way trip to the Democratic Republic of the Hopelessly Undone. She pulled her hand away and scavenged for scraps of courage to speak. Her lips were numb. "Should I continue with the story?"

Paolo drew his hand back. "Yes, of course. You were telling me about Austria."

"We stayed in the country for one more night." Shelley swallowed back the sadness of the unfolding memory. The tour's next events were almost as painful as her new reality. "At least, five of us did."

Chapter Twelve

Death and decisions

VIENNA, AUSTRIA

✿ *Five Years Ago*

Shelley learned that she had a taste for old cock, but she liked the Mozart concert Max had taken the group to after their rooster-soup dinner even better. The strains of the concerto echoed inside her as they filed out of the Vienna Opera House.

"Did you enjoy yourself, luv?" Max asked.

"Yes." She smiled at him.

"I'm glad you liked it."

"Who wouldn't? Mozart's timeless."

"Perhaps."

"Perhaps?"

"Mozart's good," he said, "but it's really too early to tell if his music is truly immortal."

Shelley was still trying to decide whether Max was joking when they stepped onto the street. They walked hand in hand in the cool evening. She was amazed by how Vienna had been transformed. It had softened, warmed by the glow of its streetlamps and the lights that illuminated every detail of its ancient architecture. It was the perfect backdrop, she thought, for the lovers who strolled in its streets.

Lovers. Shelley slipped the word under a breath that was equal parts wistfulness and fear. She looked at Max and wondered how it was possible to want something so badly and be utterly terrified by it at the same time. Why couldn't he have warts?

"Where to next, Max?" Jonathan asked. "Back to the monastery?"

"We won't be spending the night at the monastery," Max said.

"Oh?" Jonathan said.

"I took the liberty of sending our luggage ahead to our new accommodations," Max said.

Shelley looked up at him in surprise.

Max bent down and brought his lips a kiss shy of Shelley's ear. "The monks wouldn't approve of what I want to do with you tonight."

Shelley strained her neck admiring the classical murals that adorned the ceiling of the Hotel Imperial's two-story opulent lobby. It did not require much imagination to envision what the hotel had been like in its previous life as a royal palace.

"Are you sure this is our hotel, Max?" Brad asked.

"I certainly hope so," Max said. "I just followed the directions the receptionist gave me when I called to make the reservations this morning at the Holiday Inn. Although I have to say that this place looks so much better in person than in the brochure."

Vienna surprised Shelley again. It had been romantic as she walked through its streets, but now, as she looked over it from the window of the hotel's one-thousand-seven hundred-square-foot Royal Suite, it was no less than ethereal. Illumined domes and elegant spires rose above the rooftops of the old city, challenging her to find the right words to describe their magic. She settled on a sigh.

"And we haven't even seen what's inside the mini bar yet, luv." Max walked across the polished parquet floor to where Shelley was standing. He drew her hair from her shoulders and planted a trail of kisses from behind her ear down the length of her neck.

Pages of faded pink lists and yellowing scrapbooks fluttered in Shelley's mind, their edges rustled by Max's breath against her skin. Then they flapped in a hotter breeze. Shelley rushed to grab them. They slipped from her fingers, torn by the wind. She watched her defenses fly out the window and scatter over the ancient spires. She turned to face Max. An oversize bed dared her from behind him. She slipped her arms around him and pressed her lips to his.

Max pulled away and wrinkled his nose at the collar of his white cotton shirt. "I smell like soup."

"I didn't notice." Shelley pulled him to her for another kiss.

"I really need a bath." He took her hands from around his neck. He kissed her forehead and strode toward the bathroom.

Shelley threw herself facedown on the bed. She mumbled into a pillow, "Don't mind me. My libido and I will be fine right here." Just as well, she thought. She had strayed on this detour far longer than she had intended. This was the universe giving her the chance to jump off the train before it was too late.

"Did you say something, luv?" Max's voice echoed in the marble bathroom.

"Nothing." She pulled up the covers and muffled a groan.

"Shelley . . ."

"Yes?" She swore she would strangle him if he asked her to bring him his toiletry kit. She turned in the direction of the bathroom to see what Max needed. What she saw was what *she* wanted.

Max leaned, nearly naked, against the doorway, a towel draped loosely around his hips. "I was just wondering if you would care to join me."

Shelley took a deep breath. She could always get off at the next station.

Buttons. They were wonderful things, Shelley thought. In the twenty-plus years that she had been pushing them in and out of holes, it was only now that she realized what they were actually for. They heightened anticipation in a way no zipper could hope to match.

She savored how Max's fingers lingered over the tiny pearl buttons that ran down the back of her blue dress. She drew a sharp breath each time his fingertips brushed against her increasingly bare back. The last of her buttons came undone. Only two thin straps kept her clothed. Max kissed them off her shoulders. Her dress pooled at her feet. She stepped out of it.

He took her hand and led her to the tub. Shelley sank into its lavender-scented froth. She sat between Max's legs and leaned against his chest. He circled his arms around her.

She shuddered as pinpoints of electricity shot through where her wet skin touched his. She would live in this tub, she decided, happily subsisting on tap water and Max's nakedness.

"Can we stay here forever?" she asked.

"We'd shrivel into prunes and run up an obscene hotel bill, but yes, technically we could." He drew little circles on her shoulders with his thumbs.

Shelley flipped over, pressing her breasts against Max's chest. She reached down between his legs. "As long as you don't shrivel up over here, I think we could manage."

"I wouldn't worry about that." Max drew her toward him until their faces touched. He teased her lips open.

Shelley moaned.

The phone in the bedroom rang.

"Mmmmm?" she asked.

"Mmmmm." He ignored the phone.

Shelley pulled away and panted, "I think we should get that. It might be important."

"More important than this? I don't think so." He kissed Shelley and held her to him.

The ringing stopped.

"See?" he said. His lips made their way to her breast.

Max's cell phone rang from the bathroom's marble counter.

"Max, I really think you should answer that," Shelley said.

He sighed. He kissed her and stepped out of the tub. "Don't go anywhere, luv."

"I won't." Shelley studied the tension and release of the muscles in Max's legs as he walked to the sink. It was like watching a lion pace. The image terrified and thrilled her.

He picked up his phone. "Hello? Maximus Coitus Interruptus speaking."

Shelley's laugh died on her lips when she saw the expression on Max's face.

"I'll be right there." He put the phone down and grabbed a towel.

"What's the matter? What's going on?" she asked.

"That was Rose. Jonathan's had a heart attack."

A paramedic was hunched over Jonathan when Shelley and Max rushed into the room. Max gathered Rose to him. She clung to him, trembling like a tiny bird as they watched her husband's chest rise. And fall.

The stark white lights of the emergency room washed out Rose's face. Only her fingers had any color left. They were red from being wrung.

Brad took Rose's hands and warmed them in his palms. "He'll be fine, Rose."

Rose nodded. She kept her eyes on her lap.

Coffee splashed on the floor across from her, spilling from Dex's cup.

"Shit. Sorry." Dex stopped pacing to mop up the spill with a napkin. Shelley noticed that his hands were shaking. "You okay?"

Dex was as pale as the waiting area's white walls. He sat down for the first time since they had gotten there. "Yes. I . . . just have this, um, thing about hospitals."

"You really don't have to stay," Rose said. "I'm sure you're all tired. Why don't you go back to the hotel?"

"We're not going anywhere." Shelley put her arm around Rose. She felt brittle. Shelley loosened her grip and scanned the room for Max.

Max was sitting at the other end of the room. He looked back at Shelley without saying a word.

A doctor strode into the waiting area. He walked toward the tour group, keeping his eyes directly ahead of him.

Five steps, Shelley thought. Now four. Four steps left to hope. Rose stood up and split the difference. Shelley stopped herself from pulling her back.

"Mrs. Templeton?" the doctor asked.

"Yes?"

He shook his head. "I'm sorry. We did everything we could."

Shelley waited on the couch outside of the bedroom. She watched Rose clutch Jonathan's sweater to her chest through the half-open door. The image reminded Shelley of all the times Rose had all but disappeared in her husband's large arms—except that now it was Jonathan who was folded and small. Shelley wondered how long his sweater would smell like him. Rose kissed the sweater and placed it in his suitcase.

Shelley leaned on Simon. "I can't believe that Jonathan's gone."

Simon sighed.

Dex slumped on the sofa. "Poor Rose."

"I don't even want to think about what she must be feeling right now," Brad said.

"Me, either," Shelley said. Watching Rose was difficult enough. She seemed to be searching for her husband among his things. In a large white T-shirt. In an unfinished book. In a toothbrush left on the bathroom counter. Rose ran her fingers over every fold, crease, and curve, as though Jonathan might be hiding behind one of them. Shelley shared that hope, allowing it to fade only when Rose stowed away the last of Jonathan's black cotton socks. He was everywhere and nowhere.

Rose rolled the suitcase out of the bedroom. The bag had always looked too small for Jonathan, Shelley thought. But now, as Rose dragged it behind her, it was enormous. It contained more than Jonathan's things. Shelley could not imagine how much Rose's grief weighed.

"I'm ready, Max," Rose said.

Max walked in from the balcony.

Shelley averted her eyes from Max. His reaction to Jonathan's death bothered her. He appeared concerned, even sympathetic, but as hard as she searched his face, she could not find even a hint of sadness in it. He had yet to shed a tear.

Rose had not cried, either, but Shelley trusted that she was still in shock. The most Rose had managed to say since the hospital was a polite "Yes, please," when Max offered to make arrangements to fly her and Jonathan's body back to London that evening.

"We're going with you to the airport," Dex said.

"Thank you, dear," Rose said, "but I think I'd like to be alone."

"Of course." Simon took her hand. "But at least allow us to accompany you downstairs."

Rose smiled and squeezed his hand. She turned to Max. "Max, my sister is asking which airline I'll be taking. She'll be picking me up at the airport."

"I've arranged for a private plane for you."

The group raised a collective brow.

"I borrowed it from a friend," Max said without looking at them. He took Rose's luggage from her and made his way to the door.

"Thank you for your help, Max," Rose said.

Max wrapped his fingers around the doorknob and twisted it. He stopped midway. He turned around. "Why aren't you crying, Rose?"

"I beg your pardon?"

"It's taken you a lifetime to find Jonathan, and yet now that you've lost him . . . you have no tears."

Rose backed away from Max and sat down on the couch. She kept her eyes on Jonathan's suitcase.

Shelley rushed to her side. She glared at Max. "I'm sorry, Rose. I'm sure he didn't mean to be so *insensitive*."

"It's all right, dear." Rose patted her hand.

"No, Rose, it isn't." Shelley turned to Max. "I think you should apologize, Max."

Rose shook her head. "No. I'm glad he asked the question. To be honest, I've been asking it myself."

"It's because you're still in shock, Rose," Shelley said.

"No, I'm not in shock, dear. I know that Jonathan's gone. I do miss him. I can't even say his name without dying a little. But, to be honest, I haven't cried because . . ." She took a deep breath. "I've had no reason to."

"But you just said . . ."

"I have every reason to be sad, but I don't have any reason to mourn. People grieve when things end. Nothing has ended tonight. One of us has simply gone ahead as we always knew it would have to be. But there is no place Jonathan can go . . ."

"Where you can't follow," Shelley said.

"Yes." Rose smiled. "In time."

Shelley hugged Rose as tightly as she could without breaking her. She glanced over Rose's shoulder. Max was looking at her, his face straining with an emotion that Shelley had not seen before. It was strange, she thought, that when everyone else had found some comfort in Rose's peace, Max appeared as though he was about to cry.

Shelley gave up trying to sleep. CNN was delivering a muted weather report: There was a storm over China. She sat up in bed and switched off the television. The evening's events pressed closer in the darkness. She rubbed her eyes, trying to erase the image of Rose rummaging for scraps of her husband among his things. She could not. They were seared into her memory, blending into old scars left by a childhood spent watching a different woman go through exactly the same motions. She fumbled for the lamp.

The door of her room creaked open and Max walked in. "I'm sorry. Did I wake you?"

"I was up. How was Rose?"

"Calm."

"I can't begin to imagine what she must be going through," Shelley lied.

"Good." Max crawled in beside her and laid his head on her stomach. The lamplight deepened the shadows beneath his swollen eyes.

"Are you okay, Max? Have you been crying?"

"No, luv. I'm just . . . tired."

She wiped away the tear that was running down his cheek. "Rest."

Max turned away from her, his voice less than a whisper. "I wish I could."

The disco ball looked less sparkly that morning with two less passengers reflected in its mirrored tiles. The tour group drove away from Austria in silence, sipping the bottles of water they were having for breakfast. No one had been particularly hungry when they rose that morning.

Brad wiped away a tear with the back of his hand. Simon offered him a tissue.

"Thanks." Brad dabbed at the corner of his eye and blew his nose. He leaned on Simon's shoulder.

Dex looked out the window. "So much for short love stories and happy endings." He sighed, fogging up the glass. "I wonder how Rose is doing."

"Yeah, me, too," Simon said. "This trip's not going to be the same without her and Jonathan."

Max slowed the Volkswagen and parked at the side of the road.

"Why are we stopping?" Shelley asked.

"I feel I need to say something before we drown ourselves in mineral water and general misery," Max said.

Dex frowned. "Excuse me?"

"I know we've woken up to a less than cheery morning," Max said, "but I do have some good news for you."

"Good news?" Shelley asked.

"Yes. The good news is that we woke up," Max said. "Today is a new day, and I, for one, have decided to live it. I strongly urge you to do the same."

"It's not that easy, Max," Simon said. "Are you suggesting that we simply forget about what happened last night?"

"Actually, I am suggesting the complete opposite. I am asking that we honor it."

"How?" Brad asked.

"Jonathan had one wish, and that wish was to spend the rest of his life with Rose," Max said. "Would it be fair to say that he got his wish?"

"Well . . . uh . . . yes, I suppose so," Dex said.

"We should celebrate that," Max said. "Not many people can say that they spent the rest of their days with the love of their life."

"But they'd just gotten married . . ." Shelley said.

"And they were happy in that short time that they were," Max said. "If last night proved anything, it's that life is a strong drink served up in an extremely short—and fragile—shot glass. Jonathan didn't waste a single drop. Neither should we."

Brad took a deep breath. "Guys, I think Max is right. I say we try our best to enjoy the rest of this trip."

Dex nodded. "Jonathan and Rose would want it that way."

Simon raised his water bottle. "To Jonathan and Rose . . ."

"And the life they lived so well." Shelley took a long sip and felt the water wash away the tears in her throat.

Max drained his bottle and turned the key in the ignition. He flicked on the stereo. The upbeat chorus of "Stayin' Alive" filled the van. The disco ball spun, showering it with stars.

Chapter Thirteen

Ghosts and getaways

❧ *Now*

A h, the Bee Gees to the rescue," Paolo said.

"Yes, you might even say that they saved the trip," Shelley said. "Jonathan and Rose had left the back row very empty, but Max somehow managed to keep our spirits up with dangerously large doses of the Bee Gees' greatest hits."

"Scary." Paolo chuckled. "But I can relate. I grew up with a mixed tape of seventies music blaring in our car."

"That sounds like Max, all right," she said.

"Well, he is—quite literally—one of a kind," Paolo said.

The realization came without warning, much like discovering a bee trapped in your car. A black and yellow blur zipped past in her peripheral vision. Shelley gasped.

"What's the matter?" he asked.

"One . . . one of a kind," she said. The bee buzzed in her ear, waving its stinger at her. "I think that might not be the case exactly."

"What do you mean?"

Shelley shook her head, trying in vain to evade it. Shoo. Shoo. "After Austria we headed to Slovenia. Max took us to a river."

"So?"

"It was a river where a man had once lived." The bee settled on her shoulder. Damn.

"What man?"

"A man . . . ," Shelley said, "like Max."

The bee jabbed its stinger into her neck. It injected its toxin and pried itself off, leaving its bottom half embedded in her jugular. It fell dead on her lap.

Shelley felt the thick poison crawl under her skin. She hummed "Chiquitita" to keep calm. Wait. That was ABBA. The chorus of "How Deep Is Your Love" popped into her head. She sang silently, trying to soothe herself with old comfort.

LJUBLJANA, SLOVENIA

Five Years Ago

The late-afternoon sun glowed on Shelley's eyelids. It roused her from a dreamless sleep.

"Rise and shine, luv." Max fastened back the window drapes.

Shelley squinted through the glare, disoriented. The black-and-white neoclassical details of the bedroom came into focus. She remembered where she was: a riverside penthouse apartment in the capital of Slovenia. She yawned. She knew from the sandy dryness of her mouth that she had been asleep far longer than the ten-minute nap she had told Max to wake her from. "What time is it?"

"Not ten minutes later." Max sat down beside her on the bed. "The boys have gone exploring in the Old Town. We're supposed to meet by the river for dinner. Are you feeling up to it?"

Shelley cleared her throat and rubbed her eyes. "You shouldn't have let me oversleep."

"But you were snoring so blissfully, I didn't have the heart to wake you—despite having gone deaf in both ears."

She threw a pillow at him. "I do not snore."

Max laughed and gathered Shelley to him. He smiled and kissed her softly. "I thought you needed a bit more rest after . . . everything that's happened," he said. "How are you feeling?"

"Better." She snuggled closer. The events of Vienna were not far behind, but the pain in her heart was duller now, soothed by sleep and Max's embrace.

"Good," he said. "I'd hate to think my eardrums died in vain." He flipped Shelley over on the bed and tickled her until her high-pitched squeals threatened to make him deaf in earnest.

Shelley and Max strolled along the small river that circumscribed the Old Town district of the city of Ljubljana. What the city did not have in grandeur, Shelley thought, it made up for in crooked willow-shaded streets, charming rows of red-tiled roofs, and the vibrant banter of the university students spilling out from the streetside cafés. A mop of fiery red hair flashed in the corner of her eye.

"Over here!" Dex waved at Shelley. He was seated with Simon and Brad at one of the restaurant tables set on the cobblestone embankment.

Her chest tightened when she saw the empty seats where a birdlike woman and bear-size man would have normally sat. She waved back, trying to ignore the hollow ache.

Max sat down next to Brad. "So what adventures have the three of you had today?"

Brad grinned at Shelley. "I think I should be asking you that."

"I slept the day away, I'm afraid," she said.

"And I thought that you and I were up to the same thing," Brad said.

"Which would be what, exactly?" Shelley asked.

"Oh, you know, mounting something tall, strong, and massive." Brad winked at Simon.

"Er . . ." She blushed.

"Which in English means that we climbed that castle over there." Simon pointed over Shelley's shoulder to where the medieval Ljubljana Castle stood on a hill in the center of the Old Town.

Shelley laughed. "Well, I certainly have to agree that it is by far the only thing that qualifies as massive in this city."

"Isn't this place great, though?" Dex said. "A regular Lilliput. Everything's so tiny. Even the river's small."

She glanced at the green river flowing past them. It was hardly more than a stream and matched the color of the willow leaves hanging over it.

"Don't let its size fool you," Max said. "It's a small river that's overflowing with stories."

"Including a tale about one of Isabelle's Slovenian cousins, perhaps?" Simon asked.

"You know me so well." Max signaled the waiter. "But that is on tomorrow's menu. Tonight I think we should try some toasted goat cheese, whitefish with cream sauce, and a bottle or two of Renski Rizling."

"Sounds good," Shelley said.

"And perhaps a tiny slice of a popular Slovenian folktale," Max said. "Has anyone heard of the River Man, by any chance?"

A FLIGHT TO THE PHILIPPINES

Now

Hey, Nonno told me that story," Paolo said.

Shelley gave him an incredulous look. "Max told you about the River Man?"

"Yes. I grew up thinking of him as what you Americans call the boogeyman. He lures humans into the river to live with him in his underwater kingdom, right? The story my grandfather told me was the one about a young boy the River Man had taken. He offered the boy all kinds of wonderful toys and riches to convince him to stay with him, but in the end the boy chose to return to his family. The River Man took pity on him and let him go."

"Well, that definitely sounds like the Mother Goose version of the story I heard," she said.

"I take it that the moral of the story he told you wasn't that kids shouldn't talk to strangers?" Paolo asked.

"No, not quite."

LJUBLJANA, SLOVENIA

Five Years Ago

They called him Gestrin." Max took a sip of his wine. "The people in the villages believed that he was a water spirit who sometimes took the shape of a handsome young man. He had a nasty habit of dragging hapless humans into the river and drowning them."

"Gee, sounds like a fun guy," Dex said.

"One of the most well-known River Man folktales is about how Gestrin lured a beautiful girl named Urška from the middle of festivities in the old Ljubljana town square and leapt into this very river with her. She was never seen again."

Brad edged his chair away from the river. "Perhaps we should finish our meal inside the restaurant?"

"The River Man is long gone, I assure you," Max said. "And we have another one of Isabelle's ancestors to thank for that. His name was Pavel."

"But I thought you said the River Man was just a myth?" Shelley asked.

"All myths spring from truth, luv," Max said, "and tomorrow you will see the place from where they both flow. By the way, do you know how to scuba dive?"

The group walked back to their apartment under a canopy of twinkling fairy lights strung from the cafés along the river.

"So are we really going scuba diving tomorrow?" Shelley asked.

"Weather permitting, yes," Max said.

"And you're not the slightest bit bothered by the fact that my closest underwater experience has been to grasp for the soap at the bottom of my bathtub?"

"Not at all. Did I mention that I happen to be a certified diving instructor? As a matter of fact, we can practice by grabbing other things in the tub tonight." Max gave Shelley's backside a squeeze. He glanced in the direction of their apartment building and stopped midstep. His smile disappeared from his face. "Wait here."

"What's the matter?" Simon asked.

"Stay together." Max strode toward the apartment's arched doorway.

Shelley watched him walk away. The scene reminded her of one of those slow-motion hunting sequences in a Discovery Channel documentary. She couldn't tell, however, if Max was the hunter or the prey.

A tall figure stepped out of the shadows. Max staggered back from the man.

Shelley strained to see the stranger's face in the darkness.

The man took a step toward Max and into the light of the streetlamp. His silver-white dreadlocks gleamed. He looked no different, she thought, from the T-shirt-and-jean-clad college students who congregated in the cafés. Except for his face. It was a boy's face, pale and soft—with dark eyes harder than stone.

Max spoke.

Shelley thought she heard him call the stranger a name she had heard earlier that evening: Gestrin. She decided she was mistaken.

Max stood between the blond man and the rest of the group. The stranger was speaking in a language Shelley did not understand. Max's back was toward her, and all she could see of his reaction was the tension at the base of his neck.

"Do you think we should go over there?" Shelley whispered to Brad.

Before Brad could answer, the blond stranger glanced over Max's shoulder and caught sight of Shelley staring at him. She looked to Max for safety but did not see any reassurance in his eyes. The stranger shifted his gaze to Max. And then back to her. The slowest smile crept across his face. He brushed past Max. Max grabbed at his arm, but he was too late. The man strode past him and now stood in front of Shelley.

"Good evening." The stranger's voice carried a damp chill, like a fog settling over the marshes. "I'm Mihael." He extended a slender hand to Shelley, his shoulders hunched forward, ready to hug her—or pounce.

Shelley saw Max's jaw harden as she clasped the man's hand. "Hi. I . . . I'm Shelley."

Mihael pressed her hand to his lips. They felt cool against her skin. "It's a pleasure to meet you, Shelley."

Max clenched his fists at his sides.

Mihael held on to her hand. "You are a friend of Max's, yes?"

Shelley felt as if she had just let the big bad wolf in for tea. *Is your grandmother home?* the silver wolf asked. *Can anyone hear you scream from here?*

"Yessiree!" Brad came to Shelley's rescue with his best used-car-salesman impression. "We're all friends here, right? I'm Brad, by the way." He grabbed Mihael's hand and shook it as though he had just closed a sweet deal on a rusty pink Cadillac.

"And I'm Simon." Simon pumped Mihael's hand.

Mihael kept his eyes on Shelley.

Dex yawned a decibel higher than normal. "You know, it's been a long day and we were just heading back to our apartment."

"Yes, we really should be going." Brad took Shelley's arm. "It was nice meeting you."

"I am from the National Museum of Slovenia," Mihael said. "I needed to go over some last-minute details for your dive at the archaeological site tomorrow with . . . er . . . Max."

"Why? Is there a problem?" Simon asked.

"No, no problem at all. Max and I are *old* friends," Mihael said. "We lost touch after we had a—how do you say it in English? Ah, yes—a misunderstanding. But all is well now, right, Max?"

Max clenched his teeth.

"Well, I won't keep you. I believe you have an early day tomorrow." Mihael turned to Shelley. His lips curled, exposing yellowed teeth. "It was nice meeting you, Shelley."

· · ·

Ghosts. Sometimes the scariest ones were not the ones that went bump in the night, Shelley thought. Sometimes they looked like the blond girl you sat behind in history class during your pimply phase, and hopped on the treadmill next to yours years later. They were the people who left invisible bruises on you—faces you tried your best to forget and believed you had—until they showed up at your gym as perfect as they were when you were fifteen, and still as capable of making you feel like the last person picked for the volleyball team with a flip of their highlights.

But it wasn't the ghosts themselves that were scary. It was how they haunted you with old secrets. It didn't matter that you now had clear skin, had grown four inches, and wore padded bras. They would always remember how you spilled your lunch over yourself when you tripped in front of them in the cafeteria. Shelley had seen her fair share of ghosts. That's how she knew Max had just seen one himself.

Max had not uttered a word since they returned to the apartment. Mihael had stirred old feelings in him. Shelley did not know what those feelings were, but she was certain that they ran far deeper than any teenage angst about bad skin. She lay beside him in the dark, thinking how much farther away he felt than an arm's length of cotton sheets.

"Who was that man, Max?"

His breathing was shallow.

"You seemed . . . scared."

Max rolled to his side, away from Shelley. "I was."

"Why?" She remembered the coldness in Mihael's face. "Is he dangerous?"

"All men are dangerous, Shelley."

"Not you." She touched his arm.

Max stiffened.

Shelley pulled her hand back. "Do . . . you need to be alone?"

"Yes."

She stroked her cheek. It stung from the three-letter slap. The *s* left a scratch. She pushed herself off the bed.

"But I don't want to be," he said.

Shelley turned around. "Then let me help you."

"You can't."

"I'm . . . here." She fumbled for the words. At that moment, they felt so true, but she couldn't help but worry that they sounded hollow. How long would she be able to stay by his side?

"You shouldn't be." He closed his eyes and covered his face with his hands.

Shelley stood up to leave. Why did she do this to herself? Why did she make lists and not follow them? *Meet. Date. Run.* Granted, she couldn't get far without getting lost in Slovenia . . .

She heard Max sob. Damn. His tears trumped her ego. However deep his old wounds ran and whether he liked it or not, she would have to do. She steeled herself with a breath and sat on the bed. She drew Max's hands away from his face. "Believe me, Max, I'm quite the expert at doing things I shouldn't." She brushed her lips against each of Max's eyelids. "Like this." Her lips fluttered over his mouth. "And this."

Max looked up at her. "You mustn't."

"Too late." She cupped his face in her hands. He looked at her differently than when they were in Austria. She knew he had wanted her then. She had felt his hands on her. She had felt his lips on her breasts. But now his eyes held a deeper longing. Or was it an older one? It was hard to tell beneath the sheen of tears. Part of her wished they only hid lust. It was simpler. Safer.

"Shelley . . ."

"Max, tell me what you want," she whispered.

"Too much."

"Why?"

"Because I want . . ." His pain caught in his throat. "I want you to stay."

Shelley might have broken Max's egg timer, but now she was jostling inside it. Giant grains tossed her around, closer to a whirlpool of choice. Stay. Run. Stay. Run. She was falling through the funnel, tumbling against old walls: her father's death, her mother's grief, her life before this moment. But as she reached the timer's narrowest point, she realized that she knew exactly where she was. She was nowhere else but now. Looking into its eyes. Breathing it in. Kissing its lips.

Max kissed her back. He wrapped his arms around her and pulled her on top of him, tearing away at the clothes that kept them apart. Shelley felt his hands tremble against her naked back. She sat up and guided them to her hips. His fingers dug into her skin, pressing her against him. She clung to him with her thighs, urging him deeper, away from the grasp of shouldn'ts, mustn'ts, and thoughts.

They drifted away.

Then fled. Faster and farther from apron strings and scrapbooks, sickly cats and empty tombs, haunted barns and basilisks, dead friends and ghosts with silver blond hair.

Sister Margaret shut her eyes tight and held her hands over her ears.

Shelley woke up alone on a very rumpled bed. She didn't have to wonder for long where Max was. The smells drifting from the kitchen revealed his whereabouts. She threw on Max's shirt and sprang out of bed before thoughts about things other than breakfast could snuggle next to her. She didn't want to have time to think. Or regret.

She found Max standing in front of the stove, folding over a wild mushroom omelet. She wrapped her arms around his bare chest, clinging to everything that had made the night before a good idea. "Good morning."

"Good morning, luv." Max set his wooden spoon down and lifted Shelley off her feet. He kissed her on the mouth.

The identity of the blond stranger remained a mystery to her, but it didn't matter as much as seeing Max acting like himself again. He was entitled to his ghosts. After all, she had her own. She had woken up disappointed that they were still there, hovering close. Waiting. Whispering. Waving goddamn lists. She shooed them away. "Looks like someone's feeling better this morning."

"It's a choice, Shelley," Max said. "As is everything."

Brad and Simon walked into the kitchen. Dex trailed after them. He eyed Max's pajama top on Shelley.

"Hey, break it up, you two. Feed us. We're starving," Simon said.

Max set Shelley on her feet.

"Well, good morning to you, too," Shelley said.

"So, Max, are you going to tell us about your gorgeous but creepy-in-an-I-could-be-an-ax-murderer-sort-of-way friend or what?" Brad picked up a piece of toast.

"No, not really," Max said. "Coffee?"

"Okaaaaay . . . I'm glad we cleared that up," Brad said. "Boys and girls, watch and learn as I masterfully attempt to change the topic without the slightest hint of awkwardness. Observe. This is a gorgeous apartment, Max. Is it yours? Wait. Don't tell me. Another of your gazillionaire friends owns it, right? You must introduce us sometime. I'd love to know who their decorator is. I love the neoclassical aesthetic. Oh and yes, I'd love some coffee. Black with some Sweet'N Low if you have it, please."

A small cluster of white tents was pitched on the muddy riverbank. Max parked the Volkswagen at the edge of the camp. The group walked toward the tents through the damp marshes. Water seeped into Shelley's sneakers, wetting her socks.

Brad stopped to train his camera at the river. It flowed free and dark, unlike the tame stream it dwindled to in the city.

Dex took Brad's cue. He fished out his camera. "Shelley . . ."

"I know, I know," Shelley said. "Say cheese." She had given up trying to escape from the clutches of Dex's Lumix.

Dex snapped away.

A middle-aged woman with Slavic features emerged from one of the tents. She was dressed in a black wet suit that hugged her toned body. Her wet silver-gray hair was pulled back in a tight ponytail.

"Good morning." Fine laugh lines formed around the woman's eyes and warmed her sharp face. She almost looked beautiful.

"Good morning. I'm looking for Professor Gorshe. I'm Max Gallus."

"Ah, yes, he told me you were coming," the woman said. "Unfortunately, the professor won't be able to join us today. He had to attend to some important business at the museum. I'm his colleague, Marija. I will be assisting you."

"Thank you for accommodating us, Marija. We'll try not to cause too much damage." Max grinned. "This is Shelley, Brad, Simon, and Dex."

"It's good to see young people taking such a keen interest in Slovenian history." Marija shook each of their hands. "If you'll come with me, we'll get you suited up."

Max zipped Shelley into her black wet suit and handed her a full-faced diver's mask. "This will allow you to breathe as you normally would."

"You mean unlike the way I'm hyperventilating now?"

"Don't worry, luv. We'll be diving in a very shallow part of the river, no more than a few feet, really."

"Yeah, come on, Shelley. It will be fun." Brad put his arm around her.

"Easy for you to say," she said. "You guys know how to dive."

"You'll be fine." Dex smiled. "Marija said that we won't be in the water long. Her team has already surveyed and marked off the dive site."

"And I'll be holding your hand the whole time," Max said. "Just follow my lead."

"And where exactly are you leading us, Max? You haven't even told me what I'm risking my lungs and life for," Shelley said.

Max held the tent flap open for the group. "It will be worth the suspense, I promise."

"For your sake, it had better be as spectacular as the *Titanic*," Shelley said.

Marija was waiting for them at the river's edge. Two divers in blue wet suits were already in the water farther upstream.

"Are they from the museum, too?" Simon asked.

Marija frowned. "No. They are treasure hunters."

"Treasure hunters?" Brad asked.

"They scour the river and sell what they find to the highest bidder. A

horrid business. They are common thieves as far as I am concerned."
Marija put on her regulator and waded into the brown river.

"Why? What's in the river, Max?" Shelley asked. "What are they
stealing?"

Max secured Shelley's mask over her face. "Our story."

Shelley felt a knot of dread as the cold murky water rose over her head.
She could not see more than a few feet in front of her. She watched Brad's
fins disappear into the shadows as he swam after Marija. She felt Max
squeeze her hand. She turned to face him. He looked into her eyes and
held her gaze as they swam deeper. She began to relax. There was a strange
comfort in not knowing—and not being able to control—what was going
to happen next. It was freeing to be enveloped by the dark, guided only
by Max's hand. There were no railroad tracks or trains to jump from in
the water.

Time slowed in the river. Only the gurgling of bubbles from Shelley's
regulator hinted that any second had passed at all. If she could get used
to the silt swirling around her, the brown river was not a bad place in
which to spend the rest of the tour. The water was cool, she didn't feel
the extra pounds the trip had padded onto her thighs, and Max was at
her side. An added bonus was that the river was murky enough to hide
her ghosts. Or maybe they just couldn't swim, which was even better.
Dex's fins flapped in front of her, shattering her watery oasis. She ducked,
narrowly avoiding getting her mask knocked off. She drew panicked
breaths and changed her mind. She wanted to get out of the water. Now.

A beam of light cut through the river. Marija waved to the group with
her flashlight. Shelley clung to Max as they gathered around a buoy line.
Dex swam next to her and gave her a friendly nudge. She eked out a wan
smile, debating whether or not she was going to strangle him for almost
drowning her.

Marija swept the depths with her flashlight. The powerful light pierced
through the greenish haze of algae and settled on the bottom. There, behind a veil of silt, was a riddle almost as ancient as the river itself.

Shelley did not understand what she was seeing. Pieces of broken pottery littered the muddy floor, blue-green shards of weathered glass next to them. Was this a shipwreck? A drowned city? A gravesite? Where other rivers might have yielded empty tin cans and the odd leather boot, this one was strewn with the improbable.

Marija swam ahead. The puzzled group followed her. She let her light fall on a spot marked by another buoy. Ancient coins peeked through the silt, giving the group another glimpse of the river's layered past. Then she swam to a small dark object that was still partially buried in the riverbed. Carefully, she brushed back the blanket of loose sediment that covered it, blurring the water as she did. Shelley caught herself holding her breath, wondering what other treasures the river would yield. Mermaid combs and black pearls were close to the top of her wish list.

Another beam of light flashed over the river's floor. Marija turned sharply, pointing her flashlight in its direction. A diver in a blue wet suit raised his arm to shield his eyes. He spun around and darted away. She chased after the treasure hunter. Max signaled to the rest of the group to stay put. Shelley glanced back longingly at the artifact that Marija had been about to uncover. It had fallen back into the darkness.

Marija swam back to the group. Shelley could see her frustration through her mask, but a childlike glee soon replaced it when she returned to her find. She brushed back more silt. When the sandy cloud settled, a blackened cross, larger than a man's hand, jutted through the floor. Marija took its picture with her underwater camera, then cleared away more mud. There, beneath sand and time, was a medieval sword, patiently waiting to be reclaimed.

The group changed back into their clothes while Marija took the sword to another tent to be processed and stabilized.

"That's some river, Max." Dex buttoned up his shirt. "No wonder Marija has a lot of competition."

"The Ljubljanica has yielded more artifacts per square inch than any other river in Europe," Max said. "They've found thousands of items from various points in history. Roman glass. Celtic coins. Germanic jewelry. The oldest object that's been found so far is a Paleolithic flute."

"But why would so many artifacts be in the river?" Simon asked.

"I can give you two theories to choose from. One theory is what Marija and all the other archaeologists here will tell you. The other is the story the River Man told Viktor, the man who rescued Pavel from him."

Marija strode into the tent. "And what would I tell the group, Max? Although personally I'd much rather hear your story about the River Man."

"Ladies first." Max offered Marija a seat at the table where the group had gathered.

"Very well." Marija sat down. "The reason we believe that there is such an extensive trove of artifacts in the Ljubljanica is because of a very fortunate combination of geomorphic and economic factors. The river is what we call a low-energy river, which means that its current is relatively gentle. Another favorable characteristic is its narrow bed made of soft sediment. Both of these features have greatly contributed to the remarkable state of preservation of the river finds, which under other circumstances would have been swept away or eroded. Economically speaking, the river has long been a means for communication and transportation across the Ljubljana moor. Centuries of shipping accidents and battles are a very probable source of some of the artifacts we have found. Remains of settlements and graveyards may have also been washed into the river. Of course, because of the sheer number of certain types of artifacts, we cannot rule out that a fair amount of these items found their way into the river—how shall I put it? Ah, yes," Marija said, "*deliberately*."

Chapter Fourteen

Monsters and men

LJUBLJANICA RIVER

🌿 A.D. 958

Ivan watched his son. Pavel's arms sliced through the water with long, even strokes far better than most six-year-olds. It was the one lesson that he was certain he had taught Pavel well: how not to drown.

Pride pulled Ivan's lips taut across the tanned leather of his face. If he smiled any more broadly, his face would crack. He had grown used to it. Having a son set him in the seam of bliss and breaking. Hearts, he learned, were fragile things outside the chest. He was never more aware of it than when he saw his son running over rocky paths, climbing up trees, or diving into the river. It swam to him now.

Pavel grabbed onto Ivan's arm, wrapped his legs around his father's waist, and hoisted himself up for another dive. Ivan pulled him down from his shoulders and set him in the hook of his arm. He waded back to the riverbank. A chill snaked through the water, swirling around his legs. "That's enough play for today. It's getting late. I have to leave before first light tomorrow."

"Can I come with you, Papa? Please?" Pavel widened his eyes. They were amber like his mother's and just as skilled at making his father melt.

Ivan ruffled his son's wet hair. He wanted to say yes. "I'm afraid the fishing net is still larger than you are."

Pavel pouted.

"Why the face?"

"I'm not a baby anymore."

"And neither are you a man. Fishing is not play, Pavel. You will just be in the way."

Pavel wrestled free from Ivan's arms. He ran back to the village, tears streaming down his face.

It was still dark when Ivan came to say good-bye. He hovered near Pavel's bed. He had spared his son the rod but regretted that he had made him go to bed without supper. He ran his fingers through Pavel's brown hair and watched his eyelids quiver. Pavel pretended to sleep. Ivan pretended not to notice.

The night's harsh words had left a bitter taste in Ivan's mouth. He was a whisper away from taking them back. He brought his lips next to his son's ear, then changed his mind. His apology made a sharp wheeze as he sucked it back through his nose. He exhaled it with a heavy sigh. If only all of life's lessons were as easy as teaching children how to swim. He drew himself up, traced Pavel's cheek with his thumb, and left.

Pavel listened as Ivan walked into the inky dawn. Later, he would try to remember every unspoken word, breath, and footstep. *Good morning. Good-bye. I'll see you soon. I love you. Shuffle, shuffle. Creak, creak.* They were wisps at best, but he made do. He shaped them into a handful of fog, the last memory he would have of his father.

Pavel held his mother's hand. Or was it she who was clinging to his? She had kept him stitched to her side ever since his father had left more than a month ago. She had told him his father was dead. He wondered why she had lied to him. His father was coming back. Perhaps he had just lost his way. Or found a treasure. And needed a bigger boat to carry it in.

Which meant he had to find larger trees. He was hiking through a forest to find some now. Pavel wriggled his fingers. They were starting to feel numb. His mother squeezed them tighter, pulling him closer to her hip. He sighed. His mother was silly sometimes. Pavel crinkled his toes as the muddy riverbank swallowed more of his sandals. How much longer was this going to take?

Chanting hung over the water thicker than mist. The elders had not run out of prayers yet. Pavel fidgeted. More mud licked his heels. He was tired. It was difficult sleeping on his father's side of the mattress. The space was too large to fill, but his mother would have it no other way. It was just as well. He wanted to be awake when his father walked through the door.

Pavel looked at the faces of his neighbors as they chanted. They didn't seem to be getting much sleep, either. Maybe it was because of the women who had not come back from fetching water. He asked his mother about them, but she did not like to talk much lately. She was too busy checking if she had barred their door. And it wasn't just her. The whole village now kept its doors secured. He heard one name whispered behind them. Gestrin. His mother boxed his ears when he said it out loud.

Ema, the smith's daughter, had boasted that she knew all about Gestrin. She had said he was a river spirit and that he was angry because no one had brought him offerings. Pavel had rolled his eyes at her. He didn't like girls much. They were loud and cried a lot when he pulled their hair. Still, he missed her when she went away. His mother told him that Ema was visiting an aunt. Other people told lies about her. Ales, his best friend, listened to them. He said that they had found Ema. He said that she was . . . broken.

Ales tugged at Pavel's sleeve and whispered in his ear. He pointed at the ground beneath his feet. "They said this is where they found her."

Pavel tugged his arm back. "Shut up!"

His mother shushed them both.

The chanting ended. *Finally.* Pavel looked up at his mother. She nodded at him and handed him his toy. It was time. Necklaces, pots, and coins splashed into the river. The carved wooden boat joined them. It bobbed, tangled in a string of his mother's beads. It took on water. Pavel watched his favorite toy sink. It was silly, he thought. He kicked at the mud. He didn't have to do it. He didn't believe their stories. His father wasn't dead. Gestrin did not kill him. He didn't have to make an offering. He just wanted to see if his boat would float. He wasn't hoping that it was enough to buy his father back. Not really.

The clouds stirred as Pavel skipped pebbles across their reflection. "Do you believe in the River Man, Uncle Viktor?"

Viktor patted Pavel's shoulder. He no longer had to crouch down to do it. The boy had grown since his last visit. "That is an old wives' tale, Pavel."

"So . . . the River Man did not take Papa?" Pavel picked up another stone.

Viktor looked into Pavel's eyes. They were as amber as his own. "No."

"I knew it." Pavel beamed. "I told Mama that Papa was coming back."

"No, Pavel. You misunderstand. Your father isn't coming back."

"But you said . . ."

"Your father wasn't killed by the River Man. He had an accident. I'm sorry."

Pavel threw the stone. It skipped three times before sinking into the river. "You're wrong. He will come back. You'll see."

Viktor sighed.

A young woman marched toward them. The hem of her wool dress was wet from the marshes. Her brown hair swung in a braid behind her. "There you are! I've been looking for both of you. It's getting dark. Come away from the river."

"But, Mama, it's still early."

"Listen to your mother," Viktor said.

"Only if you tell me more of your stories when we get back home." Pavel looked up at his uncle hopefully.

"It's a deal." Viktor smiled and tousled Pavel's hair.

Anja and Viktor walked back to the village. Pavel ran ahead of them.

"You have a good boy there, Anja," Viktor said.

"Yes. He's just like his father." Anja dabbed at her eyes with a rough sleeve.

"I am so sorry about Ivan," Viktor said. "I regret I was not able to come sooner."

"Thank you, Cousin," Anja said, "for your company and for your help. I will pay you back, I promise."

"There is no need. That's what family is for. We take care of each other."

"But really, Viktor, it is far too much."

"And there will be more if you need it."

"But . . ."

"Anja," Viktor said, "we are blood. You are my family. I will take care of you and Pavel."

"Thank you." Anja sobbed into his chest. Viktor's help had lifted the weight of a widow's worldly burden off her shoulders. Now only the greater task of healing what was left of her heart remained.

The morning rippled over the river. Pavel squealed with delight as he jumped from Viktor's shoulders and scattered a sunbeam across the water.

"You are a boatman's son." Viktor smiled as the young boy swam back to him.

Pavel laughed. "One more time, Uncle? Please?"

"All right, but this is the last time. My shoulders are about to fall off."

Pavel clambered up his uncle's back. He looked out into the water to the place where his toy boat had sunk. He closed his eyes. It was fleeting, but the river made good on their trade. His father's shoulders were beneath the soles of his feet, ready to launch him into the sky.

Anja cleared the dinner table. She stacked the bowls without looking at her guest. "Viktor, Pavel told me that you went swimming in the river today."

Viktor smiled. "Yes, we did. Ivan taught him well. Your boy is a fish. Why don't you come with us tomorrow and watch him?"

"Cousin, please don't take this the wrong way, but you shouldn't go back to the river," Anja said. "Ever."

"Why? Pavel is a good swimmer, Anja. You have nothing to worry about. He is safe with me."

Anja's lips trembled. "No one is safe from the River Man."

"But there is no such—"

"You are wrong," Anja said. "That vile creature does exist. He took my husband. I will not let him take my son. You must promise me that you will never take Pavel to the river again."

The river blazed with torchlight. Night had fallen and Pavel was still missing. It was easy for a child his size to crouch in the nooks and crannies of the village, and easier still to hide in the tall growth of the marshes—at least this is what the villagers chose to believe as they held up their oiled flames and called out his name.

Anja tore at her cloak. "Pavel! Come home!"

"We'll find him, Anja." Viktor held her to keep her from crumpling to the mud. He knew Pavel would not answer back, no matter how loud or long his mother called for him. He was not hiding from her. He had run from Anja when she had told him that he could no longer swim in the river, but he was not a cruel boy. And neither was he a weak swimmer. Viktor was confident that he had not drowned. But what he was most certain of was that a river spirit had not taken the boy. Evil did not need make-believe monsters to do its work. There were very real men for that. Viktor knew he had to find Pavel. Soon.

Most mornings bring small miracles. They wash away shadows and chase away ghosts. This was not such a morning. The dread that Viktor had gone to bed with was the same one pounding in his chest when he woke up. He grabbed his sword and ran to the river.

Viktor did not call out Pavel's name. He could not bear the silence that would answer back. He trudged along the riverbank until the sun was high in the sky and the muddy scars from the previous night's search on the bank were far behind him. And that's when he saw it, the very thing he had hoped not to find. Peeking through the marshes was a small foot. It was paler than when it had happily leaped off his shoulders. Viktor forced himself to move, to run toward the body when everything else in him told him to flee. He knelt beside Pavel and cradled him in his arms.

A whimper. A tremble. A breath. Viktor looked down at Pavel and gasped. He was alive. But there was no time for relief. The boy's lips and chin were stained black and his breathing was growing faint. Pavel's feet stiffened. Viktor realized what was happening. The boy had not been drowned. He turned Pavel over on his knee and thrust a finger down his throat. Pavel vomited poison and bile.

Anja rushed to Pavel's bed carrying a bowl containing a mixture of egg whites, honey, and herbs that Viktor had instructed her to make. She pressed the bowl to her son's lips.

"Are you certain this will work, Viktor?"

"Yes." He said what she needed to hear. Pavel's recovery depended on the kind of poison that had entered his body, something he had no way of knowing. The bowl in Anja's hands was as much for her as it was for Pavel. It contained a small mercy: honeyed hope.

They waited for the medicine to work. Their eyes flitted around the room like restless moths, avoiding each other's gazes.

Pavel coughed.

Viktor stopped pacing.

Pavel opened his eyes. "Mama?"

"Pavel!" Anja gathered him to her breast.

Viktor collapsed into a chair, his feet swept from under him by a flood of exhaustion and relief. He breathed. His family was whole again. His arm dropped to his side. It brushed against the hilt of his sword. The metal turned his blood cold. He gripped the weapon, readying it for the task ahead—to carve out the heart of the monster that had dared to slash his.

"The River Man asked me to stay."

These words were all Viktor could coax from Pavel in the three days that had passed since he found him.

"Let it go, Cousin," Anja would say. "Pavel is safe now. Let him forget."

But it was Viktor who could not forget. Pavel had almost died and a murderer was free under the pardon of superstition. Viktor was convinced he would kill again. He sharpened his sword.

The shape of Pavel's body was still carved into the marshes when Viktor returned to the site where his search had ended. But today was not a search. It was a hunt. He combed through every reed for his prey's trail. By midday, he accepted that there was none to be found, which meant only one thing. Pavel had come here on his own. He had escaped.

Viktor's gaze fell to the stain of vomit on the bank. He remembered that when Pavel had first purged the poison, it was inky black. *Fresh.* Not much time had passed since the time it was forced upon Pavel and the time he had found him. The boy could not have been adrift in the water long. Viktor hoped that if he walked farther upstream, he would find the place where Pavel had jumped to safety. From there, he could find the trail to the place he had fled. He walked on.

Viktor knew when he stepped on it that what was beneath his feet did not belong to the river. It was solid but not firm enough to be a rock. He held his breath and looked down. There, pressed into the mud, was a small sandal. Beside it were the caked footprints of the man he was going to kill.

Gnarled branches grew over the shack and gathered it into the darkest part of the evening's shadow. Thorny vines snaked through its decaying planks, tearing them apart while holding them together. Viktor would not have seen the hovel if not for the yellow-orange slivers flickering through the gaps in its weathered walls. He crept toward it.

A carpet of damp leaves muffled Viktor's footsteps. He drew his sword and shoved his foot against the shack's door. The heel of his boot crashed through the rotting planks. Wood clattered to the floor.

"Good evening," said a thin voice.

Viktor turned in its direction.

A man was seated on a low bench in front of the fireplace, his back toward Viktor. A silver-white braid fell down to his waist.

Viktor hastened toward him and pressed the blade of his sword into his neck. "Stand up."

"Come, sit with me awhile, Viktor," the man said. "Or are you in such a hurry to kill me?"

Viktor gripped his sword tighter. "How . . . how did you know my name?"

"Young Pavel told me," the man said, "before I let him go."

"What did you say?" Viktor nicked the man's pale skin with his sword. Blood trickled down his slender neck.

"I said . . ." The man stood up and turned to Viktor. The shadows from the fire swirled over his face, unable to find a wrinkle to settle in. "I let Pavel go."

Viktor bit down his shock. It sliced his teeth. What he saw magnified the horror of the crimes. The monster was much younger than he expected, a boy no older than seventeen. "You're just a . . . boy."

"It was the villagers who gave me the name River Man." The young man smiled. "But, please, feel free to call me Gestrin."

"I prefer to call you what you really are, *beast*." Viktor raised his sword to Gestrin's chin. "In a moment you will have no use for any of your names. You and your myth die tonight."

"I hate to disappoint you, Viktor, but myths cannot die," Gestrin said, "and neither can I."

Viktor laughed drily. "A murderer and a madman."

"Ah, but that's where you are wrong. I am not mad. I know very well that I am not the evil spirit that villagers believe me to be. I am no myth. I am so much more than that."

"Is that so?" Viktor sneered. "And just who do you think you are, then?"

Gestrin edged closer until the tip of Viktor's sword drew blood from the cleft in his chin. "Your god."

A mixture of revulsion and pity rose in Viktor's throat. He spat it out.

"What's the matter, Viktor? Have you lost the stomach to run your sword through my flesh?"

Viktor held his sword steady. "I am just waiting for you to stop gibbering. Slicing your throat before then would be . . ."

"Impolite?"

"No," Viktor hissed, "messy."

"How considerate," Gestrin said. "I feel the need to return the courtesy."

"Shall you be offering me some supper then before I kill you?"

"No, but I will tell you what happens after you do."

"You mean other than me wiping your blood off my sword?"

"Yes," Gestrin said. "I will tell you how you will walk away from this grove, satisfied with your revenge."

"Not revenge," Viktor said menacingly through gritted teeth. "Justice."

"The kill is yours to reason out as you choose."

"The way you justify your murders?"

"We are talking about my death, not theirs."

"Yes," Viktor said. "Let's talk about your death."

"If you were a lesser, nameless man," Gestrin said, "I would let you go home to your village, bursting with pride that you had slain your monster. I would let you live your life with your family, wishing only that you grow in happiness and contentment in the years that pass."

"Who knew that you were so generous?" Viktor said.

"Indeed." Gestrin smiled. "And then when your heart brims with joy, I will find you. I will watch you as you kiss your wife, wrestle with your sons, and cradle your baby daughter in your arms. I will look into your eyes and see which one of them makes you smile the most—so that I will know which one to take while you are sleeping."

"Enough games." Viktor grabbed Gestrin's shoulder and shoved him to the floor. "Kneel."

"I respect your courage, Viktor. You are different from the others. You do not fear me. You do not fear . . . death." Gestrin rubbed his chin. "Perhaps you do deserve to know the truth."

"What truth?"

"About what really happens when you walk out that door with my blood still dripping from your hands," Gestrin said.

"More foolishness . . ." Viktor raised his sword, preparing to strike.

"There will be darkness and then the Silence," Gestrin said. "I do not know for how long the Silence will last, but when it is over, when the fire crackles in my ears, I will open my eyes, stand up, and walk out the door. I will find you, Viktor, but I will not kill you. Courage like yours is a shame to waste. You would make a worthy companion. I will seek you out only so that you will know what I am telling you is not a lie. I am a god and you will see me rise."

"Stop." Viktor did not want to listen anymore. "Let us end this madness."

"Very well." Gestrin knelt in front of Viktor. He tilted his chin up and looked directly into Viktor's eyes.

Viktor tore his gaze away. But he was too late. Gestrin had seen what he was trying to hide.

"Wait . . ." Gestrin gasped. "You *do* believe me. I see it in your eyes. Why? Tell me!"

"What I believe is that you are mad and that you are a murderer." Viktor tightened his grip on his sword. "I cannot let you live."

"But I did not kill them!" Gestrin said. "I simply asked them to stay."

Viktor remembered Pavel's words. He brushed them away.

Gestrin rose to his feet. "Tell me, Viktor, is that too much to ask? Even gods grow tired of being alone. They should have been honored just to stand in my presence. I gave them a choice, the same choice I gave Pavel."

Viktor's sword weighed heavier in his hand. "What choice?"

"To die." Gestrin took a step forward. "Or to live as a god by my side. Forever."

Viktor backed away.

"I can make gods of the tiniest of men," Gestrin said, "just as I became the god that I am now."

"You are not a god." Viktor flicked his sword and cut Gestrin's arm. "You bleed, just like any man."

"Wounds are fleeting." Gestrin ran his finger over the flesh wound. "I am not. I was born before a grove grew here, at a time when the river was mightier. I had a family here. A wife. A child growing in her belly. One night a man my wife had spurned carved my son out of her womb. He bound me and forced me to watch, knocking me out in the end not as a mercy but to stain me with their death. I cried for justice and instead I was accused of his crime." He smeared the blood from his wound across his lips.

"The river was our judge, receiving the innocent and shunning the guilty. My people bound my hands and feet and cast me into it. I tried to be calm, but I was a boy and I thrashed and cried for mercy, for reason.

But they did not listen. I heard their jeers as I sank. The water rushed into my nose and mouth." Gestrin took another step toward Viktor.

Viktor backed into a rotting wall.

"If my judges were fair, as was our custom, they would have pulled me out of the river once my innocence was proven by the ordeal," Gestrin said. "But they were not. My absolution became my execution. The rope that tethered me to the bank broke and the superstitious fools took it to mean that the river did not wish me to leave. They left me to die.

"But the river was more merciful. It invited me to lay my head on its soft bed. But I could not accept its invitation. I thought of my wife and the shreds of my son. I thought about the man who had killed them both, the man whose crime I was drowning for. I could not die. I would not." Gestrin stared at the blood on his hand. "What happened next is a blur to me now, because it has been many lifetimes since it happened, but I do remember this: There was pain, there was darkness, and then there was nothing at all. I rose from the river a day later, a god. Whatever battle was waged in the river, I won."

Viktor swallowed hard.

"My people feared me and worshipped at my feet—as they should." Gestrin sneered. "I had beaten death and now I was its rightful master. It was mine to give as I pleased. I gave it freely to those who laughed at my trial and slowly to the man who had killed my family." He smiled. The blood on his lips shimmered in the firelight. "Was I not a generous and patient god?"

Viktor's sword trembled in his hand.

"Time passed. A grove grew. The river dwindled," Gestrin said. "But I remained. Everything changed except for me. I did not know this new world and its new god. I did not want to be a part of it. I stayed away. I was alone. Always alone."

"You sought . . ." Viktor tried to form the word without gagging. "A companion."

"Someone worthy to stand by my side and speak my name."

"But you tried to drown them . . ."

Gestrin shook his head. "No. No. I tried to give them life! But . . .

they were all afraid. They were all weak. They flailed about, too terrified of the water to fight for their right to live. They surrendered to death. The river judged them undeserving of my gift."

"And so you gave them poison."

"I thought that it would be less frightening than the river. I thought that if they were not afraid, if their minds were clear, perhaps like me they would triumph over death."

"But it did not work." Viktor clenched his teeth.

"Many died on the floor, writhing in terrible pain, unable to think, much less fight for their life," Gestrin said. "I had to make the poison less painful and . . . slower. It needed to bind their body but not their mind."

Viktor's hand tightened around his sword. "That was the poison you gave Pavel."

"I did not give it to him, Viktor," Gestrin said. "He stole it from me."

"What?"

"I told you, I let him go. He was like you. He wasn't afraid of me. He did not believe in monsters. He asked me if I took his father. I told him that his father had met the same fate as the others who would not remain by my side." Gestrin sighed. "I told Pavel the same story I have just told you and asked him if he wished to stay. I asked him if he wanted to live forever."

"What . . . was his answer?"

"He said yes."

"Liar!"

"Pavel said he never wanted to leave his mother. He told me how sad she was when his father died. He wanted to be immortal so that she would never have to be alone," Gestrin said sadly. "It was then that I knew I could not keep him. He was too young to truly understand the gift that I could give him. He would have left me, like all the others. So I cut his binds and told him to return to his mother. That's when he stole the poison from me, to keep himself forever at his mother's side. I chased after him, but he swallowed the poison and jumped into the river."

"No . . ."

"I swam after him. I was in the water when you found him. I saw you take the choice from his hands before he had a chance to make it," Gestrin said. "I wonder if he will ever forgive you for that."

"I have heard enough," Viktor said with a heaviness in his voice. "Kneel."

"But . . . I thought you believed . . ." Gestrin implored. "I let him go."

"It does not matter either way. You are still alone. Tomorrow you will try to find someone else to be with you. Nothing has changed. I cannot let you go."

"Then stay." Gestrin held up a small silver flask. It glowed in the fire-light. "It will not hurt."

Viktor closed his eyes. "Neither will this." He felt his blade slide between Gestrin's ribs. "I'm . . . sorry."

Gestrin clutched the sword sticking out of his chest. His fingers bled on its blade. He took a step forward, burying the sword deeper inside him. He reached out and gripped Viktor in a tight embrace. His lips curled and blood gurgled through his yellowed teeth. "I will find you."

Viktor looked down at the grave. The man who believed he was immortal did not move or breathe. His silver hair was caked in blood. Viktor filled the ditch quickly, covering Gestrin's half-smiling lips with loose ground. He didn't have to do it. He threw more soil over the grave. He didn't believe Gestrin. The man was dead. He had killed him. Still, he had bound Gestrin's hands and feet, twice, and he dug a hole deeper than death. Just in case.

A young boy skipped stones across the river. Laughing children ran past him as they chased one another on the bank. The boy smiled up at his uncle.

His uncle smiled back, his sword ready at his side.

Chapter Fifteen

Gifts and gratitude

LJUBLJANICA RIVER
SLOVENIA

Five Years Ago

The tent's tarpaulin door flapped in the wind. The wet smell of the marshes drifted through and hovered over the group like the words of Max's story. Shelley felt their weight in the air. She leaned her elbows on the table.

"How sad," she said. "I don't see why Viktor had to kill Gestrin. He was clearly insane, but couldn't they have just locked him up?"

"I don't think things worked that way back then," Dex said.

Simon nodded. "What Viktor did was the kindest thing that could have been done to the man. Gestrin was a murderer and what the villagers would have done to him would have been a thousand times worse."

"But still . . ." Shelley said.

"You pity him?" Max asked.

"I do," she said. "I don't think he was evil."

"He was a dangerous man, Shelley," Max said.

"I'm with you, Max," Brad said. " 'I'll drown you so that you can live forever.' I mean how twisted is that? Nut job or not, he had to be stopped."

"So you don't think Gestrin was telling the truth?" Shelley asked.

"Why?" Dex asked. "Do you?"

"Wouldn't it be interesting if he had been?" Shelley said.

"Now that's a scary thought," Simon said.

"Why?" she asked.

"Well, for starters, while I do sympathize with his story, it doesn't change the fact that he was a homicidal maniac," Simon said. "Can you imagine how depraved he might be by now if he were still alive and desperately searching for a companion?"

"But what if he found one?" Shelley asked. "Wouldn't that change how the rest of his story would be written?"

"That still wouldn't make him less creepy," Dex said. "What if he decided he wanted to add more members to his little group? It would be like, 'Hey, would you like to join our poker club? You would? Great! We usually play out by the pool. It's really deep. We should go for a swim sometime.'"

Marija smiled and stood up from the table. "That was a very interesting story, Max."

"Thank you for all your assistance, Marija," Max said. "Please give my regards to the professor when you see him."

Shelley and Max made their way to the van. The rest of the group walked ahead of them.

"Shelley, wait." Marija strode up to her. "I almost forgot to give you this."

"What is it?" Shelley asked.

"A gift." Marija handed her a small silver vial.

The muscles in Max's neck tightened. "Where did you get this? Did you find it in the river?"

"No. It's from a colleague of mine. He said he was an old friend of yours. He told me he met Shelley last night." Marija winked at her. "I think he may have a little crush on you."

"Mihael . . ." Shelley examined the vial.

Max grabbed the vial from Shelley and twisted its cap off. He poured it out. A dark liquid seeped into the mud. He handed the vial back to Marija.

Marjia knitted her brow. "What are you doing?"

"Making a donation to the museum," Max said. "If you examine it, I believe you will find that it has some historical value." He took Shelley's hand and led her to the van. He turned around. "Oh, and please tell Mihael that if he insists on giving away such extravagant souvenirs, I shall have to look for him and thank him. Personally."

A FLIGHT TO THE PHILIPPINES

🌹 *Now*

"Whoa. Are you telling me that Gestrin . . . Mihael was immortal, too?" Paolo said. "And that he tried to poison you?"

"Frankly, I don't know what to think anymore." Shelley rubbed at her temples. "I may, however, be able to form a semblance of an opinion by raising my blood alcohol level up a few notches. What do you say? Do you think you inherited enough of Max's charm to find us a few glasses of clarity on the rocks?"

"I guess we'll find out," Paolo said.

He flashed a grin so familiar to Shelley, it made her heart leap and break at the same time.

"Max, I mean, Paolo," Shelley said, "scotch, if you can manage it, okay?"

"Sure."

Shelley watched the man with her husband's smile disappear behind the curtains of the airplane's pantry. She wondered if she would ever see Max's own wide grin again. If she did, it most certainly wouldn't be when she showed up on his doorstep. Max had been less than thrilled when Gestrin had intruded into his "new" life. She imagined that she would be met with the same reception when she stumbled into his latest one.

Shelley remembered the first time she had made love with Max, the hours her body exorcised his demons on the night he had seen Gestrin. Was she now also a ghost to Max? Would he run from her as he had from

Gestrin and into the comfort of another woman's arms—and legs . . . And where the hell was that drink?

Paolo slipped back to his seat, looking a couple of pounds heavier than when he had left.

"Feel free to applaud." He produced two plastic cups and a half dozen miniature bottles of scotch from inside his jacket.

"What, no peanuts?" Shelley feigned disappointment.

"A thousand pardons for the oversight, Your Highness," Paolo said. "Now shut up and drink."

She held out her cup. Paolo emptied the tiny bottle into it.

"Bottoms up," he said.

The contents of her plastic cup disappeared in one gulp. "One more."

Paolo opened another bottle.

Shelley drained her second cup more swiftly than the first. "Another."

"Um, maybe I should scavenge some peanuts for us first." Paolo took her cup from her.

"Honey-roasted." Shelley peered out the window.

"I'll do my best." Paolo scooped up the unopened bottles and tucked them back into his pockets.

"And where do you think you're going with that?" she asked.

"I don't want you to party without me."

"Fine. Hurry back." Shelley pulled her legs up into her seat and curled into a ball.

Paolo returned with two bottles of water and several foil packs of peanuts. Shelley was sleeping. He laid a blanket on top of her. "He was right. You do snore," he whispered.

Shelley's eyes fluttered open.

"Oops, sorry. I didn't mean to wake you."

She stretched her arms over her head. "I don't snore."

"My mistake. It must have been the roar of the engines."

"Ha ha." Shelley straightened herself up. Her head swooned from the alcohol.

Paolo settled into his seat. "So did you ever hear from Mihael, er, Gestrin again?"

"No, actually. He must have gotten Max's message loud and clear. Being buried alive is not something a person—especially an immortal one—would probably want to repeat."

"But do you think he's still out there plotting his revenge?"

"Paolo, please. Let's not go there. I don't think my brain can handle worrying about more than one immortal at a time."

"Shelley, this is serious. You could still be in danger."

"I honestly don't think I could be further from it."

"Why?"

"Because, as Gestrin said himself, he would only try to hurt Max by taking something precious from him. Max already walked away from me. Going after me would be a waste of time," Shelley said. "Besides, who says that he hasn't had a change of heart? Maybe the vial he sent through Marija really was a gift."

"Since when did poison become an appropriate gift?"

"It's twisted, I know. But think about it. Maybe it was some sort of peace offering. Maybe he was trying to create a companion for Max . . ."

"Or maybe he was just trying to kill you."

"Let's just drop it, okay? Gestrin is the least of our worries right now. Do you want to continue or not?"

"Um . . . well . . . I ditched the scotch. Drinking may not be such a good idea after all."

"What I meant was," she said, "shall we continue with the story?"

"Oh, uh, right. I knew that. Peanuts?"

"Thanks." Shelley tore open a pack.

Paolo popped a peanut into his mouth. "So, let's see now . . . we've covered Fatherhood and the French Communards, the Playboy Years and the French Revolution, Death Wishes and Swiss Basilisks, Aging and

Medieval Monasticism, Untimely Death and Celebration, Murder and Immortal Life. I honestly can't imagine how the rest of your trip could possibly top what you've told me so far."

"I thought so myself at the time," Shelley said, "until Max hypnotized a chicken."

Chapter Sixteen

Alex and apocalypses

LJUBLJANA, SLOVENIA

❧ *Five Years Ago*

More pillows were on the floor than on the disheveled bed. Max rolled off Shelley and kissed her neck. *"Petelinji zajtrk."*

Shelley caught her breath. Droplets of dawn, each a tiny snow globe swirling with the first pale rays of the sun, glistened on her breast. She had found it easier not to think about trains and lists if she kept herself busy. Luckily, Max had kept her preoccupied since returning from the river. "Did you just sneeze, or did you say something really naughty in Slovenian?"

"Rooster's breakfast," Max said. "That's what they call it over here."

"Call what?" she asked.

Brad rapped his knuckles on the wall between their bedrooms. "Early-morning-freaking-noisy sex!" he said. "Now will you two be quiet and let a guy catch up on his sleep?"

Dex parked his bag next to Brad's and Simon's in a puddle of morning sunlight in the apartment's living room. "All set, Max."

Max walked down the hallway carrying a large cardboard box. "I hope you boys can squeeze a few more things into your luggage before we leave."

194

Brad yawned. "If by a few you mean that giant box you have there, I'm afraid not. Now, however, if I had more than a couple hours of sleep and was in a better mood, I just might have offered to dump out the contents of Simon's suitcase and find you some space in there."

Shelley strode into the room. "As I recall, there were some very interesting noises coming from your side of the wall, too."

Simon grinned. "Um, so, what's in the box, Max?"

Max set the box down on the floor. "See for yourself."

Shelley peeked inside. It was filled with a half dozen hemp sacks, each about the size of a large bag of potato chips.

"Pick one," Max said.

"Well, if these are more of your gold coins, I think I'll be able to find some room for it." Brad eyed the box. "In fact, I wouldn't mind slinging a few over my back."

Shelley untied a sack and wrinkled her forehead.

"From the look on your face I take it that it doesn't contain the shiny souvenirs I was hoping for?" Brad asked.

"I'm afraid not." She held up a square piece of ocher-colored stone the size of her thumbnail.

Brad chose a sack and opened it. Simon and Dex followed suit. They each pulled out a colored tile.

"Is this the arts-and-crafts leg of the tour, Max?" Dex examined a red square. "Or are we retiling the bathroom?"

"Close enough," Max said. "Hold on to that thought—and your sack—until we get to our next stop."

"Which would be . . . ?" Shelley asked.

Max held the door open for her. "An Alpine forest, luv."

VENICE, ITALY

Five Years Ago

It gleamed in the sun like a polished grand piano, Shelley thought, and was easily the most elegant boat docked in Tronchetto Island's harbor.

Max ran his hand over the grain of its dark mahogany hull. "All aboard, campers."

She climbed onto the vintage motorboat just as the boat next to it roared to life. The sleek white boat pulled out of the dock, sending waves rolling the deck under her feet. A cloud of nausea swelled behind her eyeballs. She wiped a newly formed bead of cold sweat from her brow. She missed the van they had left in the island's parking garage. The frayed green shag on the Volkswagen's floor had seen better days, but at least it had provided more solid footing than the undulating boat.

"Well, this is quite a change from the van," Dex said. "I love boats. This beats anything I've been on, though."

"It feels strange not having a disco ball spinning in my face." Brad settled onto the wooden bench next to Simon.

Max reached under the captain's seat and fished out what could have been the Venetian twin of the van's mirrored ball. "You were saying?"

"Why on earth is there a disco ball on this boat, Max?" Simon asked.

"I think it gives it a certain pizzazz, don't you think?" Max said.

"Hang on." Brad's jaw dropped slightly. "Are you saying that this is your boat, Max?"

Max rubbed his chin. "Let me see . . . No, I don't think that's what I said. But I do know where the owner keeps the spare key." He twisted the disco ball open. He pulled out a small plastic-egg key chain. A silver key twirled in the breeze.

The lagoon's small islands were a blur of green and stone among flailing strands of Shelley's hair. Shelley gathered her hair away from the wind and tamed it into a knot. Dex took her picture. She had gotten used to having her own personal paparazzo and obliged him with a smile. The sea sprayed her face, leaving a sharp mist of salt on her lips. This is what Venice tasted like, she thought.

Max glanced back at her from the boat's wheel. "Did you know that for centuries Venice's sewage has run straight into the canals of the lagoon?"

Shelley gagged. She might have felt better if she had heard what Max said next, but she was too busy tearing through her bag for mouthwash to listen.

"But not to worry, campers. The tides wash the canals out into the Adriatic Sea twice a day."

"That's good to know, Max," Brad said, "though I'd like to point out that the Adriatic is nowhere near the Alps, which makes me wonder if we've gotten lost. You did say that we were headed for an Alpine forest next, right?"

Max slowed the boat to a stop.

Shelley pulled her head out of her bag and looked around. The boat bobbed in the middle of a wide canal.

"Our forest." Max pointed to the Venetian islands.

"Okaaaay . . ." Simon said. "Are we speaking metaphorically here?"

"Not at all," Max said. "I mean that in the most literal sense. I'd offer to give you the guided tour, but unfortunately, we left our diving gear in Slovenia."

"Why would we need diving gear?" Shelley asked.

"Our forest is underwater, as it is the very foundation on which Venice stands. The Roman refugees who built Venice pounded thousands of oak and pine logs into the lagoon to keep their sanctuary from sinking. There are mountains in Slovenia that are still sadly bare today as a result."

"And one of those refugees happened to be Isabelle's ancestor, right?" Shelley said.

Max restarted the boat. "How did you guess?"

The wooden planks creaked beneath her feet. Shelley looked straight ahead at the rocky beach, away from the murky water lapping against the posts of the small island's narrow pier. She held her breath.

Max skipped over two missing planks. He held his hand out to her. "Watch your step, luv."

Shelley took his hand and leaped over the gap. She walked onto the strip of craggy shore. A rowboat's red carcass was mired between two large rocks, crumbling with every rise of the tide. Her last hope for a romantic

Venetian interlude sank to the bottom of the lagoon with a gurgle. "I take it we're skipping a visit to the Rialto, Max?"

"I'm not a big fan of the piazza pigeons," Max said. "Greedy lot."

Brad scanned the tall cypress trees that curtained the shore. "Yeah, creepy deserted islands are tons more fun. Any chance we can stay on the boat?"

"Certainly," Max said. "I'm sure the mosquitoes will love the company."

Brad slapped his arm. He grimaced at the black mess of wings and legs that had been about to make a meal of him. "Lead the way."

"Follow me." Max disappeared through a break in the trees.

Shelley tried to keep her disappointment in check as she pushed through the branches reclaiming the narrow trail. Admiring the broad shoulders of the man happily humming a medley of Bee Gees songs in front of her made it easy.

Max stopped and shoved an overgrown shrub to the side.

Shelley gasped. An illustration from a Beatrix Potter book greeted her at the end of the path. Four rustic ivy-covered buildings were nestled around the edges of a wide, circular courtyard. The structure closest to Shelley was a quaint two-story house, with tall blue-shuttered windows and a small porch. The other two buildings were smaller and more roughly built. Farm implements and supplies were stacked around them, giving her the impression that they were storage sheds. She had a harder time figuring out what the fourth building on the far side of the courtyard was for. She peered up at it.

The tower was at least thirty feet tall and resembled a giant chess piece. Beyond it, Shelley caught a glimpse of rows of squat trees. Olives, perhaps.

A breeze blew through the courtyard, carrying the sea and the fresh pinelike scent of the cypresses. She closed her eyes to find a word to wrap around the balmy feeling expanding in her chest. She exhaled. *Sanctuary*.

Sanctuary, for Shelley, was not the lilac bedroom she had left in

Ohio. It was much smaller than that. (Which was rather fortunate since she was able to fit it into the carry-on bag she took with her to London.) The chipped floral teacup was the first thing she had smuggled out of her mother's house when she moved out. In it she found a pocket of porcelain solitude whenever she needed to get away from her mom's loneliness; it was the same quiet solace the island embraced her with now.

Max took Shelley's hand and led her to the main house. "We'll be staying here tonight."

She looked back at the tower. "Er, why is there a tower on the island, Max?"

"The same reason all towers are built, luv." Max shrugged. "Perspective."

A small dust storm rose as the group navigated their way through the welter of curios, artwork, and artifacts that carpeted the main house's first floor. Shelley tiptoed around a mummified Egyptian cat guarding a large Oriental vase. She imagined that this was what an old china shop might look like—after the proverbial bull had run through it. She stubbed her toe on a wooden sword. "Ow."

"I apologize for the chaos," Max said. "The caretakers only look after my island's farm. I prefer to keep the house locked up when I'm away."

"I'm sorry," Brad said. "I think one of those mutant mosquitoes must have been buzzing in my ear. I thought I just heard you say that this was your island."

"You did," Max said. "It's been in my family for generations."

"Are you serious?" Dex said. "You actually own an island?"

"I wouldn't be too impressed. It's not exactly the poshest address in Venice, but it's a good place to raise chickens," Max said.

Shelley stepped over a clutch of jeweled eggs nesting in a medieval knight's dented helmet. She inspected the grinning green Buddha sitting next to it. If the statue had not been the size of a barrel, she would have believed it was made from real jade. "What is all this, Max?"

"I needed a showcase for my dust-mite collection." Max blew a thick layer of dust from a lopsided stack of vinyl records. Alvin and the Chipmunks smiled back at him.

Brad sneezed. "Perfect. Just what my allergist ordered."

"Gesundheit," Max said. "Upstairs is slightly more habitable. Best get to your rooms and unpack. When you're done, bring your sacks with you and meet me outside. You're about to make history."

Max emerged from one of the sheds just as the group stepped onto the porch of the main house. He carried a bucket in one hand and four trowels in the other. He waved at the group and motioned for them to follow him to the far side of the courtyard.

Shelley could not keep her eyes off the tower and was only mildly aware that she was now standing in its shadow.

Max set the bucket down. A wave of white slush lapped against its metal rim. "If you've ever filled in a coloring book or painted by numbers, you won't have any trouble with our afternoon's amusement. I've already marked off the places you'll each be working on. All you have to do is spread some of this plaster and lay the tiles on it. No need to be perfect. Dex, this is your spot. Simon, you're over here. Brad, you'll be working right next to Simon." Max pointed to Shelley's feet. "And, luv, you're standing on your bit."

A pond of ocher, blue, red, and green tile rippled under Shelley's sneakers. It was the first time she noticed the abstract mosaic sprawled across the courtyard. She drew a sharp breath.

"Ah, I knew it was coming," Brad said. "The catch. Hard labor in exchange for board and lodging."

"And did I mention the baskets of olives you'll be pitting and jarring later?" Max said. "Holler if you need anything. I'll be in the house making dinner."

Shelley scraped the excess plaster from the tiles she had set. She stood up and examined her afternoon's work. What she felt was unexpected and, before this moment, inconceivable. Her jeans were stained with splotches of drying plaster and underneath them her bruised knees were surely an even sadder sight, but there was a warmth in the bottom of her belly, the pleasant heaviness that followed a large fudge brownie and a tall glass of milk. Not a tile was out of place, and in this tiny patch of a world she had created, everything made sense. She may have made her living by hammering out words on her computer, but it was only now that she felt what it was like to create something. It felt good.

Dex laid the last of his tiles and sidled up to Shelley. He handed his camera to Brad. "Would you mind taking our picture? And make sure you get the mosaic in the background, okay?"

Brad framed Shelley and Dex in a shot. "Smile." He switched to his Nikon and snapped his own handiwork. "I hate to admit it, but this was actually fun."

Max appeared from behind Shelley. "I think Brad's mosquito found a new ear to buzz in. I thought I just heard Brad say that getting his hands dirty was fun."

Brad grinned. "Fun? I meant 'run.' That meal you're whipping up had better be worth all this slave labor, Max."

"I'll have to check if you've earned a place at the dining table first. Let's head up in the tower and have a look, shall we?"

The steel spiral staircase shuddered each time Max heaved at the rusty handle of the door at the top of the tower. Shelley pressed herself against the cold stone wall, bracing herself for another tremor. She kept her eyes on Max's jean-clad bottom, averting them from the sheer drop inches from her cringing toes. There were, of course, other reasons Shelley's eyes were glued to that particular spot of Max's anatomy, but vertigo was a perfectly legitimate excuse as well.

Iron groaned through the tower as Max pulled the heavy door open. She followed him outside. A breeze flitted through the doorway, echoing her premature sigh of relief. She sucked her breath back in and stepped back from the parapetless ledge. She bumped into Dex.

"Ouch." Dex peeked over Shelley's shoulder. "Holy . . . Don't they have building safety codes around here, Max?"

"I ran out of bricks. Besides, if there was a wall over here, you couldn't do this." Max strode toward the edge of the platform. He plopped down and dangled his legs over it. He turned to Shelley. "Best seat in the house. Coming, luv?"

"I'll need to check my calendar." Shelley gripped the doorway. "Oops. Sorry, tumbling to a horrible death isn't penciled in for today. Perhaps we can reschedule for, say, fifty years from now and skip the horrible part?"

"Nonsense. It's perfectly safe up here. It's the ground that might cause some problems." Max held out his hand to her. "Trust me."

Shelley sighed. She bit her lower lip and reached for his hand. "If I fall, I'm taking you with me."

"Too late." Max drew her close. "You already have."

Shelley lowered herself next to him. She continued to hold his hand—not because she was afraid of falling, but because she was certain that if she did not, she would float away. She leaned toward him and anchored herself on his lips.

"Careful now, wingless lovebirds." Simon clung to the doorway.

"Yeah, we don't want to spend the rest of our holiday scraping you guys off the ground," Brad said.

"Then join us," Max said. "Let the caretakers worry about the five odd stains they'll find on the courtyard."

"Oh, well." Dex took a deep breath. "What the heck." He walked to the ledge and sat down.

"I'm going to regret this." Simon clenched his teeth over his mint gum and followed Dex. He lowered himself next to him, puffing out peppermint-scented wisps of air.

Brad rolled his eyes and groaned. He left his camera at the doorway. He crouched down and crawled to the edge. Then he sat down and hooked his arm around Simon's. "So . . . what do you do for thrills around here, Max?"

"Well, I don't know about thrills, but she's kept me busy." Max pointed to the courtyard. "Campers, I'd like you to meet Alessandra. You can call her Alex."

Shelley's gaze fell to the courtyard, immediately followed by her lower jaw going slack. The pixel pond of tiles receded and in its place surfaced . . . the largest chicken she had ever seen. The sheen of ocher tiles caught Shelley's eyes, drawing her attention to her first great artistic effort—a single mosaic feather on Alex's plump bottom.

A FLIGHT TO THE PHILIPPINES
Now

Paolo's perfectly shaped nostrils flared from the chuckles escaping through them.

"A brilliant start to my career, I know," Shelley said.

Paolo burst out laughing. A chorus of shushes erupted from behind his seat. He turned purple as he choked on the laughter he was miserably failing to stifle. He caught his breath. "Well, you've come a long way since then," he said. "I've seen your work."

"You have?"

"Yes, when you fainted and collapsed on your foyer floor."

She pushed the memory away. "Er, yes. That was my first project when I moved into Max's place."

"It was an hourglass, wasn't it?"

"Yes."

VENICE, ITALY
Five Years Ago

Simon admired Alex from his perch on the tower. "I read somewhere that mosaics have been called eternal paintings or something like that."

Max nodded. "That's why I thought it would be the most fitting way to tell Venice's real story."

"Real story?" Dex asked.

"Mosaics have been thought to be eternal because of the resilience of the materials used to make them—glass, gold, stone, enamel. Undisturbed, they can weather time indefinitely," Max said. "The same, however, cannot be said for the mosaic's foundation. A mosaic, by necessity, is set in plaster, a less hardy material that one day will crumble."

"That's not exactly something you want to hear after spending hours scraping your knees and encrusting your fingernails in glop," Brad said.

"But that's exactly the point," Max said. "It's the futility of the exercise that makes it quite remarkable, the human struggle to build something permanent on something inherently . . ."

"Impermanent," Shelley said.

And just like that, it happened.

Shelley let it slip out of her, a shade of a thought that had been hovering around the periphery of her mind since the night she and Max had become lovers. It had been waiting for an unguarded moment such as this to take form. And now she could not take it back. She had given it a voice. Her voice. It whispered the truth in her ear: That of all the great monuments people strove to build, love was the leaning tower of LEGO. It had crushed her mother and now it threatened to flatten her. *If she let it.*

"Exactly." Max nodded.

"Oh, okay, I get it. Mushy foundations. Venice is like a mosaic because it's sinking, right?" Brad said. "But what does Alex here have to do with anything?"

"Venice would not exist if not for her and a few of her friends," Max said. "And today you have completed the only monument to the truth behind how Venice came to be. As I told you on the boat, Roman refugees who fled the barbarians invading the mainland founded Venice. As the Roman empire declined, the lagoon became a temporary sanctuary during times of invasion. In 568, however, a few years after the emperor Justinian I died, their relocation became more permanent in nature. Italy, which was then under the eastern Roman empire in Constantinople, no longer had the strength to defend itself from the Lombard horde spilling over the Alps.

"Legend says," Max continued, "that the bishop of the Roman city of Altinum asked God for a sign to guide him as the barbarians drew nearer. After three days of fasting and prayer, the sign he was waiting for came in the form of a vision of birds fleeing with their young. The bishop took it to mean that they needed to leave the city as well. God then told the bishop to climb the city's tower. From there, the good bishop saw the place in the lagoon that was to become their new home—the island of Torcello."

"And how much of that story is true, Max?" Simon asked.

"Well, I suppose you could safely put your money on everything up to 'Legend says,'" Max said. "But the truth will have to wait. Dinner's getting cold."

Shelley braved the maze of clutter in the main house to return to the courtyard later that evening. She had slipped away from Max's arms and left him asleep in their bedroom. Now she was walking barefoot across the moonlit mosaic, feeling the cool, smooth tiles on her soles.

A cloud passed overhead, casting a wide shadow across the courtyard. Without any light to show her the way, Shelley let memory guide her to her destination. She reached the darkest part of the shadow just as the cloud unveiled the crescent moon. The tiled feather was pale in the evening, she thought, a cheerless version of the fierce ocher it had been when it had found its place under the sun. She knelt down and ran her hand over her work until her fingertips grazed a loose tile. It wobbled at her touch.

If someone had asked Shelley at that moment why she was crouching in the dark in the dead of night wearing only Max's pajama top, she was prepared to say that she was getting some air. But since she had the courtyard to herself, she was glad she didn't have to lie. Shelley then thought, to the satisfaction of Sister Margaret, that, technically, saying she was out for some air was not entirely a lie. She would after all be breathing in the course of pursuing her real objective. The fat nun in her head nodded her approval and rolled back to sleep. "Air it is."

"Air what is?" a voice whispered in Shelley's ear.

Shelley shrieked and stumbled back. She looked up in terror at Dex's grinning face. "You just scared the hell out of me, thank you very much!"

Dex chuckled. "What are you doing out here?"

"I . . ." Her practiced lie stuck to the roof of her mouth like a heaping spoonful of peanut butter.

"I needed some air," Dex said. "The dust in that house was killing me."

"Um, yeah, me, too," Shelley said.

"Would you like to go for a walk?" Dex asked.

"Sure. Why not?"

Shelley sat next to Dex at the end of the crumbling dock, swatting away determined mosquitoes. The rhythm of the waves washing over the beach did little to lull the restlessness inside her.

"The tour's zipped by, hasn't it?" he asked. "Do you know where we're going tomorrow?"

Shelley swallowed hard. She knew too well that Max's tour was going to end in a couple of days, and without knowing it, Dex had just put into words the very reason why she had left Max's side. The whispering in her head had not stopped, and now the ominous creaking of a tower made from colorful plastic children's blocks joined it. It was a relentless chorus calling out Shelley's gnawing fear that despite all she was coming to feel for Max, she still had no idea where she was heading tomorrow—or any fraction of time beyond the present. More than ever, she felt the urge to flee.

She tightened her fist around the ocher tile that she had pried from the courtyard. Its sharp corners cut into her hand. She bit down the pain.

Shelley had taken back a piece of herself, a tile that would remind her that once she had stayed on a train longer than she had intended and fallen in love with a man she did not know. But if she was being honest—which she was not at that moment—she would admit she had taken the tile in the selfish hope that one day that man would find himself walking barefoot on a moonlit mosaic and feel that something was missing . . . and then, perhaps, remember her, too.

A FLIGHT TO THE PHILIPPINES

Now

Shelley placed her hand on her chest and felt the small square pendant through her cotton blouse. She'd had its corners smoothed years ago, but now, as she hurtled toward a different island in search of a different man, she felt the tile slice into her heart.

VENICE, ITALY

Five Years Ago

Shelley scratched at the mosquito bites she had accumulated while sitting on the dock with Dex the night before. The red bumps on her legs, she thought, sadly outnumbered the *bricole* posts their boat was passing on the lagoon. Max raised his voice over the boat's motor and explained how the wooden pilings, topped with orange lamps, marked the shallows and kept boats from running into mud. Shelley looked at the clusters of *bricole* and wished that life were as easily charted.

Dex steered past a post. He had pleaded with Max to let him take the wheel when they set off from Max's island.

"These *bricole* are by far the best way ever devised to keep unwanted, nosy neighbors away," Max said.

"What do you mean?" Simon asked. "Aren't they supposed to mark mudflats and sandbanks?"

"Indeed, and whenever charming invaders decided to pop by for a visit, the ancient Venetians simply pulled out the posts to confuse them," Max said. "It's a pity hiding isn't as easy nowadays."

Shelley looked at Max and had the feeling that he wasn't talking about the tourist-loving Venice. "Why? Is there anything you want to hide from, Max?"

"People don't hide because they want to, luv. It's because they need to." He turned to Dex and pointed to an island rising in the horizon. "Straight ahead, my good man."

"Aye, aye, Captain."

The traffic on the lagoon thinned as the motorboat approached Isola Torcello. A brick bell tower loomed larger in the horizon. The boat slowed as the waves dwindled into a brackish soup of silt and weeds. A heron perched on a sodden islet tilted its head at Shelley, as though asking her why she had bothered to come this way.

Shelley leaned over the side of the boat. The swamp mirrored the different shades of muddy brown she was feeling. She was almost certain that she could make out the line where time had stopped and left the island of Torcello to fend for itself. It was hard to believe that only ten minutes away the city of Venice was busy plying tourists with all the accoutrements of the postcard-perfect holiday.

Dex pulled the boat over to a small dock.

If loneliness was a place, Shelley was convinced that she had found it. She stepped onto the island.

"Campers, welcome to Torcello. Follow me." Max took Shelley's hand and led the group down a trail alongside a small winding canal.

"You have a thing for deserted islands, don't you, Max?" Brad asked.

"They have their charm," Max said as they approached an arched stone bridge. "That is the Ponte del Diavolo, the Devil's Bridge. They say that the devil built it in one night."

"And I know why he was in such a hurry to get out of here," Brad said. "This place feels like a ghost town."

"Perhaps," Max said, "that's because it is."

The trail ended in a dusty piazza bordered by a handful of stone buildings. Among them was an octagonal church whose bell tower the group had seen from the lagoon. A massive, roughly hewn white stone chair was planted in the overgrown grass in front of it, a throne waiting for its forgotten king.

Max leaned against the carved chair and looked around the piazza. The broken marble columns dotting it outnumbered the people in the tiny square. "There are only about twenty people who live here now. That's about 19,980 less residents than when the island was at its peak."

Simon looked at the sparse architecture around him. "Twenty thousand people lived *here*?"

Max nodded. "After they fled from Altinum, the Roman refugees prospered here, finding their fortune in the salt trade. They took the stones from their homes in Altinum and built a city and harbor. But as you can see, they didn't stay here."

"Why not?" Dex asked.

"They were invaded," Max said.

"The barbarians followed them here?" Simon asked.

"No. The mosquitoes did," Max said. "The waters that had once surrounded Torcello gradually filled in with silt, turning its harbor into a mosquito-infested *laguna morta,* a dead lagoon. Thousands died from malaria. The island's settlers had no recourse but to once again pack up their lives and leave. They rebuilt their homes on the Rialto. You can still see the original marble from Altinum in the buildings that stand there today."

Shelley imagined the early Venetians taking their homes apart, stone by stone, until there was nothing left. She thought about crumbling mosaics and the pieces of the life her mom had never quite managed to pick up. She thought about Rose, love stories, and inevitable endings. She looked at Max and felt light-headed. She sank onto the white stone chair.

Max smiled at Shelley. "That's called Attila's Throne."

"As in Attila the Hun?" Shelley asked.

"Yes, but poor Attila must have been standing for quite a long time, because that chair was made a hundred years too late. But what makes this chair really interesting is the myth that whoever sits in it will be married"—Max smiled—"within a year or sooner."

Shelley jumped to her feet. "Well, um, that's a lovely bit of trivia. But we didn't come all this way to chat about a chair, did we?"

"You're absolutely right, luv." Max took Shelley's hand and strode toward the church. "We're here to see the end of the world."

"Surprise, surprise," Brad whispered to Simon as they entered the Basilica of Santa Maria Assunta. "More mosaics."

A communion of patterns and colors covered the floors and walls of the ancient church. Shelley stood in awe of the Byzantine mosaics. On one apse was the tiled image of the Madonna and Child, looking lovingly at all who glanced their way. On the opposite end of the church was a more disturbing scene: the Last Judgment.

"If you are familiar with Christian teaching, you will recognize this as a depiction of the day after the End of Days." Max pointed to the mosaic of a godly figure presiding over writhing souls pleading for mercy. "This is the moment when Jesus Christ passes judgment on all who have ever lived and died, and decides where they will spend eternity."

"Do you believe in the end of the world, Max?" Simon asked.

Max nodded. "Of course."

"Really?" Simon said. "I didn't take you for the religious type."

"I'm not," Max said. "But I do know that the world will end."

"What makes you so sure that it will?" Shelley asked.

"Because it has ended before," Max said, "and it will again."

"What do you mean, Max?" Shelley frowned.

"I mean exactly that," Max said. "The world has ended before. Many times, in fact."

"It has?" Brad said. "I must have missed that on the news."

"Look around you," Max said, "and tell me that the Apocalypse did not happen here. Some people think that the world will end at some point in the future in a great, unimaginable, final cataclysm. I have a somewhat different point of view."

Dex grinned. "So you don't think a giant asteroid will crash into the earth?"

"I'm not discounting that possibility. I did watch *Armageddon*. Bruce Willis was very convincing. I just don't think the world has to run into a massive rock to end. Our world, after all, is what we choose to create around us, here and now. We build homes, towns, cities, civilizations— grander than all that came before, but never enduring. Etruscans. Egyptians. Greeks. Romans. Venetians. Where are their empires now? Where are the worlds they built? Gone. Judged. Ended. But life goes on. We take our shattered bricks, spread our plaster, and build again . . . hoping that we are starting over for the last time," Max said. "This was the same hope held by Isabelle's kin more than a thousand years ago, the only thing they could carry with them when the Lombards were at Altinum's gates."

"This isn't another depressing story, is it?" Brad asked.

Max smiled. "Don't worry. Isabelle's ancestors were smart enough to own a chicken—several, in fact."

Chapter Seventeen

Hunger and homecomings

ALTINUM

༈Ꮖ *A.D. 568*

His oars sliced through the lagoon like a knife through the soft bellies of the fish he caught. Every pull on his oars brought him closer to Altinum, one of the last-standing cities of an empire near its end. He looked over his shoulder and saw its shore.

A flock of birds flew overhead, a flurry of shadows in the dusk. There had been many such flocks flying above his home on the lagoon in recent days. Too many. He knew there could only be one reason for their exodus from the mainland. It was the same reason he was rowing toward it now. Barbarians were tearing through the plain.

He had expected the people of Altinum to seek safety in the lagoon as they had done in the past. But this time it seemed to him that the birds had more sense than the people who remained locked inside their doomed city.

The fisherman had once sought the sanctuary of the lagoon and he had not left it since then. But it was not the barbarians who had driven him to the sea. It was the very people he was now trying to save.

That was a long time ago, he told himself, and they would no longer remember what he could never forget. His memory was still stained with the knowledge of how ignorance turned friends and neighbors into an angry mob. He could still remember how being different had forced him into exile.

But the fisherman also remembered one other thing. He still had family in the city that had once cast him out, and it was for them that he needed to return. That, of course, and the few feathered friends he had left behind.

The rotund bishop looked up from his favorite dish of hard-boiled eggs in pine-nut sauce. He frowned at his turkey-wattled secretary. "Who?"

"A fisherman, Your Grace, from the lagoon." The secretary chewed on his lip, feeling the heat of the bishop's glare. His master did not like being disturbed while he was dining, but what their visitor had to tell him could not wait.

"What does he want?" The bishop's breath wheezed out of him, squeezed from under the weight of his thick chest. Breathing alone caused him to break into a sweat. He wiped his brow with the back of his fleshy hand.

"He says he has news of the . . . Lombards." The secretary grimaced at the taste those words left in his mouth: honey and iron. Blood.

The bishop pushed his meal away. He did not relish hearing news of his appointed executioner. He had been strong once, just like his city. But now Altinum was decaying, rotting from the inside like the empire it was born from. He was tired and prayed only for a swift and painless end—preferably from a blow that he didn't see coming. But his fisherman visitor would deny him even that mercy. He sighed. "Let him in."

The bishop's home was a peaceful place, the fisherman thought as he followed the secretary down the hall of the villa. Within its walls it was easy to pretend that the plains were not burning. The secretary led him to the inner courtyard, where the bishop was waiting for him.

"Your Grace." The fisherman bowed to the bishop. "I am Marcus. I bring urgent news."

"The barbarians," the bishop said. "I know."

"I have scouted the plains," Marcus said. "They are drawing closer to the city."

The bishop fiddled with the gold ring that bit into his fat finger. "I see."

"But there is still time, Your Grace," Marcus said. "I have already spoken with the other fishermen in the lagoon. They are willing to ferry your people across. You just need to . . ."

"Pray, my son." The bishop looked to the heavens and clasped his hands.

"Er, pray?" Now was not the time to be petulant, Marcus reminded himself. If humoring the bishop was what it took to convince him to evacuate the city, then that's what he would do. He clasped his hands and kneeled, believing that the bishop wished him to join in a short petition to his god.

"No, no, my son." The bishop touched Marcus's shoulder and ushered him to stand. "I must pray for a sign."

"I don't understand, Your Grace," Marcus asked. "What sign?"

"A sign for what to do next."

"With all due respect, Your Grace, I think what must be done is quite clear. You must get out of the city," Marcus said, "fast."

The bishop nodded. "Fast . . . yes, yes. That is a very good idea."

Marcus sighed with relief. "I will ready the boats."

"Boats? No, my son. We should fast while we pray for guidance," the bishop said. "I shall instruct the city to do so today. Thank you for your service, Marcus. You may go now."

"But, Your Grace . . ."

"You may go."

Marcus went through a choice list of expletives, unable to decide which suited the bishop the best. He dismissed each as far too generous. He stomped down the streets of Altinum, eager to return to his home.

More birds flew noisily above him. He glanced up at the sky. It had darkened, but not by clouds. It was smoke from the villages being torched outside the city's walls. Marcus imagined a certain man roasting on a spit, but to his disappointment, he took no pleasure in the image. He wondered why he still cared about what happened to Altinum, pretending that he did not already know the answer. He was making his way to it now.

He wondered what he would find when he got there. So much of the city had changed since he had lived in it. But it wasn't the villas, plazas, or paved streets that were different. These were relatively the same despite their state of neglect. It was its people that had changed. Their eyes now held the same fear that the barbarian tribes once had when they were forced to bow down to Rome.

But the tide had turned. It was now irreversibly—and perhaps even justly—rushing back to sweep what was left of the empire away.

The small home was tucked away at the end of a short alley. Blowing in its courtyard, like brightly colored sails, were freshly dyed fabrics, drying in the sun. To Marcus, it was an oasis in a city that had faded to gray. It was just as he had left it.

He smiled as he watched two young dark-haired boys weave through the rainbow of cloth, in the thick of an imaginary battle raging in the cobbled yard. Hearing them laugh, Marcus could forget that their world was about to end. Almost. But perhaps, he thought, as the little soldiers waved their wooden swords at a retreating barbarian horde of clucking hens, there was still something that could be done.

A woman leaning a clay jar of ocher dye on her hip approached him. Her two young sons dashed past her as they celebrated their victory with shouts and cheers. "Can I help you?"

Marcus smiled. "Yes, I think you can."

Ionus, the cloth dyer, stared at his guest in disbelief when the man had finished telling him of his plan. The stranger's amber eyes were filled with worry and doubt. Ionus was now beginning to regret inviting this man who claimed to be his uncle into their home, but he had come to him with a truth he could not ignore: the Lombards were indeed upon them.

The refuge across the lagoon the fisherman offered his family was something he could not refuse. The man's other agenda, however, was more difficult to accept.

"I'm sorry, but that is simply the most ridiculous thing I have ever heard." Ionus set his cup down. Warm watered-down wine sloshed to the table.

"Perhaps you have other ideas?" Marcus asked. "I'd be happy to hear them."

"Well, no, but . . ."

"These are the facts before us," Marcus said. "The barbarians will overrun this city and you, your family, and everyone else here will die—unless you come with me. I cannot save Altinum, but I can save you. The fate of the rest of Altinum is in the hands of another man, a bishop who has chosen to starve himself while waiting for his sign."

"But what you are proposing is blasphemous," Ionus said.

"What I propose," Marcus said, "is that we answer the good bishop's prayers." He pushed his stool from the table and stood up. "And now, if you could set aside your skepticism for a moment, we can get to work saving your family."

His wife and sons were asleep when Ionus set the pots Marcus had just used for his project away. He was still not convinced of Marcus's plan, but he had very little choice in the matter. Though what the fisherman asked him to do confounded him, it had made him feel less helpless. It was better than just waiting for the end to come.

"You've been a great help, Ionus." Marcus set the basket containing their night's work aside.

"I still don't understand what we just did, but I suppose I simply have to trust you on this. I don't have any other choice."

"Of course you do," Marcus said. "You can always opt to watch the city, and everyone in it, burn."

"That's not much of an alternative, is it?" Ionus sighed.

Marcus shrugged. "But a choice, nonetheless."

"May I ask you a question, Uncle?"

Marcus nodded.

"Why do you care about what happens to me and my family? We have been strangers up until today."

"Would you care less about your sons if years passed before you saw them next?"

"Well, no. Of course not."

"You have your answer, then. Blood cannot be thinned by time or distance."

"Yes, I suppose you're right," Ionus said. "But this plan of yours . . . I fear it puts us in greater danger. And even if it does work, what happens after we leave home?"

"You won't be leaving it," Marcus said.

"But you said . . ."

"I said that you would need to leave this city. As for your home . . ." Marcus glanced in the direction of the room where Ionus's wife and sons slept. "I believe they shall fit in my boat."

"Why have you returned? What news do you bring?" The bishop questioned his decision to see this bothersome man again. It was the second day of his fast and he blamed his gnawing hunger for his poor judgment. He had originally thought dealing with the fisherman would help keep his mind off his grumbling stomach, but now it was growling louder than ever.

"Thank you for seeing me again, Your Grace," Marcus said. "I was just wondering if you have received the sign you have been praying for."

The famished bishop shook his head. "No, but God's ways are not our own. I have faith that He will reveal His plan to me in His own time."

"Hopefully, before you faint from hunger," Marcus muttered under his breath.

"Did you say something, my son?"

"I said I hope it doesn't take much longer. You don't have much time left."

"Is there anything else you wanted, my son?" the bishop said sharply.

"Yes, Your Grace," Marcus said. "I am returning to the lagoon and I wanted to give you this before I left." He handed the bishop a cloth-covered basket. "Please accept this humble gift as a token of my gratitude for taking the time to listen to a simple fisherman."

"Thank you, my son," the bishop said. "What is it?"

"Salt," Marcus said, "from the lagoon, Your Grace. And a little something that I have found to go particularly well with it."

The bishop had not eaten or drunk anything the whole day and was feeling light-headed. He stared at the basket. A half dozen hard-boiled eggs stared back at him. He licked his lips.

Just one, he thought. He did, after all, need to keep up his strength to lead his flock. Never did they need him more than in these trying times. So in truth, he decided, eating an egg—or two—was, in fact, his duty.

The bishop said a short prayer of thanks before partaking of his spiritually fortifying meal. He tapped the top of the egg on the table and began to peel off its shell. And there it was—his burning bush—the sign he had been waiting for. What the bishop held up joyfully in his hands wasn't a bush, of course, nor was it burning—just slightly warm at most. But it didn't matter. He was certain that it was the message he had prayed for, even if he didn't have the faintest idea what it meant. His fingers trembled as he hastened to peel the rest of the eggs. Written on the egg whites were the same miraculous words that would fill his dreams that evening: *Follow the chickens.*

The sun was barely up when the old secretary ran into the bishop's room. "Your Grace! Your Grace!"

The bishop bolted up from his bed. "What is it?"

"Your Grace, the chickens!" The secretary's wattle jiggled. "Look outside your window."

The bishop rose and lumbered to the window. He opened the shutters and looked out into the street. He laughed. "Of course!"

It was an impossible sight. Chickens, unmoving like statues, dotted the road. They seemed to mark a trail—a path that the bishop was determined to follow. He ran into the street.

The trail of chickens ended at the foot of the city gates' tall marble tower. The bishop wondered what to do next. A cock crowed from the top of the tower just as the chickens below began to stir. The bishop bounded up the tower two steps at a time, filled with the energy of his younger, forgotten self. The paralyzing weight of insecurity and abandonment fell away as he climbed. A lighter man emerged at the top.

The bishop looked out from the tower. The lagoon sparkled in the sun. The meaning of the message given to him became clear. In the horizon, he saw his city's salvation—an island he would later call Torcello. As he lifted his hands to the heavens and praised his god, a fisherman on the lagoon rowed his family to their new beginning. Later that day many more boats would come to ferry the bishop's flock.

VENICE, ITALY

Five Years Ago

Secret egg messages? Frozen chickens?" Brad laughed. "You're kidding, right?"

"What makes you think that?" Max replied. "I thought that knowing that Isabelle's kin were cloth dyers made the solution to Marcus's dilemma rather obvious. And of course the wooden swords and the chickens in the yard were dead giveaways as well."

"You're not going to tell us how it really happened, are you?" Shelley asked.

"You're absolutely right, luv," Max said. "I'm going to show you. But first we need to head back home."

. . .

The group waited for Max behind one of the sheds near the olive grove.

"He's a strange one, isn't he?" Dex said.

"I can't argue with you on that," Shelley said. And she was even stranger for getting involved with him, she thought.

Max reappeared with a dusty wooden sword in one hand and a struggling chicken tucked underneath his other arm.

"Um, we aren't going to sacrifice a chicken to the gods, are we?" Brad asked.

"Not in this part of the tour, no." Max crouched down and held the chicken's head to the ground. He took the sword and drew a line in the soil back and forth in front of the tip of the bird's beak. The hen relaxed in his grip and stopped moving. Max stepped away from it.

Simon stared at the frozen bird. "What did you just do?"

"She is in a trance," Max said. "She can stay this way up to half an hour."

"So that's what Marcus did?" Shelley asked. "He hypnotized the chickens?"

"Marcus convinced Ionus and his family to help him out, and I believe that the children had loads of fun doing it." Max grinned. "And technically it's called tonic immobility. It's a defense mechanism some animals have. That's why a deer freezes in the headlights. It's actually pretending to be dead, hoping against hope that the metal monster rushing toward it will be fooled and leave it alone. It's what our old bishop was earlier afflicted with, I think."

"What about the eggs?" Dex asked, his eyes glued to the entranced chicken.

"That was even simpler." Max smiled. "Vinegar and alum. The mixture seeps invisibly through the eggshell so that whatever you write on the outside of the egg magically appears underneath the shell. And, as I'm sure you all know because you are such history buffs, alum was also widely used in the ancient cloth-dyeing process to fix the colors to the fabric."

Chapter Eighteen

Egg salad and escape

VENICE, ITALY

🌿 *Five Years Ago*

Shelley woke up from a dream about petrified chickens to find Max gone from bed. Just as well, she thought. She would need to get used to sleeping on her own again after the tour was over. She dressed and went downstairs. The dusty kitchen was empty. She waded through the mine-field of clutter to get to the front door, catching cobwebs on her jeans. She stepped outside, then bent down and brushed off the silver-gray wisps clinging to her legs.

"Hey, Shelley! Over here." Dex waved from the courtyard.

She looked up. The morning sun shimmered across Alex. A picnic table was set in the middle of her tiled belly and was draped with a crisp white cloth that caught the blue from the sky. Dex, Brad, and Simon were seated around it, cups of coffee in hand. Shelley joined them and was greeted by a breakfast of toast, fruit, marmalade, and five brown eggs in silver cups. "Dining al fresco? What's the occasion?" she asked.

"I guess Max got tired of sharing breakfast with his dust mites." Brad poured Shelley a cup of coffee.

Max emerged from the olive grove clutching a spray of wildflowers. He set the bouquet in a crystal vase at the center of the table. He kissed Shelley on the lips. "Good morning, luv."

Enjoy it while it lasts, she reminded herself. "Good morning. This is lovely, Max."

Max sat down. "Let's eat, shall we? I hope you like soft-boiled eggs."

Shelley tapped her egg with a spoon. Nothing happened. She tapped harder, but with the same lack of result. She looked up. Brad, Simon, and Max were already dipping pieces of toast into sunny yolks. She chipped at the eggshell with her fingers. A firm white top peeked from under it. "I think mine might be a tiny bit overdone."

"My apologies, luv. My egg timer met an early demise in Austria. You can have my egg if you like."

"Oh, right." Shelley smiled guiltily. "But, you know, yesterday's story has actually put me in the mood for hard-boiled eggs." She peeled off the eggshell and gasped.

"What's the matter?" Brad asked.

Shelley continued to stare at the egg in her hands.

Brad reached for her shoulder. "Shelley?"

The strength drained from her fingers. The egg began to slip from her grasp. Shelley squeezed her fist around it. A warm mush seeped between her pale knuckles. She opened her hand. Egg salad. Her heart sank. She prodded the mess with her fingers, searching for the two words she thought she had seen. They were gone. Perhaps they had never even been there.

"Are you okay?" Simon asked.

"I . . . I thought I saw something."

"Huh?" Dex arched a brow. "Where?"

"On the . . . uh . . . egg," Shelley said. "There was something written on it . . ."

"The egg?" Simon asked. "What did it say?"

Shelley bit her lip and turned to Max.

Max looked into her eyes and took her mush-filled hand in his. "It said . . ."

Shelley held her breath.

" 'Marry me.' "

A FLIGHT TO THE PHILIPPINES

❧ *Now*

"Wow. So that's how the two of you got engaged," Paolo said.
Shelley looked out the window. "I didn't say we got engaged."
"But I thought you said . . ."
"I said that's how Max proposed to me."

VENICE, ITALY

❧ *Five Years Ago*

It seemed like it was only yesterday that Max had proposed to her. Oh,
it was. Shelley sighed. Many things had changed since then. For one, she
had become a thief earlier this morning. She hoped the island's caretakers could forgive her for stealing their boat. It was the only way she could
flee Max's island.

"Don't answer. Not yet." Those were Max's exact words, she recalled,
right after he said *"Marry me."* Perhaps, she thought, if he hadn't said
them, things would have been different. She would not have paused. She
would have said—screamed—yes! But Max had given her time to think
straight . . . out the door, onto a stolen boat, and onto a train leading to
nowhere.

Shelley shrank into her train seat and stared at the ticket in her hand.
She wasn't quite sure how it had gotten there. She vaguely remembered
standing in front of a ticket booth and babbling about hard-boiled eggs,
tumbling LEGO towers, and not wanting to end up like her mother. How
the bespectacled clerk in it had come to any conclusion about her desired
destination was rather remarkable, she thought, considering that she herself had had no clue. She had just wanted to get a ticket. Any ticket.

Letters swam in front of Shelley's eyes as she attempted and failed to
remember how to read. She gave up trying to decipher the words printed
on her ticket. The fact that she had no idea where she was going didn't

matter. All that mattered was that the little slip of paper in her hand took her as far away as possible from Venice—and Max. Maybe then, she hoped, her higher brain functions would start working again.

The hours that followed the proposal had grated on her, rubbing her raw with reason. She had survived them by going through the day pretending that it was still possible to answer yes. It was the lie she clung to as she made love to Max and kissed him that last evening on the island.

He had tasted bittersweet, like the last piece of dark chocolate cake lurking in the fridge the night before a lemon-and-apple-cider-vinegar cleanse. The memory was still in her mouth as she sat on the train wearing only the clothes she was able to grab while Max was sleeping.

Shelley had quietly pulled on Max's gray cotton shirt and her own pair of jeans as she padded out of the house before the sun was up. That she had managed to leave with her pants was a stroke of sheer luck. Finding her clothes after Max had ripped them off her was always challenging. She had already lost almost half of the underwear she had packed for the trip and several shirt buttons. Leaving her handbag containing her phone and wallet on the island, however, was considerably less fortunate. Thank goodness for Dex and the money sewed into his underwear.

"So, are you planning on telling me why you've kidnapped me?" Dex asked from the seat across from her.

"Pass. Next question, please." Shelley was feeling guilty about dragging him along. He had been a necessary accomplice when she realized she had no idea how to steer, much less start, the caretakers' motorboat. He had been taking pictures on the dock when she ran into him during her escape. Holding his camera hostage as she herded him to the boat had not been one of her finer moments.

"Fine, then just tell me why we're going to Rome." Dex waved his ticket in front of her.

Ah, Rome. Mystery destination solved. He was proving useful already, Shelley thought. He could read. "Because it's not Venice?"

"Try again."

"And you can take a lot of nice pictures there?"

"I see that you've really thought this through." He rubbed the freckled crease on his forehead.

"I'm sorry. I really am." Shelley handed his camera back to him. "There's still time to get off the train."

Dex sighed. "It's okay. Who would I take pictures of if I went back?" He pointed his camera at her. "Say cheese."

Shelley mustered a smile. This wasn't exactly a time she wanted to remember.

Rome was still about four hours away. Shelley was exhausted from nearly thirty minutes of dodging the subject of Max and smiling for Dex's camera. If she said "cheese" one more time, she was certain she was going to become lactose intolerant. Still, posing for pictures was a good way to keep Dex happy until they could get to the embassy in Rome and replace their passports. She was determined to stick to that plan as they rode the train. It was either that or answer Dex's questions about Max. She chose cheese.

"That looked great," Dex said, checking her photo on his camera screen.

"Um, do you mind if we take a break?" Shelley's mouth was beginning to ache from all the false smiles.

Dex stretched his long legs. His foot brushed against something beneath the seat across from him. He crouched down. "Well, look what we have here." He pulled out a worn guidebook. He sat back down and flipped through its tattered pages, stopping at the section on Florence. "Too bad we're not going to be able to see Florence. That's where the Uffizi museum is." He handed the book to Shelley. "It would have been nice to see the statue of David."

A penis. Just what she needed, she thought as she stared at the picture of the naked man on the dog-eared page. The tension and movement in his cold marble muscles stirred memories of the much warmer body she was aching for. With the exception of a certain carved body part (that Shelley objectively felt was less endowed than its real-life counterpart), the massive statue of David was a veritable stone replica of the man she loved.

Shelley sighed. She did love Max; this she knew without question. That was the problem. Saying yes to Max's question was easy. Saying yes to what he did not ask was not. To have said yes meant she consented to a beginning—and an end. Till death do us part. There was a very real reason for this wedding vow. It proclaimed the infallible truth that all marriages ended in one of two ways: spouses died or love did. She refused to be widowed by either. She read the caption beneath the photograph of the statue silently.

Michelangelo chose to depict David at the point when he had already decided to fight Goliath, but before they had engaged in battle. It represents the journey across cognizant choice and deliberate action.

Shelley looked at the statue's eyes and was struck by the determination and courage she found there. But there was also something else. Something she had not expected to see. Peace.

Her choice had not left her with the same serenity. Perhaps, she thought with a sigh, it was because running away was actually the opposite of a decision. It was procrastination. She had yet to make a real choice. She needed to find Max. Having no clue where the tour group was headed next, however, posed a slight problem. She looked at Dex. "Um, you don't suppose this book would have a section on prominent chickens in history, would it?"

Dex took a nap after making a valiant though vain effort to scour the guidebook for chickens. Shelley watched him sleep. A tiny stream of saliva dribbled from one side of his mouth and pooled on the green sweater he had balled under his neck. She smiled. Dex was sweet and simple, the kind of man her mother had always wanted her to marry. So unlike Max. When she had looked into Max's amber eyes, there was an easy charm in a flicker, depths of strength in a glint. Sometimes, when Max thought she wasn't looking, she caught a glimpse of a longing so devastating, she had to look away. And yet she would always look back, unable to resist what haunted her the most: the reflection of an extraordinary new world.

Shelley wondered where Max was now, even as she accepted the

futility of finding him. Having also failed to find any reference to historical chickens or eggs in Dex's guidebook, she decided that the logical
thing to do would be to find her own bearings. Max would return to
London at some point. She would contact him then and give him the
answer he might not necessarily want but at least deserved to hear.

Dex whimpered. "Sheil . . ."

Shelley turned to Dex. Had he called her name? His eyes darted
after a dream beneath his lids.

"Sheila. Please. Stay!" Dex jolted awake. His sweater fell to the floor.

"Dex, are you okay?" Shelley touched his arm.

Dex grabbed his sweater, looked away, and wiped his eyes with its
sleeve. He turned back to face her. The fractured smile Shelley had first
seen when they met in Max's van had returned. It reminded her of a flan-
nel robe, the kind people throw over their pajamas when they rush to
answer the door. Rumpled and slightly askew.

"Sorry, was I talking in my sleep?" Dex asked.

Shelley nodded, noticing that his lashes were still wet. "Who's Sheila?"

Dex swallowed and looked out the window. He dug his fingers into
the sweater. "She's my wife," he said to his reflection in the glass.

"Wife?" Shelley's head jerked back in surprise. "I didn't know you
were married."

"This trip was supposed to be our honeymoon. Sheila . . . couldn't
come."

"I don't understand . . ."

Dex looked at her and sighed deeply.

"Sheila doesn't know me anymore," Dex said, "on most days at least.
She's sick. Familial Alzheimer's disease. It's an extremely rare form of
Alzheimer's that afflicts younger people."

This was it, Shelley thought. This was the pain that had been peeking through the cracks in Dex's smile the entire trip. "Oh, Dex, I'm so
sorry."

"We had always dreamed of traveling around Europe. But Sheila got
sick and the disease progressed more rapidly than anyone expected. The
changes were small, almost unnoticeable at first. She started forgetting

little things . . . her keys, her purse. But later, more things started to fade. Hours, days, faces. Me. It was like I was dead to her . . . just . . ." Dex choked on his tears.

"Just what?" she asked quietly.

"Worse. It was like I never even existed." Dex swallowed back his pain. "But there were still good days to look forward to . . . days when we could talk, laugh . . . dream. It was on one of those days that I asked Sheila to marry me."

Marry me. Max's voice breathed into her ear. Shelley fought back tears.

"And she turned me down," Dex said.

"But I thought . . ."

"I managed to change her mind. As you may have noticed, I can be quite persistent." He tapped his camera. A shy smile flickered in his eyes.

Shelley smiled back. Dex had taken more pictures of her on this trip than anyone ever had on all her vacations combined. "I have."

"In time, Sheila came to understand why I needed to be with her."

"And why did you?" Shelley regretted the question as soon as the words had tumbled out of her mouth. She had not meant to be crude, only honest. In staying, Dex was choosing to be left behind. He was either a fool or the wisest man she knew.

"Because I don't believe in jumping off trains, Shelley," he said. "Do you remember what Jonathan said about Rose when we were at the monastery? How he wanted to make memories with her while he could? That's how I feel about Sheila. I want to be with her while I can. I want to remember as much as I can: the funny squeak she makes when she hiccups . . . the way her skin smells like peaches . . . the way she curls into a ball next to me when we sleep." His voice grew softer. "These are all I'll have of her after she's . . . gone."

"That's why you were so upset that night we took Jonathan to the hospital."

"Yes," Dex said, "except that I remember thinking that Rose had it slightly better than me. Rose could at least hope that things were going to be okay, even for just a little while. I don't even remember what that's like anymore. Sheila isn't going to get any better. I'm sitting in the waiting room—all day, every day—knowing that every second brings us closer to the end. Can you imagine what that feels like, Shelley?"

Shelley bit her lip. She didn't have to imagine it. She was very aware that people and relationships had expiration dates. She had watched her dad wither and her mom fade next to him. It was exactly why she had fled from Max. Things couldn't end if she didn't let them begin.

"But you know what? I'd do it all over again," Dex said. "Losing someone to F.A.D. is extremely rare, but finding the other half of your soul is rarer. Any man, at least any man who had found what I had, would do the same, which leaves me wondering why . . ." He paused, looking hesitant.

"Why what?"

"Why you're on this train."

Shelley blanched from the punch to her gut.

"I honestly thought you and Max had something—"

"Terrifying." The word slipped out in a whisper from her lips, but it rang loudly in her head.

"But isn't that the point? Isn't that what everyone hopes for? To find a passion so great that it scares the hell out of you? Why are you so desperate to run away from it, Shelley?" Dex asked.

"Shouldn't you be asking yourself that same question? Why did you leave your wife's side to go on this trip? What are you running away from?"

"What? No. You've got it wrong. I never left her, Shelley. Sheila's been with me on this entire trip." He took a deep breath. "And I have pictures to prove it."

"What are you talking about?"

"I . . . took pictures of you so that Sheila could see her face on them when I got back home. I'm making the memories she can no longer make for herself. This is our trip, memories we can reminisce about on good days and hold on to through the bad," Dex said. "I'm sorry I didn't tell you. I was afraid you wouldn't . . ."

Shelley regretted her poses. She wished he had told her the truth. Dex could replace her plastered smile, but she was worried that Sheila might still see the reluctance in the arms folded across her chest and the awkwardness weighing down her hunched shoulders. She did not know Sheila, but she knew that she deserved so much more. Shelley threw her arms around Dex and hugged him tight. "I understand."

"Do you?" Dex sighed into her shoulder.

She pulled away. "Of course I do."

Dex clasped her hand. "Then I'm asking you again, Shelley—why are you here? If you really understand the value of making memories with someone you love, why are you throwing yours away so easily? You don't know how much I envied you . . . all of you on this trip. Everyone had someone to experience the journey with. You shared everything, from the best eggs to the worst kind of pain. One day these memories will fade, but you'll always have someone to argue with about what the name of that monastery in Austria was and to laugh with about that creepy guy we met in Slovenia. Do you know how special that is?"

Shelley wanted to give him an answer, but she knew that nothing she could say would make a difference. He had not spent his childhood learning how cruel scrapbooks could be, watching a woman find—and lose—her husband every time she turned a page. If he had, perhaps he would think better of jumping off trains.

"I know that there's no magic potion to preserve my life or Sheila's," Dex said, still holding on to Shelley's hand. "And I know that the time will come when her voice won't be as crystal clear in my head. But even when every detail has dulled, I know that I'll always have something that not even time can take away. Pain."

Shelley's hand stiffened against Dex's palm. "And that's a good thing?"

"Yes, because when I've forgotten everything else, I'll feel that ache . . . that tightness in my throat . . . that heaviness in my chest . . . and know that I loved a woman once and she loved me back. It's proof that I existed and so did she."

Chapter Nineteen

Choices and cholesterol

ROME

❧ *Five Years Ago*

It was Saturday and the embassy was closed. The recorded message on the phone stated a number to contact in case of an emergency. Shelley deliberated about whether her situation qualified as one. She wasn't in-carcerated, no one had been murdered, and her passport had not fallen into unscrupulous hands. She wondered if leaping from imaginary trains counted.

Dex knocked on the phone booth. "Well?"

She hung up. "I think we need to find a place to stay until Monday."

Dex had left their hostel to do some sightseeing. While his persistence had paid off in getting Shelley to pose for his pictures, it had little effect on getting her to talk about why she had run away. She wasn't trying to be stubborn; she just didn't know what to say. She was staring at a brick wall. Literally. She drew the threadbare orange curtains shut, blocking out the view.

She flopped onto the bed. The rolling landscape of lumps and springs jabbed at her ribs. Shelley rolled on her stomach and buried her head on the stained pillow. She gagged and flipped over. Death by wet dog.

Shelley would have fled, but her feet had gone on strike. They demanded rest. But the bed refused to cooperate. A spring stabbed her in the back. She scrambled off the mattress and dashed out the door.

It was the third cup of espresso that quieted the protests of Shelley's exhausted appendages. Even her toes were now buzzing with borrowed energy. But the Olympian sprint they wanted to run would have to wait. Shelley was channeling the caffeine rush for other purposes.

She took the last paper napkin from the dispenser and began to scribble down the second volume of possible answers to Max's question. She looked at the tall stack of napkins beside her. She signaled the waiter for another cup.

The waiter narrowed his eyes under a hedge of dark brows at the pile of napkins on the table.

Shelley didn't notice him. She was engrossed in reviewing her latest list.

It's not you. It's me . . . Blech.

If only love were enough . . . Pathetic.

It just wouldn't work . . . Ugh.

Absolutely not! . . . Psychotic.

No. Hmm.

No. Not bad, not bad at all. Swift, like a bullet to the head. Shelley hoped it would be just as painless. She was well aware that when she squeezed the trigger, it would not be Max who would be standing at the end of the barrel. "No," she practiced out loud.

The waiter frowned. "No espresso?"

"Huh?" She looked up at him. "No. I mean yes. Another espresso, please."

The waiter nodded. "One espresso." He turned to leave.

"No." Practice would make perfect, Shelley told herself. She was already beginning to sound more convincing.

The waiter walked back. "No espresso?"

"What? No. No. One espresso. Please."

The waiter rolled his eyes. "One espresso."

"No!" Shelley smiled at the depth of her delivery, seconds before being kicked out of the café.

Shelley would still have been wandering aimlessly around Rome if not for Sister Margaret. The heavyset nun had suggested that every good Catholic schoolgirl should make a visit to the seat of her faith. Shelley did not want to disappoint her longtime boarder by telling her that the only thing she now had in common with the pink-cheeked schoolgirl she had once been was that she still occasionally put her hair in pigtails. She conceded to touring the Vatican, deciding that this would at least delay her return to the forest of mildew she had to sleep on. She walked up to St. Peter's Basilica and took in its scale.

The large church dominated the sprawling colonnade of St. Peter's Square. The elliptical line of pristine white columns surrounding the square symbolized the church's embrace of all humankind, but in that moment Shelley felt the colonnade defy its vastness to give her the hug she desperately needed. Maybe she hadn't changed so much after all.

When she was a young girl, there was one image that had fascinated Shelley from the first time she had seen it on a postcard stuck on their refrigerator door. She was gazing up at it now.

"*The Creation of Adam,*" said the recorded voice in her headphones.

Shelley switched off the Sistine Chapel's audio tour. She wanted to keep the moment to herself—at least as much as she could, standing shoulder to shoulder in a chapel full of tourists. She stared at the two hands outstretched toward each other, one giving life, the other receiving it. It spoke to her now as much as it had when she was younger, when she had not yet known that the hands were part of a much larger painting and what they actually depicted. She had simply seen them as two hands lovingly reaching out to each other, desperately close but unable to touch. They had made her feel sad. They still did.

But as Shelley looked up at the masterpiece, she realized that something was different. She wondered if it was because she was now craning her neck up to see it and not straining on her tiptoes to view it in its honored place beneath the pot roast recipe her mom had cut out from a magazine. She studied the ceiling, ignoring the pain throbbing in her neck. Something else had changed, not just her perspective. The colors were much brighter than those in the picture in her head. The painting had been restored.

The conservation work was meant to reveal Michelangelo's original palette—and it did—but at a cost. Shelley missed the depth the painting had when it still wore the patina of age. It was in the eyes of the saints that this was the most obvious. They were flat, stripped of all they had witnessed through the centuries. They appeared so young now compared to . . . Max's? She dismissed the thought just as quickly as it had popped into her head. She blamed it on the cocktail of mildew spores, caffeine, and longing in her system.

"And that concludes our tour, campers." A deep voice sliced through the crowd.

It punched Shelley in the throat.

"So, you see, if not for Isabelle's lovely ancestor and her brave rooster, you would not be standing under this great masterpiece today."

"That was the best story on the entire tour, Max," Brad said. "No cats, lots of sex, and a happy ending."

Simon nodded. "That really was an eye-opener. What a finale!"

Max smiled. "I'm glad you enjoyed the tour."

Shelley fumbled through her pockets for the volume of napkins she had written on. Her fingers found another list. She pulled it out. It was tattered and stained from a cycle in the wash. Her words had melted into inkblots, but she remembered them well.

Meet. Date. Run.

She prepared for a sprint. Max had not yet seen her. There was still time for her to slip out of the chapel. She glanced at Max. He was walking away. A rock fell in Shelley's gut. She could not bear to watch him leave—at least not before she had given him her answer. She tried to go after him, but her feet were welded to the floor. She tried to call him back, but her voice abandoned her. She looked to the painted heavens for help. The blue sky turned into night and a halo of stars twinkled around Adam's head, signaling the inevitable. She was going to faint.

Shelley peeked through her lashes. The sky. White feathery clouds were brushed across it. Michelangelo was a true master. Very realistic, she thought. A bird flew overhead. She choked. It *was* the sky—and she was being carried away beneath it.

Max grinned down at her. "So, have you thought about your answer yet, luv?"

Shelley stared back at him openmouthed. There was no trace of bitterness on his face. "You're . . . you're not mad at me?" she asked.

"Should I be?" He set her down on her feet. "I asked you to think about it, didn't I?"

"But . . ."

"When you left the island, I assumed that you had taken some time—and poor Mrs. Bianchi's boat—to think about my question," Max said. "Was I wrong in that assumption?"

"Well . . ."

"My only fear was that you didn't fully understand what I was asking you. It was physically impossible, you see, to fit the entirety of my question on one hard-boiled egg."

Max smiled and got down on one knee. He took Shelley's hand in his.

"Once, in front of a sundial, I asked you not to run from the seconds you stood upon. Later, I showed you an egg timer and asked you to hold on to the moment in your hands. On one of the darkest nights of my life, I asked you to stay by my side," he said. "I know that I have already asked far too much and have no right to ask for more, but I must ask you this one more thing."

She inhaled sharply.

"Shelley, will you let me hold your hand as we outrun reason, brush past elephants, race up steps, tumble down hills, roll in the hay, leap over crumbling walkways, and dangle our legs over ledges?"

"Max . . ."

"Wait, luv," he said. "Let me finish. What I'm really trying to ask you is . . ." He took a deep breath.

Shelley's heart pounded in her chest, pumping blood to her head, away from her legs. Her knees began to buckle. She gripped Max's hand tighter for support.

"Shelley Sullivan, will you let me be the one who makes you eggs for breakfast—only on Sundays mornings, of course, because to be honest, I've been feeding you far too much cholesterol on this tour—and kiss the spot behind your ear before you sleep, till death do . . ."

Shelley drew a sharp breath as she silenced Max with her hand. She felt his lips against her palm. She had grown up with the words he was about to say echoing in her head. She could not bear to hear them again. It was what she had spent her entire adult life avoiding: her mother's pain. But as she stood still, locked onto Max's eyes and unable to run, it crashed into her—a wave that found every empty space inside her. It filled her to the brim with every moment she had shared with Max. Eggs. Sleep. Mornings. None of these would ever be the same. She could spend a lifetime wringing him from her memories without extracting a drop. He was a part of her now.

She exhaled. Her only choice became clear as the air rushed out of her chest. A peace settled in its place. Decision bridged action as a well-rehearsed answer rolled off her tongue. "No."

Max dropped his hand to his knee. He turned his face away from Shelley.

She had thought that Dex was being naive for welcoming the wound Sheila would leave him with. As the tragedy of a life without Max washed over her, Shelley began to think otherwise. Dex's and her mom's pain was not because their lives were without love. It was because their lives had been drenched in it. She had believed her mom was the saddest person she knew. Now she saw that her mom was, perhaps, also one of the luck-iest. She had known a love worth mourning, a love worth remembering.

Shelley knelt down beside Max and cradled his face in her hands.

"What I meant, Max," she said, "was will *you* let *me* remind you to floss every night for richer or for poorer, in sickness and in health?"

The question was the only honest answer she could give him, the only answer worthy of what he had asked. Shelley asked Max to marry her because simply saying yes fell short of how she felt for the man who cared about her arteries and wanted to hold her hand through the adventure they were already having. She was still very aware that this journey would inevitably end one day, but if they watched what they ate, took care of their teeth, and held hands as they crossed the street, it would at least be a long one. She remembered Dex and swore to take lots of pictures along the way.

Max's face lit up with a grin. He gathered Shelley in his arms and kissed her. "I thought you'd never ask."

A FLIGHT TO THE PHILIPPINES

Now

And that's how Max and I got engaged."

Paolo smiled. "I suppose that more than made up for missing the last stop of the tour."

"That wasn't the last stop."

"But weren't Brad and Simon raving about Max's last story at the Sistine Chapel?"

"They were, and technically it was the last stop—for them at least," Shelley said.

"Why? What happened after the proposal?" Paolo asked.

"You mean after the scandalous standing ovation Brad and Simon gave us in St. Peter's Square?"

"Er . . . yes."

"We called my mother to share the wonderful news, and afterward, we all went out for an enormous celebratory Roman feast." Shelley smiled at the memories of her mother's squeal of delight and the heaping plates of pasta and bottles of red wine. "And then Max booted Dex, Simon, and Brad out of the van."

"What? Max stranded them in Rome?"

"Not exactly. Max took them as far as the airport, gave each of them a hug and a first-class airline ticket back to London. After Max and I got married and I started helping him out on the tour, I learned that while the stops in the middle of the Slight Detour would change, the tour always started at Isabelle's tomb and ended at the Sistine Chapel," Shelley said. "There was only one time that Max made an exception."

E R C O L A N O

I T A L Y

Five Years Ago

Shelley sat next to Max as they drove out of Rome and through the back roads of Italy. She couldn't help but feel a little strange being alone with him. It was, however, a strangeness that she was utterly happy to be befuddled by every day for the rest of her life. She and Max weren't completely alone, though. They still had Barry, Robin, and Maurice Gibb for company. By now, she knew all their songs by heart. She smiled and hummed along.

"Why the smile, luv?" Max squeezed her hand.

"I was just thinking of the funny little road we've been on."

"What happens when the road gets less funny?" he asked.

"I think this van can handle a few potholes," Shelley said. "I don't know about you, but I'm strapped in for the ride."

Max put his arm around her. "I'm here until the end."

She leaned into him. "So how much farther until we get to our hotel?" It was late in the evening and she was looking forward to room service and a large bed.

"Not much, but we have to make a slight detour first."

"A detour? At this hour?" Shelley asked. She ran her hand over Max's thigh and smiled naughtily. "Wouldn't you rather, well, you know, *sleep*?"

"Oh, I am most certainly planning on catching up on a *lot* of sleep tonight." He grinned.

"So let's leave the detour for morning and head to our hotel now. I'm sooooo sleepy," she purred into his ear.

"I'm afraid this can't wait, luv," Max said softly.

"Why not?" Shelley leaned back in her seat.

"This is something you need to see before we go anywhere else."

She looked up at him, puzzled. "What do you need to show me, Max?"

"The beginning."

HERCULANEUM EXCAVATION SITE
ITALY
🌿⚬ 11:30 P.M.

Shelley held Max's hand as they walked through the quiet seaside town. It would have been a charming moonlit stroll, she thought, except for the fact that Herculaneum was no longer a town, nor was it by the sea, and she and Max weren't so much strolling as they were darting through the shadows like thieves.

It was as quiet as the grave.

Shelley heard the volcanic ash scrape against the soles of her sneakers. This was the ash that had buried the Roman town and pushed away the Bay of Naples, Max had told her. It had been spewed by the same eruption that had obliterated Pompeii on the other side of Vesuvius. Until Vesuvius erupted, the people living by the bay did not have any idea that it was anything other than a mountain whose surrounding fields were extremely well suited for farming. That's why they lived next to it. They did not even have a word for volcano. She wondered if this had made the catastrophe more horrible; it was like being betrayed.

"Are we supposed to be here, Max?" Shelley whispered.

"What makes you think we shouldn't be, luv?"

"Oh, I don't know," she said, "maybe because the sign at the gate said the excavation site closes at four P.M.?"

"We're in Italy, luv. Signs like those are like traffic lights. They're just suggestions." Max scanned the dusty street with a small flashlight, illuminating the irony that surrounded them.

The eruption that had entombed Herculaneum in A.D. 79 had also preserved it. In the darkness, Shelley could easily imagine that the town was sleeping rather than dead. The shells of the ancient Roman houses stood in rows along the small paved road. A number of homes, two stories high and still covered by tiled roofs, were virtually intact. Their wooden doors, though scorched black, remained bolted, just as they had been left almost two thousand years ago. She could not help but wonder if she was the intruder they were trying to keep out. "Seriously, Max, are you sure this is okay?"

"Absolutely. We're free to roam where we please," he said, "as long as the guards don't see us." He turned a corner.

"Please tell me you're joking."

"If I say yes, will that help you keep your voice down?"

She tugged on his arm. "Are we or are we not trespassing?"

"No, of course not," Max said. "Not really."

"Max Gallus, if we get thrown into a miserable Italian jail, don't hold your breath for any conjugal visits," she said. "Why couldn't we have just come in the morning?"

"I told you," he said. "I wanted to show you where the story of Isabelle's family began."

"In the middle of the night?"

"There are things in Herculaneum that you can't see when the sun is up, luv."

"Like what? The inside of a police car?" Shelley said. "I'm pretty sure that there are perfectly legal tours of these ruins during the day."

"But that's just it," he said. "In the daytime, you will only see ruins."

"What else is there?"

"Life," Max said, "as it was."

"Here?"

"No." He trained his flashlight to the left side of the road. A crumbling portico emerged from the shadows. He took her hand and walked over to the entrance of what had once been a seaside villa. "Here."

Shelley crossed over the threshold and tripped on a loose paving stone. "Ouch. I can't see a thing, Max."

"Good. That's the idea."

Chapter Twenty

Beginnings and boathouses

HERCULANEUM

August 24, A.D. 79

1:00 P.M.

Veneria was summoned as soon as Livia's birthing pains started. She was a wall of a woman with thick wrists and even thicker ankles. She was the most competent midwife in the whole of Herculaneum and commanded the birthing room with military precision.

She never smiled. Or cried. Or frowned. She simply twisted the lobe of her right ear. No one knew what that meant exactly, and they were not supposed to. Veneria thought it best to keep her feelings to herself. Midwives like her brought only two types of news: good and bad. She did not have the luxury to be touched by either. Both required tears and she was too old and tired to shed them for other people. And so she twisted her earlobe and didn't smile. Or cry. Or frown.

Veneria twisted her ear a lot today. This was not the first time she had been called to Livia's side. She had been to the birthing room of the seaside villa three times in the past twelve years. Each time had been more difficult than the last, and each time she was the bearer of news. It was never good.

Livia reclined, naked, on a low wooden bed, a small pillow under her hips. It was her fourth hour of labor. Her knees were bent and her pale thighs were parted for Veneria's inspection. In truth, she no longer needed Veneria to tell her what to do. She was all too familiar with the steps of birth. And burial. Three small clay amphorae containing the bones of her sons had already been laid to rest under the eaves of her house.

Livia surrendered every decision to the midwife. She did not trust herself with even the smallest action. She was able to endure the pain only because she clung to the hope that this time—if she was stronger, if she could be braver, if she followed the midwife's every instruction perfectly—her baby would live.

Veneria massaged Livia's swollen belly with a soft cloth soaked in warm olive oil pressed from her husband's vast groves. She looked at the young woman's face. Livia was no longer the rosy sixteen-year-old Veneria had first attended to. She had lost three sons since then and her body had paid the price. But though her body had grown brittle and thin, her hope had not. It was this hope that made Veneria twist her earlobe purple, more than all the dead children she had laid in Livia's arms. She did not enjoy seeing it crushed.

Veneria wished Livia was more like her husband. Maximus no longer seemed to hope, and this made it easier for her to bring him the news. She would find him waiting for her on the terrace overlooking the bay, watching the waves wash onto the narrow beach. He never said a word, but his eyes told her that he already knew what she was going to say.

Veneria continued to rub Livia's belly. "Breathe," she said.

Livia hastened to obey. She opened her mouth. Her chest tightened. She drew a breath and sucked in dread. It was happening again.

Veneria wiped the cold sweat from Livia's forehead. She signaled her assistants to refill the sheep bladders with warm oil and lay them at Livia's sides.

Livia could not feel their heat. She could not feel anything other than fear.

Veneria held her firmly by the shoulders. "Look at me," she said. "Do you want your baby to live?"

Livia nodded through her tears.

"Then breathe."

Maximus watched the waves roll to the shore. He thought about his wife in the birthing room. Her fears on their wedding night thirteen years ago had been unfounded. He had grown to love her more deeply than he thought was possible.

Possible. Maximus sighed. The word seemed foreign now. The borders of the possible had shrunk with every dead son. When he was younger, it had stretched before him, vaster than his olive groves. Now he could hold it in his palm. He inhaled deeply. He needed this time to mourn. He already knew what was going to happen next. He tightened his fist around the *bulla* intended for his child. Protective charms clinked inside the golden amulet. Maximus knew the token was premature, that it was to be given to a child only upon *dies lustricus,* the day of naming. But he could not wait. Eight days was too long to wait to give his son a name, nine days an eternity to name his daughter. His children never lived that long. He needed to give his child all the protection he could. Perhaps then the baby would live long enough for him to hold it in his arms. He rested his hands on the low wall overlooking the beach. He had never felt so old or tired.

It seemed a lifetime ago that he had stood at the altar, a haughty eighteen-year-old boy, scowling at the veiled young girl who stood before him.

"*Quando tu Gaius, ego Gaia,*" his bride vowed before the priest.

When and where you are Gaius, I then and there am Gaia. Maximus wondered what that was even supposed to mean. Whatever it meant, it sounded suffocating. He adjusted the wreath of flowers that was slipping off his head. He had not wanted this marriage, and from the pained look on his bride's face, neither had she.

But their lives and choices were not their own. Maximus was his father's only child and Livia her father's only daughter. They were their families' most valuable commodities, and their union made for excellent commerce. And so Maximus and Livia stood under bands of wool and flowery boughs, sealing the most unbreakable of business contracts in the atrium of Livia's father's house.

Maximus sighed. This wedding was just the beginning of his doom, he thought. Hordes of noisy children were demanded of him and his wife in great haste. He did not like children and thought they were the utterly inconvenient by-product of an otherwise enjoyable act. He was very aware that as a Roman father it would be his ultimate duty to be the guardian of his family and secure his children's future. In return, they would secure his. Through them, his name and legacy would live forever. Immortality, he was convinced, was not a fair trade for having to fill his home with clumsy short people with runny noses.

Maximus's only consolation was that he and his new bride would be making his family's holiday villa in Herculaneum their permanent residence. His father had acquired more farmlands near Vesuvius, and he was to oversee the estate. He could not decide what he loved most about Herculaneum: the fact that its distance from Rome would deter his in-laws from visiting or that it overlooked the sea. He drifted off into a daydream of fishing boats, water, and escape. He would find an island, he imagined, where he could hide forever from the thinly veiled misery standing in front of him. When and where this Gaius went, he sneered, would be none of Gaia's business.

The lavish dinner reception at Livia's family home was over. The wedding procession that followed ended at the door of Maximus's house. Hymns had been sung, sesame cakes eaten, and nuts showered on the couple. All that was left was for Maximus and Livia to enter their home as husband and wife.

Maximus carried Livia over the threshold. It was forbidden for a bride to walk into her new home. If she did, she risked tripping, a very bad omen for the marriage.

He, however, did not need any omens to make him feel worse. Though his bride was far from heavy, his knees nearly buckled under the weight of the world he felt he now carried.

Maximus watched as Livia kindled the atrium hearth with the wedding torch. The hearth blazed and she tossed the torch to the gathered guests. They scrambled for the lucky souvenir. An ember flew onto Maximus's cheek. He flinched as his future burned into his skin.

Maximus studied Livia as she stood at the foot of their bed. The light from the oil lamps bathed her in a golden glow, revealing her silhouette beneath the white wedding tunic. His eyes lingered on the embroidered woolen band around her waist. It was the knot of Hercules. Livia's stepmother had tied it around her when she helped Livia dress that morning. He alone would have the privilege of unknotting it. If only love came as easily as lust, he thought. "Come here," he said.

Livia walked toward him. Maximus thought that she looked like a deer he had once killed: beautiful and terrified. "Unbraid your hair."

Her lips trembled as she pulled the ribbons that held the six thick plaits of her dark hair in place. Her long hair fell over her shoulders.

"You're a goddess." Maximus said this softly, not to seduce her but because it was true. He reached out to untie the knot at her waist. This part of his duty was not so terrible.

"But you do not love me," Livia said.

He pulled his hand back. In that moment he envied the gods. They snatched mortals from meadows and loved them wantonly. Perhaps, he thought, immortality gave them no other choice; their mortal lovers withered in a blink of their eternal eyes. But people loved differently. They loved slowly and cautiously because their hearts broke more easily than clay. Maximus sighed and looked away. "No," he said, "I do not."

She took her husband's hands and pressed his fingers around the knot that kept her clothed.

"I thought you were scared."

"I am."

"Then why . . ."

"I am scared that you will not love me, husband," Livia said, "as I already love you."

MAXIMUS AND LIVIA'S VILLA
HERCULANEUM
🌿 A.D. *67*

Within a few months of their wedding, all of Maximus's fears and expectations had evaporated more quickly than the foam left on the shore by the crashing waves. If someone had told him nine months earlier that this is how he would feel about starting a family, he would have said that too much cheap wine had addled the person's mind. But perhaps it was he who was drunk and it was Livia who filled his cup.

His wife's youth was deceiving, he thought. Livia had lost her mother early in life. She had been too young to be scarred but was old enough to remember the fleeting joy of her mother's embrace. He was convinced that her mother's death had taught Livia how to live—and love—as breathlessly and boldly as any goddess. He knew this as surely as he knew that he was the mortal she had stolen from the meadow.

Maximus struggled to imagine a happiness greater than what he felt at this very moment. This was impossible, he decided, since every crevice of his life was already filled to overflowing with joy. And yet he knew, as he stood on his terrace and watched the fishing boats return from the coast, that he would be a happier man before the sun set on this day. This was the day he would become a father.

His thoughts drifted to how he had made love to his wife that morning. He remembered opening his eyes and being drawn immediately to the roundness of Livia's breasts and pregnant belly. She had never looked more beautiful and he had never wanted her more. He would have lived in those seconds forever, but his longing for the child told him to be patient. Until his child was born and his family was complete, forever would have to wait.

Livia stirred in her sleep as he drew circles on her belly. She peeked at him through half-open eyelids and smiled. "You'll wake the baby," she said. He grinned and told her that he was sure his son wouldn't mind a visit. He kissed her deeply.

The sea wind blew through his hair and brought Maximus back to the present. He glanced at the beach and saw that the fishing boats had been stowed away in the arched vaults by the shore. Their leathery crews were now climbing up the wide stone ramp built into the wall of the town. The men were tired but smiling. They were on their way home to their children. Soon, he thought, there would be children running to greet him at the door, too.

Footsteps shuffled behind him. It was the midwife. He smiled so broadly, it hurt. He did not yet see that she was tugging at her ear, begging him to be strong.

MAXIMUS AND LIVIA'S VILLA
HERCULANEUM

August 24, A.D. 79

Maximus dried his eyes with his tunic. They appeared less amber through his tears. He looked at the courtyard, expecting to see Veneria soon. She would bring him her news just as she had done three times before. He practiced standing tall, willing himself to be the pillar his wife soon would need. But his legs crumpled beneath him. The *bulla* slipped from his grip and clattered to the ground.

Maximus struggled to get up, surprised by how much his grief had weakened his knees, but he could not. A vase shattered on the floor next to him, and its clay pieces continued to rattle on the tiles, jostling against one another in a race to his fingertips. He realized that he was not the one who was trembling. It was the ground.

The quake stopped as suddenly as it started. It had been the strongest of the tremors plaguing Herculaneum in recent days. Maximus snatched the amulet from the floor and secured it in the folds of his toga. He sprinted to the birthing room, skidding over broken clay.

"Livia!" A wave of relief washed over him when he saw his wife lying on the bed. She looked terrified, but she was safe. And so was the child inside her round naked belly. He ran to her side. He pressed his face against her stomach and wondered why children had to be born. He had felt no greater joy than when his unborn sons had moved under his cheek. He was a father to them then, much more than he was when he held their lifeless bodies in his arms.

Veneria tugged at her earlobe and rolled it between her fingers. The tremor had shaken her courage but not her focus. She checked between Livia's thighs and saw that she was ready to be transferred to the birthing chair. "It's time," she told her assistants.

The three sturdy tan-skinned women stared at her blankly, frozen by the shock of the quake.

"Now." Veneria did not raise her voice, but its gravity brought the room to attention.

Maximus stepped aside as two of the assistants hurried to Livia. They hooked their arms around hers and helped her off the bed. The third readied the wooden birthing chair.

Livia clung to the women. They lowered her onto the crescent-shaped hole in the chair's seat. This was where her baby would be pulled through, she thought. She leaned against the chair's thick back and gripped its curved armrests.

Maximus turned to leave the room, as all men were expected to. His heart screamed for him to stay. And so did his wife. She reached out to him and Maximus took her hand. Another tremor, stronger than the first, pulled him from her and threw him to the ground.

Veneria's assistants screamed. They grabbed hold of the birthing chair and one another.

"Silence!" Veneria ordered.

The assistants looked at her, unsure if her command was meant for them or the ground.

"The baby is coming now. I can see the head." Veneria wiped her face with her apron. She pressed down on Livia's belly. "Push."

The tremor subsided as Livia's pain grew. She strained against the arms of Veneria's assistants. She felt her body ripping apart with every push.

"Be strong, love." Maximus gripped Livia's hand. His palm was as icy as hers. He closed his eyes and prayed to Nona, the goddess of pregnancy, the spinner of life's thread. But it was her sister's wrinkled face that Maximus saw in his head. Morta sneered at him, holding up the shears that she used to cut what Nona spun. She ran her crooked finger over its dull blade, a cruel promise of how the pain would be slow.

Veneria positioned her hands around the baby's crowning head. "Just one more push," she said.

An animal-like cry rose out of Livia's throat.

No one heard her.

A thunderous roar drowned out her scream. It echoed in the arcaded streets of Herculaneum and rumbled through the ground, bringing the town to its knees.

Maximus was not sure if the ground had stopped shaking. His body had not. He unclasped his trembling hands from his ears. The terrible roar had stopped. And so had Livia's screams. There was only a hollow ringing in his head. It was like being underwater, he thought. He watched a mute scene unfold before him.

Veneria led the pantomime. She held an infant in her arms, its body staining her tunic with blood. Maximus could not see its face or hear its cry, but his deafness gave him hope. As long as he could not hear Veneria's condolences, he could pretend that his child was alive.

Veneria approached Maximus and Livia, but her eyes were not on them or the child she carried. Her gaze was fixed on the sky outside the window. Wordlessly—because she was no longer capable of speaking—she laid the baby, as was the custom, at its father's feet.

The ringing in Maximus's ears faded. He could now hear the lusty cries of the child. The sound was new to him. He had never heard anything so puzzling. It made him want to laugh and cry at the same time. And so he did. The baby had been laid at his feet to be judged if it was worthy of life. He took the bundle from the floor and looked into her bright brown eyes. He knew then that the real question was whether he was worthy of her. He turned to his wife. "Livia, we have a daughter—"

That's when he saw it—the abomination that already gripped Veneria and her assistants by their throats. His daughter slipped from his arms. Livia caught her. Maximus knelt beside his family.

The mountain outside his window had spawned a demon. It writhed upward toward the sky, taking the shape of a black and gnarled tree, more enormous than any myth's imagining. Its sprawling canopy scorched the daylight from the sky, gorging itself on the sun and a town's shattered peace. It was this demon's birth cry that had roared through Herculaneum, Maximus thought, and it was its mother's labor that had shaken the ground.

He held his family close. He kissed his daughter's head and asked for her forgiveness for the choice he was making for her. He would let her live in a world that was about to end.

The tremors were growing stronger. Blue lightning ripped across the dark clouds spewing from the mountain. It was clear to Maximus that the nightmare was not about to fade away. Things were only getting worse.

He walked over to his daughter on the bed. She slept soundly. Livia lay beside her, too weak to move. Maximus kissed both of them lightly on their foreheads before leaving the room.

From his terrace he could see the sea churning. Its convulsions almost matched the chaos on the shore. The town of five thousand was spilling onto the beach, neighbors and friends trampling one another for the remaining boats. Fishermen held their ground for the highest bid.

The panic below was no place for his family, but as the sky grew darker and the thunder louder, Maximus accepted that he had no other choice. Livia was in no condition to flee the countryside by foot as many already had. Their only possible escape was by sea. If they didn't leave now, they never would.

One fisherman was now tenfold wealthier for the trade he had just made. The sea-weathered man waited for his passengers at the end of the shallows. His fishing boat rocked against the jetty, pummeled by the rising waves. Two grim-faced slaves drew their swords and kept the crowd gathering on the dock away from the boat for their master.

Maximus carried Livia from their villa to the teeming beach. Veneria followed him closely, clutching their newborn daughter under her cloak. They pushed through the swarm of people. Their clothes and skin became stained with the sweat and tears of the frantic throng. They made their way to the jetty.

Maximus set a barely conscious Livia down on the fishing boat. Veneria squeezed next to her and propped her upright with her shoulder. The baby wriggled against her chest, searching for a breast to suckle. The women servants and their children boarded the boat next. The crowd on the dock pressed closer. Maximus's men waved them away with their swords.

Maximus stroked his daughter's pink cheek and climbed back to the jetty. He took his place beside his men and drew his sword. He ordered the crowd to move back. He knew that if he dropped his sword even slightly, the crowd would swarm the boat—and all that was important to him in this world would be lost to the sea.

The fisherman called to Maximus and urged that they cast off. The waves were swelling and soon even escape by boat would no longer be possible.

But Maximus was not yet ready to leave. There was enough room for four more people. He searched the faces of the crowd around him and struggled to make the impossible choice.

A woman raised her small child above the horde and begged him to take her son. He reached through the wall of bodies between them and pulled the woman and her child from the frenzy. The pleas and screams of the crowd grew louder. They edged closer.

Two more, Maximus thought. An old woman stumbled, struggling to get up. He lowered his sword and bent down to take her hand. A large man burst from the crowd and rushed toward him, his sword pointed at Maximus's chest. Maximus parried his thrust and knocked the sword out of the man's hand. It fell into the water. The man spat and tackled him to the dock. Maximus's men jumped on the attacker and tried to pull him off. The crowd surged toward the boat.

Maximus felt the man's grip tighten around his neck. He gasped for air. One of his slaves pressed his sword against the man's throat and sliced it from ear to ear. Blood gushed into Maximus's nose and mouth. He choked and shoved the man off him. The corpse fell into the water next to the old woman Maximus had tried to help. She was floating facedown, her tunic swirling in the roiling sea.

His attacker's blood splattered from Maximus's lips as he begged the crowd to stop pressing forward. He pointed his sword at them to keep them at bay and ordered his men onto the boat. The crowd edged closer, inches from his sword. He thrust his sword forward. The mob stumbled back against one another. A man fell into the water. Maximus swung his sword again. He was all that stood between the mob and his family. Reason had left their eyes. They were going to rush the boat.

A large wave crashed into the fishing boat. Maximus heard his daughter cry. There was no more time. He looked at his family and tried to remember their faces. Livia opened her eyes and he gazed into them for the last time. The fisherman screamed for him to cast off over the roar of the surging mob. Maximus raised his sword and cut the rope that tethered the boat to the dock. Then he spun around, his blade meeting the wall of flesh.

The mob lost their taste for blood when the boat carrying Maximus's family sailed away. They were too broken to hate or hope. Maximus crawled to the shore. He had fallen into the water when the crowd pounced on him. He clung to the timbers of the jetty and waited for them to disperse.

He took shelter in one of the vaults where the boats were kept in the harbor. They were all empty now. He had no desire to return to his villa. The emptiness of his home would kill him sooner than any demon would.

The chaos on the beach was gone, a dense silence taking its place. People no longer shoved and clawed at one another. There was nothing left to fight over.

Maximus warmed his hands by the fire at the mouth of the boathouse. He looked around the room and into the faces of the people crouched inside it. He wondered if any of those huddled there had been among the mob on the jetty earlier. If they had been, he did not recognize them, and nor, it seemed, did they recognize him. Perhaps this was because they were all different people now, stripped of everything but their names. He was now a husband without a wife, a father without a daughter, a man without a life. He bowed his head and folded his arms around the cold pit in his stomach. Charms tinkled in his toga. He reached inside the folds and pulled out the *bulla,* the protection he had failed to give his nameless child. Hot tears welled in his eyes.

He heard a child whimper against his mother's pregnant belly. The woman bundled the young boy closer to her and soothed him with a lullaby. Two more, he thought sadly. The boat could have carried two more. A raspy voice whispered in his ear. He jerked his head back. An old man was speaking to him.

"She is a widow," he told Maximus.

Maximus looked at the widow's swollen belly and thought that she could not have lost her husband too long ago—seven months at the most.

"Her husband was killed today," the old man said.

"Today?" Maximus asked. "How?"

"I heard people say that he was murdered by runaway slaves on the jetty," the man said. "They sliced his throat before stealing his boat. Now his family is stranded here with the rest of us."

"Oh." The truth behind the man's death dawned on Maximus. There was no point correcting the old man, he thought. It would be easier for the man's widow to grieve her husband as she remembered him. The man Maximus's slave had killed had attacked him out of desperation, and if their roles had been reversed, Maximus knew that he would have done the same.

"But I'm sure we will be rescued," the old man said. "The boats will come back for us, you'll see."

Chapter Twenty-one

Shears and silence

HERCULANEUM EXCAVATION SITE

🌿 *Five Years Ago*

Shelley and Max walked down the stone ramp that led to the ancient waterfront. The eruption of Vesuvius had pushed the sea over half a mile back from where it used to lap at the shores of Herculaneum. Now, instead of a view of the coast, a seventy-foot wall of hardened volcanic flow stood at the harbor's edge, marking the boundary of the excavation site.

Built into the wall at the bottom of the ramp was a row of large, arched stone vaults. Max pulled back the tarpaulin cover from one of the vaults and ushered Shelley inside.

She sat in the hollow of the vaulted boathouse next to Max, looking out into the darkness where the sea once was.

"They found three hundred bodies huddled together in these vaults. One of the skeletons they found was of a pregnant mother still clutching her son," Max said.

Shelley leaned against his shoulder. "Tell me how they died."

"That's not necessary."

"I want to know."

Max sighed. "Shortly after midnight, the pressure that held up the massive volcanic cloud column over Vesuvius collapsed, sending a tidal wave of superheated gas, ash, and molten rock crashing down the mountain. It hurtled toward Herculaneum at a speed of one hundred kilometers per hour, scorching everything in its path. It took only about four minutes for the burning wave to engulf the town and reach the shore.

"Based on the contorted limbs of the skeletons they found here, scientists say that the people died from intense thermal shock. Plainly speaking, they were cooked to death. The extreme heat—around four hundred degrees centigrade—caused their hands and feet to contract into a death grip. Their bones and teeth cracked and their flesh vaporized. Their brains boiled in their head and their skulls exploded."

Shelley covered her mouth with her hand and tried not to be sick.

"But the scientists believe that all this happened in the blink of an eye," Max said. "The people were incinerated instantly and their death was painless and swift."

"Thank God," she said. "They didn't even know what happened to them."

"Shelley," he said, "I said, that's what the scientists *believe*."

"What do you mean?"

"Death is never swift, luv," Max said, "no matter how those left behind would like to comfort themselves with the thought."

HERCULANEUM

  August 25, A.D. 79

1:00 A.M.

The dark cloud over Vesuvius bled seamlessly into the night sky. Maximus stood on the beach and waited for a flash of lightning to reveal where it ended and where it began. He wanted to see the face of his enemy before it struck him down. He did not have to wait long. Before the next flash struck, the demon was racing down the mountain to meet him.

Maximus watched the broiling tree trunk collapse upon itself and surge toward Herculaneum. The beach shook as heated gusts of wind blew down from the mountain and pushed back the sea. This is how he would die. Interesting, he thought, surprising himself at his detachment. He did not know if his family was alive, and without them, he did not wish to live. He welcomed the end. Perhaps in the fields of Elysium he would see his wife and daughter again.

A child began to cry. The sound came from inside the boathouse. Maximus peered in. It was the child of the man who had attacked him. No lullaby could quiet him now. His mother rocked him against her breast. The people in the boathouse huddled closer together. If they had seen what was coming for them, he thought, they would not have bothered. No vault or embrace would save any of them.

Maximus looked up at the black wave sweeping over Herculaneum. He felt its heat on his skin. It rose over his villa, engulfing it. It surged over the stone ramp leading to the shore. And then it fell upon him. In the corner of his eye, he caught a glint of metal. It was Morta raising her dull shears.

A friend had told Maximus once that his entire life had flashed before him when his horse threw him, and he thought he was going to die. Maximus now knew that his friend was a liar. Death was not as kind as his friend had led him to believe. What Maximus saw as the wave cooked him from the inside was not the life that he had lived—it was the life he would not have. He watched the fishing boat carry his family to safety. He watched his daughter grow into a beautiful stranger with amber eyes just like his own. He watched his widow find comfort in another man's arms.

Livia.

Her name was going to be his last thought. Maximus wondered if there was still time to say it out loud.

He had difficulty telling which came first: his lungs roasting, his tears broiling his eyes, or his skin flaking into ash.

Maximus did not know what came next because he no longer had a body to feel the pain. But there were two things he did know.

It was now silent.

And he did not want to die.

HERCULANEUM EXCAVATION SITE

❧ *Five Years Ago*

1:00 A.M.

Shelley sighed as they made their way out of the ruins. "I can't decide."

"Decide what?"

"I can't decide which was more tragic," she said. "How this family began or how it ended."

"Dying is not the real tragedy, Shelley."

"It's not?"

"Forgetting is."

She thought of Dex, his pictures, and the train he refused to jump from. He had said that being forgotten was worse than dying. She now wondered if what he was really afraid of was being the one who would forget. Perhaps he had taken those photographs for himself as much as for Sheila. It was the same reason, she realized, that Max took people on his tour. Isabelle and Livia were long gone. They would not care if they were remembered or not. It was Max who did not want to forget—and she did not know why. But she did know that she and Max would now remember their story together. She reached for his hand. "There was no tragedy here, then."

Max smiled and pulled her into an embrace.

"You know, something just occurred to me," Shelley said.

"What?" he asked.

"There weren't any chickens or eggs in this story."

Max smiled. "You're right," he said. "And look what happened."

Chapter Twenty-two

Shells and seasickness

A FLIGHT TO THE PHILIPPINES

❧ *Now*

Shelley fastened her seat belt as the plane began its descent to Manila. She wondered how much of what Max had said about Herculaneum was true. She hoped that he was lying. Imagining how a stranger suffered in those final moments on the beach without feeling some measure of empathy was impossible. Realizing that the stranger was her husband . . . She couldn't bear the thought. Her eyes darted around her, searching for a distraction. She glimpsed Paolo's face. Something was wrong.

It was a change so subtle, she thought, that if Paolo hadn't looked so much like her husband, she would have missed it. But Paolo did look like Max, and Shelley knew their shared face well enough to see how the laugh lines around their eyes could deepen ever so slightly, how the back of their throats could constrict, and how the muscle behind their brow could tense up. It was the same way Max had looked after he had seen Mihael. She could tell that Paolo was scared. "What's the matter?"

"Huh?" Paolo pasted on a quick smile. "Nothing."

"No," she said. "Something's bothering you. It's written all over your face."

He sighed. "It's . . . it's just that I didn't expect it to happen like that."

"What are you talking about?"

"Maximus was on the beach," Paolo said. "I think that's when it happened."

"What happened?"

"That's when he became . . ." he said, "immortal."

"Oh . . . that," Shelley said softly. She pulled her seat belt tighter.

Paolo turned away and took a deep breath. "I just didn't think you actually had to die," he said, "to live forever."

"I . . ." Shelley grasped for a lie to comfort them both. She felt the landing gear being lowered and gripped Paolo's arm. Her heart raced. It was her turn to be afraid.

"Are you okay?" he asked.

"No." Shelley's voice trembled. The island of Boracay was still two hundred and seventeen miles across the sea and another plane and boat ride from Manila, but the thought of standing on the same ground as Max drained the last of her courage.

BORACAY, PHILIPPINES

🌿 *Now*

You can tell a lot about a place by how it feels between your toes.

Shelley's ten digits took great pride in their astute ability to judge an area's character. Her left big toe was an especially thoughtful observer. By instinct, it could tell within seconds of touching the ground if a place was rough, slippery, or soft. Now it decided, as Shelley waded to the shore, that this particular island required a whole different category of praise. *Paradise* came close, but that rang a bit trite. *A happy accident*, it thought—a string of mishaps, to be precise—suited it much better. Shelley's toe was utterly convinced that Boracay had not come about on purpose. If it had, it would be forced to accuse God of favoritism— something that the Catholic in it refused to let it do.

Shelley, however, was less reverent than her appendage. God, she decided, as she waded away from the outrigger that had ferried them to the island, was selfish, and this was where He hoarded beauty like a secret stash of chocolate. Boracay was His kitchen drawer.

Powder-fine sand caressed her bare feet. The smooth, weightless grains swirled in the water and settled in the spaces between her toes. This was what life was supposed to be like, she thought—before she stubbed her toe on a piece of driftwood, hopped on one foot, and fell into the water. Salt water shot up her nose. She choked and pulled herself out. She grunted from the weight of her waterlogged jeans as she fished her backpack from the shallows. Her dignity was harder to recover.

Paolo chuckled. "Good form. Smooth entry. I'd have to give that a solid eight point five."

She smoothed back her dripping hair and wrung the water from her blouse. "Well, I find that a swim always clears the head before confronting an immortal. You should give it a try."

Paolo was staring at a startled yellow-and-black-striped fish before he realized that Shelley had shoved him into the sea.

Shelley stood under the shower of the small bamboo hut she and Paolo had rented. The water was as warm and salty as the sea she had dragged herself out of. She unwrapped a small complimentary bar of green soap and rubbed it between her palms. It refused to lather. She rubbed it again and coaxed a bubble. Getting clean was going to take longer than she had expected. But she had time. Unless she wanted to traipse around the island dressed in Max's plaid bathrobe and gym socks, she would have to wait for Paolo to return with some dry clothes.

Shelley was beginning to think that the green brick would catch fire before it yielded another bubble. She gave up and set the bar down. She ran her hands under the stream of water falling on her shoulders and neck. Something hard brushed against her fingers. It was the mosaic tile from Torcello. Her fingers shook as she fumbled with its clasp. The ocher tile clattered on the bathroom floor. For a moment, she considered leaving it there. She steeled herself and picked up the tile, then set it on the tiny glass shelf above the sink. She stuck her head under the shower and covered her face with her hands. A cold band of metal pressed against her cheek. She pulled off her wedding ring and placed it next to the tile pendant.

Shelley stared at the two tiny objects. They were the last reminders that she had once trusted and loved a man completely. It broke her heart to leave them, but she refused to let Max see her still wearing the relics of his illusion. She had never felt more naked. She wanted to dash out of the shower and throw on whatever she could find. Even a palm leaf would have been better than her emotional undress.

"I'm back," Paolo called through the bathroom door. "I have your clothes. The lady at the store said I could take them back if they didn't fit."

"Great. Thanks." She grabbed a towel and rubbed herself dry, then stuck her hand through the door.

Paolo handed her the plastic shopping bag. "I got you some flip-flops, too."

"Thanks." Shelley opened the bag. "Um . . . Paolo?"

"Yes?"

"A blue bikini? We're not exactly on vacation, you know."

"I figured that you'd prefer swimming in that rather than the sundress I bought for you to wear over it," he said. "Unless, of course, you really do enjoy jumping into the water with all your clothes on."

"Swimming?" Shelley poked her head out the door.

"Yup," Paolo said. "Remember? The website said that we needed to swim over from the boat to The Shell."

"Brilliant." She was already nauseous thinking about what it would be like to see and talk to Max again. Confronting him wearing a tiny blue bikini was not going to help. She wondered what she would say to him. She should have made a list.

Hi? I don't know if you remember me, but I'm supposed to be your widow. Maximus the Immortal, I presume?

Sorry to drop in like this, but I was just desperate to find out what you put in your baked eggs.

"I hired a boat to take us to The Shell," Paolo said. "We can leave as soon as you're ready."

"Paolo, if we wait until I'm ready," Shelley said, "we'll never leave."

. . .

The small outrigger bobbed in the water, balanced by a pair of bamboo poles that stretched from its sides like wings. The boatman, a solidly built man named Manny, helped Shelley to her seat.

"How long will it take us to get to The Shell, Manny?" Paolo settled onto the damp wooden bench next to Shelley.

"Ten minutes," Manny said. The lines on his face deepened as he spoke, mapping his life across his coffee-colored skin. He switched the motor on and steered his boat away from the shore.

Manny's voice rang in Shelley's ears above the motor's rumbling. Ten minutes. She couldn't decide if it was too short or too long. All she knew was that it made her want to hijack one of the bright yellow banana boats zipping past them and head in the opposite direction. A group of screaming tourists bounced past her on a yellow inflatable tube. Their cheeks flapped in the wind, making their faces look like the clay art project she had made in kindergarten. Shelley didn't have to speak Korean to know what they were saying. Their high-pitched shrieks translated into fun in any language. Of course they could have been screaming for help, but she chose to believe the former.

Shelley sighed.

These were people who lived in a world that was governed by all the natural laws, she thought. If the speedboat pulling the inflatable craft happened to take a particularly sharp turn, physics dictated that the large yellow tube skidding behind it would take a nasty tumble and send its passengers flying through the air. And if one of those passengers—bless his soul—happened to crash into the water at a horribly wrong angle and break his neck, biology dictated that he would die—and not click his head back into place, towel himself dry, and hide from his grieving widow on some remote island.

Manny steered their boat down the coast and left the yellow blurs behind. There were no screaming tourists there. There was only aquamarine. Shelley realized that it was the color of quiet.

A man straddling an old surfboard paddled toward their outrigger.

A small pyramid of green coconuts was piled in front of his knees. He held up a coconut and a plastic straw and waved at Manny.

"Would you like to buy one?" Manny asked Shelley.

She shook her head and managed a weak smile. Unless the coconuts were filled with scotch, she didn't think they were going to do her much good.

The coconut vendor paddled away.

Shelley held her breath as their boat rounded the limestone cliffs at the end of the coast. Lush vegetation cascaded over the rocks, softening their rugged beauty. Where the sandy yellow stone was barefaced, the sun set it ablaze with a golden glow. She shielded her eyes from the glare.

"There it is," Manny said.

Shelley turned in the direction Manny was pointing. She bit her lip. Stubby trees and wild bushes sprouted from the cliff wall. Peeking through the green drapery was a small thatched hut. She heard Paolo take a deep breath.

The boat came to a stop several yards from the rocky shore. "What time should I come back for you?" Manny asked.

"We . . . uh . . . don't really know how long this will take," Paolo said.

"Would it be possible for you to wait for us here?" Shelley asked. She thought that it would be a good idea to have Manny nearby in case she needed to be fished out of the sea after the nervous breakdown she was going to have shortly.

Manny nodded.

"Oh, and do you know CPR?" she asked.

Manny gave her a puzzled look.

"That's okay. Never mind," Shelley said. She wasn't sure if she wanted to be revived, anyway. She just wanted to make sure that her mother got her remains.

"Let's go." Paolo stood up and pulled off his shirt. He dove into the water, emerging a few feet away, waving at Shelley to follow.

Shelley looked at him and then glanced down at her feet. They remained firmly anchored to the outrigger.

"Come on!" Paolo called.

She apologized to her appendages, slipped off her sundress, and jumped overboard.

A glittering swirl of iridescent fish scattered around her. Shelley briefly thought that she was seeing stars, which was never a good thing in her case. She swam toward Paolo.

He reached the cliff first. He climbed onto a narrow limestone ledge and helped Shelley out of the water.

She shivered in her blue bikini. The Shell was now just twenty feet directly above where she stood. She gripped Paolo's hand to keep from diving back into the sea. A rope ladder dropped behind her, sending a breeze through the fine hairs on her neck. She lunged forward. Paolo caught her before she fell. Shelley wrestled free of his grasp and prepared to jump away.

Paolo grabbed her arm. "It's too late to back out now. He's seen us." He handed the rope ladder to her. "Ladies first."

"Absolutely not." Shelley thrust the ladder back at him. "You go first."

"So you can be halfway back to London by the time I reach the top?" Paolo said. "I don't think so."

Shelley knew that he was right. If Paolo made the mistake of letting her out of his sight, she would not hesitate to make her getaway. She gripped the rope and planted a foot on a rung. "Fine."

Shelley climbed with her eyes shut, finding the sight of the jagged rocks below and the hut above equally terrifying. She reached upward for the next rung. Her hand closed around thin air. She pried her eyes open and looked up. A rung was missing. But this was not what made her freeze. A shadow moved across the slits between the hut's bamboo floor. Her knuckles turned white as she gripped the rope tighter.

"You okay up there?" Paolo asked.

Shelley chose not to answer. If she opened her mouth, she would start crying. She reached for the next rung. The open hatch in the hut's slatted floor loomed closer. She pulled herself up the last rung. Stars twinkled in the corner of her eye and this time Shelley was certain that it wasn't a school of sparkly fish. Damn it. Not now. She reached for the bamboo handlebar next to the hatch. A hand closed around hers.

Warm fingers clasped Shelley's clammy palm and pulled her into the hut. Shelley clambered up on her hands and knees.

A pair of bare feet stood in front of her—Shelley swallowed—attached to the longest pair of shapely bronze legs she had ever seen. She jerked her head up only to see the last thing any woman searching for her husband wanted to see. Draped in an orange tie-dyed sarong and smiling at Shelley with sensuous lips was the reason the word *jealousy* was coined. The woman was the island—a shore of caramel skin, a sea of blue-black hair, a stream of sunshine sparkling in bright honey eyes. Shelley hated her instantly.

"Hi." The woman offered Shelley her hand. "Welcome to The Shell. I'm Sari." Her lilting voice fell in time with the reggae beat playing softly in the background.

Shelley took the woman's hand, suppressing the urge to twist it behind her back and demand to know where Max was. Her eyes darted around the empty café.

Vines grew into the crevices inside the hut and entwined themselves around its bamboo posts, making the hut look more organic than manmade. Man's touch, however, or more accurately, a woman's touch was still evident in the mismatched collection of batik drapes, tablecloths, and pillows strewn around the café. The eclectic decor gave the hut a laidback bohemian feel. Shelley, however, was anything but relaxed.

"So what would you like for breakfast?" Sari asked. She ushered Shelley to one of the café's three bamboo tables.

Shelley sat down at a table overlooking the sea. She wondered if she had made a mistake. Perhaps she had just imagined seeing the picture of Max sipping coffee and looking out of this very window.

"I recommend the baked eggs." Sari handed Shelley a menu. "My husband's an excellent cook."

Shelley blanched. She was about to throw herself and Sari out the window when she heard Paolo clambering through the hatch. She turned to him to say a quick good-bye.

Sari ran to Paolo and gave him a tight hug, then tiptoed and kissed him on both cheeks. "It's so good to see you again, Paolo."

Shelley choked, too confused to put questions into words.

Paolo inhaled deeply. "Shelley . . ."

"Shelley?" Sari's eyes widened. "You're Shelley?"

Shelley froze. How did this woman know her?

"I've heard all about you," Sari said. "Please wait here while I go get my husband. He's in the kitchen." She disappeared through the curtain of seashells at the back of the room.

Shelley stared at Paolo, paralyzed by his deception. She wasn't sure if she wanted to punch him in the face or burst into tears.

He took the seat across from her. "I can explain."

"Please do," she said between clenched teeth.

"It's not what you think . . ."

"Really?" Shelley glared at him. "And what do I think?"

A buttery earthy scent wafted through the seashell curtain, bringing with it memories of Parisian grandes dames, Bee Gees mixed tapes, Venetian islands, and the smell of Max's skin against hers. Shelley could already picture its bubbling yellow crust. The curtain parted to reveal the dish that had spurred her journey. Sari carried it out on a wooden tray together with two cups of coffee.

"Sundays with Shell," Sari said as she set the dish down on the table. "On the house."

Shelley averted her eyes from the plate, half expecting to see cheese melting over her hot and still beating heart, freshly hacked out of her chest. She scrambled to throw up out the window. She knocked her chair to the floor.

A hand closed over Shelley's shoulder as she hung over the ledge, desperate for the fresh sea air.

"Shelley, are you okay?" a warm voice asked her.

Shelley spun around. He was just as she remembered him.

"You don't look too good," he said. "Do you need a doctor?"

She staggered back. "Dex?"

"You must be seasick," Sari said. "I'll get you some water." She disappeared into the kitchen.

Dex set Shelley's chair upright and helped her sit down.

Shelley stared at him. "What . . . what are you doing here?"

Dex smiled and sat next to her. "My wife, Sari, and I own this place. Our house is just farther up this cliff."

"Hang on. Sari's your wife?"

"Yes."

"But what about—"

"Sheila died soon after I returned home from my European tour."

"Oh."

"I met Sari here in Boracay when I was doing a piece for my website. It's called the Back—"

"The Backpacking Gourmet," Shelley said.

Dex grinned proudly. "You've heard of it?"

She nodded and glanced at Paolo. He looked away.

"After Sheila died, I decided to travel again," Dex said. "I felt closer to her that way. I felt like I was still making memories for the two of us. Eventually, I started writing about my travels. Boracay was the last place my dart landed."

"Dart?" Shelley asked.

Dex pointed to a hole-riddled map on the wall and smiled. "Ta-dah. My very scientific navigation system," he said. "I followed my dart, met Sari under a palm tree, and decided not to leave. Can you imagine my surprise when I saw Max here? I'm so sorry things didn't work out between the two of you. I had always thought that you two were perfect for each other. Max didn't like to talk about it when I asked about you, so I don't know any of the details. It's a pity we weren't able to stay in touch after the tour. My life got pretty crazy for a while . . ."

"Dex." She tried to steady her voice. "Where is Max now?"

"Well, I don't know, actually. After Sari and I convinced him to sell us this place, he packed his bags and left."

Sari walked back into the room and handed Shelley a glass of water. She turned to Paolo. "That was about two weeks after you left."

Shelley heard Paolo's breath catch in his throat. She searched his face for answers. It didn't seem so familiar now. She looked at Sari. "So you've met each other . . ."

Sari smiled and sat beside Paolo. "Yes. We had never seen a person so desperate for baked eggs and cheese. Paolo got in touch with Dex through the website. We were the ones who introduced him to Max."

Shelley glared at Paolo. "You've seen him," she said slowly, struggling to control her rage.

Paolo dropped his eyes.

"Hey, but don't worry." Dex grinned. "Max taught us his baked eggs and cheese recipe before he left. That's why everyone comes here."

Shelley's heart sank.

"Honey, didn't Max leave something for Paolo?" Sari asked Dex. "And Shelley?"

"Oh, yeah, that's right. I almost forgot. I'll go get it." Dex stood up and slipped through the shell curtains.

"That's how I knew your name," Sari told Shelley. "Before he left, Max told us that he expected Paolo to return with you."

Dex walked back to their table. He was carrying two white envelopes. He handed one of them to Shelley and the other to Paolo.

Shelley's hand shook as she took the envelope from Dex's hand. "Um, Dex, do you think you could give us a moment?"

"Of course." Dex squeezed Shelley's shoulder again.

Shelley looked into his eyes. Dex did not need words to reassure her that he knew exactly what it was like to lose the person you loved the most.

Shelley tried to smile, but a tear rolled down her cheek, betraying her true feelings. As scared and confused as she had been, she had expected Max to be there, waiting for her. The fact that he had moved on . . . It hurt more than she could have imagined.

Dex turned to Sari. "Hey, hon, um, could you help me sort things out with that new inventory program you installed on the computer? I inputted the latest stock this morning and it says that we have ten years' worth of coffee creamer."

"Oh, er, certainly," Sari said, standing up. "Please excuse us, Shelley, Paolo. We'll be up at the house if you need anything."

"We might be a while. I'm horrible at numbers." Dex gave Shelley a meaningful smile. "Enjoy your breakfast."

"Sari, Dex," Shelley called after them. "Thank you."

Dex looked back and gave Shelley a wink.

Shelley heard the back door of the hut open and shut. Dex's and Sari's footsteps grew fainter as they made their way up the steps carved into the cliff.

"Shelley," Paolo said, "I need to explain—"

She glared at him.

"I thought that Nonno would be here waiting for us," he said. "That wasn't the trade."

Trade? The word stung Shelley like alcohol poured over a fresh wound. "What trade?"

"The trade I made with him when I first found him," Paolo said.

"I don't believe you." She crumpled the envelope in her fist. "Everything you've told me is a lie."

Paolo looked directly at her. "I didn't lie to you. I saw Nonno's picture on Dex's website and in Brad's book. That's how I discovered he was alive."

"And you went looking for him," Shelley said, "without me."

"Yes."

"So what was this charade all about?"

"It wasn't—isn't—a charade," he said. "I really needed to find you."

"Why? You had already found Max," Shelley said.

"I found him, yes," Paolo said, "but finding him alone wasn't everything that I was searching for." His eyes darkened. "I came here with the same questions you have. I wanted to know who Nonno was, how it was possible that he was still alive, and why he left me." He inhaled deeply. "But I had one more question for him."

Even in the balmy Philippine sun, Shelley's skin turned to ice.

"I wanted to know," Paolo said, "how I could be like him."

Shelley clenched her fists to keep from flinging the eggs in Paolo's face.

"But he wouldn't give me the answers," he said. "He said that we would have to make a trade."

"What did Max want from you?"

"He didn't want anything from me," Paolo said. "He wanted you."

"What? Why—"

"He said that you would have the answers I was searching for—that he had already shared them with you. If I wanted to learn the truth," Paolo said, "I had to bring you here."

Tears scalded Shelley's face. "So where is he?"

"I'm sorry; I don't know."

Shelley looked down at the thin envelope in her fist. She turned it over.

Shelley

Seeing her name written in Max's hand was like hearing him whisper it in her ear. She threw the envelope away. It landed next to the open hatch.

The wind chimes stirred. The breeze lifted a corner of the envelope off the floor.

Shelley dove for it. Her fingertips grazed the edge of the paper just as it fell through the hut's entryway.

"No!" Paolo lunged toward the hatch.

Shelley slumped to the floor. Max's letter was gone. She buried her face in her hands and began to cry. She had come all this way to get answers and now she had just thrown them away.

She had been so fearful of the words she and Max would exchange when she confronted him, afraid that they would be horrible and scarring. And now she wept desperately for the soggiest scrap of half a word. She didn't even need to read it. She just wanted to have something to show for her search other than a palmful of tears.

Paolo sat next to her. "Here," he said.

Shelley looked up. He handed the crumpled envelope to her.

"But how . . ."

"It got caught on a rung," Paolo said.

Shelley could not have survived losing whatever it was the envelope contained, but she could not bring herself to thank Paolo for saving it. He had betrayed her trust just as Max had, and in that way, she thought, he was already like the man he sought to become.

"Are you going to read it?" he asked.

"No," Shelley said. "You read yours first. Aloud."

Paolo opened his envelope. Inside it was a letter and a second envelope. The smaller envelope was yellowed with age. He set the older envelope aside and unfolded the letter.

Chapter Twenty-three

Context and consequence

Paolo,

This is the tenth sheet of paper I have written your name on. Hopefully this time I will know what to write after it. (Don't worry, I recycle. I am very concerned about the planet the next generations and I will continue to inherit. I used one of the pages to write down the baked eggs and cheese recipe for Dex and Sari.) As I have not yet crumpled this sheet, I believe I am making progress, even if only by pushing this pen across the paper and writing gibberish about how environmentally conscious I am. (Did Shelley tell you about the time she won a gift voucher for banning plastic coffee stirrers in the office?)

If Shelley is with you now, then you would understand why I sent you to find her. You would know why there was no way I could have possibly told you all that you wished to know when you first came to me. I was not being cruel, as you had accused me. (You used a more colorful term as I recall, but since there is a large chance that you are reading this letter to Shelley—hence my use of English—I have taken the liberty of toning down your language.) But I deserved your anger—just as you deserved to know the truth with all its layers and context.

I asked you to find Shelley because the truth of who I am is not so much a story but a journey—a journey I had already shared with Shelley—and a journey that you, in turn, needed to *take with her to understand fully. To rattle it off to you over a cup of coffee (or even a round or two of Boracay's best mojitos) would have robbed you of the depths of a history that is as much mine as it is yours. But believe me when I tell you that it is a legacy that I wish you did not have to inherit. I kept my lifetimes from you so that I would not deprive you of your own.*

I wanted you to have your boring summer afternoons, your teenage angst, your days when your life's meaning depended solely on whether you scored a goal in soccer. I wished the mundane for you, the small and unnoticed, the simple memories painted in black and white. The gray I live in was too cruel to share.

Paolo blinked back a tear. The letter shook in his hands.

But please do not think that I kept who I really was from you. The past isn't a coat you check at the door. I raised you in the full presence of my strengths and numerous faults. I shared with you all the lessons my lifetimes have taught me with the hope that you would be spared the pain of learning them for yourself.

But, I suppose, a father cannot protect his children forever. I could not even protect my first daughter long enough to give her a name. This is the one law of the universe I have had the greatest difficulty accepting (even more than coming to terms with the fact that the world is not flat). This is perhaps the reason why it is something I have constantly had to relearn. When you found me, I realized that it was a lesson I had failed to grasp yet again. And so here you are today, released from the last of my protection, free to face the answers to all you wish to know—on your own—as it was always meant to be.

You asked me who I am. I would like to think that you have always known the answer to this, as I have never hidden it from you. I am and always will be Nonno, the man who raised you as a son. As for who I was, you now have your answer. I was Maxi-

mus, Julien, and all those lives in between—stops on my journey to become the man I am today—a father who loves you still.

By knowing who I am, the answer to your second question should become clear as well. Why did I leave you? I loved you too much to stay. You did not need my choices altering the course of your life. You had enough decisions of your own to make. I should have known though that the consequences of our choices would one day intersect. That is their nature, just as surely as the earth is round.

That is why I taught you how to trade, because that's what life is—a barter of choices and consequences. Nothing you have is without a price paid by yourself or someone else. Some days you will get more than what you paid for and on others you will pay more than what you should. (For the record, your blue stuffed elephant was always the standard price for a cup of water. I only charged extra if you wanted juice.) Our family has had a long history of getting more than they bargained for—I tried to raise you to be shrewder.

Isabelle chose love and paid the price by dying alone.

Adrien traded a moment's pleasure for his youth's years.

Uri won wars to feed his family and lost his mind.

Pavel tried to be a child forever and drowned his innocence.

Abbot Thomas worked tirelessly to strengthen the spirit and wore his body to the bone.

Ionus helped build a new world but had to leave all he knew behind.

And Maximus . . . he wanted life. And for this I continue to pay the price.

Today another trade will be concluded. You have chosen to accept the terms for the answers you wanted. You found Shelley and have brought her here. In return you have most of what you set out to find. You also, perhaps, have Shelley's hate. That, unfortunately, is part of the cost. I hope that she will find it in her heart to forgive you, but her forgiveness is yours to earn—in the same way that I have to make my own amends.

But the trade is not yet complete. You require one more an-
swer, but I will give you two.

Can you be immortal? If you had asked me that question
before I met Mihael that night in Slovenia, I would have been
very relieved to tell you that this was not at all possible. Until I
saw him, I lived with the comfort that the cruelty of my life was
mine alone to endure. Mihael—Gestrin—robbed me of that
peace. Seeing him again confirmed the fear that had been shad-
owing me for centuries—that he was indeed immortal and that I
had buried him alive. But while I was greatly pained by what I
had done, I knew it had been necessary. He had become a mon-
ster and had to be stopped.

What Gestrin said to me that night rekindled an ancient
fear. He told me that he had searched for me ever since he escaped
from his grave. That I had bound his hands and feet even in
death had meant one thing to him: he had finally found a person
who truly believed he was immortal, the companion he was long-
ing for. But when years passed without finding me, he assumed
that I had died.

But as I said, all choices intersect.

Gestrin never strayed far from Slovenia, returning now and
then and sometimes staying for the course of a lifetime. Sentimen-
tality always drew him back to the river where he was born. He
reinvented himself as a researcher of its history. It was around this
time that I had started bringing tours to the river as well. On one
of these tours, he saw me. It was then that he discovered why I
had believed him that night in the marshes: I was immortal, too.

Gestrin waited before making his presence known to me, fi-
nally choosing that night I was in Ljubljana with Shelley. You
cannot imagine the terror I felt when I saw him and realized the
danger I had placed Shelley in. In my eyes he was still the mur-
derer who had tried to take Pavel. I did not doubt his promise to
find me and take those whom I loved.

But he said he did not want vengeance. He said that he

wanted to set things right between us. He wanted to give me a gift. The next morning at the river, I discovered what he meant. He sent Shelley a vial of his poison. He planned to give her to me—a companion to spend eternity with. It was a trick and I refused it.

Can you be immortal? Your grandmother asked me the same thing before she died. I never spoke to you about her and now you will know why.

I met your grandmother in March 1944, right before Vesuvius erupted—again. I had volunteered to help evacuate the villages in the path of the eruption. I wanted to help spare whomever I could from my old demon. That's where I saw her. Pale, crying and calling my name from the stream of dusty and frightened refugees. But she was not Livia, though it was her face that I saw in the crowd. And it was not my name she was calling, though it was what I heard.

It did not matter. What I saw and heard was the chance to make things right.

She told me her name was Sophia. She had a broken ankle. I put my arm around her and never let her go.

A part of me knew that I was marrying her for the wrong reasons, that I was marrying a ghost. That's why I decided to tell her who I was—I wanted at least one of us to be marrying the truth.

I was taken aback at how easily she had accepted what I had laid before her. I suppose it was at that moment that I began to love her. Or at least I tried to. Her faith was what endeared her to me, but it was ultimately how I lost her as well.

Sophia and I did not speak of my secret again until long after your father was born. Ten years had passed. Sophia was older and I remained the same. She was no longer the young girl I had met, but in my eyes the passing of the years had only made her more beautiful. Sophia saw things differently. The fine wrinkles that were beginning to line her face reminded her that she was bound to time—and that I was not. She asked me if she could be like me.

The answer I gave her is exactly the answer I am giving you now: all you know of death is a lie.

I stood on a beach in Herculaneum waiting for death to take me away. I saw it hurtle down the mountain, devouring all life in its path.

I imagined that dying was a battle. I was wrong. It is a trade.

Morta will invite you to sit with her. She lays the cards of your life in front of you, but there is no point in looking back. You already know what has happened. What you do not know is what will be. This is what she brings to the table.

Life will go on without you just as it did before you were born. It has not stopped for the passing of the greatest of men and it will not stop for you. At death's table, you watch it leave you behind.

There is the part of you that will look at the future unfolding without you and be at peace. There is another part that will not.

Morta hands you the shears. You are given the choice of severing yourself from what anchors you to this world or staying behind. The halves of your soul take sides. They wrestle for the shears.

Looking at the world you know, it is not hard to guess which side always wins.

But I cared little then of what the world expected of me. If death had not shown me that Livia and my daughter had sailed to safety, I would have cut my life's thread in an instant. But what I saw was the cusp of my dream. I was not about to give up without a fight. I claimed the shears and stabbed the part of myself that dared to abandon my family. It bled into nothingness. I made my choice—and it was binding. I did not know and could not know then what I had just traded for my dream.

There was darkness.

And Silence.

I clawed out of the grave Herculaneum had become that evening. My body was whole again, but I knew that inside it, I was not. I had killed the half of my soul that knew the way out of this life. The Silence was the void left by my own voice, the voice you hear when you have conversations with yourself, the voice that tells you that you are never alone.

I bartered death for a dream I could never live. I decided then that it was better that my wife be a widow to the man I had been than wife to the monster I thought I had become. Through the centuries I watched my dream unfold from a distance, stepping in only when my children needed me the most. I learned to be content. I learned to make peace with who I was. But when that dream ended with Isabelle, I was left with nothing but the memory of the choices I had made.

When I met your grandmother, I dared to dream again. But Sophia could not be with me. She was not content with what I could offer her. She wanted forever, but this was not mine to give.

What happened next is her story to tell, and her words are enclosed in the second envelope I have left for you. Perhaps after reading her letter you will be able to answer your last question yourself. Choose well.

I love you.

Forever,
Nonno

BORACAY, PHILIPPINES

🌺 *Now*

Paolo set the letter down. Tears streamed down his cheeks. He let them fall. He looked like a man finally coming to terms with the fact that he had lost his entire family and his dreams, all at once. Shelley could not help but go to him. She would not leave him now.

"I forgive you," she said.

Paolo and Shelley held each other, sobbing in each other's arms until they were too tired to cry. They cried for themselves and for Max, the choices they had made and had not, and for their shared loneliness. The envelope containing Sophia's letter was now wet with their tears. Paolo opened the yellowed envelope, already knowing what it contained. He translated it for Shelley.

Chapter Twenty-four

Failure and forever

Amore mio,

If you are reading this then it means that it is morning, you have woken—and I have not. I have failed. To me, the chance I took was worth it. To be with you forever was the only life I have ever wanted to live.

I beg you, do not hate me. In failure I am selfish, but had I succeeded, what I would have gained would have been for both of us. We would have had each other for always.

I know I have no right to ask you this, but please do me the kindness of keeping the truth of my death from our son. He is a boy and will not understand. Tell him and the world that I died peacefully in my sleep. If not, others will judge what I have done as an act of weakness and desperation, a coward's escape out of life. I do not want to taint our son's life with what the world calls suicide. Only you and I will know that when I took my life, I was not seeking death. Immortality is a choice, but perhaps not a choice meant for all.

You told me once that you had half a soul. I thought that if I surrendered half of mine to death, the half that was left I could give to you. Together, we could be whole for all eternity. I am sorry for placing too much faith in destiny. It appears that you were meant to be mine only for a little while.

Do not blame yourself or regret telling me the truth about

who you are. What has happened is a consequence of my choice, not yours. You gave up death for your dream, I gave up my life for mine. My only regret is that in pursuing my dream of being with you for always, I have left you forever. But you are not alone. I have given you a son and restored the family that was once torn from you. You are the father you have always wanted to be, and no one will ever take that away from you again.

Though it shatters my heart to say this, find love again. Perhaps one day a woman will be born who can be with you forever, a woman strong enough to make the same choice that you have made.

I am looking at you now as you sleep soundly by my side and I am hoping that when the sun rises I will be alive to shred this letter into a million pieces. Perhaps tomorrow will be the first morning I wake up and not feel my body withering next to yours.

I have read that the poison I will take is painless and I would like to believe that it is. I will kiss you in your sleep for what I am praying will not be the last time, but if it is, know that in this kiss I am promising you a love to last all your lifetimes.

Forever,
Sophia

BORACAY, PHILIPPINES

❧ *Now*

S he killed herself." Shelley was frightened by how much she understood Sophia's intentions.

"Because she thought she could be immortal." Paolo shook his head sadly.

"And what about you, Paolo?" Shelley asked slowly, uncertain that she would like his answer. "Do you still want to be like Max? Do you love life so much that you are willing to die for it?"

He walked to the window and looked out at the sea. "No, it's not what I want anymore. At first I envied him. Who wouldn't? He has no deadline to accomplish his dreams, to have adventures, to experience everything tomorrow has to offer. But I'm beginning to see things differently now. I'm part of a larger story and I was not born to be its end. It is too ancient to squander for my vanity. I will not be the last leaf to fall from the tree."

She watched the waves turn to froth against the rocks. "Then what will you be?"

Paolo smiled. "With any luck, I will be an old man who cooks baked eggs and cheese for his grandchildren on Sundays. I will have chickens— lots of them. And when I am gone, my family will remember me and wonder what I put in those eggs to make them taste so wonderful," he said. "There are other ways to live forever."

Chapter Twenty-five

Letters and lies

BORACAY, PHILIPPINES

❧ *Now*

Shelley's letter fluttered in her hand.

"Aren't you going to read it?" Paolo asked.

"I don't know," she said. "I don't think I can."

"Why not?"

"I'm only here because you needed a storyteller. I already know what my letter says—an apology, a thank-you, a good-bye."

"You don't know that."

"But I do, Paolo. If the letter wasn't a good-bye . . ." Fresh tears stung her eyes. "Then he would be here."

"Shelley . . ."

"I already mourned my husband once. I can't do it again. I won't."

Paolo took her in his arms. "I know it's difficult, but not knowing will be worse."

Shelley chewed on her lip. For all the pain she was feeling, she had to admit that she was still glad that she had learned the truth. Max was alive and he had left her—but he had not meant to be cruel. Those were simply the terms of the trade he had unknowingly made.

"You don't have to read it to me," Paolo said. "But clearly he had something to say, something he wanted you to know. He asked me to find you, and I know in my heart that he did it as much for himself as for me."

Shelley knew that Paolo was right. She retreated to a quiet corner while Paolo went outside. She ran her fingers over the creases of the letter and imagined Max's fingers pressing them into place. She unfolded the paper slowly. Beneath the folds were the last words Max would ever say to her. It was the good-bye that she did not want to hear. She closed her eyes and pressed his letter to her lips. It smelled like a place she had once been to. Salty. Faraway. She smoothed it on the table.

> Shelley,
>   It is barely morning and the bed is still warm from where you lay in my arms.

Shelley stopped reading. What was Max talking about? When had he written this letter?

>   I watched you creep outside, careful not to wake me. I listened to you dress in the hallway and walk out the front door. I listened— until there was nothing left but the sound of my own breathing. I do not know where you are going. I do not want to know.

Tears burned Shelley's eyes. This was the night she had run away from Max, the day after he had asked her to marry him.

>   Yesterday, I asked you to be my wife. I asked you to think about your answer. I wanted to give you the chance to do something that I could not do myself—to run away. I could never willingly leave you, Shelley, though I know this is what a less selfish man would do. But I am half a man, wholly in love, and so I have chosen to let you leave me instead.

Was I hasty in asking you to marry me? In my eyes, I could not have been slower. In a blink, you will be gone. I see the sand of your life flowing—fast and freely between my fingers. I am not a god, but you are mortal. I wished only to snatch you from the meadow before time laid you beneath it.

You make me laugh, Shelley. You also make me cry. Your heart is so soft that it pities monsters. Basilisks. River Men. You see beyond their crimes. It filled me with the hope that you would see beyond the one I have just committed—because make no mistake, asking you to be my wife is the sin of a madman.

I am writing all this because I know I have no intention of ever giving you this letter. I just needed a place in this universe to tell the truth, even if only on a page that will never be read. But I have never lied to you. All the lies I have ever told have been to myself. I have never promised you anything I couldn't give. The lie was that I didn't want more.

I want forever with you, Shelley.

I want your days to be as long and endless as mine.

I want to hear your voice next to me on the nights I fear to dream.

I want you to choose me, to choose us, every day, and always.

But the price is too high for what I want, and I will not let you pay it. And so I have let you steal a boat—and my heart— and pray that we shall never meet again.

Run, Shelley. Run away with your thoughts, your answer, and your heart while you can. Run from me and my hopeless secrets. Run and hide, Shelley, because if I find you, I will never let you go.

So leave me, my love, on this island, my sanctuary in every apocalypse, and let the world I dared to dream for us end.

Max

Chapter Twenty-six

Tea and tomorrow

WHERE SHELLEY IS

Now

The chicken was noticeably quiet as it sat in the back of the rented motorboat. The fact that it was lying between a generous layer of mayonnaise and a soggy lettuce leaf might have had something to do with its demeanor. But the cold sandwich was the closest thing Shelley could find to a chicken at this time of the night and she needed all the luck she could get. She had also stuffed two hard-boiled eggs in her coat pockets for good measure. (She had no idea what she was going to do with them or the sandwich, but she thought that taking them with her was probably the least mad thing she was doing that evening.) She rubbed her chest. It hurt.

It had been two weeks since she and Paolo parted ways. She had flown back to London while Paolo lingered at The Shell to perfect the fine art of making baked eggs and cheese. Dex had become quite an egg expert and was happy to share Max's elusive secret ingredient with them. Shelley was more than mildly stunned when she learned that the great mystery behind the dish was actually just a few drops of—

A fortress of cypress on the horizon caught Shelley's attention. She inhaled sharply. She pointed in its direction. "Over there."

The rugged man behind the helm nodded. He smelled as salty as the lagoon he made his living on. He steered the boat toward the crumbling dock.

Shelley stuffed the sandwich into the back pocket of her jeans and climbed onto the walkway.

"Should I wait for you?" the man asked.

"No," Shelley said. The boat sped away.

She shivered. She turned her collar up against the sea wind and shoved her hands deep into her pockets, jostling the hard-boiled eggs. The wooden planks creaked as she made her way to the shore. Not much had changed, she thought. She took another step forward. Her foot shot through a gap in the walkway. She stumbled forward and grabbed onto a post, then pulled herself up and rolled back onto the dock. Her sandwich talisman smashed into a pulp under her weight. She groaned. Still, squished chicken salad was better than nothing.

The path was overgrown with wiry branches and shrubbery. Shelley pushed her way through. The caretakers had stopped coming to the island when Max died. They had never forgiven her for stealing their boat despite her profuse apologies and the Christmas cards she sent them every year. She had not bothered to replace them and now had several sufficiently arduous minutes of getting snagged and scratched along the bristling path to regret this decision. She emerged from the thicket with a nest of twigs and leaves hopelessly entangled in her hair. She pulled off what she could, thankful that there weren't any house-hunting seagulls in the vicinity.

The moonlit courtyard opened in front of her, opalescent like a fading dream. Alex looked paler than she remembered. She took a breath and walked across the mosaic chicken. Her shoe scraped against a hole where a loose tile had been. Her heart stopped, then began racing.

Shelley reached the threshold of the main house. She dug into her pockets for a key and unlocked the door. She ran her hand across the wall, feeling around for the light switch.

A Murano glass chandelier sparkled to life. A prism of colors fell over the room, and Shelley narrowed her eyes at what she was seeing or, rather, what she was not.

Unlike the dock's familiar state of disintegration, in this room everything had changed. The grinning jade Buddha was not smiling at her from his temple of vinyl records. Fabergé eggs and ancient armory no longer littered the floor. The marble floor glistened. The maze of Max's past was gone.

Shelley felt colder. She blew into her hands and rubbed them together.

She walked to the foot of the stairs and looked up. She gripped the carved wooden banister and braced herself for the climb.

Every step sent a sharp pain shooting through her body. Shelley stumbled over the last step and crumpled to the floor. She lay on her back and waited for the world to come into focus. It never did. Her vision remained blurred like a fogged-up window. But what she did see was enough to let her know that she was now just a few feet away from her destination. At the end of the hallway was the room she had fled from a lifetime ago. Behind its wooden door was what she had come to find. She picked herself up and dragged her numb feet toward the door. It was ajar. She peeked through.

The wrought-iron bed lay in a pool of moonlight, white cotton sheets draping over it like frosting. The pillow on which she had laid her head five years ago remained slightly rumpled. It was exactly the same.

He was exactly the same.

Max's face was nestled next to her empty pillow. He still slept on his side of the bed, Shelley thought. She pressed her frozen palm against her heaving chest. She walked to the bed, emptied her pockets on the nightstand, and undressed. She climbed into the bed and slipped under the warmth of Max's arms, melting into every curve of his body.

"Shelley . . ." he whispered into her nape.

Her name. His voice. It was a marriage of sound and meaning that she thought she would never hear again. She turned to Max and saw that he was still asleep. She began to cry. Hot drops fell on the back of his hand. He stirred from his dream.

"Max . . ." Shelley's heart broke in her voice.

Max reached out to touch her face. "Shelley, you look so real."

She wondered if any of this was real. Her vision remained blurry. The room was fading into mist and only Max's arms around her kept her from flitting through the window. She heard Max calling her back.

"Are you?" Max asked.

The pain in Shelley's chest was greater now. She dove into Max's eyes, searching for some place where it did not hurt. She had to say something— anything—while she still could. "Max," she said, "you . . . cleaned the house."

"Well, um, yes," he said. "I did. It was making me sneeze."

Shelley winced through another wave of slicing pain.

Max looked at her worriedly. "Are you hurt?"

"I was," she said. "Not anymore." There was no part of her body that was not in pain, but she was not lying to Max. Max's death hurt. Learning he was alive hurt. But finding him and lying in his arms—that did not hurt at all.

"Shelley . . ."

"Max, please," Shelley said. "No more words." She pressed her lips against his, and for a moment she forgot the pain.

Max kissed her back.

And then there were no words spoken between them for a long time.

A very long time.

Max and Shelley caught their breath, gasping from all the words they didn't exchange.

"I never wanted to leave you, Shelley." He rolled on his back. "You don't know how many times I had to stop myself from going back. One time I even got as far as your doorstep. I knocked . . ."

Shelley's breath caught in her throat.

"But you weren't home."

She regretted for the second time in as many weeks that she had not listened to Brad and hired a butler.

"I was glad," Max said.

Shelley's heart crumpled. "Why?"

He cupped her face in his hands and gently ran his thumbs over her cheeks. He wiped away her tears. "I wanted you to be happy."

"I wasn't." She looked away.

"In time you would have learned to be."

"Like you?" Shelley asked. "In your little café in the Philippines?"

Max took a deep breath. "Did you see the water, Shelley?"

"The water?"

"Around the island," he said. "Did you notice the color of the sea?"

Shelley remembered the aquamarine that had lapped against Manny's outrigger.

Max tilted her chin to face him. "It is the color of your eyes," he said. "It was the reason I hid there. I built a home on a cliff so that whenever I felt selfish enough to return to you, I would look out onto the water, see the peace in your eyes . . . and find the will not to disturb it."

Tears brimmed in her eyes. "Until Paolo found you."

"Yes." Max sat up in bed. "And I knew it was just a matter of time before he found you, too—whether or not I had asked him to."

"What do you mean?"

"No one wants to be alone," he said. "Paolo would have eventually sought you out to share the burden of his discovery. That's why I decided that the kindest way for both of you to learn the truth was . . . at the same time. He needed the context only you could provide, and you needed to come to see the truth in all that I had already told you." He swallowed. "But there was also another reason."

Shelley stiffened. She pulled the sheet over her breasts.

"I would not have admitted it then," Max said, "but deep inside I knew that I had asked Paolo to find you as much for my sake—if not more. I realized, however, that if I ever saw you again, saying farewell would never have been an option."

"And so you came," Shelley said, "here."

Max nodded. "But how did you know where I was?"

"You told me," she said.

"Told you?"

"In your letter," she said. "You wrote that this place is your sanctuary." The pain caught up with her. Shelley clutched her chest and cried out. She rolled to her side.

"What's wrong, luv? Are you all right?" Max sat up and switched on the lamp on the bedside table. A sliver of metal flashed in the light. The silver vial lay next to the eggs and the rest of the contents of Shelley's pockets. "Shelley"—his voice was laced with panic—"what is this?"

"A snack?" She smiled weakly. The pain was subsiding now, like a rip that had reached its end. She was drifting away.

"No." Max snatched up the vial. "What is *this*?" He tore its silver cap off. It was empty. "What have you done?" His face crumpled with despair.

"I made my choice." Shelley saw a table set before her, and she was being called to sit in front of it. "Gestrin . . . he was . . . very helpful." Her voice was growing fainter with each word.

"No!" Max cried. "Shelley! Why did you do this?"

"It will work." She took his face in her cold hands. "It has to."

Max pulled her hands off his face and held her by the shoulders. "When did you take the poison? You need a doctor—"

"No, please," Shelley said. "This is what I want."

"You would kill yourself . . . on the word of a madman for the chance to live forever?"

"No, not for . . . ever, Max," she said. "For you. I would die to live for . . . you."

He was sobbing now. "You didn't have to do this. I would have stayed . . ."

"But I wouldn't have," Shelley said. "I don't want to ever have to leave you, Max."

"But that's what you're doing now." Max's voice shook with fear and grief.

"I'm not leaving you."

"You're dying, Shelley."

"I am," she said. "But I will make the right choice in the end. I already made it once before."

"I don't understand . . ." Tears streamed down his face.

"You made me a widow. I've already been torn in half. I chose to live then. I know I can do it again," Shelley said. "I'm just very . . . tired . . . right now . . ." She closed her eyes. "Let me sleep . . . just for a little . . . while."

Max gathered her to him. She was growing limp in his arms, but her face remained full of hope. He kissed the secret spot behind her ear. "Good night, luv."

"Good night, Max." Shelley curled into a ball against him.

He pulled her closer. "What do you want for breakfast?"

"Breakfast?" Shelley asked. Her voice was barely a whisper. Time was slowing. There were cards being laid before her, pictures of places. Faces. She saw her mother, Paolo, Brad, Max . . . but not her own.

"Yes," Max said, "for tomorrow."

Tomorrow. Shelley was beginning to forget what the word meant. She just wanted to sleep. She was so tired. She nuzzled closer to Max. A blank Scrabble tile brushed her cheek.

Tomorrow, she remembered, from the Old English *to morgenne*, dative of *morgen* or "morning." Written as two words until the sixteenth century and then as "to-morrow" until early in the twentieth century. "To morning." Shelley repeated the words in her head. To morning—this was the direction she needed to go in. She found the strength to speak. "It's Sunday tomorrow," she said. "Do you have to ask?"

"Baked eggs and cheese it is, luv," Max said, "and tea . . ."

Jasmine.

It was not Shelley Gallus's top choice for her last thought, but it would have to do. She wondered if there was still time to say it out loud.

Epilogue

A sprig of tarragon lay next to broken eggshells on the counter. In the oven, cheese melted into cream. The kettle whistled, calling to a chipped floral teacup waiting patiently on a picnic table set for two. It was Sunday morning.

Acknowledgments

I have now come to the part of the book that I believe is the hardest to write. It is difficult because I know that I will never be able to come up with the words to sufficiently express my gratitude to all the people who have helped to put this book in your hands.

The first ones that I will fail miserably to thank enough are my family.

Grandma, you never got tired of playing with me when I was little and because of you a part of me will always be the five-year-old who believes in fairy tales.

Dad, this novel is here because you taught me that things happen twice—first in our minds, second in reality. (So if you feel that you've read this before, you know why.)

Mom, you are the true author of this book. The journey toward *Before Ever After* began when you told me stories about elephants that loved ice cream and little engines that could. It continued when you bought the "newspapers" I made and told me that my imaginary mice were brilliant. Finally, you patiently read Max and Shelley's story far more times than the safety limit set by the International Proofreaders Union until it became fit for human consumption. All the dotted i's, crossed t's, and well-placed commas of this book thank you from the bottom of their Times New Roman hearts.

Vince, you braved the first draft of this book and showed me the importance of happy endings.

Derek and Trina, you challenged me to write a book that you would read. Here it is. No skimming allowed. There will be a quiz later.

Second, I would like to thank my wonderful circle of friends, both online and off, who have been so generous with their time, support, and happy-dancing bananas. Rez, PV, Pinky, Dino, Johnny, Cathy, Tina, Jebot, Rochelle, Fino, Mutya, Jinggoy, Kris and Jake, thank you so much for enduring countless dinners with me where the menu often featured my endless writing rants and rambles as the starter, main course, and dessert. To my blogger friends and AW family, thank you for sharing this journey with me. Virtual hugs feel just as warm as real ones. Bopet and Cecile, you rock. The photos you shared for the book's trailers were incredible. Reich, my fellow happy camper, I will never forget the "real" Slight Detour we took together. There's no one else I would have rather spent a homeless night on a bridge with. And for the record, I owe you a gyro.

My deepest gratitude also goes out to my amazing agent, Stephanie Kip Rostan. Steph, you were the first person who did not share my last name to fall in love with Max and his chickens. Thank you for staying up late to finish reading his story and for believing from day one that it was worth sharing with the world.

And of course, none of this would be possible without my brilliant editor, Kate Kennedy, whose insight, passion, and patience have enriched this novel beyond anything I could conceive. Kate, you've taught me so much. Thank you for taking a chance on me and for championing this story.

I would also like to extend my heartfelt thanks to the wonderful and dedicated team at Crown Publishers who have helped bring this book into the world. Julie, Justina, Chris, and Molly, thank you for your expertise and tireless efforts.

Finally, I would like to say thank you to the man I married, the co-author of this great adventure we began fourteen years ago over a couple of beers and a shared love for striped caterpillars and Polgara's hard bread, bacon, and cheese. You are my before, ever, and after.

Ad majorem Dei gloriam.

About the Author

SAMANTHA SOTTO fell in love with Europe's cobbled streets and damp castles when she moved to the Netherlands as a teenager. Since then, she has spent nights huddled next to her backpack on a Greek beach, honeymooned in Paris, and attended business meetings in Dusseldorf in the pleasant company of a corporate credit card. *Before Ever After* was inspired by her experiences living, studying, and traveling in Europe. This is her first novel.